P₁

D0873542

Soapsuds

"A wild ride through the outlandish universe of soap-opera starlets." —*Cosmopolitan*

"It's got sex! It's got intrigue! It's got hot women, hot men." —KELLY RIPA in *US Weekly,* July 2005

"*Soapsuds* is funny, smart and spot on about the industry. Finola Hughes pulls off something I wouldn't have thought possible—she maintains a sense of humor about the medium, but never lets it become a joke or the characters become cartoons." —LOUISE SHAFFER, author of *The Three Miss Margarets* and *The Ladies of Garrison Gardens*

"A bubbly good time." —Toronto *Metro*

"Talk about drama!" —*All You* magazine

"If you've ever been at home during the day, you know how easy it is to get involved in watching the soaps. The first day, you watch figuring you're only going to watch for a minute. . . . By the fourth day, you're hooked. . . . *Soapsuds* is just like that. Three or four pages in and you're a fan." —*The Aiken Standard*

"A fast-paced and humorous look at daytime drama . . . a fascinating behind-the-scenes glimpse of daytime television." —*Romance Reviews Today*

"An excellent drama that will have you laughing often." —*Huntress Reviews*

Soapsuds

A
N
O
V
E
L

Finola Hughes

and

Digby Diehl

Ballantine Books   New York

2006 Ballantine Books Trade Paperback Edition

Copyright © 2005 by Finola Hughes and Digby Diehl

Published in the United States by Ballantine Books, an imprint of The Random House Publishing Group, a division of Random House, Inc., New York.

BALLANTINE and colophon are registered trademarks of Random House, Inc.

Originally published in hardcover in the United States by Ballantine Books, an imprint of The Random House Publishing Group, a division of Random House, Inc., in 2005

LIBRARY OF CONGRESS CATALOGING-IN-PUBLICATION DATA

Hughes, Finola.
    Soapsuds / Finola Hughes and Digby Diehl.— 1st ed.
        p.   cm.
    ISBN 0-345-47083-4
    1. Soap operas—Fiction.   2. Television actors and actresses—Fiction.   3. Television programs—Fiction.   I. Diehl, Digby.   II. Title.
    PS3608.U35S63 2005
    813'.6—dc22

Printed in the United States of America

www.ballantinebooks.com

9 8 7 6 5 4 3 2 1

Text design by rlf design

For our spouses,

Russell and Kay

And for our children,

the two Dylans and Cash

Acknowledgments

Few people understand the many creative contributions, the sacrifices, and the much-needed love that partners provide to authors. We want to express our deepest appreciation to Russell and Kay for that and so much more.

Our wise and diplomatic literary agent, Rich Barber, kept our boat on an even keel during the uncharted journey to publication, and Peter Iannucci, personal manager extraordinaire, boosted us with unfailing enthusiasm and wine as we navigated our way.

Rarely in the history of publishing has an editor lived up to her namesake as well as the genial, witty, and perceptive Allison Dickens. We are grateful for her wisdom and her sharp editorial eye.

Our thanks, too, goes to a remarkable publishing team, including Gina Centrello, Tom Perry, Gillium Hailparn, Ingrid Powell, and the rest of the ink-stained gang at Ballantine/Random House.

Finola's personal assistants, Francesca Nunez and Sejal Patell, have been helpful models of efficiency and calm in the midst of sometimes chaotic storms.

Thanks to our hard-working transcriber, Julie Wheelock. No one could have given transcripts of our conversations back to us more quickly or accurately.

Special thanks to our talented photographers Deniz Uzunoglu and Brigitte Lehnert, and to the entire crew of the Style Channel's *How Do I Look?* for their support.

Soapsuds

A Monday in October

"You're a very fortunate woman, Ms. Merrick," the petite blonde nurse with the bouncing boobs tells me as she pushes my wheelchair down the corridor. "They did a heroic, even a miraculous job after your accident. You were touch and go for a while there."

With my entire cranium swathed in gauze like some latter-day mummy, I nod. Not just because I understand what little Miss Perky Tits, RN, has said, but because there's nothing else I can do. I'm wrapped so tight that there is no way to do much more than grunt or hum.

"You lucked out. When a woman goes through the windshield like you did, she is often scarred for the rest of her life. Of course, with all your broken bones, there was no way to rebuild your face *exactly* the way it was before." She pushes me through the door into a tiny examining room. "Nevertheless, when Dr. Schroeder comes in to remove your bandages, I think you'll be pleased," she says in a tone that's a bit too bloody cheerful for me. "I'm gonna leave you for just a moment while I go get him. I'll be back real quick," she adds over her shoulder with a wink and a jiggle as she's halfway out into the corridor. "I'm sure you're dying to see 'the new you.' "

Alone for a moment, I go back over what happened. Cruising in the vintage Mercedes convertible that had been so lovingly restored . . . Laughing and carefree, enjoying the balmy summer night, the full moon, and the sound of the Pacific lapping at the shoreline. Burke at the wheel of his pride and joy . . . No seatbelts—"it's more 'authentic' that way," he said.

He'd been doing such a great impersonation of a sober person that I hadn't realized how much he'd been drinking until he suddenly slammed on the brakes, even though the traffic signal was still a quarter mile up ahead. The SUV behind us couldn't stop until it was somewhere in the back seat. By that time, however, I had been turned into a human projectile launched through the windshield.

Lying in a crumpled heap on the highway, I became aware of sirens and flashing lights, the squawk of walkie-talkies . . . and many faces hovering overhead. "Devon . . . Devon . . . Devon . . . **Devon Merrick.** Don't try to move. Blink twice if you can hear me. I'm a paramedic. First we're going to stabilize you, and then we'll take you to the hospital. They'll take good care of you there."

What followed is still a blur: the frenzied trip to the ER . . . the urgent voices of doctors and nurses. "On my count . . . one . . . two . . ."

Then it all goes blank for a while. Waking up numb and cold with my lips wrapped around a plastic tube . . . *I must be underwater, but how the hell do they expect me to scuba dive in this headgear? And where's my mask and flippers?*

I hear muffled bustling sounds around me. "She's regained consciousness."

Okay, so I got a bump on the head and I'm a little disoriented, but I really must get this huge radiator hose out of my throat. It's not as if I'm a '55 Buick. "Please don't try to remove your breathing tube, Ms. Merrick. A nurse will help you shortly."

My eyes come to half mast and I become increasingly aware of my surroundings. "Too soon to tell how much permanent damage there will be."

Clearly I wasn't supposed to hear that—my eyes bulge in alarm. The recovery room nurse answers the questions I'm unable to ask. "You were in an automobile accident. When you were ejected from the vehicle, your cheekbone and your eye socket were shattered. Your jaw was broken in four places and your nose was smashed. You were rather a mess. Since then you've had surgery to rebuild the bone structure of your face. You're all held together with plates and screws—right now you'd set off metal detectors in every airport in the country. Miraculously enough, your companion walked away without a scratch. At least we think so—he seems to have disappeared. If he ever shows up, the cops would like to have a little Q&A with him about what happened."

That conversation seems like ancient history as the peppy little nurse returns with Dr. Schroeder, who gives me a faux-cheery "And how are we this morning?"

I glower at him. I try to manage a "Fuck you" through my bandages, but "Mmmmph" is all that comes out.

Officious toad. Wait, that makes me sound like an ingrate. Okay, surgically proficient officious toad . . . but how condescending of him to refer to me in the first-person plural—unless of course he really does see two of me.

"You must be dying to see what you look like. We're going to get those bandages off you right away now."

Dr. Schroeder and the nurse begin snipping at the gauze and unwinding my shroud. "There's never a good time for an accident like yours, Devon, but if you had to have it, you're lucky that it happened when it did. You are truly a miracle of laser microsurgery. Even two years ago, I wouldn't have been able to give you nearly the result that you have."

Snip. Snip. "That's the last of it." Schroeder steps back and looks at my face with a critical eye. "Yesssssssss!" *I bet he says the same thing when he sinks a twenty-foot putt.* "Devon, you're wearing some of my very best work!" The smug, self-satisfied look on his face should be reassuring. It isn't.

Schroeder nods to the nurse and pats her on the ass, even as she pats my face with a moist cloth, then holds a mirror up to my face. "Aaaaaaaaaaaaaaaaaaah!" I gasp.

* * *

"Cut!" The disembodied voice booms over the set. "Very nice, all of you. Way to get your feet wet, Kate—you give great gasp. Welcome aboard as the new Devon Merrick. . . . Now *mooooveit,* people! Some of us would like to go home tonight before we have to come back tomorrow. I don't give a shit about seeing my wife, but I have to walk my dog."

The lights snap out in the hospital, and like giant R2-D2s the cameras roll onto the next set. A cameraman gives me an encouraging wink and says, "Welcome to Hope Canyon." Makeup and Hair pick up their massive beauty kits and lumber wearily toward their next heart-stopping dramatic venue, dragging their chairs like spectators on a golf course.

I extricate myself from the hospital bed, peel back another layer of sticky bandage to be able to locate the exit, and make my escape. Prop guys and stagehands go about the business of tearing down parts of the set until someone bellows, "Shutthefuckup. We're taping here!"

I feel deflated—plagued by the usual overexposed, vulnerable, nagging doubt that inhabits every moment of every job I've ever had. Ever. I stagger toward the EXIT sign, holding my hospital gown shut, so that my dimpled, cellulite-riddled ass doesn't put in an uncredited cameo appearance.

As I peer blinking into the dimly lit hallway, I make out several people apparently lined up to welcome the new guy—*moi.* As my myopia struggles to focus, I begin to discern that these people are . . . *girls.* Actresses. Hollywood girl actresses. A species that strikes fear in my soul.

A searing hot poker of anxiety shoots through my gut, spreading out into my limbs and sending a tremor of terror into my brain as I recognize the gaggle of women for what they are . . . *perfection.* They are each and every one of them perfect—perfect specimens of youthful femaleness, caught in fleeting moments of prime, succulent ripeness. It's disgusting and wildly mesmerizing—thick golden flesh covering miles and miles of divine bone;

skin so taut it seems ready to spill its luscious contents onto the hallway carpet. What a waste.

They grin—in unison. Their size 2 bodies sway precariously in the air conditioning. I shudder. It is a Victoria's Secret catalogue tableau come to life. They each have a (to the tune of "The Twelve Days of Christmas," all together now—)

> Fiiive-yeeear con-traaact,
> Fo-ur goll-den limmmbs,
> Three-car-rat die-mondz,
> Two-oo purr-fect breasts
> and a boy-freh-end in a T-V show.

My fight-or-flight mechanism kicks in, and I choose flight.

To the dressing room—save yourself, Kate, before you're revealed as the fraud that you are. There will be time enough for greetings and small talk when you don't look quite so much like a woman who's survived a car wreck.

Too late.

I'll never get through that thicket of women without saying something.

As full-blown panic sets in, the thunder noise that I hear inside my head whenever I yawn gets louder and louder. The voices in the corridor sound like they're coming from the bottom of a soup tureen—or a toilet bowl.

Worst of all, a dreadfully familiar pneumatic sensation comes over me as I feel myself start to inflate. Suddenly I am Alice in Wonderland, and I have nibbled off the wrong corner of the cookie. Growing, growing . . .

I'm feeling unmistakably warm, and surprise, surprise—my thighs have become immense. I've also become aware of my pubic hairs lying darkly beneath the hospital gown. They too have begun to grow, germinating menacingly beneath the low-rise Cosabella teal mesh thong in which I secreted them earlier this morning. Their tendrils have already escaped the confines of the thong and are threatening to curl out into the world, like time-lapse footage of an overgrown forest in Blair Witch III.

My pubic hairs mock the system, and they're going to betray me. "She's dark," they say, "she's brunette! She's a big, sweaty, Irish witch with thick thighs, brown eyes, and a brown heart. She's an imposter—an imposteress!"

Growing, growing . . .

If you wait any longer, Katiegirl, you'll be too enormous to even fit through the dressing room door. Run!!!! Run before your pubic hair gets so long you trip over it. Get your waaaay-bigger-than-size-2 Irish ass out of this wretched hospital gown, and into something flattering. And while you're at it, lose the celadon green "recuperating sickie" makeup.

If I felt vaguely cowlike before, now I feel positively Brobdingnagian in comparison to these impossibly small, perfectly formed human beings. I slump, I hunker, but no amount of slouching can make me invisible.

Busted. I don't belong here. Why are they all smiling at me? Shit—even their teeth are perfect . . . straight and dazzling white! No one in the UK has those—an obscure Act of Parliament forbids it.

"You're Kate McPhee." A honeyed voice emanating from a deeply tanned, highly cleavaged Britney-Spearsian twentysomething blonde intrudes into my hysteria from the depths of the hallway/commode. "Hi. I'm Tiffany Duquette—Fallon Salisbury."

Oh please—perfect names, too? It rolls off her tongue smoothly, rhythmically even, like a lyric from a Broadway show tune. What mother's malice aforethought would name a child "Tiffany Duquette," unless she knew from the moment of birth—or maybe from conception—that her offspring would be a soap star?

Of course, in my unnerved condition, the possibility is lost on me that her name, like her boobs, could be a complete fabrication.

"It's so *wonderful* to meet you in person, Kate. I've heard such *wonderful* things about you. I just know you'll be a *wonderful* Devon, and I'm looking forward to working with you. You're going to love being part of our *Live for Tomorrow* family."

"Mmmph." I'm so stupefied by all the *wonderful* that I can't talk. It's as if my jaw is still draped in the gauze from the last scene.

"Kate, I'm Alison Goodwin—Taylor Daniels." Alison has perfect features reminiscent of Grace Kelly, but just slightly more cheesy Wisconsin. She is creamy, liquid, and lush, her face all spread like a bowl full of freshly churned butter. She has a cupid's-bow mouth, and her very long straight blonde hair falls in a silky milk curtain over one creamy shoulder. As she smiles a creamy-dreamy, wispy half smile at me, her sky blue eyes give me the message: *It is impossibly nice to be me.*

"And I'm Amber Hartman. I play Jennifer Abell." Amber is well named, with honey blonde, rather than blonder-than-blonde hair, and is so tan that she looks to have been dipped in cocoa. It's all warm and chummy and Southern-California-friendly among just-us-girls here in the corridor.

Except that I'm still growing. By now I'm the size of a battleship-class Lane Bryant dinner lady—one of those 44DD uniform-clad hairnetted aunties who plop enormous portions of mashed potatoes and meat loaf on your plate at the cafeteria. . . . or used to. This is Southern California, home of the bean sprout and the no-foam soy latte, and although dinner ladies still abound in Britain, this place hasn't seen them since Jane Fonda was still in leg warmers.

The hen party is broken up by the very welcome arrival of some testosterone. "Right—you must be Kate. I'm Trent Winterfield—Philip Salisbury on the show."

Alrighty then. About thirty-two, dark wavy hair. Twinkly green eyes with what I perceive to be a puckish nature behind them. Puckish and sexy, too, in a you-bet-I-know-where-this-soft-leather-restraint-should-go kind of way. Yup. That works. Peachy—I'm looking like such a piece of doggie doo.

"Oh shit," he says. "Places, everyone! Here comes the Queen."

*The queen? She's in America? What in the world is Queen Elizabeth doing on a soap opera set? Oh, of course, not **that** queen . . .*

Our quintet prepares for the imminent arrival of Meredith Contini. Even people who don't follow the soaps know Meredith and her character, Regina Abell. She started on *Live for Tomorrow* as the ingénue thirty-plus years ago. Now she's become the franchise—the most recognizable face in soaps. A vision in puce ruffles, every perfectly coiffed burnished copper hair in place, Meredith is moving with regal grace up the hallway toward us.

Ah, the prima donna.

Her Majesty docks herself at our cluster, but it's clear she could never, ever be mistaken for one of the gang. Petite but curvaceous, her perfectly pedicured feet balance on tiny Jimmy Choo sandals with a four-inch heel. She is almost but not quite chubby. Her legs touch at the thighs, and when she walks they rub together with an ultrafeminine rustle, a sound enhanced by the Vera Wang soufflé of a dress she's wearing. And she has a legendary JLo-class ass. Meredith is almost as famous for her derriere as she is for her deep copper hair. Despite her roundness, her face is a cheekboned perfection. Through the play of light and shadow, her makeup artist has given her the illusion of cheekbones where none exist in nature. She has large liquid grey eyes, with sweeping eyelids topped by eyebrows that are perfect dark slashes in her kabuki mask. Skimming the brows is a cylinder of henna-sunset bangs, a look that has remained virtually unchanged over the score-plus-ten of years she's been on the show.

"Kayyyytte," she says with self-consciously pear-shaped tones. "I'm Mehrreddithhh. How delightful that you are joining us."

I try not to register alarm—or pleasure—as I feel Trent's strong masculine fingers grip my shoulder, firmly pulling me backward till my ear is just inches from his lips. "Don't take it personally, Kate," Trent whisper-breathes into my ear. "That's what she says to everyone on their first day."

"Forgive me for not staying longer," Meredith continues, "but Regina Abell is needed on set, and I have to save her voice, so I'll just say 'Welllllllll-commmme to my worrrlllddd.' "

"Remember that and you'll be fine," Trent murmurs . . .

—Ooooooooh! Sexy murmur!—

. . . as she glides away, "as long as you recognize that it is indeed her world, or her 'Gahrden Pahrty,' as we've all come to know and loathe it. And darling, if you are to remain a guest at her Gahrden Pahrty, there are just two rules:

1. Know your place;
2. Stay in it."

Whatthefuck have I gotten myself into?

* * *

On the double, a ruggedly handsome older man with a full head of silver hair sails past our little gaggle with a hearty wave. "Can't stop now," he says in a rich, perfectly enunciated mid-Atlantic baritone. "I'm up next."

"That's Richard Blakeley—Mason Salisbury," explains Amber helpfully in a little-girl voice that is equal parts Melanie Griffith and born-again Betty Boop. "He's our Imminent Grease."

I know that, against my volition, my eyes register anxiety as my brain goes on Thesaurus Autosort in a desperate effort to decode Imminent Grease.

Trent saves me the trouble. "Richard is the *éminence grise* of *LFT*—our patriarch, who has a liver the size of Montana and an ego to match. And for those of you keeping score, that's one point for him—he and Meredith have been having a late-off, and he's arriving at the Gahrden Pahrty after she's already up there. She really hates that!"

"Now, Trent," says Amber with a Valley Girl giggle. "You behave yourself."

There must be a factory in East Pasadena that turns out these blonde Barbies by the boatload: perfect blue eyes, perfect hair, perfect bodies, flawless skin—and fuckall for brains underneath. Of course, when you're a 38D—by means fair or foul—in this town it really doesn't much matter that you're a nincompoop.

As I proceed down the corridor, I feel as if I'm still getting larger and larger with each step. By the time I get to my dressing room door, I'm the size of one of those giant balloons in the Macy's Thanksgiving Day Parade—it's all I can do to squeeze through the door frame and gain the safety of my private space. Worse yet, I'm sweating like a pig. My hospital attire is drenched, so I take all my clothes off and start soaking my various appendages in the sink in an effort to cool down and shrink back to my normal—but still elephantine—size.

As I balance precariously on my left foot, my right calf and left forearm are marinating in ice water when there's a knock on the door. I look in the mirror, expecting to see just one eyeball and a portion of a giant nostril, but the image looking back at me is surprisingly familiar. Draping a towel around my fishbelly white midsection, I open the door to admit a gnome, who without saying a word deposits a pink-and-silver gift basket on my dressing table and departs.

The card reads,

> *I just know we'll become the greatest of friends.*
> *Welcome again to my world.*
> *—Meredith Contini*

Tied into the pink bow at the top of the basket is an eleven-inch Meredith replica—a Meredith Barbie dressed in cherry red taffeta, with tiny matching jeweled sandals and Meredith's own perfectly reproduced garnet-cinnamon hairstyle. Setting the Meredith Mini-Me aside, I tear at the shrink-wrap and the pink ribbon to find that I'm looking at a reject from the Worst of QVC, or a Lovely Parting Gift for an unsuccessful game show contestant.

Oh Gawd. Girlie-girl stuff.

Meredith has bestowed on me some samples of her eponymous edible beauty products—Capelli di Regina Shampoo (grapefruit-lavender), Texturizing Rinse (blackberry-starfruit), and Velvet Glove hairspray (blood orange–mint). Hair is obviously a biggie at her Gahrden Pahrty.

But do I ever really want to smell like a fruit salad from the neck up?

But wait, there's more. . . . Regina's Eyes self-curling mascara in Chianti, Regina's Lips ultrashine gloss in Tuscan Melon, Contessa di Contini body lotion ("carefree and casual"), and Contini di Notte cologne ("elegantly transitions from the boardroom to the bedroom").

Why would I want to smell like Meredith Contini—especially in bed? Come to think of it, why would I want to smell like any celebrity—Jennifer Lopez, Elizabeth Taylor, or God forbid Celine Dion—between the sheets?

The *pièce de résistance,* however, is a lace-trimmed waltz-length nightgown and matching edible peignoir from Boudoir by Regina in Relentless Raspberry. If you'd given someone the task of putting together a gift assortment that was as unlike me as possible, you'd scarcely have done better.

How the fuck can I write anything that can even masquerade as a sincere thank-you note?

I'm so not a girlie-girl. There isn't a ruffle anywhere in my psyche. My family is Irish—I see myself as having potato-picking hands and childbearing calves; if necessary I could squat in a field, give birth, catch the newborn with the left hand, and continue picking potatoes with the right.

Oh, the leftover baggage we carry with us from childhood.

I remember being ten years old. My friend Sophie and I were sitting on the stoop in front of our house. This is the age when kids discover how different they are, one from the other. Sophie was beautiful—Brooke Shields gorgeous—with a luxuriant mane of curly chestnut hair, finely chiseled features, and wild eyebrows that framed emerald green eyes. I remember looking at her legs—they were delicate, skinny little beautifully shaped legs, with a teeny little calf, showcased in a cute espadrille. Me—I was wearing sensible clumpy brown boots, and I had my enormous calves stuffed into them.

While we were sitting there, my mom came home with her shopping bags. At that age it was all about comparing, so I asked her, "Who's prettier, Sophie or me?" And my mom looked at us and said, "Sophie is beautiful, but you're just Irish, Kate, you're just Irish."

After all these years, that one still stings.

Even before I asked the question, I knew that Sophie was prettier than I was, but a mother's not supposed to say so, and of course when we went inside I had to badger her about what she meant.

"It doesn't matter who's prettier, Kate," she tried to explain, "because Sophie's got a junkie mom and her parents split up. Worse yet, between her mother and her mother's abusive boyfriend, she's getting no good role models at home. Because she's learning such a terrible way of living, it's important for me to tell Sophie that she's beautiful. She needs to hear that, but you . . . you don't need it, Kate, so I'm going to tell you that you're Irish."

No amount of explaining could keep "You're just Irish" from searing its way into my psyche. In her defense, my mother was a staunch feminist, and I'm sure she was trying to jump-start me out of this mind-set of comparing myself to other girls. That's how she brought me up—no bullshit—not even when I really needed some to smooth out the bumps of adolescence. What she did made me strong, but I can't help but wonder whether maybe if she told me I was pretty even just once, I wouldn't feel myself inflating like the Michelin Man whenever I come up against the Barbies and Bambis and Brandis—or in this case the Alisons and Tiffanys and Ambers—who inhabit daytime television.

See, when you become an actor, a part of you reverts to being ten years old—and freezes that way. The comparing of faces and bodies starts up all over again, and it never really goes away. Insecurity is the actor's lot. You spend a great deal of time looking over your shoulder to see who's gaining on you—and there's *always* someone there. And that someone is *always* younger and prettier than you.

I grab the basket and tomorrow's script and head for the parking lot.

* * *

Slogging my way up into the canyon, I realize that my driving instincts are still way off—*why are all these sons of bitches coming at me from the wrong side of the highway?* It's as if I left what little sense of self-preservation I ever had back in London.

I wonder whether anyone ever found my car. . . .

When I came to the United States, I'd left a perfectly good vehicle—a jaunty little maroon Morris Minor with wood paneling—in the car park at Heathrow. After Rafe left me for my ostensible best friend, Leslie, I walked around with my broken heart bleeding on my sleeve, feeling as if everyone knew I'd been made a fool of. When I was first offered the part on *Live for Tomorrow,* I'd intended to turn it down, but when my life with Rafe fell apart, I grabbed at it and took off for Los Angeles. Without thinking at all about what it meant to transplant oneself across eight time zones, I uprooted myself from the theatre people who flock to London's Notting Hill Gate, a world that was light-years from the never-ending melodramas of *LFT*. I had always thought that these were my people—witty, urbane, cosmopolitan, and all those Hugh-Granty things Americans believe about them. The car was a reminder of everything I was leaving behind. I couldn't deal with it, so I just drove to the airport, gathered up my bags, and got on the plane.

Home, such as it is, finally looms into view. I wedge the rented Honda into a parking space of dubious legality, start to pick up the gift basket, then have second thoughts. I finally choose to leave it on the seat in plain sight, in the sure and certain hope that someone will covet it enough to make off with it. Just to make it easy for them, I leave the Honda unlocked.

After climbing the rickety stairs, I open the door to the genteel squalor of my canyon bungalow as Drusilla, in a terrific impersonation of the World's Most Pissed-Off Feline, comes crying to the rattle of the key. She has cause—her dish is empty. Come to think of it, it was empty when I left this morning, too.

"All right. All right. It's your turn." Except that when I tip the box of dry food upside down, nothing comes out. It had never been my intention to get a cat—Drusilla pretty much insinuated herself into my life by meowing on the doorstep with great persistence . . . so much persistence that at some point it was easier to take her in than to put up with her plaintive yowling at all hours. It's a technique that works with me—I've ended up with a couple of boyfriends who started out that way, too.

With Drusilla's angry supervision, the cat food scavenger hunt begins. Foraging in the refrigerator, I find cocktail olives, maraschino cherries, fudge sauce, some moldy brie, half a bottle of very flat Perrier, and an assortment of leftover takeout bags, boxes, and plastic clamshell containers. Drusilla spurns the sausage from the week-old pizza, but deigns to accept the chicken I glean from a very tired tostada. But wait a minute . . . what's this in the cupboard? Bingo!! Hidden behind the tomato sauce, cornstarch, balsamic vinegar, and organic couscous (the only reason it survived), I find a Chicken of the Sea bonanza. We split the can of tuna fish, even as I make myself a sticky note that says BUY CAT FOOD and affix it to the bathroom mirror—right next to another one that says exactly the same thing.

Sticky Note to self: You are completely inadequate at your own life.

Tossing the unopened day's mail on a pile of more of the same, I give Drusilla permission to cocoon herself in my lap (not that she thought she needed it) and settle in with my script.

```
INT.—ABELL ESTATE LIVING ROOM—EVENING

                   MINISTER
      Dearly beloved, we are gathered here today. . . .
```

Oh shit—they just took off my bandages and already I'm in a wedding.

2

Tuesday in October/the next day

5:31! 5:31!! 5:31!!!

The alarm goes off and the clock flashes the time on the ceiling. As I fumble to reach for the snooze button, there is a crackling, crumpling noise because I'm rolling over pieces of paper—the pages of the script that I'd arranged on the bed around me. I settle back onto the pillow, setting off a sound of complaint from Drusilla, who had arranged herself around my head like a helmet and is peeved about being rearranged.

It feels like it takes me three hours to get dressed. Getting the right balance between avant-garde and devil-may-care ain't easy, and by the time I'm done there is a huge pile of clothing on the floor of the bedroom, discarded efforts at mix and match. I finally settle on avant-garde on bottom and devil-may-care on top. Donning excruciatingly tight Dolce & Gabbana cigarette-leg sandblasted blue jeans over a pair of lace-up Cesare Paciotti stiletto-heeled boots that are the color of roasted veal, I top the look with a unisex vintage black cashmere sweatshirt (maybe Zegna, maybe Jhane Barnes—I vaguely remember scoring it on supersale from the men's department at Barney's) whose V-neck is so overstretched that it falls artlessly off my shoulder, revealing my bluish-white deltoid and, if one looks closely, a flash of my tit.

Crap—nobody stole the gift basket.

Meredith's magnanimous offering has survived the night in the Honda, and is now about to make the round trip back to the studio. Driving through the studio gates on this, my second morning as a soap star, I'm still feeling very much the outsider.

The cheerful guard at the gate has to repeat his instructions on where to park, which I had already forgotten in one day. As I wheel the anonymous Honda sedan in that general direction, a two-bit thrill ripples through me when I notice KATE MCPHEE in fresh paint on the wheelstop of a parking space—"my" parking place. At least somebody thinks I'm going to be around long enough for the paint to dry.

• • •

Actors are all emotional yo-yos—it doesn't take much to send us either up or down. With the vote of confidence of seeing my name in concrete if not in lights, I bound through the door marked *Live for Tomorrow* with new enthusiasm. The reception area smells of new carpet and freshly brewed coffee. I wave cheerily to the receptionist with the Ladybird Johnson hairdo as I make my way down the corridor toward the dressing rooms.

"Knock. Knock." Yes, there is a tapping at my door, but it is accompanied by a breathless voice that underscores the act of knocking and enunciates the words like the preamble to a knock-knock joke. Rather than following up on the joke and saying, "Who's there?" I fumble for the knob and open the door to an enormous pair of—knockers.

"Hi, I'm JJ, your makeup artist," they say. "We were hoping you'd come join us." These tits are perfect, each the size of a normal person's head. They've been bronzed and oiled to a seductive sheen, and they stare powerfully back at me like a pair of Israeli smart missiles. I try to tear myself away from the vision before me, and am magnificently unsuccessful. I've never seen such enormous body parts restrained in such an impossibly small infant's T-shirt.

If she sneezes, that Ace bandage she's wearing will surely explode. When that happens, there's gonna be T-shirt shrapnel everywhere.

Desperately trying to drag my eyes away from them, I am caught by another vision—that of JJ's wet-look disco pants in Day-Glo melon, sporting the world's most obvious camel toe.

"Oh my," I exclaim, which had not been my intention—actors are supposed to be able to hold all that stuff in. I quickly scan her body to find her face, hoping against hope that it has not been surgically removed and replaced by a cute bunny head. But no, there sits the prerequisite blonde, blue-eyed, button-nosed mask—which in this case is actually a relief.

"Shall we walk, honey?" she mews.

I'm not at all sure that I can. I check my thighs for any signs of pubic hair tendrils, and actually feel myself start to move out of the dressing room and down the corridor to my fate.

"Do you like your eyes dressed or not?"

What is she talking about? "I beg your pardon?"

"How much stuff do you want on your eyes? Best to go heavy, at least this time—everyone else will be, and you don't want to fade into the background."

Actually, that's exactly what I want to do.

We arrive at the Makeup room. "Welcome to Gossip Central!" says Trent upon our arrival. "This is where everything happens, where all the gossip gets swapped. Everyone hangs around here, because if you're not present, you're a target of opportunity."

I follow chirpy JJ toward a makeup chair and sit reluctantly. I feel like I have gone to the gallows. She pulls a lever at the side and I'm flung unceremoniously backward. Yep, that was the trap door. I flail my legs like a cockroach, trying to find a foothold, and catch sight of myself in the multitude of mirrors lining the walls. JJ now has me pinned with a wrestler's grip and is plucking my eyebrows.

"We need to get rid of some of this hair," she coos up my nose. "Too bushy, hon." I feel so self-conscious, so achingly present and burdensome. I try to hold my breath. Above all, I try very hard not to think about who else might be witnessing my dying bug act.

Next I hear mixing and squelching noises, and I peer over my gut at JJ, now sporting glasses on her surgically enhanced button nose. She is slapping together half a gallon of foundation, concealer, and Spackle. I shut my eyes and pray she stops short of Baby Jane.

In the background, I hear the low drone of a dreadful oldies station playing a Hall & Oates song. They are dribbling on about lost love.

What do they know about it? I think disdainfully. As if in retribution for my cynicism, a Rafe-and-Leslie pang rises up unbidden and jabs me in the heart.

Shit. That one sort of snuck up on me. Usually I'm a little better at seeing them coming. Focus on the work, Kate. The work—the actor's life—is what's going to pull you through this.

The work, or in this case the breathless urgency of today's episode, is being fed through the monitors; coffee is gurgling and smelling delicious; here in Makeup there is gentle laughter and chatter. I begin to relax. I take deep breaths and slowly drift into the actor's daydream box, where I run scenes in my head, search for inspiration, and compose Oscar acceptance speeches. It is a cozy place.

JJ has a very soft touch, and she slowly massages in face cream and ever so tenderly applies foundation, rouge, eye shadow, rouge, lashes, mascara, and rouge. Now, soaps are not known for their subtle makeup, so my throat catches when JJ murmurs, "You can open your eyes now."

I fully expect Bozo the Clown, or at the very least full-on Joan Collins, but actually what I see is . . . a Goddess. Well, me, but a very, very well madeup and slickly glossed me. She hands me a pink lipstick and smiles. "D'ya like it?"

I grin at her. "Yeah," I say. "I look good."

I came in a troll, but my God, they are doing their damnedest to put me on that stage if not a Barbie, at least a contender.

Next up: Hair. And I have masses of it. "Fancy a trim, cherub?" A short

Kewpie doll of a man sidles up to me. "Let's talk hair, shall we?" He grabs my hand and dances back to his barber chair to the strains of "Lady in Red." I giggle and do my best not to trip over my feet, the floor being a deceptively flat surface. I snuggle into his leather chair and he flits around me like a lawnmower, chopping and cutting and slashing and blowing and spraying and . . .

"Ta da," he says.

Shit, I look like Bonnie Raitt. There is so much volume and fluff you could hide a small child in there.

"Um, could we bring it down a bit?" I say, patting it nervously.

"Sure, hon, whatever you want. We want you to feel comfy." He combs and fusses and then stands back. "Better?" He winks.

Well, now I have moved on to Madonna in the "Lucky Star" video. I figure I'll settle for that, in case Flock of Seagulls is still lurking somewhere. I stand up and give him a hug.

"My name's Charlie," he says. "We're very pleased to have you with us. Come in here anytime you want—there's always coffee, a smoke, and a chat. Okay, cherub?" He has such a warm smile that I love him instantly. The Makeup room is about to become my home, and everyone in it my confidant. I feel good. I dance back to my room to get into my outfit.

I am instantly depressed.

My heart sinks when I see what I'm to wear for the wedding. Amber is marrying Trent, or more properly, Jennifer Abell is marrying Philip Salisbury. And me, I'm a bridesmaid. They've decided to stuff me into this ghastly floaty chiffon number with huge cabbage roses. Worse yet, I'm to be flanked by Alison and Tiffany in matching cabbage rose attire—two sizes smaller than mine, to be sure.

* * *

INT.—ABELL ESTATE LIVING ROOM—EVENING

                    MINISTER
    Dearly beloved, we are gathered here today . . .

                    JENNIFER
    Wait! I need time to think.

She flees the ceremony. After a moment's pause, all the bridesmaids go after her.

INT.—JENNIFER'S BEDROOM—EVENING

                    DEVON
    What's the matter, Jen? What's wrong? You've got to go
    back to the ceremony. Everyone's waiting.

Shit—do I really have to say this drivel? Weddings are the stock-in-trade of the soaps. They've got me being a girlie-girl, and I'm hating every fucking minute of it. The rest of them are all in their element. Meredith is flitting around the periphery in a Scarlett O'Hara chapeau and a ruffly pink froth of a dress, whose hue if I'm not mistaken is the very same Relentless Raspberry of the peignoir set she gave me.

I'm so uncomfortable in my skin that I'm fighting off another panic attack. I struggle with the picture hat, which they seem to wear effortlessly. These women instinctively know what to do—how to wear a bridesmaid's dress, how to set their hats, how to do the flowers. I'm not surprised. If you're a very pretty girl, you grow up knowing you're pretty, and you learn how to work it. Beyond that, there's a certain body of knowledge that just comes naturally to them, a body of knowledge I clearly do not have—and never will.

Just then something catches in my throat, a feeling of dismay. I realize, slowly at first, that I've been had. The camaraderie in Hair and Makeup wasn't real. It couldn't be, because I'm an interloper who'll never measure up. The look on their faces tells me I've been found out, and that I'll be receiving official notification shortly:

> *Dear Ms. McPhee: We regret to inform you that you do not meet our standards. Thank you for applying. Don't get full of yourself just because you came in and saw your name painted on a piece of concrete in the parking lot—we had to paint out someone else's name to put yours there; it's no problem to do it again. You may come and be in our throng, but do **not** make the mistake of imagining yourself a member.*

"Cut! Set up for Scene fourteen. Kate—that's you and Kirk."

* * *

"Kate, I'm Kirk Marlowe—Burke Chaney."

Jeez! Nobody is this good-looking.

I'm so awestruck by his physicality that I almost miss the fact that this handsome come-here-and-I'll-fuck-you-standing-up guy is extending a burly mitt to shake my hand. Nope, nothing but sheer animal magnetism here. I'm actually embarrassed by his open sexuality. He's carmel blond, with those squinty blue eyes that would look so amazing if viewed from beneath, should one be lucky enough to be on the receiving end of his expertise.

"Oh ya-yeah," I stammer stupidly. "Pleased to meet you. You're the football player . . . catching passes, right?"

"Was," he replies with a smile. "Had to hang 'em up after I had my bell rung once too often—at least once too often."

"Quite a career change," I say, wondering if I look as awkward as I feel.

"Yeah, well, everyone expected me to fall on my face in the acting business, but I took it seriously. I studied hard—didn't want to make a horse's ass of myself on camera."

As he turns and walks toward his mark for the beginning of our scene together, I note appreciatively that he is still very much a tight end.

INT.—STONY POINT BAR—NIGHT

The bartender slides the cognac down the long bar toward Burke. As his Armani-clad arm reaches out to intercept it, he looks quizzically at the bartender, who nods over his shoulder toward the opposite end of the bar, where Devon is seated. Burke grabs the glass and rises to join her.

                    BURKE
     I thought you were dead.

                    DEVON
     You did your best to make me that way.

We're in mid-scene when I hear the noisy clip-clop of heels on the studio floor, making haste for a Destination. "Oh Christ, we're in for it now," Kirk whispers. "You know you're in trouble when She comes down to the set."

My heart sinks. We are the Destination, and the heels are attached to Daphne del Valle, the doyenne of daytime, and our executive producer. Part genius, part obsessed lunatic, part network cash cow, she originated three of the longest-running daytime dramas on television, just pulled them right out of her ass, and is credited with saving two others when they were foundering. There are something like twenty-two Emmys crowding her mantel, but right now she doesn't care about any of that. Right now she's a woman on a mission.

With a withering stare, Daphne strides past, or perhaps more accurately over, the director and comes right up to the corner of the bar where Kirk and I are seated. "No, Kate. No, no, no, and no." She grabs my shoulders. "That's not how you talk to people. You're flat and you're smug"—she shoots a look at Kirk, just in case he has the idea this is only about me—"both of you.

"Shake it up out there. I want it sharp. Improvise if what's written doesn't make sense—change the words if you have to. Make it work."

An invitation to ad-lib—in daytime television? You've got to be kidding.

"But Mom . . ." Kirk's protestations are cut off in midair by a death ray glower.

Mom? He calls her Mom?

"Kirk, I'll deal with you in a moment." And she backs him off with another lethal glance. "Kate, I'm like a hawk. I see your weak point, and when you let your guard down, I attack. But don't take it badly. I do it because I want something human . . . something genuine to put out on the air. I do it out of looooooove—looooooove for you, looooooove for your character, looooooove for the show."

To look at Daphne del Valle, looooooove is hardly the first thing that comes to mind. The woman is a Grade A fright . . . but, to be sure, a Grade A fright in a Chanel pantsuit. Over the years she's evidently tried to make various accommodations to the passing of time—God knows, Los Angeles is a hard town on older women, hard in a way that New York and London are not. There, wit and intelligence are "well-but" compensating factors, as in, "*Well,* she's fifty-seven—*but* she's extremely bright and very funny." In LA your brains and your sense of humor count for zippo: "*Well,* she's fifty-seven—*but* that's too bad."

She looks like a short man. Indeed, there is the aura of a small and very intense man about her. She has Bad Hair—not just occasionally, perpetually. If she'd really been a man, she'd have been sporting the mother of all comb-overs. Instead, her thinning hair has been frappéd into a stiff meringue; mousse-laden peaks cover her head like inverted exclamation points. Coiffure by Cuisinart.

I can only assume she has a guy's table manners as well. It's obvious that she ate something right before coming to the set, because anyone can read her menu just by looking at the Chanel. There are bits of croissant (okay, foccacia maybe) adorning the lapel, coffee drips on the pussycat bow blouse, dabs of jam on the pocket (mostly black currant, with occasional punctuations of orange marmalade), a speck of scrambled egg (not necessarily from today) on the sleeve. It had to be that the last thing she did before coming down to give us grief was to reapply her lipstick—and I figure that she was still chewing when she did so, because it looks as though she threw the Bobbi Brown in the general direction of the slit in her face and then ran downstairs.

Daphne has a brief conference with the director, rips the script from his hands, peruses it briefly, then shakes her head. "Never mind. This is a crucial scene, and we really must make something happen here, but it's not going to happen today. We'll shoot this again tomorrow. Kate, darling, I need you to come and have drinks with me this evening. Bel-Air Hotel. Eight P.M." And without even waiting to hear whether I had a prior appointment for root canal surgery, she turns on her heel and leaves.

Now, there's a new record, Katiegirl. Called on the carpet by the producer on this, the second day on the job.

A creeping regret starts somewhere around my flushed Irish farmgirl cheeks and slowly, sadly moves down my body, pushing out any remaining infantile hopes and innocent expectations. I wonder whether anyone notices the puddle of my dreams that has slithered down my body and is now hanging around my ankles like Peter Pan's shadow.

• • •

I arrive early at the Bel-Air, and after nodding an anxious greeting to the swans, I go immediately into the loo to see about sopping up the perspiration that is pouring off my body in buckets. Terror-generated flop sweat. If I'd mummified myself in Saran Wrap and dressed in a garment bag, I'd have been drier. By the time I dab off the worst of it and emerge, she's already there at a small table, mantling a scotch.

Now that I can study her at close range, it's apparent that Daphne has had more than a little work done around her eyes—work that predates the Botox Era. I can only assume that her plastic surgeon's office had been running a three-fer special, because they'd also slipped her some cheek and chin implants at the same time. The cheek implants have more or less stayed in place, but over the years the chin implant had obviously slipped its moorings and become something of a free agent, since it is now floating around the southern portion of her mandible.

When she speaks, she fiddles with it nervously, moving it around to various venues on her chin. In keeping with her soft-butch persona, the effect is not unlike a man stroking his beard. "Kate," she begins, her index finger earnestly wiggling the implant in circles, "I stopped you and Kirk today because it wasn't *costing* either of you to do what you were doing, and if it doesn't cost you, it's going to be a vapid scene." Her first scotch goes down fast. She orders another.

"To do a show like this, there has to be pain—a lot of pain. And I will drive you and Kirk and everyone else toward that pain, that torment, because torment is what makes people want to be better, makes them want to better their lives." She's so completely consumed by her story that every word she speaks seems to be bitten out in a kind of aggression.

She drains the second scotch and orders another. "Kate," she says, putting her hand over mine earnestly. "What I want from you—what I want for Devon Merrick—is for you to put her vulnerability out there for everyone to see.

"You are passionate on a really strong, deep level about this man. Whatever dialogue I give you is rooted in this passion, but if the lines don't work, please—improvise. There are actors on the show to whom I would not say that. But you—you can do it. So can Kirk. That's one of the reasons why both of you are here." Her index finger is now working overtime on her jawline, toggling the implant up and down, like a light switch. "Whatever you're saying doesn't matter nearly as much as getting across the emotional subtext—that all-consuming passion—beneath it. So both of you—strip everything else away until you're left with something raw, something *organic*. Get the emotion out there, let everyone see that it's *cost* you to get to this point."

Intense as it was, what she was saying was also more than vaguely familiar. It reminded me of the acting exercises I'd had to do when I was still a drama student. *And* she didn't want to fire me, which was a relief. It was now safe to try to pin her down, to make sure I knew exactly and specifically what she wanted from me tomorrow. "Daphne—tell me more about what it has cost me."

"You just survived a horrific car crash. You spent months recuperating. You trusted Burke to drive safely and he betrayed you by getting drunk—secretly." At this point she is all but vaulting the tiny table at me. "But you loooooove him so dreadfully." It's as if her obsession is leaving her body via her mouth, and she needs to have one last big bite of it before she finally spits it out. She is literally in my face—and my face is getting damp.

No choice but to just suck it up and take it, Katiegirl. Even though you're on the receiving end of an ongoing atomizer jetspray of saliva, if you move to sit back out of range or wipe your face with a cocktail napkin, you do so only at extreme peril to your job security.

"All the while you were in the hospital, he never came around," she continues. "Your life hung in the balance—you went through all the agony and uncertainty over whether you'd be scarred for life *alone*. He never even called, even though he was responsible for what you were going through. You don't know how to handle your rage over the accident. You are hurt—wounded, both physically and in your heart—*and* you are angry, exxx-**quizzz**-itttleee **anggg-gry**. And yet . . ." Daphne pauses for a big gulp of Glenfiddich.

"And yet . . . ?" I say from the edge of my seat, waiting for her to continue. By this time I'm all body English, eagerly leaning forward and willingly moving deeper into her Splash Zone.

She takes another swallow of scotch.

"And yet . . . ?" I repeat anxiously. *How can she leave me hanging here like this?* I am completely caught up in her story, in her magnetic intensity.

Never mind her bizarre appearance—this is Daphne's genius: her fervent belief in the validity and the triumph of naked human emotion, and her determination to communicate that on the air, is so powerful that it drags us all into it, actors and audiences alike. She may be crazy, but she's good crazy, and when it all comes together, it makes great television.

"And yet . . ." One mo' time.

For chrissake get on with it! This must be what waiting out the commercials is like for viewers at home.

"And yet . . ."

And yet another mouthful of scotch.

"And yet, on a deeper level, all that really doesn't matter, because you loooooove him, Kate—you loooooove him so much. He's the greatest person you've ever slept with, but it's been months since he's touched you—since anyone touched you. All of these emotions are at war within you, rubbing together like dry kindling till you become a woman ablaze—on fire with the searing white heat of anger, and on fire with desire. Sell it. Sell the hurt. Sell the rage. Sell the hunger. Sell the loooooove. And to sell it, you have to **believe** it."

Quite by accident, Daphne del Valle has stumbled on my acting "technique"—which is to say that I have no technique at all. I just agonize over it all and then torture myself into believing everything my character does.

3

Wednesday morning/the next day

6:37! 6:37!! 6:37!!!

The alarm goes off again, to the accompaniment of staccato time flashes on the ceiling. This time I'm on the bed but not in it—*and* I'm still in my street clothes. When I got home from the session with Daphne, I was so wrung out that I pretty much dropped in my tracks. In the morning gloom Drusilla stares at me through emerald slits of accusation and reproach, not because I'm dressed, but because we're now at three days and counting of no Science Diet, no Purina, no Friskies. Post-it notes that say BUY CAT FOOD cover my bathroom mirror.

The two of us share a bowl of cereal and milk as I gather up my script pages and peruse my closet for appropriate attire. I shower fast, skip the leg shaving (I'll wear pants), and rush back to the agonizing wardrobe process that is in danger of making me late for a very important date. Unfortunately the only thing I'm in the mood for is a 1920s flapper dress in black, which hits my knees. Crap. I'll have to shave after all. I dive back into the shower and quickly drag the Gillette over my prickly calves. Ouch! I snake my hand out of the shower stall and scribble another note to add to the collection on the bathroom mirror—BUY RAZOR BLADES.

Leaving my thighs hairy and me resembling a Minotaur from the knees up, I throw on my '20s dress and a Mobil station baseball cap, leap into the Honda (and yes, the damned basket is still there), and charge through the traffic and into the parking lot at the studio.

The bouncy but adenoidal strains of George Michael singing "Wake me up before you go-go" faintly trickle toward me as I gallop down the hallway for my date with JJ. I slow my gait down to a swagger and try to layer on a veneer of cool as I enter the Makeup room. The room is a hive of activity, with worker bees intent on readying their flowers for a close-up at the Garden Party, either restoring the blossoms to their true beauty—or if need be inventing it out of whole cloth.

I pour myself a coffee and try to appear nonchalant as I lean against a wall that bears a poster of Meredith with a couple of jailbait suitors. My coffee is sweet and hot. I have a feeling of excitement in my stomach. I'm feeling really good. My talk with Daphne has inspired me. Everyone seems to be in my corner; JJ is about to work her magic; Kirk is waiting to rehearse; even Wardrobe is cooperating, having lined up a really cool cream Burberry dress for me to wear for the next scene. I am close to happy.

All the chairs are full, so I sip and varda the action up and down the Hollywood assembly line. The airhead blondes are being curled and sprayed into the various Malibu Barbies that they are. I don't envy the worker bees this task—making them distinct on the surface when they're so much alike underneath can't be easy. They are each squealing about the amount of chocolate they consumed last night. Dinner, I suppose. To me chocolate was what one ate while finding the car keys.

Nearby an extraordinarily stunning African American actress is having some goop put in her hair. A little farther down, Trent waves to me as JJ wields an electric razor and mows any hint of stubble from his chin. Next door a blond hunk is getting a full Joan Rivers makeover.

Meredith herself inhabits the center makeup perch. I hide behind my coffee cup and watch. As she reclines completely in her Queen Bee throne, her own personal chubby worker bee silently fills in the faint creases and ravines that a thousand years in the public eye have generated—at least the ones that plastic surgery has not yet expunged. There is something oddly embalming about the process. The Queen's eyes are shut tight and she wears a peaceful look. I imagine she is planning tea parties in her head, or formulating lists of more edible cosmetic products to develop.

I know for a fact she ain't thinking about acting.

She is uncannily beautiful. Her copper bangs are rolled into a perfect soft hot dog bun of hair, a look she has borrowed from Bette Davis—and quite frankly should have left with her. There is a softness about her small frame. Everything about Meredith is round, as if someone had puffed air right under the dermis, everywhere. Her bones are buried deep in her flesh; they are invisible. There is not a muscle to behold either—except in her calves, which are surprisingly firm and defined, as if reaching on her tiptoes to capture stardom has required a little physical effort after all.

She stirs and sits up to apply mascara. Like a submerged synchronized swimmer, her movements have a uniquely fluid grace; there is nothing jarring or sudden. Her water ballet gestures are sensuous but stop short of a satisfying completion, as if it were vulgar to express oneself fully. Meredith is intoxicating. I'm spellbound, a drowning captive without enough willpower to come up for air.

Meredith has briefly paused in her own preparations. Her eyes narrow slightly, zero in on their target, then recover their equanimity. She sizes up the willowy black actress. "LaTrisa, that is an extraordinary shade of lipstick," she says appreciatively, with an almost flirtatious laugh. "Step back—let me get a better look at you. Gorgeous. And I simply love that red dress on you—absolutely stunning," she coos huskily.

"Uh, thanks. Thanks, Meredith. Gotta go." Not sure of what just happened, LaTrisa extricates herself awkwardly and stumbles out of the room.

As soon as she is out of sight, the Queen's face hardens. "Phone. Now!" Meredith barks to the makeup fairy, who quickly acquiesces.

"LaTrisa is wearing MAC Bombshell lipstick. I don't know what they are thinking in here," she hisses into the mouthpiece. "Excuse me?" She pauses to listen, but only briefly. "What? No. I don't care that it looks different on a black woman. . . . Besides, if it looked that different, how come I still recognized it? That is *my* color. Exclusively. **And** she is in a fucking **RED DRESS**! I wear red, not every other fucking actress on the show. Capish?" she adds in a voice dripping pure poison. "Change her."

With that, she hangs up the phone and snuggles peacefully back into her cocoon as if nothing had happened. But in the aftermath of her tirade, the entire room is in freeze-frame—everyone is stuck in place, and no one dares be the first to move. Even the oldies music station is on pause. Suddenly Meredith claps her hands, and without a word everyone jumps to attention and the room recommences business. The music resumes; it is "We Built This City" by Starship.

From my fly-on-the-wall vantage point, I breathe a sigh of relief. I cannot formulate any thoughts, so I just stare. Trent walks past me.

"Close your mouth, Kate. JJ is all yours," he murmurs.

Damn, he's sexy.

He pours a cup of coffee and dribbles creamer in.

Okay, how does he do that? How does he make that action compelling? Is it the pouring . . . the dribbling . . . the stirring?

Sensuality just oozes out of him. Trent is a living, breathing example of something every actor knows—that the camera just loves some people more than others. It can't be taught—either you got it or you don't. He's got it and he knows it. Then the bastard saunters out with all the confidence the universe can summon up. My eyes follow him till he disappears from view as I plant myself on JJ's toadstool.

"Hi, hon!" she tweets brightly, and begins the arduous half-hour Troll-to-Barbie conversion process.

Next door the blond male, who has been lounging in his transformation pod entirely too long, stirs like a large tawny lion emerging from his afternoon nap.

"MAC Spice pencil, please," he growls, stretching out his paw. He has an ample carpet of straw-colored hair poking out from his guinea tee, on which a Saint Christopher nestles comfortably. He is muscular, but in that workouts-of-the-past way, he has gone slightly to seed. He had probably been fighting fit in his prime, but it is obvious that he now spends a greater percentage of his time in the La-Z-Boy, or more precisely, the makeup chair.

Clutching a large pink mirror that states, OBJECTS IN THE MIRROR MAY BE LARGER THAN THEY APPEAR on the back, he is outlining his Kenneth Branagh lips—which is to say his lack thereof. He follows the Spice lip pencil with a light pink gloss, and a dusting of rouge in Orgasmic.

Honestly, he would make a drag queen proud.

He squints at himself in the mirror. He slowly puts his chin one way and then the other. He scowls. Disappointment momentarily furrows his brow. He stands. He clears his throat. "Debra, could you just dab a touch more eyeliner, huh?" he mewls.

The weary makeup artist complies. Tawny Lion thrusts his chin forward and pouts at himself in the mirror. He preens. He struts a little. He nods approval and points at himself, grinning. Under his breath I think I hear him say, "You da man!" He ambles away from the chair, picks up a sponge and foundation, and begins to paint his hairy paws and arms Suntan Number 4.

Clean cups! Clean cups! Move down! Move down!

I am mesmerized—literally hypnotized—by his naked self-adoration. If he had dropped to the floor and started to lick his balls, I wouldn't have registered even the remotest surprise.

An image on the TV monitor catches my eye. It takes a moment for me to realize that it is LaTrisa, now dressed in a drab brown wool suit. An ugly dark gloss now sits on her lips where Bombshell used to be.

It's okay, I want to say to her through the screen. Don't let her get to you—you've got something they can't cover up. You're so beautiful, they could put you in a hair shirt and you'd still look like a goddess.

Suddenly, a Bambi of epic proportions bursts into Makeup. Her body has been engineered into an exotic dancer's wet dream—a twelve-year-old boy's frame supports two gigantic motorbike helmet knockers.

Oooh—with those puppies, how does she sit up in the morning?

She is Amazon Barbie come to life, a six-foot-tall frosted sundae of vanilla swirls piled upon a plate of smiles, balanced on endless limbs of toffee. "Hi, Baybeee-Waybeee!" she squeals. Tawny Lion turns, slowly. He strikes a John Wayne pose and raises an eyebrow. Amazon Barbie throws her arms around his hairy neck and appears to impale herself on his crotch.

"Mind the makeup, babe," he growls.

"Oooh, sowwy!" she giggles, as if to a two-month-old. "Doo Bee Doo

Bee's all made up, is he?" She wriggles and writhes, trying to stabilize herself on her stilettos while maintaining contact with his pubic bone.

"Let's go, babe. You can help me run lines," Tawny Lion leers. He turns her about and slaps her none too softly on the ass. Oddly enough, as he leaves, he gives an insecure and astoundingly fey little skip. Her baby talk recedes down the hallway.

Easy, Tiger! Methinks maybe Baby's Doo Bee has a little more testosterone on the outside than he has on the inside!

"Close your mouth, hon," JJ snaps, pulling me back into what passes for reality and gently putting my head back in the neck rest so she can finish my makeup.

"Who was that?" I try to keep the awe in my voice to a minimum.

"Priscilla," she sighs, bored, delicately penciling in my eyebrows.

"No—the guy, the actor, who is he?" I persist.

"Priscilla," she states with finality. "He plays Gallagher Molloy, the bartender, who may or may not be an undercover federal agent."

"But Priscilla? It's a good handle, and it surely suits him, but c'mon, JJ . . . that can't really be his name."

"Well, it oughta be. He's got one of those forwards-backwards names—where it doesn't really matter which one's first and which one's last. I think it's Shelby Garrett, but maybe it's Garrett Shelby, and since we just call him 'Priscilla,' it never really matters to me."

"Fair enough."

* * *

Kirk and I run lines, trying to bring Daphne's vision to life. We sit in his tiny dressing room, a broom closet much like my own. We are dismembering the pages. We are talking over each other excitedly about our characters. He is bringing me up to date on his history, and I'm telling him what I've created for my backstory, totally ignoring the fact that before I got here, Devon Merrick had been played by another actress. Fuck her.

He drones on, "Then I married Taylor Daniels, that's Alison's character—for the third time—and discovered that she was lying about the paternity and divorced her again, and then had a rebound affair with Regina."

"You slept with Regina?" I gasp, even as I'm thinking, *You slept with Meredith?*

"It was out of pain—I was suffering. . . ." He shrugs meekly.

"So, basically, your character is weak and has no scruples?" I raise my eyebrows in mock horror.

"Basically," he admits as he moves in closer and lowers his voice an octave . . . "but I'm a hell of a lay."

Right. Where does the Stanislavsky come in?

"So, do you think you left me for dead out of fear?" I ask, my heart thumping.

Kirk's eyes snap open wide, and a look of excitement comes into them. "Yes, yes, exactly! I was too scared you were dead. I didn't know how to go on, so I tried to forget the biggest love of my life."

He seems pleased with himself. It's almost tragic watching a grown man try to make sense of it all. However, we soldier on—vulnerable actors trusting each other, willing to expose our souls, even for silly plot twists. Otherwise, what's the point? If you show up for work, you might as well bleed a little and attempt to shine some light on the Human Condition, even if we are just bookends for detergent commercials. We run the scene.

INT.—STONY POINT BAR—NIGHT

The bartender slides the cognac down the long bar toward Burke. As his Armani-clad arm reaches out to intercept it, he looks quizzically at the bartender, who nods over his shoulder toward the opposite end of the bar, where Devon is seated. Burke registers shock as he seizes the glass and quickly rises to join her.

                    BURKE
    I thought you were dead.

                    DEVON
    You mean you left me for dead—you did your best to
    make me that way.

                    BURKE
    Devon, please! It's not like that.

                    DEVON
    Isn't it?

                    BURKE
    You have no idea.

                    DEVON
    Bastard! You abandoned me!

The loudspeaker interrupts us. "We are moving to the Stony Point Bar. Scenes ten through fifteen. Burke and Devon to set, please. Bartender and Background also. Scenes ten through fifteen. Thank you."

We are silent as we walk to the set. Actors in their own worlds, thinking, thinking, preparing emotional pathways deep in our souls, ready to be ripped open at the slightest provocation. We are certain of our newfound camaraderie.

As Kirk and I position ourselves on the set, I catch a glimpse of Daphne headed for the control room. She's dressed in the same Chanel suit that she was wearing last night, except that quite uncharacteristically, she is barefoot.

Marty, our stage manager, stands with his script in hand. "Places, please," he barks. The director, an enormously large, sweaty individual, stands fidgeting with his headset. I know how you feel, pal, I think, but I put all thoughts of swelling and exploding out of my mind. I am calm. I am prepared. I am in the zone.

"Right, right," the director mumbles, "so, stick to the blocking you did yesterday, er, you sit there, and you sit there and, um, well, then you get up and go to her, right, Kirk?"

Kirk is not listening to him; he's staring at me. I know what he's thinking. I lock eyes with him, I don't blink and I am breathing hard. We are matadors, Olympians. We are preparing for the greatest game on Earth. God, I love acting.

"Eh, right then . . ." The poor sweaty one scurries back to the booth, mumbling something about Daphne. He is a crushed man. In the distant recesses of my brain, I wonder whether Daphne reduces everyone to that blubbering mess. My instinct unfortunately tells me, yes, she does.

"Alrighty then," Marty announces in a singsong voice. "From the top, Scene ten. Can we have quiet? Places, please. Final touches, please."

The cameras glide noiselessly into place, their little red tally lights extinguished to lessen any distraction. A lighting guy swiftly moves onto the set and gently adjusts a gel. A makeup person dabs my nose with powder and tries not to make eye contact. She smells of peppermints.

I feel my emotions building, held in check by concentrating on the mantra in my head:

> *I looooove you . . .*
> *I loooooove you . . .*
> *You left me for dead.*

I run this over and over, until I am so tortured that I want to grab the crewmember who is scratching his nuts in my sightline and yell, *Sit the fuck down!*

"Clear sightlines, please. Take a seat, people!" Marty bellows. God bless him. He looks at me. "Tell me when, Kate." He is all business, but I detect tenderness and understanding. I love him.

I quickly look up toward Kirk. His jaw is set. There is a nod, almost imperceptible. I look at Marty. There are tears in my eyes. I fight them off. I nod ever so slightly.

"On the count . . . These are delicate scenes, people—no moving around. . . . Thank you. . . . We are rolling. In . . . five . . . four . . . three . . . two . . ."

The gates open. We are off.

INT.—STONY POINT BAR—NIGHT

The camera tracks on the glass as the bartender slides the cognac down the long bar toward Burke. As his Armani-clad arm reaches out to intercept it, he looks quizzically at the bartender, who nods over his shoulder toward the oppo-site end of the bar, where Devon is seated. Burke registers shock as he seizes the glass and quickly rises to join her.

The second camera shot slides up my arm, across my small, heaving breasts, and comes to rest on my face, half obscured by luxurious waves of hair, albeit brunette. A tremulous glossy mouth and one tearful eye complete the picture of a woman wronged.

                    BURKE
Devon! I . . . I . . . I . . . I thought you were dead.

                    DEVON
                 (curtly)
You mean you *left* me for dead—after you did your best to make me that way.

                    BURKE
You have no idea what I've been through.

                    DEVON
              (her voice rising)
What *you've* been through? How dare you? You all but killed me, and now you want me to care about what *you've* been through? My face is held together by bolts and plates. . . .

                    BURKE
You look beautiful to me.

                    DEVON
           (unnerved by his response)
Don't try to change the subject. You abandoned me!

                              BURKE
          Devon, please! It's not like that.

                              DEVON
          Isn't it?
          Devon raises her hand to strike Burke. He catches her
          wrist in midair . . . . and then uses it to pull
me close to him. "Before you start pummeling me," he says in a
seductive whisper, "won't you give me a chance to explain?"

   Okay, the script just went out the window.
   Kirk closes the distance between the two of us. He strongly pulls himself up against me—*damn, that feels good*—and nuzzles into the deep tri-
angular hollow above my clavicle—which means his mouth cannot be
seen on camera. I feel his soft lips and hot breath on my skin. "Stay with
me, Kate," he murmurs in a voice only I can hear. "Go with it. Just trust
me."
   "What . . ." I start to breathe heavy sighs, responding to his manly presence. . . . "What . . ." He raises his head, and as his lips move closer to mine,
he cups my cheek in his hand. I feel desire steaming off his body . . . and
my own temperature starts to rise as well. I emit the tiniest sex-starved
whimper-sigh—"Unh . . ."
   Yowzah. We're flying without a net now.
   "Devon . . . I missed you so very much." He moves in closer and is just
about to kiss me when my anger reasserts itself. I pull back from him and
let my eyes—*yeah they're brown, not blue; get over it*—flare.
   "Then why did you leave the scene? Why didn't you come see me afterward?" Every part of my body has become an accusation.
   "I barely remember staggering away from the wreckage. I guess I stumbled into a homeless encampment, because the next thing I know I'm
wearing an ice pack wrapped in a filthy rag, and all these craggy, toothless
faces are looking back at me saying, 'You okay, buddy?' "
   *Homeless encampment? Where is all this coming from? More important, where
is it all headed? Do I trust him? Yeah, I guess I do. I'm just going to keep it spinning
till someone tells me to stop.*
   "Indeed," I say, dripping cynicism, "and after that it was just too much
trouble to find out if I was dead or alive?"
   "I must have hit my head pretty hard, because when those old rummies
asked me what my name was, I didn't have an answer for them. Eventually
they went through my wallet and called Fallon—she hid me away in the
convent till everything calmed down."
   What . . . Convent? If he mentions aliens or an evil twin, I'm outta here.
   "Ah," I say ever so cynically, "the only convent in America where cell

phones don't work. Dammit, Burke! What possible explanation can you give me to make what you did okay?"

I raise my voice almost to a shout. "You left me for dead! What were you drinking. . . . No, wait!" I increase the emotional distance by moving around behind my barstool, so that it's now between us, like a barricade. "Let me guess." My voice turns sarcastic. "Was it cognac, like this?"

His large masculine hand reaches out for the fragile glass.

"No, that's not it," I continue acidly. "It was vodka, wasn't it, Burke—otherwise I'd have smelled it on your breath."

I'm spewing these words out now in a venomous fury of righteous indignation. Meanwhile, he is clutching the brandy snifter so tightly that his knuckles have turned white and his hand has started to shake.

This is no time to let up. Go for it, Kate.

"So," I say, resuming the attack. "How many did it take—how many did you toss down before you felt brave enough to take my life in your hands?"

The glass implodes under the continued pressure of his hand. Its amber contents spill across the bar, and his hand begins to bleed, but he pays no attention. "Devon, stop," he begs. "Please stop. I wasn't drinking at all. You have to believe me."

Curve ball. Major curve ball. Not only are we off the script, we're off the plot. At this point he's entitled to a storyline credit.

"I . . . I don't understand." My eyes register shock and dismay. "That's not possible." I sense the guy on Camera 2 creep in closer behind me.

Back over to you, Kirk. I'm vamping till I get a clue. If you've got something in mind, let's hear it.

"I . . . I was set up."

I can't wait to hear what happens next.

"What do you mean?"

Lead me on, Kirk. I need a little more to go on than that.

"Regina put something in my iced tea."

Holy Fucking Moley.

Out of the corner of my eye I see the director in the booth start to raise his right arm in prelude to yelling "Cut," but before he can do so, Daphne quickly but forcefully catches his wrist in midair. It is a move that exactly mimics what Kirk had done when I tried to strike him.

"You're telling me that she wanted the accident to happen?" I ask.

He nods, ever so slowly, and then gathers me in his arms.

"She sees you as a threat. She knows how strong my feelings are for you."

"Tell me, Burke," I whisper. "After all that's happened, I need to hear you tell me about those feelings."

"All the time I had amnesia," he says softly, his eyes boring into my soul, "I was completely disoriented in place and time—I didn't know who I was. I didn't know where I was. The only thing I could remember was how much I loved you."

Suddenly I'm looking into Kirk's amazing blue eyes, and our bodies are pressed together. He plants a huge kiss on my slightly parted lips. I feel his tongue halfway down my throat, and I don't mind a bit.

Sweet Jesus. That's a huge hard-on!

A small trickle of perspiration runs down between my boobs. After what seems like forever, he pulls away reluctantly. A single tear rolls down my cheek, which he wipes away with his bleeding hand, leaving a slight streak of O-positive behind.

"Cut!" I hear from the control room, but the voice is not that of the director.

It's Daphne. Everyone else is too dumbstruck to move.

"I hope that was okay, what I did," Kirk whispers to me.

Okay? Okay???? My knees are still weak, and I have this colossal wet spot between my thighs.

"A lot better than okay," I say, still breathless. As I start coming back into the present, I see Tiffany, Amber, and Alison standing in the wings, mouths agape. From the control room, a very satisfied-looking Daphne gives Kirk and me a huge thumbs-up, puts her fingers to her lips, and then lets them fly as if to say, *Magnifique.* Exactly what I wanted. That's how it's supposed to be done.

"Kate, we're going to have so much fun," Kirk says as he walks me off the set.

Suddenly, I'm aware of a horrendous screeching coming from the corridor. Meredith is steaming up the hallway in full cry. I know my imagination is working overtime, but I'm positive that she's wielding a plastic flamingo like a croquet mallet, and screaming, "Off with her head!"

* * *

I stumble back into my cubbyhole to wring out my underwear.

Note to self: On the days when you work hot and heavy with Kirk, bring a spare thong.

Maybe this comes from his background as a football player, but as an actor, Kirk is a risk taker, a tightrope walker, which in a leading man is a very good thing indeed. Even if you're just on the ground watching, your heart's in your mouth every minute, because you know it's more than a little dangerous up there—but to be out on the high wire with him, that's the best thing in the world.

Damn, that was fun!

A gnome knocks on my door and pokes his head in. "I'm sorry, Kate, but you're wanted on the . . . *Third Floor.*" The dire look on his face matches his funereal tone of voice, both of which imply my impending doom, as if he were telling me that the governor had turned down my eleventh-hour request for clemency.

The third floor of the building holds the executive offices, including Daphne's office. I'm still trying to figure out whether I'm supposed to be scared or not, when I'm ushered into her aerie.

"Sit down, Kate," she says, offering me a chair. The office is expensively and tastefully furnished in the very finest Knoll International style, but a bit sterile. It's clear that she hired someone to decorate it. There's nothing really personal in it, probably because Daphne's heart is in Hope Canyon. The remains of a meal sit on the credenza, and the office still smells faintly of raspberries. Not surprisingly, the Chanel has been festooned with yet more food—the croissant crumbs of yesteryear have been joined by some lettuce shreds, bits of hard-boiled egg, and tuna shards.

A bizarrely whimsical observation arrives unbidden: if Daphne were to arrive at my door with that much food on her clothing, she'd have the protein-deprived Drusilla, in hot pursuit of the egg and tuna morsels, draped across her bosom like a furry bustier.

That mental image spawns the hint of a giggle, which I fight off furiously, like an inopportune sneeze. It would never do to appear to be laughing at Daphne del Valle. The only way I can suppress the chortle is by getting into character.

DEVON
(à la Joe Friday)

Yes, your honor. My suspicions were immediately aroused when Sergeant Drusilla came upon the egg and tuna, which she pounced upon and took into her personal custody. I knew we were getting warmer when on closer inspection I saw more evidence—couple of capers in the vicinity of the lapel—but the key that broke the case wide open was something suspicious on the Dior silk blouse. I thought at first it was a piece of bad jewelry. Turned out to be an AWOL anchovy. I concluded that the subject had hastily consumed a salade niçoise. I'd say probably a raspberry tart for dessert.

Case closed.

"Kate, you know how pleased I am with what you and Kirk did out there," she begins, tapping on her chin implant. "I just loooooove what you did so much, but it's given us a problem."

*Aaaaah . . . I breathe sigh of relief. If **we** have a problem, it is so very much better than if **she** has a problem—or worse yet, if she thinks **I** have a problem. You know how to work this, Kate—now is the time to be a team player.*

I summon up a furrowed look of concern from deep within my brow and lean in sympathetically. "Daphne, you know I'll do whatever I can to help."

Acting 101 and Corporate Politics 101 are in fact the same course of study. Body language is everything. This stuff works whether you're onstage or off—as long as you don't start believing your own bullshit. Otherwise you end up like Meredith.

"I just had a visit from Meredith Contini," she says, twiddling her chin.

Speak of the devil.

"She was very upset about your scene with Kirk."

"Did she say why?"

"Not exactly. She did a great deal of flapping without being specific. But I believe she sees you as some sort of threat. She demanded that I fire you."

"Or else . . ."

"Or else she would leave the show."

"Can she do that?"

"In a way, yes. It's complicated, but her contract gives her a lot of say."

Well, that's that. The gnome was right. That's sometimes how it goes—do good work, step on the diva's toes, and get your ass canned in three easy steps.

"So I'm out, then?"

"I don't take kindly to threats, Kate. Ms. Contini is a star not just because *Live for Tomorrow* made her one, but because it *keeps* her one. Even though we pay her a bundle to be Regina Abell, she makes even more selling her lines of cosmetics and clothing on cable."

"The junk in my gift basket?"

"Indeed, but fans are fickle and their memories are short. No one is going to want to buy that Contessa di Contini crap if she's off the air. Meredith has to stay in the public eye. She may not realize that, but I know it, and her agent surely knows it."

"What are **we** going to do?"

*Acting 102: I stuff as much sincerity into selling that **we** as I can muster.*

"**We** are going to give you a little camouflage, Kate, at least until Madame Butterfly has stopped flapping."

"Excuse me?"

"In the weeks to come you'll find that I'm making Devon Merrick a little . . . edgier—not overtly gay, at least not at first, but ambiguous, more like an action heroine, really. I've already started reworking the storyline," she says, tossing a doorstop-size script at me. "Kate, it's going to be a fantastic challenge for you, but I know you're going to loooooove it!"

Edgy? Gay? Challenge? Her idea certainly gives me plenty of acting to chew on in this hotbed of hetero fantasy, but I'm not so sure it will throw Meredith off my scent. . . . And we'll see if I loooooooove it. . . .

• • •

"So, Kate—let's go grab some dinner." On the way back from my audience with Daphne, Kirk's arm has encircled my waist in the hallway.

"Let me go get my stuff," I say. "I won't be a minute."

Okay, it's official. I'm giddy. Giddy, but nervous. Giddy at the prospect of picking up in private where Kirk and I left off onstage. Nervous because if events continue to unfold, tomorrow has every likelihood of turning into one of those days when I come to work still wearing the same clothes I have on today.

"Great," he says with a pat on the shoulder. "Meantime I'll figure out the venue—someplace dark, quiet, and casual. Come by my dressing room when you're ready."

A barrage of personal appearance uncertainties comes at me—each and every one of them entirely self-inflicted. How good a job did I do shaving my armpits? Is my all-too-brown pubic hair tendrilling down as far as my broad Irish calves, or has it stopped discreetly at my knobby kneecaps?

Dear Lord, please don't let me puff up again. And tell me, God, are there glunks of petrified mascara in the sunken blue-purple hollows under my eyes? Do I have any color left on my mouth whatsoever?

I look in the mirror and groan—what could this man possibly see in me? I clearly need divine intervention, or at least professional help. . . .

JJ!

I'm halfway out the door, headed down to see her for a touch-up, before I realize what a monumentally stupid idea that would be. I'd be waltzing into Gossip Central. I may as well broadcast an announcement over the intercom:

Attention Garden Party cast and crew:
Be on the lookout for Kirk Marlowe and Kate McPhee, who will be leaving the studio together to go get something to eat, with the further intention of fucking their brains out later this evening.

I settle for brushing my teeth and adding a little more blush and lip gloss. One final pee before heading down the hall and knocking on his door.

Knock knock.

"Oh . . . Kate! It's you!" A somewhat flustered Kirk opens the door just a crack. Obviously not ready to leave, his hair is marvelously tousled and he is shirtless.

"You were expecting maybe Margaret Thatcher?"

"No, it's just that I . . . I . . ." he stammers. A peculiar sweet, fruity aroma wafts out the door from behind him.

"What's that smell?" I ask.

"I don't smell anything," he responds.

"How could you not?" I say with an incredulous grin. "If you crossed Juicy Fruit, Mr. Bubble, and that vile berry air freshener they use in bus station bathrooms, you'd be close."

"I guess I'm just nose-blind. I spilled some hair stuff in the shower and it got all over the place. . . . You know what? I got a bunch of errands and shit I've gotta do later tonight. Give me a raincheck for dinner, will ya?"

"Uh, sure. See you tomorrow, Kirk. G'night."

I'm puzzled. What happened to dark, quiet, and casual? Not sure what to do now, I head for the parking lot, alone.

So . . . I'm not going to need the extra thong just yet, I think to myself as I point the Honda out of the parking lot and begin weighing the pros and cons of my new on-air persona.

On one hand, it gives me a chance to stretch as an actor—never played anyone quite like this before. **And** *I may get some real writing to work with—no more girlie-girl dialogue to gag on.* **And** *it should be a Get-Out-of-Jail-Free card for Wardrobe— liberation from those abominable foofy mother-of-the-bride chiffon atrocities they trot out for every celebratory occasion.*

On the other hand . . . On the other hand . . . Other than not having any more of those steamy sessions with Kirk (at least on camera), I actually can't come up with a downside.

As if to endorse my okayness with the idea, Boy George and Culture Club hit the airwaves on the oldies station as I jump on the freeway, and we all croon "Karmakarmakarmakarma karma ka-mee-lee-onnn" together.

*   *   *

Drusilla's accusatory yowls greet me at the door, but this time I have what she wants in my bag from the supermarket. I throw some Friskies in her direction, and as the two of us hunker down in bed to learn my lines, something keeps nagging at me. Without quite intending to do so, I replay the day in my head like a detective—like Devon Merrick.

Camouflage . . . Daphne is making me gay to deflect the wrath of the Queen. Why? And Meredith is upset about the scene with Kirk. Why? She couldn't be that unhappy about the idea that Regina slipped Burke an unscripted mickey—Regina has been doing villainous stuff like that on the show for years. The fans love it, and love her for it.

"Maybe she was upset about the fact that I showed her up, proving I can act and she can't." I propose my theory aloud to Sgt. Drusilla, my sidekick, who is severely nonplussed by it.

"I know exactly what you're thinking, Sergeant. She's so bad at it that she doesn't even know that she can't act. Anyway, that threat isn't going to stop just by making me butch."

Nope, this was specifically about Kirk, and whatever it was, it was serious and immediate enough to make her march straight up to Daphne's office, rather than leaving it for her lawyer or her agent to take care of.

And what was up with Kirk at the end of the day? How weird was that? Twenty minutes after making a date, he's not finished changing his clothes, and won't open the door to me. Then there was that powerful mystery berry smell.

Berry smell . . .

"Drusilla . . . I'm on to something. Follow my logic here. Even though Daphne had been wearing salade niçoise, her office smelled like raspberries. I suspected at the time that she'd consumed a raspberry tart, but think about it, Sergeant—she wears everything she eats . . . **everything.** If she'd actually eaten that tart, some of it surely would have been on her clothing."

"But of course, Sergeant! That has to be it!" An electric shock of recognition fires all my synapses, and my eureka moment badly startles Drusilla, who bolts from the bed.

"And I can prove it!"

I jump out right after her, grab my keys, and head for the car, not caring whether or not my Bialystock & Bloom T-shirt is long enough to cover my bare ass as I begin rummaging in the trunk. Beneath a pile of unopened mail, Meredith's gift basket still remains. From it I extricate the Contini di Notte perfume, and as I return inside, I flash back to what Kirk had said when we were running lines in the dressing room.

"I had a rebound affair with Regina. . . ."

"You slept with Regina?" I had gasped, but even at the time I thought, *You slept with Meredith?*

Suddenly it all makes sense. "It's not that he had slept with Meredith—past tense. He's **still sleeping** with Meredith!"

Drusilla wrinkles her nose as I open the vial (how appropriate); the cloying smell of bubble gum and black raspberries fills the room.

"And now the Queen is raging jealous. She went upstairs to crab at Daphne about me, then came straight down to reassert her *droit du reine* over her paramour. My arrival interrupted an on-demand assignation."

Raspberry tart indeed. And of course, Daphne knew all about it. No wonder she felt she had to give me some protective coloration.

Early November

I CAN'T POSSIBLY WEAR THIS," I say to Ruben, rejecting the outfit he's put out for me. Ruben is the Wardrobe czar, and with a slew of Emmys to his credit, no one crosses him very often—not even Meredith.

"But it's Dolce & Gabbana!"

"And a woman cop is not. Save the designer labels for the invited guests at the Garden Party, Ruben. I don't want to be a pain in the ass, but Devon Merrick wouldn't be caught dead in this stuff."

"I think it's lovely!" Amber interjects.

"I know, and that's exactly the problem," I say, trying to invite her out of the conversation with a hairy eyeball.

"Okay, we'll go understated," Ruben counters. "Simple Armani suit, Burberry trench."

"Nope. No Armani. No Burberry. Devon Merrick wouldn't spend that kind of money on clothes. "

"J. Crew then," says Amber, like it should be the Final Answer, the lowest one could possibly go.

"No J. Crew. No Banana Republic. Not even Talbot's."

"Gap?" says Ruben hopefully.

"Maybe. But mostly it's too casual. Buy me a couple of cheap suits and rotate them with alternating shirts and tees."

"Booooor-ring!" says Amber.

. . .

"I need Laszlo Szekely and Fallon Salisbury. Laszlo and Fallon only. Everyone else off the set now, please." The voice of Marty, our stage manager, booms over the loudspeaker.

Trent and I are on the couch in Gossip Central as Tiffany Duquette and

Vladimir Kovacs streak past us. Tiffany gives us a cheerleadery little wave, but Vladimir blows right by as if he doesn't see us at all. In fact, he might not. The dude is focused. Dark, edgy, powerful, and perhaps slightly dangerous, he oozes sexuality in a Viggo Mortensen meets Sean Penn sort of way—Vladimir Kovacs is nothing if not intense. His character, Laszlo Szekely (pronounced ZAY-kay), is our number-one resident cad—our love-'em-and-leave-'em millionaire heartthrob with mysterious gangland connections. Like an emotional tornado, Laszlo has been cutting an erotic swath across Hope Canyon, leaving a string of broken hearts—and vindictive women scorned—in his wake.

"The set is closed for this scene," Marty's voice repeats firmly over the PA.

"Too bad," I say to Trent. "I would have liked to see it."

"You curious about Tiff's new fake boobs, Kate?"

"Nope."

No more than I am about Amber's . . . or Alison's.

"I am," Trent admits with mock chagrin.

"Oh, don't be coy, Winterfield. It does not become you. If you're trying to convince me that you're ashamed of yourself for wanting to have a peek at what's under there, it's not working. You're a guy—and for guys it's all about skin. I'm still not interested. Adipose tissue and milk ducts—jacked up high enough to defy gravity courtesy of a plastic bag full of silicone—hold no fascination for me whatsoever."

"Aha! So you've got the hots for Vladimir, too, then."

"Too? *Too? TOO??* Pooh! I find him . . . interesting."

"Bleah!" Trent exclaims, wrinkling his nose cutely. "Interesting?"

"You would prefer maybe 'intriguing'?" I ask.

"Absolutely. 'Interesting' is a kiss-of-death descriptor for a man."

"Like 'sews-her-own-clothes/fun-at-parties' for a woman?" I ask with a smile.

"Precisely," he laughs. "They're both code for 'butt ugly.' "

"Seriously . . . it's just that I've never really watched them tape one of these hot-and-heavy scenes," I explain. "I've heard that it's all technical and not really sexy at all. I would like to see how it's done."

"Perhaps I didn't make myself clear," Marty intones from overhead. "Laszlo and Fallon only."

"Your wish, milady . . ." Grinning widely, Trent jumps up, grabs my forearm, yanks me off the couch, and pulls me along behind him as we take off down the corridor at a trot.

We stop running when we get to the sound booth. "Kate," he says, "you've met Mzee Lubega?" Mzee is a black man with lively dark eyes, unwrinkled skin, and a striking corona of grey curly hair. He also has Perfect Teeth. I have no idea how old he is—he could be thirty-five; he could also be seventy.

"Seen him. Haven't yet had the pleasure," I say, extending my hand. "How do you do?"

"It's certainly a pleasure for me, now, Ms. McPhee," he says warmly, with a delightful Brit-tinged South African lilt.

"*Mzee* means 'Old Man' in Swahili," Trent explains. "So Old Man, can we . . . ?" Trent completes the sentence by casting his eyes upward.

"You were not here. She was not here," he chants cryptically by way of reply. "I did not see you. And you did not see me."

"Mzee is the Yoda of *Live for Tomorrow*," says Trent. "He's seen 'em all come and go. He's been around since the Flood—or since Meredith began, I forget which came first. If you want to know where all the bodies are buried around here, he's your man."

With an almost Santalike twinkle, Mzee puts his index finger to his lips, then slowly draws his thumbnail across the bow of his mouth and winks. "Not a word, Kate," he says in clipped tones. "Not one. Whatever it is, talk about it later."

With a great show of gallantry, he sweeps into a bow and gestures toward the base of a ladder. "Thank you, and yes I can keep quiet, and yes my lips are sealed," I promise in a whisper, as I begin to climb up into the lighting grid.

Once up top, Trent and I make ourselves as comfortable and as inconspicuous as possible. It's totally *verboten* for us to be up here, but we have a commanding bird's-eye view of the proceedings. Management has also thoughtfully provided us with a monitor, so we can see it the way the audience will see it at home.

"Laszlo and Fallon," Marty's voice reiterates decisively over the PA system. "Everyone else is eighty-sixed . . . out . . . OUT!"

By the time Marty, now extremely exasperated, adds, "This means you, Priscilla . . . and take the cucumber and that remote control vibrating egg with you!" I not only hear Marty over the loudspeaker, I look down on his bald spot. And the guilty thrill of it all is enhanced mightily by the knowledge that if Daphne catches us up here, we are so toast.

INT.—HOTEL BEDROOM SUITE—NIGHT

Fallon and Laszlo enter already intertwined, almost as if dancing. Laszlo had pinned Fallon up against the door as he put the card key in the lock, and as the door swings open, she all but falls into the room, with Laszlo still pressed up against her. She is wearing a powder blue ballet neck cashmere sweater, tight black pants, and stilettos. He's in a navy blue blazer, white shirt, and tie. Laszlo pulls back from full contact just long enough to ask her a question.

LASZLO

What did you tell Molloy about where you were going?

She opens her mouth to answer, but he resumes kissing her before she can get the words out.

FALLON
(pulling away from the kiss to reply)
Gallagher? I told him I was going to help Philip with the last-minute details of the hospital gala.

A fleeting emotion clouds her face—it may or may not be guilt.

FALLON (CONT'D)
That man is so trusting—he'll believe anything I say.

They go back to kissing, still standing up.

LASZLO

What are you going to tell him when you don't get back till morning?

He cups her face in his hands and kisses her some more.

FALLON
(pulling back)
I'll figure that out tomorrow. Philip will cover for me, whatever it is.

Laszlo brushes her hair away from her face and begins working on her earlobe.

LASZLO
(whispering seductively into her ear)
And if you don't get back till next week?

FALLON

Right now the only thing that matters is you and me, right here, right now.

More kissing, still standing up, but it's heating up quickly. Laszlo stops kissing her, unglues their bodies, and faces her at arm's length. Grabbing her shoulders firmly, his eyes bore into hers.

LASZLO

Are you sure, Fallon?

```
                        FALLON
              (definitive, but in a sexy whisper)
          Yes. Yes, Laszlo. I'm sure—
```

```
    Even as the last syllable is leaving her lips, Laszlo
    swiftly and forcefully pulls down her sweater, and begins
    ravishing her bare shoulders, her neck, and her cleavage
    with increasing ardor.
```

Oh my God! I think to myself. I haven't been laid in so long, and what's going on down there looks sooooooooooooooo good!!

"Unh!" Despite my best intentions, my jaw drops open and a little moan escapes from my throat. Oh shit! If anyone heard that, we are found out for sure. Trent raises one eyebrow, glowers, then pinches my forearm. I bite my lip in response.

```
                     FALLON (CONT'D)
         Unh!
```

Tiffany has covered my moan with one of her own. Fortunately, we synched up perfectly—I was right on cue.

```
    With her lips glued to his, Fallon loosens Laszlo's
    necktie and places it around her own neck. She then
    opens his shirt. Pants fall away. The audience at home
    will see airborne shoes and lingerie—Trent and I see
    them thrown past the camera by stagehands.
```

```
    As Laszlo walks backward into the room, he tugs on the
    tie to reel her in. When he reaches the foot of the
    bed, he lets himself fall backward and uses the tie to
    pull her down on top of him.
```

```
    What follows is a slow-mo wrestling scene—the audi-
    ence will see Fallon's naked back, then Laszlo's.
    From our vantage point high above the action, we get to see Fal-
    lon's naked front as well . . . as the room light goes golden
    and the lovers roll over each other.
```

Although Tiffany began the scene in one of those flesh-colored tube tops designed to make it look like you're naked, it's nowhere in evidence now. Her new and improved 38DDs are right out there for one and all to enjoy. Vladimir is certainly not complaining. Neither is the guy on Camera 2, who is close enough to the action to be classified as a participant.

Looking over at Trent, all I can see in the dark is a very wide grin.

Alice was a little startled by seeing the Cheshire-Cat sitting on a bough of a tree a few yards off. The Cat only grinned when it saw Alice.

```
The two lovers roll up to a sitting position. The bed
is a mess—this is an athletic session. They sit fac-
ing each other in a full-contact embrace, chest-to-
chest and hip-to-hip, legs interlaced. The sheet now
winds through and around their legs, covering every-
thing from the waist to mid-thigh. Fallon leans back,
lips parted, eyes closed, and shakes her blonde mane.
Vladimir juts his hips forward . . .
```
And the two of them begin rocking in unison.

OhmyGod . . . It looks like they're . . . Are they? . . . Nah . . .

The rocking continues with escalating urgency. I look over at Trent—he is wide-eyed, and his smile has ossified on his face. I lean over and tug on his sleeve.

"Cheshire-Puss," she began, rather timidly, as she did not at all know whether it would like the name: however, it only grinned a little wider. "Come, it's pleased so far," thought Alice. . . .

It can't be, can it? . . . It sure looks like they're really doing it!

I start to feel pain in my index finger and am surprised when I discover the source—I seem to be ferociously biting my own knuckle. I look over at Trent once more—he is still smiling. In fact, not one muscle on his body has moved. Much like a four-year-old with an urgent question, I again tug on his sleeve.

Without taking his eyeballs off the action, he inserts his right index finger into his left fist several times.

A glisten, then a sheen of perspiration at the small of Tiffany's back confirms Trent's diagnosis.

"And cut! Break! Good job, you two. Almost looked like the real thing."

Trent and I wait till everyone has cleared the set before coming down from the rigging.

"Swell field trip, Trent."

"Wasn't that special?" he says, in a Dana Carvey *SNL* Churchlady voice.

"Does that happen often?"

"The bar is always raised to see whether you can actually screw on camera," he says. "It's TV's answer to the Mile High Club. Lots of people have tried, no question. This is the first time I've actually seen anyone pull it off. Of course, if anyone on *LFT* was gonna do it, it would have to be Tiffany. Most people consider modesty a virtue—not her. She's pretty much of an exhibitionist, and she's been gunning for Vladimir for a while."

"He didn't seem to be objecting too strenuously."

"No, but don't read anything into that. He was just staying in character. Vladi's pattern of romantic liaisons and entanglements pretty much mimics Laszlo's."

We cross the deserted set to the recently abandoned bed. "Well, Trent, this explains it!" I say with amazement.

"Explains what?"

I straighten the rumpled sheet and hold it up for his examination. It is not rectangular; it has been notched into an L-shape along the top edge. "It explains one of the great mysteries of Daytime—how it could be that when two lovers lie on their backs side by side in bed after a sex scene, the sheet covers the woman's breasts, but leaves the man naked down to his waist."

"The things you learn from television," he says with a grin. "Let's get outta here before we have a great deal of explaining to do ourselves."

Mid-November

JEEZ, KATE! Close your eyes, will ya? I keep askin' you to shut 'em, hon, but they keep flappin' open!" says JJ with more than a touch of exasperation. "If you don't want to look like a raccoon by the time you go back upstairs," she chides, "you gotta stop twitchin' and let me work on you."

I'm in Makeup getting touched up, but I can't take my eyes off the monitor. Bradley Peterson, the new actor debuting today as Nicholas Duncan, is lying on a gurney in the morgue. He's replacing recently departed Bradley Robertson, who left (via a boating accident) when he got the second lead in a WB sitcom. Like Bradley I, Bradley II is quite the hunk—extremely handsome, even when he's dead.

Medical examiner Mason Salisbury—Richard—is standing over him, preparing to conduct the coroner's inquest . . . make that swaying over him. Listing slightly to port, then to starboard, he looks as if he's standing on the deck of *Old Ironsides* in heavy seas.

"Whoops there," says Trent from the pod next door.

"Does he have an equilibrium problem?" I ask, somewhat naïvely.

"Only when he doesn't have a drink in each hand," cracks LaTrisa from the opposite side.

"Yes, indeed," adds Trent, "the good Dr. Salisbury is none too steady on his pins today."

All three of us look expectantly at the monitor, even though we know what's coming next. In a soap, no one is ever dead—not even if you see them buried and dismembered. Or dismembered and then buried. Or blown up, or cremated and their ashes scattered at sea. It just means that they come back again as another actor. . . . It's Daytime's way of recycling.

Sure enough, just as Richard turns on the high-speed oscillating autopsy saw, Bradley/Nicholas opens his eyes—his beautiful deep blue eyes.

                    MASON
(at a shout, dropping the saw and wheeling the gurney on the
                run through the double doors)
    I need an ambu bag and twenty ccs of lidocaine, **stat**!
    We got a live one. We got a live one!

Moments later, Bradley is back in Gossip Central to exchange his dead guy makeup for some hospital pallor—"recuperating" pallor, as compared with "last rites" pallor. Despite the pasty blue-grey complexion, he is absolutely gorgeous. Unlike many actors, he's actually more attractive in person than he is on camera, if that's even possible.

"Hi, I'm Bradley Peterson," he says as JJ eradicates the last of the shine on my nose.

"Kate McPhee—Devon Merrick," I answer as JJ pronounces me finito. "We've been watching you come out of your coma."

"I've admired your work," he says, flashing a smile. "You really liven things up around here."

"Why, thank you, I try," I reply coyly but flirtatiously. "It's nice that someone notices."

Unsolicited praise from a coworker—be still my heart.

I'm trying hard not to bat my freshly mascaraed eyelashes (lest they leave little birdie tracks beneath my eyes)—and failing—but how the hell can you flirt without them? Before JJ has to start over, the summons comes over the loudspeaker: "I need Devon Merrick, Jamila Benton, and Jennifer Abell to the floor. Devon, Jamila, and Jennifer, on set now, please. Richard, don't go wandering off."

"That's my call. I've gotta run, Bradley. It was a pleasure meeting you."

"Hey—before ya go . . . I understand we'll have some scenes together coming up," he says. "Maybe you'd like to have dinner on Saturday?"

"Oh!"

My first reaction is one of surprise, shock, and dismay. I'm astonished that this very attractive man is actually asking me out—moi. Recover, Kate—quickly—so you don't look like quite such a horse's ass.

"Oh! Oh, yes! Yes . . . I think I'm free then."

And if I'm not now, I'll make it so.

"Let's meet at Musso and Frank, say, 8:30?"

"Great. I'm looking forward to it."

INT. ABELL MANSION—NIGHT

                    DEVON
                (all business)
    So Mason, until we get to the bottom of this, I have
    to ask you not to leave town. You too, Jennifer.

                            MASON
Shomuch for my big weekend in Palm Shprings.

                          JENNIFER
                      (uncertainly)
But I don't understand. . . .

                          JAMILA
It's like this, Jennifer. We don't know who the real
target of the voodoo cult is yet, or who's behind it.
Until the picture becomes clearer, Lieutenant Merrick
believes that both of you may be in danger.

                            MASON
Either that, or you think we're part of their nefari-
oushplot.

                          DEVON
A few safety precautions. When you're at home, keep
your doors and windows locked. Avoid going out alone
at night—even to walk the dog. And this is most important. Both of you—no manicures, no pedicures, no haircuts until I say so.

                          JENNIFER
But I have a standing appointment with Clarice. . . .

                          DEVON
Cancel it. Voodoo priests don't have to be with you in
the flesh to cast their spell. They just need a piece
of you—they can do their evil work using hair or finger-
nail clippings.

                            MASON
Showhat yurr shaying, D'teckive, izzat wurrunder un-
offissshull housh arrrrresht.

"Stop right there." From the booth, Daphne's icy voice interrupts the
scene. "You seem to be having a bad tongue day, Mr. Blakeley."

"Mmmph? Oh. Shorry."

"Get the marbles out of your mouth, Richard. You may think you're
Demosthenes, but you're not."

"Who?" says Amber blankly.

"Dem-ahss-then-eez," says Daphne with precision, as if to the class
dunce.

"I don't understand."

"I thought not. D-E-M-O-S-T-H-E-N-E-S. Look it up, Amber. It's a fucking shame that stupidity isn't painful. And by the way, back off on the tanning sessions. Either that or I'll tell them to use clown white as foundation on you."

Amber's eyes well up with tears, and her jaw begins quavering. "Oh shit, Amber, don't start blubbering on me," Daphne continues with great exasperation. "Someone wipe her eyes before her mascara runs." Even as poor Amber looks crushed, for a moment Richard brightens in the hope that Daphne's tirade is over and that he's escaped.

A false hope, as it turns out. "Richard," she continues, "if your teeth are loose, I'll send out for some Fixodent. And if it's that other problem," she says acidly, ". . . . *again* . . ." Daphne lowers her voice an octave, and she loads the word *again* with a distinct tone of menace, ". . . have your agent call me in the morning."

He'd hidden the swaying well enough during the autopsy scene, but it is now obvious to everyone that it is indeed that other problem . . . again. Richard has been nipping at the cooking sherry—so much so that now his normally impeccable diction is impaired.

"Ten-minute break," calls Marty. "Everyone pee and come right back." The man is a human tourniquet—it's his duty to stop the bleeding and get the job done.

"Psst! Kate!" says Amber as she looks around furtively for Daphne. "Who is Demos—Demosth—?"

"Demosthenes?" I ask.

"Yeah, him. I know I'm supposed to look it up but . . ."

But you have no idea how to do that.

"Demosthenes, Amber, was an ancient Athenian statesman and orator," I say. "To improve his elocution, he practiced speaking with stones in his mouth, making sure he pronounced each word distinctly."

"Wow! Thanks, Kate," she gushes. "You're a terrific suppository of information!"

I quickly catch up with LaTrisa. "Tri, was that a veiled threat I heard?" I ask.

"Girl," she says, "there wuddn't no veil about it. That was an out-and-out threat, pure and simple."

"You mean Daphne would really can our Imminent Grease?" Amber's malapropism for Richard has been assimilated into the lexicon of Gossip Central.

"You bet your sweet English ass she would, sugar. Daphne will use the IG's drinking as a leash to rein him in, but if Richard starts costing the show money with flubs and retakes, she'll cut the cord. Right now she's really pissed at him—what we have to do is get him through this scene."

"And Amber's no help. Okay, we'll divvy up his lines between us. He really has much more reacting than acting to do in this scene anyway.

And LaTrisa, whatever you do, for Chrissake don't leave him any sibi-
lants!"

"Underrrrrsssshtood," she says with a thousand-megawatt smile.

> DEVON
> (all business)
> So Mason, until we get to the bottom of this, I have
> to ask you not to leave town. You too, Jennifer.

> MASON
> Ahh . . .

I nod to LaTrisa—this one's yours, dearie.

> JAMILA
> (jumping in quickly)
> Which means your big weekend in Palm Springs is out.

Truly bewildered, Amber looks back and forth between Richard and La-
Trisa because her cue is coming from the wrong actor. Even this minimal
bit of improvisation is entirely beyond her.

> JENNIFER
> (uncertainly)
> But I don't understand. . . .

> JAMILA
> It's like this, Jennifer. We don't know who the real
> target of the voodoo cult is yet, or who's behind it.
> Until the picture becomes clearer, Lieutenant Merrick
> believes that both of you may be in danger.

> MASON
> Either that, or you think we're part of their nef—

LaTrisa looks sharply at me. Oops—my turn.

> DEVON
> (stepping on Mason's line)
> It's also possible that one or both of you might be
> involved in their nefarious plot.

Richard looks at me quizzically but has enough theatrical savvy to keep his
yap shut.

> DEVON (CONT'D)
> Assuming that you are not, it would be wise for both
> of you to take a few safety precautions. When you're

at home, keep your doors and windows locked. Avoid
going out alone at night—even to walk the dog. And
this is most important. Both of you—no manicures, no
pedicures, no haircuts until I say so.

                    JENNIFER
But I have a standing appointment with Clarice. . . .

                    DEVON
Cancel it. Voodoo priests don't have to be with you in
the flesh to cast their spell. They just need a piece
of you—they can do their evil work using hair or fin-
gernail clippings.

                    MASON
So what you're shaying . . .

Oh gawd . . . There's no way he'll be able to spit that out. One more syllable puts him in jeopardy, and if the words *housh arrrrresht* leave his lips, he's
fired.

                    JAMILA
              (curtly cutting him off)
I know exactly what you're thinking, Mason. You're
thinking that you're under unofficial house arrest.

                    MASON

Richard gets as far as opening his mouth before LaTrisa runs right over him.

                  JAMILA (CONT'D)
But that's not how it is. This is being done for your
own protection, and it will be over soon enough. Is
there anything you don't understand?

                    MASON
No.

    "Cut!" says Marty quickly.
    "I don't understand. What just happened here?" asks Amber. She is
truly clueless.
    "Thank you all. That's a wrap, people," Marty continues. "Return to
your homes and villages until we gather at the clearing once again to *Live
for Tomorrow.*"
    Emerging from the booth, Daphne stares hard at LaTrisa and me but
says nothing and keeps walking.

                    • • •

LaTrisa hooks her arm through mine as we head back to the dressing rooms. "Kate . . . we have to do something about Richard."

"I think he's safe from Daphne's wrath, at least for the moment."

"No, not that. He's gonna go and get in his car and drive home. If he picks up a cop, it's gonna be bad."

I feel almost as stupid as Amber. Here I'm still thinking about how to protect him within these four walls, and LaTrisa is already thinking about how to protect him in the real world.

"Yeah, I know," I say. "He's slammed. What do you want to do?"

"We could follow him home."

"Tri, if we do that and something goes wrong, we'll be trying to fix it after it happens, not before."

"There's no way he should be behind the wheel, but Kate, you and I both know he doesn't believe he has a problem. I don't think he'll let us drive him home, will he?"

"He will if he can't find his keys."

A great and sunny beam of recognition lights up LaTrisa's already lovely face. "I'm on it, Kate!" she says over her shoulder as she heads for his dressing room.

Damn! God sat back and had a beer after that one. Look out, Halle Berry! Look out, Julia Roberts! With that smile, that face, that body, and that luminous warmth and intelligence, this woman's too big for Daytime.

Just then the Good Ship Richard looms into view at the end of the long hallway. He must have been tippling from a secret stash somewhere. He's now noticeably more in the bag than he was on the set—we got through the scene not a moment too soon. He begins tacking his way down the corridor, careening first into one wall, then the other. Even drunk, however, there's a certain majesty about him. To give LaTrisa the time she needs to ferret out the keys, I stride down to intercept him; we meet up on one of his starboard reaches. "Hey, Richard!" I say, spinning him around and pointing him in the opposite direction. "I need to ask you about one of our scenes tomorrow. . . ."

Before he can protest too greatly, LaTrisa comes up behind us and wishes us both a good night. As she does so, I distinctly hear the melodic jingle of keys in my ear—damn, she's good. "Prepare to come about!" I say, grabbing Richard by the shoulders, pushing on the left and pulling on the right. With LaTrisa on one side and me on the other, we execute the 180. Then like a pair of tugboats we half nudge/half drag him to his dressing room.

"He'll be back out soon," she whispers once we're back in the corridor.

We loiter in the hallway, a discreet but convenient distance away from Richard's door. We don't want to be hard to find. He opens it noisily, right on time. "I shay," he begins, of necessity leaning his full weight against the doorjamb for support, "you haven't sheen my keyshanywhere, have you?"

● ● ●

We bundle him into LaTrisa's car, and as I'm about to jump into the back seat, she shakes her head and slips me his keys. "Black BMW," she whispers.

The gates to the studio lot are manned by a night watchman, who tips his hat cordially, first to LaTrisa, then to me in the chase car, as we leave the lot. If he finds it odd that Richard is with LaTrisa and I'm creeping along behind in his Beemer with the lights off, his face doesn't give it away.

I follow LaTrisa to his condo; as we approach, she pulls to one side and waits. Obviously she expects me to do something, but what? She points her index finger upward until it dawns on me to look where she's pointing. Duh! His garage door opener is on the visor. Our mini-convoy pulls into the garage and the two of us maneuver Richard through his front door and into his bedroom.

I scavenge a couple of Tylenols from the medicine cabinet, throw them down his gullet, and get him to swig a little water to wash them down. At least his head won't be quite so bad tomorrow. LaTrisa and I look at each other and ask the unspoken question: leave him in his clothes or undress him?

"Right." I work on the shirt buttons.

"Thish musht be my ducky lay!" he says. Those are his last words before passing out.

LaTrisa goes for the belt buckle. "Commando," she whispers as she opens his fly. "And no wonder!"

"Woohoo!" I reply softly. It's clear that our IG is well equipped.

"That must be quite something under combat conditions," she says appreciatively as she slips off the trousers.

"I dunno, LaTrisa. I suspect he's got a pretty serious case of ADD."

LaTrisa shoots me a puzzled look. "Attention Deficit Disorder?"

"Nope. *Ascension* Deficit Disorder," I respond. "If he's chugging this much single-malt, it's gotta leave him . . ."

"Hydraulically impaired?"

"Bingo. What should we do with his keys?"

"I say we set up the coffeepot in the kitchen and leave them next to it," LaTrisa says as we tuck him in. "I want him to wonder how he got home, how he got naked, and how his keys got there. Maybe it'll be a clue that he needs to get sober. At least I can start a conversation with him about it."

As we drive back to the studio I ask, "LaTrisa, how did you get so good at this?"

She shakes her head sadly. "Practice. Practice. Practice. There are alcoholics hangin' from every branch of my family tree."

"Mine too," I reply, "but I never got very proficient at dealing with it. What I did do was try to shield my brother, Daniel, from the worst of it."

"I've been coping since I was a little girl. Mama had her first flute of Cristal at about ten in the morning, and my daddy spent many, many years looking up from the bottom of one of those damned Crown Royal purple drawstring bags."

"I know exactly what you mean. There were a whole lot of days when I never knew who was gonna show up," I volunteer.

"Or if anyone was gonna show up."

"Exactly."

LaTrisa nods to the ever-cheerful guard and wheels into the studio lot. "We did good today," she says.

"We did indeed," I respond. We hug like the sisters we have become and I jump into the Honda, start the car, and then turn it off again. It would be nice to have the script to study. I race back into the building, hoping to fetch it and escape unseen.

● ● ●

I grab my script and allow myself the luxury of thinking about the weekend—I'm gonna have two days of free time. I can do some laundry; clean underwear would be nice. I can buy more cat food. Drusilla would be pleased. I'm almost to the main door to the parking lot when I hear the assertive and all too familiar clip-clop of Daphne's Ferragamos coming up the long corridor behind me. Doesn't this woman ever go home? Worse than that, I can tell without turning around that she's gaining on me. Shit.

Bogey at six o'clock! Opportunities for evasive action—nil.

"Kate—before you leave . . ."

She's got me in the crosshairs and she's got tone.

"I just wanted to make sure you were all prepared for your first session tomorrow."

Fire one.

"I beg your pardon? Prepared? What session?"

What I'm all prepared for tomorrow is a session in indolence—a gorgeous wallow in blatant sloth, if you will—sleeping in and doing absolutely nothing until midafternoon at the earliest.

"Your first session with Jay Park, the master who is going to teach you tae kwon do. Didn't you get my note?"

"Why, no."

Well, yes, come to think of it, there was something in an envelope which may have had your handwriting on it, Daphne, but if I remember correctly it's now buried under several days' worth of scripts, a couple of Starbucks cups, two pairs of shredded pantyhose, some Tarte cheek stain (in Flush), and a cylinder of Kevyn Aucoin mascara, which has petrified since the brush/cap went missing. Oh, and it's all topped with a light dusting of Prescriptives Magic Liquid Powder—I sneezed as I was putting it on.

"You're to report to the Dojang—"

"To the doe-what?"

"Dojang—the tae kwon do academy—at eight tomorrow morning. I've booked you for two all-day sessions, just to get started. After that, he'll come to the studio for regular lessons for the next several weeks. We have to make Devon Merrick look like the martial arts master that she is."

So much for blatant sloth.

6

Mid-November Saturday morning 8:10 A.M./the next day

H I, I'M JAY. You must be Kate McPhee."

"Am I supposed to bow or something?"

"It's traditional, and it's a sign of respect, but let's not worry about it—especially since you don't look quite awake yet."

"How perceptive of you—the coffee should kick in shortly. I'm sorry, this is not my best hour."

"When and if you do bow, don't put your head all the way down. Your opponent could kick you in the chops while you're staring at the ground."

Sheesh—the ninja mindset—who the hell thinks like this?

"Even with your head lowered, Kate, be aware of your surroundings. Try to see everything around you with your peripheral vision . . . but actually, for you . . . for this morning," he adds with a wink and a radiant grin, "I'll settle for a little *jip joong*—concentration. I'll be happy if you can keep your eyes open and really focus in on what I'm saying."

"Right."

Jay is a slender Asian man with long black hair and a straggly, Brad-Pitt-starter-kit goatee. There is an air of intensity about him. He is dressed in what looks like black pajamas; there is a black belt with ten stripes on it around his waist. When I finally got around to reading Daphne's note last night, I learned that he is much in demand to do stunt work on big movies, and that he has made time in his schedule to be able to work with me. Given the pathetic state of my fitness and the fact that I'd really rather be back in my bed, he has his work cut out for him.

"I'm not going to turn you into a crouching tiger in just a couple of sessions. What I'm going to teach you is some basic tae kwon do movements, and how to use them to work with the stuntmen—and -women—whose job it is to make it look like you know what you're doing. Once you get the hang of it, you may get to a point where you actually do know what you're doing, and I think you may even get to like it. I hope so. We'll start with *chagi*–kicks. I'm going to ask you to take off your shoes. It's considered impolite if the soles of your feet are dirty. Go wash them in the ladies' room. And while you're in there, put these on." He hands me a set of pajamas that are as white as his are black, with a white belt.

Peachy.

When I return, Jay must be able to read my enthusiasm—or lack of it—in my face. "Don't be like that! Kicks as a weapon make a lot of sense. Look at yourself in the mirror—your legs are longer than your arms. Stronger, too. Everyone's are. Your quadriceps and your hamstrings are the strongest muscles in the body. If you want to test that theory, do a handstand and see how long you can stay up there."

"Thank you, no. I believe you."

"Now the front kick, the *ap chagi*, is the easiest to learn. Lift your right foot, about knee-high."

I comply to the best of my ability—which at present seems severely limited—and struggle to keep my equilibrium.

"I'll take that effort as the best you can do for now, but we're going to have to work on your balance. Okay—now kick out with the ball of your foot."

I extend my foot toward the long cylindrical punching bag and look to him for approval. "Right motion, Kate, but waaay too slow. Kick out sharply—and don't just leave your foot there long enough to contemplate your toenails. Pull it back quickly, or your opponent will grab it and use it against you. Again."

I kick out, and then retract my foot. (And yes, I'm overdue for a pedicure.)

"Not bad. You'll get better with practice. Again."

I kick out, again . . . and again . . . and again, without feeling like I'm making any improvement from one kick to the next.

"Again!"

"I can't."

"Never say that to me!" he yells, then kicks the bag sharply.

I recoil, not so much because he shouted at me, but because it came on so suddenly. "I don't want to hear it," he continues softly. "Yes, you can. And if I yell at you, it's because I give a shit. Now, again."

"Wait a minute—how'd you get into this, anyway?"

"I grew up in East LA. Look at me—I'm the ninety-eight-pound weakling poster boy. All through grade school, I was always the smallest kid in my class—and I paid for it on the playground, every bloody day. There were some huge badass motherfuckers in my neighborhood. If I had to go one-on-one, pound-for-pound on the street, I was doomed. About in fifth grade, I realized that the only way I would survive was to be quicker, stronger, and smarter—and if I had to, to use their size against them. That's when I discovered tae kwon do."

"Did it work?"

"Not at first—I still got beat up, but less often as I got better at it. And eventually they stopped messing with me. Now I really don't have to use it at all, except on camera. But I still love the mental discipline of it . . ." At this point his eyes get a faraway cast to them. ". . . and the spirituality of it even more."

"I can see that," I said.

All of a sudden he snaps back to the present. "Besides, being able to surprise people and do outrageous stuff with your body is the best. Here, watch." After a startling shriek, Jay becomes virtually airborne and in a flurry of movement he attacks the bag, using both his fists and his feet. He's a true athlete, and his slight build belies tremendous strength and even greater agility. He is every inch of him a warrior. It's not only impressive, it's, well, cool.

Okay—you convinced me—I wanna do that!

I smile. He beams. He's not even breathing hard, but when he looks at me, he can tell he's got me hooked.

"Shit," he says, "if I'd known that's what it would take to get you really into it, I'd have done the demo first thing!"

I can see why he's so much in demand. He not only makes you do it, he makes you *want* to do it. I'm surprising myself—the idea that I am capable of liking this is a revelation to me.

He gives me a little hug of encouragement—*that feels good,* his body is like a brick—and I pull away reluctantly.

"Okay," he continues. "The roundhouse kick. This is the one you have to do really well, Kate, because it's the money shot in any TV or movie action sequence. It's big. It's dramatic. Audiences love it. But it's also the one that, if you miss, you could really hurt somebody—including you."

"Including me?"

"Yes, including you, especially if you lose your balance, land on your keister, and break your coccyx—tailbone. Talk about having your ass in a sling. Now, stand with your left foot slightly in front of the right. Pull in your abs—it'll help your balance. Be aware of your center of gravity. Raise your right leg—now bend your knee. Okay—at the same time, rotate sideways—pivot on that left foot—and strike out with your right leg, like this."

As Jay demonstrates the move, his extended foot is positioned to catch Clint Eastwood upside the head. When I try to imitate it, it becomes clear that my extended foot would score a direct bull's-eye on Danny DeVito's groin.

"Your extension and your flexibility will get better, Kate, but you're gonna have to work on them. Remind me to give you some exercises to do at home. Again."

At least this time I don't fall over.

"Okay, take a break."

I run to the ladies' room because I don't want him to see what a wimp I am. I sit on the potty and watch my legs shake for several minutes until it's time to resume.

"Okay, punches. Now, make a fist."

I ball up my right hand, and he makes a face.

"Not that way. To keep from hurting your knuckles when you punch, you have to know how to make a fist. Fold your fingers in tight, then wrap your thumb over them. Good—but on the days when you fight, you should trim your fingernails close, or you'll gouge your palm when you strike. Now punch out. Hit with just your first two knuckles. The last knuckle will break if you hit something hard with it. You can also attack with what we call a hammer-fist—use the side of your fist, like driving a nail. Make sure to strike with the fleshy part of your hand, below the knuckle—if you make contact with your pinkie finger, you're gonna break it."

I punch out, and he scowls.

"Rotate your entire arm from the deltoid—your shoulder—as you hit. The punch should screw itself into the target. . . . Again . . ."

I punch.

"Better . . . Again."

I punch.

"Better still . . . Again."

I punch.

"Ah, Kate . . ."

"What is it now?"

"It would help a *great* deal if you didn't close your eyes while you were punching. 'See. Think. Do.'" He says this softly but firmly, like a mantra. "See it; think it; do it. This gives you one extra beat and makes your punch look stronger. You absolutely *must* lock eyes with the stuntman. They know that you can gauge how far away you are. If you kick or punch randomly, and you haven't stopped for a second, then it's out of control. Again."

I punch.

"Better. Keep in mind where the camera is when you're doing this. There will be a camera behind the person you're fighting, so that when you throw a punch, it will look like it passes across his jaw. Likewise, when he hits you, the camera behind you will show your punch or kick and give the impression of making contact. It's all about camera angles that make you look good, because if you see some air between a foot and a face, it's a reshoot.

You have to know exactly where the person is and where the camera is to make it work. Now, again."

And so it goes, for the rest of the day. The sun is going down when he tells me to be back again at eight A.M. tomorrow.

Saturday night 8:27 P.M.

I wheel into the parking lot of Musso's and check myself in the mirror—not bad, for once, I decide. I'd gone through my usual dither about what to wear before settling on a little black silk Badgley Mischka cocktail number that has a certain vintage Hollywood glamour-funk to it, much like Musso's itself. Saucy little Manolo CFM sandals that tie at the ankle (natch). Emerging from the car, I see Bradley out of the corner of my eye. He's on his cell phone, leaning up against a white Corvette.

Well now, that's a bit of a disappointment. The white Corvette is a bit effeminate, and not at all what I'd imagined he'd be driving—a black Porsche Boxster would have been more like it.

As I get closer I realize that he's wearing tight white jeans, and my heart sinks. Perched against the 'Vette like that and yakking on the phone, he looks for all the world like some gay cabana boy straight out of West Hollywood.

Once inside Musso's we are seated in one of those cozy mahogany booths. The place reeks of history, and since it dates from the end of World War I, by Hollywood standards it is positively antediluvian. I peruse the menu. No one seems to know why, but Musso's menus always have a date at the top, even though the food never changes from one day—or year—to the next. Neither do the venerable red-jacketed waiters. Legend has it that Chaplin and Fairbanks once raced each other down Hollywood Boulevard on horseback—loser buys dinner and drinks—and many of the waiters look like they've been here since then.

Taken in by the dusty charm of the place, I peer over the top of my menu at Bradley. Perhaps I've misjudged him. He is still so pretty. Right now all I can see is the area from the bridge of his nose to the top of his head, and even that's cute, but somehow he looks different. Something's changed.

Wait. His eyes. They're a different color now than they were on the set—no longer indigo, more like electric teal. Sonofabitch!! He's wearing colored contact lenses!

"What would you like to eat, Kate? There's all kinds of stuff here that no one else serves anymore."

"Indeed. When was the last time you saw any restaurant offering Shrimp Louie? This menu belongs in the Smithsonian."

"Where is that, exactly?"

This date has disaster written all over it. I can't wait to introduce him to Amber.
He has the pounded steak with country gravy. I order Welsh rarebit, just because it's a such a relic—and maybe because it's something of a comfort food, and I need all the help I can get to survive this meal.

I conjure up a scenario for Devon Merrick, wherein her cell phone rings with news of some catastrophe urgent and compelling enough to give her a reason to get up and leave.

                         DEVON
                 (answering her phone)
        Hello?

Devon strains to hear the person at the other end of the line, and furrows her brow.

                      DEVON (CONT'D)
        Henry, is that you? You sound terrible. What's wrong?

A look of shock and dismay crosses her face.

                      DEVON (CONT'D)
        That's terrible! No, I'll be right there. I'm leaving
        immediately.

She hangs up her cell phone. The look of shock and dismay has now turned to grave concern.

                      DEVON (CONT'D)
        Terrible news, Bradley. I must take my leave of you.
        My dentist's Schnauzer has a hangnail. I'm leaving for
        Rancho Cucamonga at once.

Somehow we get through dinner, but the lapses in conversation grow longer, and by the end of it I'm so desperate that I order the tapioca for dessert—and eat it.

After he pays the check, I all but run to my car at a speed that's about as fast as a woman on three-inch stilettos can motor. He trots alongside to keep up. "Thank you so much for dinner, Bradley. I had a lovely time," I lie. "I'll see you at the studio on Monday." I begin fishing in my purse for my keys.

"Uh, Kate . . ." he says.

"I can't seem to find my keys."

"That's because they're still in your ignition."

"Oh."

Note to self: Get a spare key made. Make that several—and put one in every purse and one in one of those magnetic box thingies that attaches to the bottom of your car.

"Don't feel bad," he says in an effort (unsuccessful) to console me. And the date ticks on. He stands there looking about, waiting for a tow truck to magically appear. He pulls his keys out of his pocket, and anxiously jingles them.

"Right," he says nervously. "I'd better go. Gotta meet my trainer at five A.M." He pecks me on the cheek, but even then he doesn't really look at me. He is fixing his cyber-blue eyes over the top of my head, perhaps toward his enterprising future. "Great date, Kate," he calls over his shoulder as he ambles past me and over to the white 'Vette. He climbs in and drives off with a hearty wave of farewell.

I stand there fuming in the dust and exhaust he leaves behind. *Un-fucking-believable. He's left me to deal with this all by myself.* I stare through the window of my car, trying to will the keys to leap out and into my hand, like Rose McGowan in *Charmed.* No luck. They dangle serenely in the ignition, the stupid Prada robot key chain looking *so* last season.

A beautiful young Latino parking attendant with a wide smile and the whitest of teeth is standing by the trunk of my car. He looks me up and down appreciatively, looks at the car, then winks knowingly.

"I locked myself out; my keys are inside," I inform him artlessly. I point at the Prada key chain for emphasis.

"Okay. No problem," he says, removing what looks like a small leather manicure kit from his pocket. He opens it to reveal an assortment of picks and other paraphernalia, then looks once again at the Honda and grins broadly but expectantly. I hand him a twenty; he removes the folded Slim Jim from the kit, opens it, finagles briefly with the door on the driver's side, and I'm literally gone in sixty seconds.

· · ·

Even though I'd been eager for this date to end, I'm feeling weird, unceremoniously dumped for an early night to bed . . . or at least so he said. I drive along Wilshire, then Beverly Glen, and then take Sunset to look at all the lights and billboards and remind myself I live in Hollywood. So far away from London and the mess I left behind. But not far enough away. Like uninvited guests, Rafe and Leslie come plowing into my mind, battering down walls and plonking themselves neatly on my frontal lobe. Damn.

Defenseless, my thoughts drift back to a Sunday last summer. Rafe ceases to desire me. He no longer makes love to me. I put down his lack of sex drive to laziness and artistic temperament. He gives me no excuse, but I surmise that five years out of work for an actor could take its toll on the libido. His lack of motivation and productivity must basically suck him dry of all life force, even if he does still have his music. And his music seems to be all he has left—when he doesn't tinker around on the piano keys, most days, including this Sunday, he lies around the apartment, watching old movies and endlessly fiddling with his gold Moroccan puzzle ring. He is pale and wan. And beautiful.

My friend Leslie calls us for dinner. He jumps at the opportunity. She says she needs to move some furniture to accommodate a new table. Rafe volunteers and drives over to her place. When I arrive later on, I am astonished to find Rafe deftly maneuvering a vacuum cleaner around her apartment. His sleeves are rolled up, and he wears a red bandana around his head to keep his long, dark locks off his sweaty brow. Never, ever in all our time together has he lifted a finger to wash even a single dish. He grew up with household help, and the long stint at public school destroyed any semblance of chore responsibility. (I, on the other hand, have no good excuse for my general household apathy.) Anyway, I stare open-mouthed at the domestic scene. Leslie cavorting around in a low-cut, *Butterfield 8* slip, the Eurythmics on the CD player, and Rafe happily cleaning.

I shake the image out of my head and concentrate on a billboard of Angelyne up above the old Spago. Well, things could be worse. I wonder for the nine hundred and fifty-first time how long the affair had gone on before I found out. I can't believe it didn't dawn on me then and there.

"Fuck 'em." I pull over for a late-night decaf Starbucks. The usual pale Goth *barista* isn't on duty, and I buy a Venti vanilla cap, extra hot with two shots of decaf espresso, and sit in the corner letting the scalding liquid travel down to my stomach and quiet the dinner lying there. I stare out at the lights and cars of Sunset. I feel like I belong. That's good. Right now I belong here in Hollywood, California, the U.S. of A. I feel strangely patriotic toward my new home. I stand with my drink and walk out into the cold bite of the desert air. As I near my car, I see I have a parking ticket on my windshield. Who gives tickets at midnight on Sunset Boulevard? I read it and realize I acquired it several days ago in Westwood. Stupid little village. I jam the ticket into the glove box with the other nine or ten I've received in the last couple of months and drive home.

Sunday morning

7:02! 7:02!! 7:02!!!

When the alarm goes off in the morning, it takes me all of three seconds to realize that there isn't one part of my body that doesn't ache—right down to my toes. As part of my balance and flexibility training, Jay had given me some homework. I was to practice flicking a light switch on the wall on and off with my feet. After I got home, it seemed like as good a thing to do as any, but now I'm as creaky as the unlubricated Tin Woodman in *The Wizard of Oz*.

A warm shower helps, as do a couple of Advils, but not enough. I feel like someone attacked me with a baseball bat while I was sleeping. My legs are the worst. Stairs are a bitch, and as I get into my car I discover that I can either stand or I can sit, but getting from one to the other is severely problematic. Nevertheless, at eight I report back to the Dojang for round two with Jay.

"Today it's all about forms."

"Good morning to you, too. It was all I could do to wash my damned feet. Why didn't you tell me I was going to be this sore?"

"Because if I had you'd have quit on me. I had to baby you along as it was. Now let's get on with it. Forms are like ritualized dance, Kate. I happen to think they are beautiful. What you are doing is learning the movements, both offensive and defensive. I like them for short action sequences because in a way they're like a script. If I tell the stunt guys what form you're using, they know exactly what move is coming next. Your job is to perfect your movements and memorize the sequence."

And so I am introduced to Song Ahm One. *Chun-bi*—ready position. Block. Punch. Kick. Block. Punch. Block. Kick. With each kick, my thighs are screaming.

"Higher."

"You've got to be kidding."

"Nope. Again."

I start burning the sequence into my brain. *Chun-bi*. Block. Punch. Kick. Pu—

"Stop there a second.

"What I want you to do is put the weight of your body into it when you punch. . . . No, don't lean; twist your hips—like this." Jay puts his hands on my hips—*that feels very good*—and gives them a goodly amount of torque. His touch is purposeful, directive—there's no doubt what he wants me to do. . . . Makes me wonder if he would be that strong and, um, assertive if we were doing this horizontally.

"No no no—don't hit like *a girl*, Kate. Do it like you mean it. Pretend it's an ex-boyfriend."

Jay has no clue that with those few words, he has set off a raging argument in my subconscious.

"Well, what are you gonna do, Katiegirl?" says my internal referee. "They say the first step in recovery from a broken heart is when sadness turns to anger. Do you have that anger inside you? Do you have it in your heart to strike at him?"

What's left of the proper young woman I was brought up to be speaks first: "Oh, I couldn't possibly. . . . When Rafe left me, it made me sad, but could I hit him? Never."

"Why not?" counters the street-smart cynic, the one who survived all those

"Thank you. Next!" *auditions in the West End before landing a part in* Cats. *"Look at the mess that's become of your life because of him. You used to consider yourself a serious actress—and here you are playing an edgy, almost gay character on an American soap opera. Your best friend in the world is your cat. It's like you ran away and joined the fucking circus."*

Whaap! *Take **that**, Rafe! That's for not sleeping with me for six months while you were screwing my best friend Leslie.*

Whaap! *That's for spending my money while you were not sleeping with me for six months and screwing my best friend Leslie.*

Whaap! *That's for letting me make a fool of myself with our friends while you were spending my money while you were not sleeping with me for six months and screwing my best friend Leslie.*

Whaap! *That's for that miserable vase of flowers that you bought with my money that was meant to make up for letting me make a fool of myself with our friends while you were spending my money while you were not sleeping with me for six months and screwing my best friend Leslie.*

"Easy there, Grasshopper!" says Jay, intruding on my annihilation of the punching bag. "Give it a rest, Kate. You're not Bruce Lee yet!"

"Oh, sorry. I got carried away."

"I noticed. However, your technique was excellent. Notice how the twist at the hips makes your punch uncoil—like a spring, or a snake. Again."

* * *

As I plop into the front seat to go home, I am exhausted, but at the same time strangely exhilarated. Christina Aguilera's "Fighter" comes into my brain—and, as so often happens to me, it shows up on the radio shortly thereafter:

> Makes me that much wiser
> So thanks for making me a fighter.

As soon as I get home, I grab my script and begin marinating in a super-hot tub full of Epsom salts (turning the faucets with my toes). I have to be back on set for a day-long day, a day that's going to begin with Meredith.

Mid-November Monday morning

"TRENT—YOU IN THERE?" I knock on his dressing room door. "Open up, Winterfield. You gotta help me run lines."

Trent has become my pal on set. We rehearse together and talk about the others, and he makes sure I'm in the loop on everyone's foibles.

I become aware of a great deal of activity going on behind the door. Still, it does not open.

"I spent the weekend with Jay Park and fell asleep in the bathtub," I continue from the hallway. "Wait . . . that didn't come out right."

I knock again, this time more insistently. "Hey—it's me, and every muscle in my body aches. It's all I can do to lift my arm high enough to knock on the door. Give me a break."

Nothing.

"Okay," I say, deciding to make a scene. I knock again, this time really pounding, adding a couple of *ap chagi*s for good measure. "This is Lieutenant Devon Merrick of the Hope Canyon PD." I continue beating on the door, making a true racket. "I know you're in there. Come out with your hands up!"

Finally, Trent opens the door. His hands are held shoulder high, open palms forward, but he is shirtless and his hair is mussed.

"What the . . . ?" I ask.

He puts his fingers to his lips. "Something-something-something," he says. Well, not *says*, exactly. Not a sound escapes his lips. He just mouths what I think is a three-syllable word.

"What?" I ask again, whispering.

"Something-ssss-something," he mouths again.

All I get is the middle syllable. "Why are you hissing at me?" I hiss back.

"Lllllll-ssss-nnnn," he mouths.

"I *am llll-ssss-nnnng*, if that's what you're saying," I respond peevishly, trying not to let my voice creep up in volume while pronouncing each syllable distinctly, "but if you haven't noticed, no sound is coming out of your mouth. . . . Don't tell me—you've got laryngitis." He shakes his head furiously, then pulls downward on his ear.

"Sounds like?" I ask. He nods furiously. "Crap, Trent—I feel like a contestant on *Pantomime Quiz*."

He then runs his hand down the side of his head, down almost to his waist.

I look puzzled and say quietly, "You're petting yourself? No, that's not it."

He repeats the motion, this time more languidly, tugging at his chestnut curly locks on the way down. "Hair?" I guess. He nods and repeats the gesture. "Long hair." He nods again, and points to the closet.

My eyes narrow and I lower my voice so that I am barely speaking. "There's something with long hair in your closet?"

He nods once more, vigorously this time, then outlines the shape of a curvaceous woman with his hands.

"And it ain't Willie Nelson."

Trent smiles, cups both hands in front of his chest, and bounces them slightly, as if comparing the heft of two weighty cantaloupes.

"Don't tell me it's Amber!" My voice rings out louder than I'd intended.

Trent scrunches up his face, puts his index finger to his temple, and squeezes off a round with his thumb. He makes the long-hair gesture again, tugs on his ear, then puts his finger to the end of his nose and pushes it upward.

"Nose in the air—snooty. Long hair," I whisper. "Sounds like." He cups his hands in front of his chest again, but now waves his fingers toward himself in the classic "come on, you're getting warmer, give me more" gesture.

"Damn . . . I suck at charades. Okay," I say, half to him and half to myself. "What was I saying when you tugged on your ear the first time . . . ?" I think back through the conversation. To remind me, Trent puts one hand to his ear as if straining to hear.

" 'Listening!' I was saying, 'listening'!"

He nods, tugs on his earlobe once more, and waits for me to put it together. Finally, it dawns. "Alison is in your closet?

"Why the fuck would Alison be in your cl—" I stop in mid-sentence and have another look at the half-naked, tousled man before me. Until now it hadn't really registered that he was also barefoot and wearing only silk boxers—taxicab yellow at that—with smiley faces on them.

Note to self: You not only suck at charades, your powers of observation are for shit, too.

"Trent . . ." I insert my right index finger into my left fist.

Trent taps his index finger to his nose and smiles sheepishly.

"Leave her in there," I whisper. "You have to help me with my lines. I'm working with Meredith today. You know how she thinks rehearsing is beneath her. Unless she's in Hair and Makeup, she stays holed up in her dressing room until she's on the set."

I sweep past him into the room. "Why, Kate," he bellows. "Do come in!"

I pick up Alison's lacy bra. It's pink, no surprise there, but it's a padded push-up which, considering her surgical enhancement, seems to me to be twice redundant. "Pardon the mess. . . ." says Trent, as I twirl it over my head like a lariat and fling it into the corner. "Sure I'll run lines with you," he continues as I repeat the process with the matching pink lace tanga, "but first things first. I'm famished."

"Can't think why." I smile.

He phones out to the Italian deli. "They say it'll be thirty minutes. Meanwhile . . . what's this about Jay Park and sleeping in the bathtub?" he asks.

"Jay kicked my butt all weekend long teaching me tae kwon do. Last night I was so sore that I climbed into the bath with my script. I fell asleep and woke up several hours later in ice cold water, all wrinkly and pruny and freezing my ass off. It was all I could do to haul myself into the bed, and the next thing I knew it was morning and here I am. I really hate being unprepared."

"Okay," he says as he steps into his cargo pants, "let's get started."

"Take my script," I say. "Let's see how much of this I've got down cold."

INT. CORAZON PRISON—CELLBLOCK D—DAY

TRENT AS MATRON
(raps on the iron bars with her nightstick—or in his case, with Alison's high heel)

Abell. Visitor to see you.

TRENT AS REGINA
(with a dismissive wave of the hand—which Trent exaggerates into a wild wave. He also adds a pout.)

Send them away. I don't want to see anyone.

TRENT AS MATRON
You don't have a choice, señora.

The matron throws open the door, and Devon Merrick enters the cell. The matron, however, does not withdraw.

DEVON
Could we have some privacy, please?

> TRENT AS MATRON
>   (to Devon)
> *Lo siento mucho, mi cucaracha.* But I yam on suisite
> watch, Deetective Merrick. I have orders not to leave
> Ms. Regina alone.

>   DEVON
> Idiot! She's not alone if I'm here now, is she? At
> least stand out of earshot.

> TRENT AS MATRON
> We thoughtfully provide our special inmates with Dolce
> & Gabbana belts with which to hang themselves.

"Trent, stop it, please. Just read the script." I lean over and swat him with my pages. "And put a shirt on, please? I'm sick of staring at that soap opera six-pack." He dutifully pulls on a Von Dutch T-shirt, which he has personalized with TRUCKERS DO IT BETTER, in black Sharpie.

"You drive a Beemer, you fuckin' fashion victim," I snap.

He smiles, blows me a kiss, and continues reading.

>   TRENT AS MATRON
> You have ten minutes.

>   DEVON
> Thank you.

Matron slams door and stands a little way off.

>   TRENT AS REGINA
> (waving his hands grandly once again, sticking out his chest,
>   and pouting like a beauty queen)
>
> Just go away and leave me in my misery.

>   DEVON
> You should be happy to see me. Are they treating you
> okay?

Devon nods up and down as if to say *yes* as she speaks— except that I speed it up a bunch—so much that I look like a sea lion swallowing a mackerel during the eleven A.M. show at Sea World.

>   TRENT AS REGINA
>   (shaking theatrically and pouting)
> It's awful here. They are awful . . . (Regina is a
> little slow on the uptake, and Devon shakes her head

no until Regina gets it.) . . . awfully nice to
me . . . considering . . .

Devon nods and gives her a thumbs-up. . . .

And then I sit there without a clue as to what I'm supposed to say next.
"Okay, I'm up," I say to Trent.

"You ask Meredith how the accident happened. 'Tell me . . . ' yada yada
yada."
   "Oh, right. Of course. Thanks."

                    DEVON
Tell me what you remember of the accident.

                 TRENT AS REGINA
I was driving the Bentley. I wasn't speeding when I
took the curve on the Mount Soledad road, I swear it.
Suddenly the car began to skid and I lost control.

                    DEVON
Had you been drinking?

                 TRENT AS REGINA
Absholutely not . . . hic.

Trent holds an imaginary bottle to his lips and does some extraordinarily
bad drunk acting. I scowl and throw Alison's stiletto at him.

        TRENT AS REGINA (CONT'D but now whining)

What is it?

 Devon sees the matron coming back, then removes a pad and
paper from her pocket and begins writing. I hold up the back of
my script, on which I've written:

DID YOU KNOW THAT MALLORY WAS PREGNANT?

"Hey, hey now," Trent says officiously, as if he'd caught me cheating on an
exam. "Before you show her the paper, you're supposed to ask the matron
to give you a few more minutes."
"Oh yeah, duh!" I quickly glance down at my script and then cover up the
words once again.

                    DEVON
                 (to matron)
So, bitch, we need some more time—police business . . .
okay?

Trent giggles.

>   TRENT AS REGINA
>   (whining, pouting, and tossing his imaginary curls)
>   I don't quite understand why I'm in lockdown for a
>   traffic accident. They told me that the Bentley was to-
>   taled, and Mallory is in a coma, but . . . why?

Devon removes a pad and paper from her purse and begins writing.

>   TRENT AS REGINA (CONT'D)
>   What is it?

I hold up a small piece of paper on which I have written: IS SHE ANY GOOD IN THE SACK?

Trent mimics my sea-lion-with-mackerel nod in reply.

* * *

I hear a muffled woman's voice—I point to the closet, but Trent shakes his head no and points to the wall instead. Grabbing my note pad, I write MEREDITH? on it. He nods again and shapes his hand like a telephone receiver. Meredith has the dressing room next door, and even from the muted tones I can hear, it sounds like there's a meltdown in progress. I can't make out the words clearly enough to figure out the source of her displeasure. I put my ear to the wall in an effort to hear better, but Trent waggles his finger at me and disappears into the bathroom. Seconds later he returns with two water glasses, the better to hear the conversation.

"Renato . . . Renato . . . you wouldn't believe what I'm going through. I'm so stressed out. I'm having a fuckin' nail emergency. My French manicure is chipped, and the worthless chick from Jessica's salon can't get here till four P.M., but I'm shooting the prison scenes right after lunch."

There is a short pause. Trent has his hand over his mouth by now. Good idea.

"OF COURSE it matters if Regina has perfect nails in jail. I have to hold the goddamn prison bars. It frames my face so much better. Besides, I'm fucking MEREDITH CONTINI and I sell nail polish on QVC. ARE YOU COMPLETELY STUPID?"

There is another pause, during which I pretend to put my finger down my throat.

"WHAT?" she resumes. "Of course it has to be someone from Jessica's, asshole. I wouldn't dream of letting anyone else touch them. . . ."

"Renato, what I need is a break. I need one day off. I need a massage, a spa day, a manicure. I need to work out. I cannot put on one more pound.

You never should have let me have that dessert when we were skiing last week. I have lingerie scenes next week with Laszlo and I need to get my ass into my own Contini boudoir sets—and I'm FAT!"

One more brief pause.

"Fat, Renato, I'm fat. . . . *Fat,* do you hear me? F-A-T. FAT FAT. DO SOME-THING ABOUT IT! FIX IT!!!" she screams, then slams down the phone.

There is silence. Trent and I hold our breaths. Soon there is the noise of tiny footfalls—Meredith has started running in place in her stocking feet. But wait—there is another noise, too. She has started singing to accompany her dressing room aerobics. At first I can't quite make out the tune, but it almost sounds like "Anything you can do, I can do better. . . . I can do anything . . . better than you."

I pull my glass away from the wall. "Who's Renato?" I ask.

"He's the unfortunate toad who married her."

"Poor slob. Jesus, Trent—why didn't you tell me you get to hear all that shit?"

"You never asked," he replies offhandedly. "Let's finish this off, shall we?"

● ● ●

INT. CORAZON PRISON—CELLBLOCK D—DAY

                    TRENT AS REGINA
            (with watery eyes, at a whisper)
    Mallory, pregnant? She's not old enough. . . .

"Stop!" I say. He has started delivering Meredith's lines in a ridiculous matronly falsetto.

                         DEVON
            (dismissively, at full voice)
    Does she have periods?

                    TRENT AS REGINA
    Well, yes.

He's making me laugh now

                         DEVON
                      (roughly)
    Then she's old enough.

                    TRENT AS REGINA
    But she's never . . .

                         DEVON
    Been with a guy? How do you know that?

> TRENT AS REGINA
> (with sanctimonious theatricality)

> A mother knows her daughter.

"Stop it!" I say laughing.

> DEVON
> Do you really? (giggle)

> Then how is it that you didn't know. . . . (giggle)

"Cut it out! You sound like Nathan Lane when he dressed up as the mother in *The Bird Cage*."

> DEVON
> . . . that you didn't know about this?

"Oh, thank you!" he says, still in character, hands fluttering like a butterfly. "You are so terribly kind. I'll have the houseboy make us some soup. Agador . . . Agador!"

> TRENT AS REGINA
> There's no way. No one's come to the house. She doesn't have a boyfriend.

> DEVON
> But *you* have a boyfr—

I can't continue. I'm laughing much too hard.

> TRENT AS REGINA
> Laszlo? That's unthinkable. He would never . . .

"Ooooooooh!" he exclaims, flapping his hands madly, à la Meredith, but still in the persona of Nathan Lane's Albert. "I've pierced the toast!"

The two of us collapse in a heap, literally weak with laughter.

There's a knock on the door. "Lunch!"

As we're finishing up the last few bites it occurs to me—we've quite forgotten about Alison in the closet.

"Trent?" I say, gesturing over my shoulder toward the closet.

"Oh? . . . Oh, yeah!" He nods.

I grab the roll that had accompanied my antipasto salad, open the door a crack, and peer in. Alison is sitting wrapped in Trent's *LFT* cast robe. She looks up, blinking at the light. "Hey Alison—I thought you might be hungry," I say, handing her the roll.

She shakes her head nonchalantly. "Oh, thanks, but I don't do carbs." I close the closet door, wave goodbye to Trent, and head out into the corridor.

• • •

Meredith keeps me waiting for a good twenty minutes before she shows up on the set. I'm sure it's my imagination working overtime, but on the wall I see the huge black shadow of a Chinese dragon as she approaches. When she arrives, the shadow dissolves into a petite figure in a cranberry-colored prison jumpsuit, which has been altered to enhance her femininity, complete with a belt and Manolos. In a "normal" prison, both would be considered suicide implements and removed, but not, apparently, in the fashion-savvy detention center of Hope Canyon.

"Hello, Kate," she says grandly. "How are you?" she asks, adding a flick of her hair. "Love your work in that scene yesterday, by the way."

"Ah, thanks."

Ah shit. All this phony crap makes me crazy. This is just like what she did with LaTrisa. Her MO is to pay you a compliment, because she wants to make you feel obligated to give one back. That's how it goes at the Garden Party. But life ain't a garden party, and anyway I can't do it. I don't have the charm to do it. I don't have the chops to pretend to do it—I can't blow smoke up someone's ass to that degree. I'm so uncomfortable around her I don't fit in my skin. It's like there's nothing genuine in her life anywhere—not on the set, and not off it, either.

INT. CORAZON PRISON—CELLBLOCK D—DAY

Regina is reclining on her cot in her cell. Two sets of footsteps are heard approaching, followed by the jangle of keys.

                    MATRON
        (raps on the iron bars with her nightstick)
    Abell. Visitor to see you.

                    REGINA
        (with a dismissive wave of the hand)
    Send them away. I don't want to see anyone.

Out of the corner of my eye I see Trent's grin in the shadows. Wearing what appear to be a pair of lavender satin opera-length gloves, he is clearly mimicking Meredith's hand gestures.

                    MATRON
    You don't have a choice, señora.

The matron throws open the door, and Devon Merrick enters the cell. The matron, however, does not withdraw.

                    DEVON
    Could we have some privacy, please?

                    MATRON
I am on suicide watch, Detective Merrick. I have orders not to leave this prisoner alone.

                    DEVON
Well, she's not alone if I'm here, now, is she? At
least stand out of earshot.

                    MATRON
                  (to Devon)
You have ten minutes.

                    DEVON
Thank you.

Matron slams the door and stands a little way off.

                    REGINA
Just go away and leave me in my misery.

As she speaks, Meredith puts the back of her hand to her forehead—very
Blanche DuBois—and tosses her perfect toasted-henna mane.

    Offstage and out of her line of sight, Trent apes the gesture perfectly,
as I

1. fight off the urge to laugh; and
2. search my memory bank to figure out what he reminds me of while
   he's doing this.

                    DEVON
You really should be happy to see me. Are they treat-
ing you okay?

Devon nods up and down as if to say *yes* as she speaks.

                    REGINA
              (a little slow on the uptake)
They're awful . . . (Devon shakes her head no until
Regina gets it.) . . . awfully nice to me . . . con-
sidering . . .

Devon nods and gives her a thumbs-up.

                    DEVON
Tell me what you remember of the accident.

                    REGINA
I was driving the Bentley. I wasn't speeding when I
took the curve on the Mount Soledad road, I swear it.

Meredith shakes her hair again, then runs her fingers through it.

> REGINA (CONT'D)
> Suddenly the car began to skid and I lost control.

Overcome by the emotion of the recollection, Meredith crosses her arms in front of her chest, hugs her shoulders, and shudders—or pretends to. *Shit! I haven't seen a gesture that wooden since we did* Julius Caesar *in the church basement.*

> DEVON
> Had you been drinking?

Lavender gloves in the air, Trent repeats the chug-a-lug movement from rehearsal. *That's it—he's doing Regina as Miss Piggy!*

> REGINA
> Absolutely not.

> Devon's face clouds, as if debating whether or not to speak.

> REGINA (CONT'D)
> What is it?

> Devon removes a pad and paper from her pocket and begins writing.

> REGINA (CONT'D)
> Although they've been very . . .

> (Devon looks up from her writing with a cautionary glance.)
> . . . very nice to me here, I don't quite understand why I'm in lockdown for a traffic accident. They told me that the Bentley was totaled, and Mallory is in a coma, but . . . why?

> Devon holds up a small piece of paper on which she has written:

> DID YOU KNOW THAT MALLORY WAS PREGNANT?

"And cut!" says Marty, the stage manager. "Time to pay the bills. Insert commercial here for a) laundry detergent, b) peanut butter, c) tampons, d) laxative, or e) that miracle product—all of the above. We're back up in five, ladies. Don't go wandrin' off."

"Touch-up and Hair, please," Meredith says.

The on-call makeup woman quickly appears and sizes up the situation. "Ms. Contini, I really don't think you need—"

"Like Nike says: just do it!" Meredith snaps commandingly. The makeup lady shrugs, then adds a little more tint to her cheeks, a touch of MAC C-Thru gloss to her lips, and a light dusting of finishing powder to her nose. She then holds the mirror up to Meredith for her approval. "Thank you ever so much," Meredith says effusively, now all sweetness and light.

The Hair worker bee arrives next. After giving her tresses a quick brush and a light misting of Head Rush Shine Adrenaline, he likewise holds up a mirror so that Meredith can scrutinize her loveliness in the looking glass. He stands there expectantly, waiting for her seal of approval.

"Two minutes!" yells Marty. "Places. Let's move it, peeps."

"Arturo, can you puff up my bangs just a little more, please?"

Arturo fiddles with the individual hairs that comprise the hot dog bun that Meredith has worn on her forehead for at least two decades.

"One minute," calls Marty.

"If you're not Regina or Devon, get the fuck off my set!" Daphne's no-nonsense voice booms from the booth. I see Trent making haste, even as Arturo grabs his brush and spray and skedaddles as fast as his scrawny bird legs can carry him. "Meredith," Daphne continues crisply, "need I remind you that you are not at the Emmys or the Queen's Ball? You are in prison—you're **supposed** to look like shit. Stop fussing. Let's get to work, people. And lose the belt!"

Meredith pouts ever so slightly and stands to allow a Wardrobe fairy to remove the belt/suicide device. After pulling the zipper on the jumpsuit down a couple of inches to better show off her cleavage, she lifts the edge of the prison mattress and removes a small, well-worn piece of paper before resuming her place. Turning away from me and the rest of the crew, she unfolds it carefully, places it behind her, and stares at it.

"On the count.... We are rolling. In ... five ... four ... three ... two ..."

```
INT. CORAZON PRISON—CELLBLOCK D—DAY
   On Regina
```

> REGINA
> (with watery eyes, at a whisper)
> Mallory, pregnant? She's not old enough. . . .

> DEVON
> (dismissively, at full voice)
> Does she have periods?

> REGINA
> Well, yes.

Wait a minute. . . .What's that back in the shadows?

> DEVON
> (roughly)
> Then she's old enough.

It's Trent—he's snuck back up into the studio. All I can see is his smile.

"I wish you wouldn't keep appearing and vanishing so suddenly," said Alice. "You make one quite giddy."

> REGINA
> But she's never . . .

> DEVON
> Been with a guy? How do you know that?

> REGINA
> A mother knows her daughter.

> DEVON
> Do you really? Then how is it that you didn't know about this?

> REGINA
> There's no way. No one's come to the house. She doesn't have a boyfriend.

"All right," said the Cat; and this time it vanished quite slowly, beginning with the end of the tail, and ending with the grin, which remained some time after the rest of it had gone.

> DEVON
> But you have a boyfriend, don't you, Regina? He comes to the house.

> REGINA
> Laszlo? That's unthinkable. He would never . . .

"Well! I've often seen a cat without a grin," thought Alice; "but a grin without a cat! It's the most curious thing I ever saw in all my life!"

> DEVON
> (with disdain)
> He's a guy, right? Guys don't always think with their cranium—sometimes their thought processes originate . . . farther south.

                        REGINA
    Are you insinuating that Laszlo Szekely is the father
    of my unborn granddaughter?

                        DEVON
    Not anymore.

                        REGINA
    What do you mean?

With the camera on me, Regina steals another look at the unfolded piece
of paper that is just beyond my field of vision.

                        DEVON
    Mallory lost the baby in the accident.

    On Regina.

                        REGINA
            (her eyes all but brimming over with tears)
    No! No!

Meredith's hands fly up from her lap—her fingers flutter next to her ears,
even as the matron's footsteps are heard coming down the hall.

                        DEVON
    I'll be leaving now, but, Regina, just one more
    thing. . . .

Metaphorically speaking, I'm folding a rumpled raincoat over my
arm. . . . Peter Falk, somewhere your ears should be burning. Thank you,
Lieutenant Columbo!

                        REGINA
            (as a solitary tear trickles down her cheek)
    What is it?

                        DEVON
    If you didn't know Mallory was pregnant, how did you
    know the child was female?

    On Regina, as tears fill her eyes.

"And cut! Thank you, ladies."

                        ◦ ◦ ◦

    Trent comes up to me while I'm still on the set. "Way to go, Lieuten-
ant!" Meanwhile, Meredith is reaching for her crypaper. "Whatcha got

there, Mer?" Trent asks playfully, as he nimbly snatches it out of her hand.

"Trent Winterfield! Give me Fluffy this minute!" she says imperiously, with a stamp of her foot and a regal toss of her hair.

Fluffy? Fluffy?? My God!

"Cute dog, Meredith," says Trent with a smile. "How old is she?"

Somewhere in the back of my mind I remember that seventy years ago, they used to make Shirley Temple cry by telling her that her dog was dead.

"Fluffy would have been, uh, twenty-five next month."

"No offense, Mer," says Trent, "but isn't the mourning period over by now?" With mock gallantry, he hands the photo back to her—except that the "mock" aspect is entirely lost on Meredith.

"Thank you." Sniffling ever so daintily, she looks wistfully at the photo one more time, folds it carefully, and swans off.

After this performance, the ghost, not of Fluffy, but of Neville Charters, my first acting coach, must be doing about 78 rpm in the boneyard. Mind you, I don't think Neville's even dead yet . . . and if he's still alive, this surely would be enough to kill him.

What he instilled in me about acting and emotions has become ingrained to the point that it's no longer technique. You didn't survive his classes without getting it—and getting it on his terms. "Kate," he'd say, "acting is a noble profession. Trying to bring emotion to other people—trying to impact people's lives—is a noble profession. A painting, when it is compelling to you, is so because it impacted the artist when it was created. He cried tears that went into the oil. You must do the same thing onstage—absorb your material so completely that it impacts you as a human being. **That's** what you share with the world. And sometimes you succeed, more often than not."

"Kate?" Tapping on my shoulder, Trent intrudes on my personal flashback. "Kate, are you in here? Hello? Anybody home?"

"Huh? Oh . . . sorry, Trent."

"You look upset."

"I'm astonished, angry, and appalled, I suppose."

"Meredith affects a lot of us that way—nice alliteration, by the way."

"What she did was just not . . . authentic."

"Badoom-sssshhhuh! Why, Kate McPhee! It's Meredith! Why on earth would you possibly be surprised?"

"I'm horrified that I was a participant in it. There was not a real moment to be had in that entire scene. I mean, if you're crying in a scene about a lost baby and the only way you could get to tears is by thinking about your fucking dead dog, that's not genuine. In fact, it's abysmal."

"Keep those A-words comin'!"

"Sorry—I seem to be stuck at the beginning of the alphabet, but it doesn't matter. The bottom line is that you've got to cry about the circumstances you're dealing with in the scene, right? Help me here, Trent . . . right?"

"Nice try, Kate, but in the Gahrden Pahrty, that's not how it works. What went on here was so perfectly her—so in-*A*-ppropriate, but she gets away with it. She's been getting away with it for decades."

"A photograph to get you into the right space is fine as an actor's tool, but she's got it all wrong. You can't use a dead dog. It's ridiculous."

We can just see the last of Meredith as she glides down the corridor. "Would you look at that?" I rant. "She can't even walk naturally."

"Of course not. That's beneath the Queen." Trent smiles his Cheshire Cat grin.

"No, that's not it," I proclaim. "It's much worse than that. In her mind she's really not walking at all. She's **playing the part** of someone who is walking!"

"Well, it was either that or demand to be carried in a sedan chair," he replies seriously.

8

The next day

JAY FINDS ME IN THE HALLWAY. "C'mon, Kate, I'm headed upstairs. You'll wanna see this." When Jay says a scene is interesting, it is worth paying attention. In addition to being the martial arts coach, he is an unofficial assistant director—one with Daphne's ear.

As I hustle along beside him, I ask, "See what?"

"Fight scene. Vladimir and Shelby."

"You mean Priscilla?"

"Yeah, him. The two of them are gonna go at it, and he's supposed to lose. He really hates that."

"So? Like it or hate it, he still has to lose—Daphne wouldn't let him go that far off script, would she?"

"Probably not, but as soon as you get two guys in a fight—even a play fight—the egos take over. I was rehearsing them and it was really tough blocking out the moves. Priscilla doesn't take direction the way a stunt guy would."

"From my observation, Priscilla doesn't take direction much at all."

"There ya go."

* * *

Jay and I find a good vantage point in a corner, lean back against the wall—and vanish. Since all the attention is focused on that very small, well-lit place that is the set, we are all but invisible. It's amazing how inconspicuous you can be in the shadows around the perimeter.

As is their custom, Vlad and Priscilla are staying loose by telling bad jokes. Today the topic is blondes.

"Hey Shelby," says Vladimir, "what does a blonde say when you ask her if her blinker is on?"

"I don't know, Vladimir," says Priscilla, deliberately exaggerating his role as straight man. "What *does* a blonde say when you ask her if her blinker is on?"

"It's on, it's off, it's on. . . ."

Hope and Crosby they ain't.

"Okay, I got one, I got one," says Priscilla. "What do you do when a blonde throws a hand grenade at you?"

"I give up, Shelby," responds Vlad. "Tell me."

"Pull the pin and throw it back."

Vladimir grins, not so much because he thought Priscilla's joke was funny, but because he's come up with a better one. "So then, what do you do when a blonde throws a pin at you?"

Before Priscilla has a chance to respond, Vladimir answers his own question. "***Run!*** She's got a grenade in her mouth!"

That one actually gets some open laughter from the techies. In their little two-man game of one-upmanship, Vladimir takes that as a ringing endorsement, and victoriously raises both hands over his head, *Rocky* style.

It's no coincidence that this is more than a little juvenile. Actors—both men and women—are something less than fully fledged adults, and not just because we play house for a living. Some of it has to do with how we are seen by the public—we don't grow up because we can't. We're not allowed to get older at anything like a normal rate of speed. (Meredith, of course, has taken this concept to dizzying heights.) Much of it, however, is self-imposed. We are all of us stuck on the brink of puberty in one way or another. Actresses of any age size one another up—"My waist is smaller than hers, but she's got bigger boobs, *and* she's got an ass to die for"—just like we did in gym class.

Actors, like athletes, compare speed, strength and, well, length (okay, diameter counts, too). I can just imagine the furtive peeking and measuring that goes on in the loo when all present are supposed to be going about their own urinary business, eyes front. (And if the IG isn't boss of the beach in there, I'd be real surprised.) As for guys at the less well-endowed end of the size spectrum, I bet some of them only pee when they know the potty is deserted, just to avoid coming out on a short end of the stick, as it were.

INT. STONY POINT BAR—NIGHT

Gallagher Molloy is at his usual post, tending bar. He bristles as Laszlo Szekely enters in a well-tailored top-coat, white silk scarf, and tuxedo, but Szekely is unaware of it. Laszlo has been at the fund-raising gala for the Hope Canyon Medical Center all night, and now wants noth-

ing more than a nightcap before going to bed—alone, for
once.

> GALLAGHER
>
> Would . . . you . . . like . . . a . . .
> drrrrrrrrrrrink?

As usual, Priscilla is hogging screen time by speaking extremely slowly.

> LASZLO
>
> (doffing his topcoat and tossing it over a barstool)
> Bloody Mary, please.

"Over the next coupla weeks, Daphne's gonna turn Laszlo into a vampire," Jay whispers. To avoid disrupting the scene, he puts his lips right up against the side of my head and speaks straight into my ear canal, producing world-class goosebumps. "There will be increasingly frequent references to vampire stuff. Hence the Bloody Mary, get it?"

> GALLAGHER
>
> It's two A.M. and you're ordering . . . that? . . .
> Where do you think you are, pretty boy? . . . At some
> foo-foo society . . . brunch?

"Chance of nightfall, with increasing probability of blood and fangs?" I respond in similar mouth-to-ear fashion. "How come she tells you that and not us?"

> GALLAGHER (CONT'D)
> (mockingly)
> Your eggs benedict . . . will be along shortly,
> your . . . lordship.

> LASZLO
>
> Why are you behaving this way? Does rudeness run in
> your family?

"Need-to-know basis," Jay replies. I can hear but not see the smile on his face.

> GALLAGHER
>
> Oh . . . I dunno, Mr. . . . Szekely. . . . Maybe it
> has . . . something to do with . . . you seducing . . .
> Fallon.

This is truly nauseating. The speed at which Priscilla is delivering his lines is so slow that he could put a lemming fired up on coke to sleep.

                          LASZLO
               (Glares at him but says nothing.)

                         GALLAGHER
What's the . . . matter, Laszlo. . . . Cat got
your . . . tongue?

"I'll be sure to bring my garlic and my crucifix," I whisper to Jay.

                          LASZLO
                (attempting to be diplomatic)
Fallon Salisbury is a lady, and I'm very fond of her.

                         GALLAGHER
                (with a chip on his shoulder)
She's **my** lady . . . and I'm . . . fond of her . . . too.

                          LASZLO
                        (stiffly)
I refuse to have this conversation.

                         GALLAGHER
Oh, but we are . . . having it. . . . You . . .
were . . . seen . . . groping her . . . in the elevator of the . . . Esperanza Regency.

Laszlo is troubled, not only because Gallagher has him dead
to rights, but by the level of detail of his information.

                          LASZLO
Opens his mouth to reply, but Priscilla runs right over him.

                         GALLAGHER
Sixteenth floor . . . Corner. . . . suite . . .

                          LASZLO
(Opens his mouth again, but Priscilla is not done hogging the
                     camera yet.)

                         GALLAGHER
I mean . . . really.

                          LASZLO
                        (bristling)
Fallon is a grown woman. I greatly enjoy her company,
and she enjoys mine.

                         GALLAGHER
Did you . . . think you'd get . . . away . . . with it?

```
                    LASZLO
              (with increasing anger)
I did not coerce her in any way. If you have issues
with Fallon's behavior, I suggest you take them up
with her. Nobody "got away with" anything, Molloy, and
I resent the inference.

                   GALLAGHER
We'll see what Regina . . . Abell . . . has to
say . . . about that.

                    LASZLO
                 (intensely)
You know, actually, I've changed my mind. I don't want
a Bloody Mary. What I want is to punch your lights
out.

                   GALLAGHER
Fine. . . . Let's take this out back. . . . I don't
want to be cleaning . . . up my bar . . . after I'm
done with . . . you.
```

"And cut," says Marty. "We are moving to the alley. Let's go."

* * *

"I'm gonna kick your buh-utt! I'm gonna kick your buh-utt!" Vlad taunts in a singsongy voice that is straight off the playground.

Can we please grow up a little here?

"You and whose army, Kovacs?"

Probably not. Jeez. If actors have a lot of Peter Pan in them, then these two are surely the Lost Boys.

```
EXT. ALLEY BEHIND STONY POINT BAR—NIGHT

Gallagher and Laszlo circle each other warily. As arranged,
Priscilla gets off the first punch,
```
but what was supposed to be a glancing blow to the jaw gets a bit more of Vladimir's cheekbone than it was supposed to. He staggers backward, rubbing his cheek.

"Not the face! Not the face!" Vladimir exclaims. "I need some ice."

"Cut!" Marty yells. "Ice pack!"

"Makeup!" shouts Priscilla in counterpoint. "I need some Orange Number Five for my knuckle."

There is a bustle of activity behind the cameras as Vladimir tries to walk it off.

"Shouldn't lead with your chin like that, Vladi my boy," Priscilla continues. There is an unmistakable note of condescension in his voice.

"Dammit, Garrett! That hurt!"

"Ding! Neutral corners, please," says Marty, trying for damage control.

For his part, Priscilla seems entirely unfazed by the idea that in his "carelessness" he inflicted pain on his pal. "The script may say I have to go down," he says, "but if you think I'm gonna roll over for you, you'd best think again."

"Oh, and by the way," Vladimir retorts, "you still have to pay up."

"For what?" Priscilla asks.

"I told you before—you lost the bet. Tiffany and I pulled it off."

So that's why Priscilla kept hanging around the set—the Lost Boys had a private wager going about the sex scene. No wonder Marty couldn't get rid of him: he had money riding on it.

"Yeah, yeah, yeah," Priscilla taunts. "Sez you."

"And sez Tiffany," Vladimir spits back. "Ask her yourself."

"I don't believe either of you. You got no proof, Kovacs," says Priscilla.

Oh but he does, you moron!! I saw it. So did Trent. I want to jump up and shout, but I stifle the urge to blurt it all out.

"You got no witnesses. You got nuthin'."

A little spastic twitch goes through my body as the desire to stand and the need to protect Mzee fight it out within me. Jay looks at me quizzically but doesn't say anything.

"Oh, so it's gonna be like that, is it? Fuck the ice, let's go. . . ." With that, Vladimir removes the white scarf from around his neck and whips it across Priscilla's cheek.

> *Tweedledum and Tweedledee*
> *Agreed to have a battle;*
> *For Tweedledum said Tweedledee*
> *Had spoiled his nice new rattle.*

"And we're rolling," says Marty. "Action!"

Jay peers forward intently as the scene resumes.

Gallagher and Laszlo circle one another warily. While they are circling, Vladimir removes his tie and his tuxedo vest, and roughly pushes up the sleeves of his white shirt. He now looks incredibly dashing in a darkly brooding, Brontëesque sort of way—like Jane Eyre's Edward Rochester, the master of Thornfield Manor, whose homicidal maniac wife is up in the attic.

As arranged, Gallagher gets off the first punch, but Vladimir blocks it before it "lands."

"Hey!" says Priscilla. "You were supposed to take that one!"

"Sez who?"

"Cut!"

"That was a mistake," Jay says, now in a normal voice, since the cameras have stopped. "Did you see what happened there, Kate?"

"Yeah, neither one of them is following the script. And the best thing about a fight scene is that Priscilla can't jack up his face time by slowing it down."

"No, not that. Priscilla telegraphed his move by bobbing his head," Jay explains softly. "That made it easy for Vlad to block him. When you fight, keep your head level and steady, even when you move forward. Otherwise your opponent will know you're coming."

"Are we ready to roll again, people?" Marty asks. "One mo' time . . ."

"No—one **last** time." Daphne's voice fills the studio. "If assholes could fly, right now this place would be an airport. This is your final take, gentlemen. I suggest you make it a good one. Play it the way I wrote it, or have your agents call me in the morning."

> *Just then flew down a monstrous crow,*
> *As black as a tar-barrel;*
> *Which frightened both the heroes so,*
> *They quite forgot their quarrel!*

Late November

6:48! 6:48!! 6:48!!!

When the alarm goes off, I stare at the ceiling, pound the snooze button with my fist, and attempt to go back to sleep, but instead of nodding off I sit bolt upright in bed and watch the perky dawning of a new day. As the sun drifts dreamily toward her sinecure at anchor above Southern California, a colossal shadow of self-doubt creeps across my countenance, like a shade-loving vine.

Fuck morning—all this sunny optimism pisses me off.

I would like the sun to show at least a glimmer of uncertainty about her appearance, instead of the searing confidence that yes, she is gorgeous, and yes, people here bask in the glow of her reflected light and feel infinitely better about themselves. But no. Suspended up there, she's just another blonde Barbie with a sense of entitlement.

I recognize her unwavering exuberance as the same relentless cheerfulness that infects all of Los Angeles. The place is an ongoing experiment in positive thinking. There is a jolly, robust energy in Southern California, often in the face of every conceivable reason to be otherwise. Everyone here is so alarmingly upbeat. This is not my natural state.

In Southern California, happiness is the norm—sadness is a departure, and outright melancholy is a deviant behavior. Chalk it up to the prevailing clouds and gloom of the motherland, but those of us ruled by Britannia, like natives of Seattle, find happiness to be an aberrant state of mind that only occasionally intrudes upon our normal saturnine demeanor.

Which means that today as on most days I am a trespasser on the campus of the University of Happy, a gate-crasher at the House of Doan-Gimme-No-Bad-News. And it's hard to be up when you're exhausted. Of course, the plus to this grueling schedule is that I'm too tired to dwell on my awkward, oversize presence in a world of perfect Barbies. Thank God, Devon's personality change has been well received by the fans, but fourteen-hour days at the studio have been the norm, not the exception. Daphne's been a tiger on the set, mauling if not devouring all who falter, and she's achieved the desired result. Our numbers are up and we're getting good ink in the press, but my Starbucks jones has increased tremendously. I've been pouring lattes down my throat in an effort to caffeinate myself sufficiently to respond at least halfway to the city's manic giddiness.

Into the car and hurtling down the freeway. I do like the feeling of hurtling. This is the free, easy, *Thelma & Louise*-y part of my day, a few moments of precious me-time alone in my personal space, before the frenetic day at work. It is peculiarly Californian. Everywhere else in the world, one drives. In London you drive, park in massive traffic jams, and politely wait to drive again. In Germany you're homicidal—a rocket on the autobahn at speeds up to two hundred clicks per hour. In Paris, if you drive a car, you're suicidal, if only because everyone else is nuts—you're lucky just to survive. In New York you drive like a boxer—you bob, weave, and curse. But in Southern California, you hurtle.

Th-thump. Th-thump. Th-thump. The Honda is making a dreadful noise and steering so much like a truck that I abandon the freeway for surface streets. I pull to the curb and circle the vehicle warily. The right front tire is flat, very flat, and I've got all of, oh, twenty-seven minutes to get to the studio.

"Aha!" I say to no one in particular. "This is why Triple-A was invented." But I'm not nearly organized enough to have the auto club on my speed dial, and I don't seem to have the card with me, either.

Note to self: Find the Triple-A card.

Amended note to self: Nah. Just call and get a new one.

The good news is that the car died right in front of my favorite Starbucks, and I need a fix. Not only that, it's a place full of people with time on their hands—time enough, I'm hoping, to change a flat.

"Can I help you?" asks the neo-Goth *barista* blankly, with no glimmer of sincerity whatsoever.

I gaze across the counter at an individual whose inky black hair is plastered like *al dente* vermicelli to her (I think this is the proper pronoun) translucent, albino-pallid, almost blue skin. Multipierced eyebrows frame a vacant Idontgiveashit stare.

"I'll have a Venti vanilla latte and a maple-oat scone," I say, looking around for someone to help with the car.

"I'll have what she's having!" effuses a brittle tenor over my right shoulder. "Sorry, but I've been waiting for a chance to say that since *When Harry Met Sally.*"

I turn to the source of the remark. In a perfect world I'd be looking at a guy in mechanic's overalls, but instead I get that familiar growing sensation. I'm just not ready to deal with a guy who's coming on to me. I'm looking for Mr. Goodwrench, not Mr. Goodbar.

"My name is Erwin Saunders. What's yours?"

Even though the face isn't repulsive, something about Erwin is a bit . . . off. The remark was much too glib, and the pants are much too plaid. I suspect he's been rehearsing that pickup line daily in front of his bathroom mirror ever since the movie came out in, what . . . '89? It wouldn't have mattered if I'd said, "Grande extra hot soy hazelnut cappuccino with an add-shot of hemlock." As I feel my torso continue to swell, I'm so horrified at being ambushed that I neglect to give him a false name.

"Kate McPhee."

"What do you do?"

"I'm an actress on *Live for Tomorrow*."

"The thoap! Ith yooo! Yohre on my thories!" exclaims the Goth. Her smile exposes the braces on her teeth, but that's just the beginning. There is enough metal in her mouth to more than match what she has in her eyebrows—as she speaks, the industrial bolt in her tongue clacks against her incisors, at least until gravity gains its inevitable victory, pulling it back with a sploosh into the font of accumulated saliva in her lower jaw, giving her a Daffy Duck thufferin' thuccothathsh underwater lithp.

"Yeth—yes." A lithp that is unfortunately contagious.

"I don't follow the thoaps—soaps," says Erwin. "What character do you play?"

"Thee'th Debbin Mewwick, uffta Hohppe Cangyong PD," the Goth volunteers brightly. "I luff thith thow. . . ."

My God, our fans are truly everywhere.

"Thpethially theh noooo Nick-th-olath-sch."

"Oh, you mean Bradley," I say. "I'll be working with him today."

Erwin has remained right behind me. I feel his warm, eager breath on my neck, followed in short order by his warm, equally eager hand on my ass.

Men are so predictable.

By the time my latte is up on the bar, I'm larger than a Shaq-size Pillsbury Doughboy because Erwin has done his level best to remain glued to my posterior—and it's really creeping me out. Ready as I am to dash out the door, I still have to solve my transportation problem. Casing the joint, it's clear that there isn't anyone else around who looks ready or able to help.

Like it or not, Katie, you're a damsel in distress and he's the only white knight on the horizon.

"Um, Erwin," I turn toward him with a smile, placing my hand lightly on his forearm, "there's something I have to ask you. I have a flat and I can't be late to the studio. I need someone to help me change a tire."

"I'd be happy to do that to you, er, for you, Kate."

"My car is just out front."

. . .

"So you go after the bad guys," he opens, making the obligatory chitchat as we walk toward the car.

"Yeah, that's me."

"I could be bad . . ." he offers with a smirk that I choose to ignore.

Pushing aside a jumble of used coffee cups, under which Meredith's gift basket still lurks, we exhume the little toy spare from the subbasement of the trunk.

"I'm a detective," I reply, trying to keep conversation to a minimum. I don't want to do anything that might distract him from the task at hand.

"You figure out who did it and arrest them, right?" he asks as he places the jack under the rear of the car.

"You could put it that way."

"Oh, I'd love to put it that way," says Erwin with a smarmy leer. "Meet me at the Rite Spot for a drink tonight and we'll get to know each other better [wink, wink], if you know what I mean."

*Yeah well, you knew that was coming, didn't you, Kate? I briefly contemplate the thought of Erwin Saunders **without** his plaid pants. Eeeewww. It's so unimaginably repellent that a shiver rolls up my spine.*

"I can't tonight, Erwin, sorry."

"Tomorrow night, then."

"I . . . I . . ."

"It's the least you can do for getting me to change your tire."

No, it isn't. Ah, the desperation guilt-trip ploy. We clearly have very disparate notions of how much of my companionship this kindness is worth.

"Well, actually, Erwin, I don't think this would work out."

"Why not?"

He doesn't seem to want to take no for an answer. I grab for my last straw and pull out Devon Merrick's identity.

"Because . . . I'm . . . I'm gay, that's why."

"It was nice meeting you, Kate. I'll look for you on TV."

. . .

"Morning, all!" I say as I slip breathlessly into JJ's chair in Gossip Central.

"You're late," she says. "We were getting worried, hon."

"Yeah, I know. My car had a flat. And my cell phone died and I look like shit. *And* I need a miracle—sorry, JJ—I'm due upstairs in ten minutes."

Luckily enough, my scenes today are night shots shrouded in fog, and a wide-brimmed Dick Tracy fedora will hide my unwashed hair and leave most of my face in shadow.

"What happened to you?" asks Trent from the next pod over. "You look like you just escaped from the clutches of Snidely Whiplash."

"Just a close encounter of the weird kind," I reply. "A tire on the car went flat and then this strange duck hit on me in Starbucks."

"Oh Kate, I know exactly what you mean!" Tiffany clucks sympathetically from the pod on the other side. "It's getting so I can't go anywhere. I get hit on awwll the time!"

I'm sure you do, sweetness. I'm just sure you do. And I'd be willing to wager that you flap those baby blues until it happens, too. It's as basic a skill for girlies as fly casting is for fishermen, and one I never learned properly, more's the pity.

"This guy in plaid pants was the only one who offered to help with the flat, and then I couldn't get rid of him."

"How'd you deal with it?" asks Trent.

"Told him I was gay."

"Tiffany," comes the disembodied voice over the intercom, "Wardrobe needs you on the double."

"Again?" Tiffany looks bewildered, a not uncommon state of affairs. "I was just there!"

"Is this the LaTrisa problem? Did they pick out something red for you, too?" Trent asks waggishly.

"Nope," says Tiffany with finality. "And anyway, it's not like she can claim the entire red side of the color wheel for herself, ya know."

"Well actually, she can," responds Trent, eyes twinkling. "You didn't read the fine print in your contract, Tiff. Everything between Barbie pink and ultraviolet belongs to the Queen."

Tiffany looks at him blankly.

My God! It's impossible to tell whether or not she knows Trent was kidding.

"But Ruben said we'd be okay with blushing plum!" A look that will have to pass for exasperation crosses Tiffany's face as she leaves for Wardrobe.

"So you told him you were gay . . . and then what?" Trent continues, without skipping a beat.

"Poor Erwin couldn't flee down Cahuenga Boulevard fast enough . . . but after that I had to tighten the lug nuts myself. Take the jack off, too."

The banter in Makeup always flirts with sexual innuendo—always.

"But that's exactly what he wanted you to do for him—tighten his lug nuts and . . . you know," he says merrily.

Game, set, and match, Mr. Winterfield.

"Smartass."

"So you noticed!"

"Turns out changing a tire isn't that big a deal."

"We guys try to keep that a secret."

"Next time I'll be able to do it myself—with my teeth."

"Devon and Nicholas . . . upstairs, now. Set up for scene three," comes the page over the intercom. I fidget in the chair, but JJ tightens her surprisingly strong grip.

"Almost finito, hon," she says.

"Gotta book it, JJ," I say. "The Borsalino will cover a multitude of sins."

"There—close enough," she states. "They'll give you a touch-up on the floor."

"Uh, Kate," says Trent as I'm halfway out the door.

"Yeah?"

"Watch out for the Black Hole."

"Excuse me?"

"You'll know it when you see it." He grins.

```
EXT. NICHOLAS DUNCAN'S BOAT—MISTY NIGHT.
A FOGHORN IS HEARD IN THE BG.

                    DEVON
    Nicholas? Nicholas Duncan? It's Lieutenant Devon Mer-
    rick, Hope Canyon PD. I have some questions to ask
    you. I'm coming aboard.

                    NICHOLAS
    What is this about, Lieutenant?

                    DEVON
    Where were you last Tuesday night?

                    NICHOLAS
    I was here on my boat. Why?
```

A shiny brand-new Nicholas stands immobile in a pretty boy stance on the "deck" of the boat, as if modeling for the Abercrombie & Fitch catalogue.

Shit! Casting has done an exemplary job of finding an exact duplicate of the last one.

Where he has come from is anyone's guess. Perfectly vapid, this is not the Nicholas of the date at Musso's, Nicholas of the colored contact lenses and white Corvette. This is a Stepford Nicholas, provided by the Nicholas warehouse, batteries included.

```
                    DEVON
    I hope you know someone who can corroborate that. Who
    was here with you?
```

>   NICHOLAS
>   No one. I was . . . alone.

I get the feeling that he's afraid to reposition any part of his face because it would make him appear less handsome. Nevertheless, I soldier on with the scene.

>   DEVON
>   What do you know about the disappearance of assistant
>   DA Jamila Benton?

>   NICHOLAS
>   (with alarm—or not. There is no alarm on the new Nicholas's face.
>   There's no emotion on his face whatsoever. Thus far in the scene, his
>   facial expression hasn't changed at all. No frown, no questioning look.
>   Rien. Nada. Botz.)

>   Jamila? . . . Missing?

>   DEVON
>   She hasn't been seen since the two of you had dinner
>   on Tuesday.

Actually, LaTrisa was offered a cameo in a film, and Daphne let her take it. Hence she has "disappeared" for a week.

>   NICHOLAS
>   How . . . terrible.

So terrible, apparently, that even his eyebrows, like those of his immediate predecessor, refuse to move.

The newest Nicholas—played by, oddly enough, the newest Bradley, Bradley Jameson—may be great eye candy, with chiseled cheekbones, a perfect profile, and a Tom Cruise wannabe killer smile, but it's all veneer and no substance. This latest Bradley is so stiff, so stilted, that there is nothing for me to play off. I may as well be out there all by myself. Actually that would be better, since I wouldn't be in danger of being swallowed up into his abyss. I now understand what Trent had meant about the Black Hole.

"Cut! That's it, thanks."

Whaddaya mean "Cut. Thanks"?? Daphne would have French-fried me for a performance like that! And she'd have been right to do it—so how come he's gonna get away with phoning it in like that? I expect her to come roaring in here, screaming for him to show a bit more emotion—something—anything—but I guess when you're that gorgeous, you get a free pass. Or maybe, just maybe, she knows he can't do any better.

"Set up for the next scene," says Marty. "I need Fallon and Philip Salis-bury, Jennifer Abell and Taylor Daniels. Jennifer, Taylor, Fallon, and Philip to the country club set, please."

Nobody mentions the Nicholas recasting; it's as if the old one had been sucked into a void and a new one beamed up. I'll have to make Trent spill the details.

As Amber, Alison, Trent, and Tiffany motor toward their places, Tiffany, now regarbed in avocado green, looks me up and down, elbows Alison vig-orously, then murmurs as they go by.

· · ·

"Do I have spinach in my teeth or something?" I ask Trent when he re-turns. "The three Barbies barely speak to me—not that I really miss their sparkling conversation—except that they seem to be whispering behind my back constantly."

"I've noticed that," he concedes.

"I had to console Taylor about Mason and the curse of the voodoo cult," I say in script shorthand. "When I tried to give Alison a comforting hug, she jumped back about ten feet, as if I had some horrible contagious dis-ease. What's going on here anyway? And why is Richard suddenly on hia-tus? And who's the new guy?"

"Those are three separate questions, dear Ms. McPhee. To answer the third one first, ol' blue eyes got a lucrative offer from Spelling. There's no justice. As to the second, our IG is off drying out—again. I don't expect this latest 'spiritual retreat,' as the network's PR department is calling it, to really cure his elbow-bending on a permanent basis—the first three sure didn't. But on the other hand, it *will* give the mother of that sixteen-year-old they found in his dressing room a fighting chance at coaxing her daughter to return to Cedar Rapids."

"Did Richard say anything about what she was doing in his room?" I ask. There was maybe a 2 percent chance that this was entirely innocent.

"Claimed to be helping her run lines for some pilots she was up for," Trent replies. "You know, working on her diction . . . trying to get rid of her midwestern *A*."

"Pilot season is over," I say. "And if little Lolita has been swigging name-brand scotch and her midwestern *A* has been screwing a name-brand lead-ing man, why would she want to go back to Cedar Rapids?"

"Let me guess—she has to hustle back to Iowa because she's the lead in her high school production of *Bye Bye Birdie*?" he hypothesizes.

"Perhaps, Higgins," I counter sardonically, breaking into a tony upper-crust English public school voice, "Eliza Doolittle in *My Fair Lady* would be more suitable."

"Indubitably, Pickering," he says, picking up the game with an entirely creditable imitation of Henry Higgins, "but, I say, Colonel, it's still a tough sell."

Oh, we actors are a hoot, always trying on voices or swapping snippets of well-known movie and stage dialogue in the midst of normal conversation. Part of it is humor; part of it is one-upmanship—checking out what's in the other guy's acting bag of tricks. In this crew, the only ones worth playing the game with are Trent, LaTrisa, and Richard, and him only when he's sober.

"Same old story," he continues, shaking his head. "How ya gonna keep 'em down on the fahm, don't you know? And Pickering, do I need to point out that that's a rhetorical question?"

"Haha! Only if Amber is present, Higgins," I say with a stage laugh, "but then we'd have to explain to her what it means."

"No kidding around, Kate," he says, reverting to his normal speaking voice, "the real reason to get the nymphet home is that Daphne's offered the mother, in truth a stage mom from hell, a pisspot full of money to keep the whole thing quiet."

"Wow. Okay, back to the first question. Why is the trio of goddesses is avoiding me?"

"You mean the sorority sisters?" he says, eyeing me carefully. "You really want to know?"

"That is in fact why I asked the question."

"Our three blonde lovelies are scared shitless of you," he pauses for a deep breath before continuing, "because they think you're a lezzie."

"You mean me, *Kate,* for real, not just Devon?"

"Yeah."

"You're kidding, right?"

"Nope."

"And you didn't tell them I wasn't?"

The silence goes on a bit too long.

"Trent . . . ?"

"Well, someone saw you and LaTrisa embracing in the parking lot very late at night."

"There must be spies everywhere."

"And you told that guy who fixed your tire that you were butch. And you said it in front of Tiffany. . . ."

"Who takes everything at face value."

Because she has no clue that there is anything else beyond face value.

"Right, and after that I really wasn't sure," he says sheepishly, "and then I told myself you were so much fun it really didn't matter."

"Thank you, I think."

"Well, you *are* the only chick in the cast who turned down Kirk Marlowe."

"A fail-safe indicator, to be sure. What is he, the official litmus test for newbies?"

"Something like that. And you do play Devon pretty much gay. Very convincingly."

"That's called *acting*, Trent."

"That's why Alison didn't want any part of you hugging her."

"Seriously, Trent, you need to take your gaydar in for a major tune-up. It's flat-out busted. And for the record, he's the one who begged off."

I decide to keep what I know about L'Affaire du Raspberry Tart to myself, at least for the moment.

"Worse yet."

"Shit. And let me guess—this has now made the rounds of the entire studio?"

"Basically, yeah."

"Perfect."

10

Early December

7:15! 7:15!! 7:15!!!
The alarm goes off and I peel back my cool cotton sheets, in the process displacing Drusilla from her cradle around my rump, drag my carcass out of my comfortable womb of a bed, and stumble into the shower.

I try to force alertness by singing Elton John's "Don't Let the Sun Go Down on Me," but I don't seem to be able to help turning it into "Don't let your son go down on me." Proof positive that there hasn't been a man in my bed for way too long.

You're overdue for a roll in the hay, Katiegirl. I mentally round up the usual suspects.

Vladimir? Do I really want to be another notch on that gunbelt?

Priscilla? Oh please. Even though he thinks I'm gay, he's so full of himself that he'd do me—just to prove he's so hot that he could turn a dyke straight.

Richard? He's lived a quarter-century longer than I have, but the way he looks at it, I'm too old for him. And then, if it's another one of those days when he's drained his bottle of single-malt, there isn't enough Viagra in all of Palm Springs to revive that particular dead soldier.

Trent? Trent's a pal.

The new Bradley? Much too wooden.

Kirk? If he's still boffing Meredith, Kirk is off-limits. Besides, he's too pretty for me. . . .

Just like Rafe.

Ouch! In my morning stupor I've let my thoughts wander into a briar thicket that I'm usually more clever at avoiding, at least when I'm fully awake. Now I've hooked my psyche on a particularly thorny bramble and ripped open a scab that is far from completely healed.

No doubt about it, Rafe was too pretty for me.

Tall and rail slender, with world-class cheekbones, Rafe was Jude Law gorgeous—even with the two-day stubble he took to sporting as he got deeper into his "consumptive anguished poet" vibe.

My closest friend, Leslie, was as voluptuous as Rafe was angular. She was effortlessly beautiful, with ivory skin, luminous violet eyes, and dark brown, almost black hair. She reminded me—and others as well—of a young Elizabeth Taylor. When we went out for coffee together, men looked past or through me to stare at her, even if I'd gone to some pains to get myself all painted and gussied up and she'd just waltzed out the door in her naked face and her sweats.

When I finally figured out that Rafe and Leslie were having this red-hot affair behind my back, there was a part of me that understood. Devastated as I was, on one level I knew it was right.

Pretty people seek each other out. That's not good or bad; that's just how it is.

Like water seeking its own level, we all tend to hook up with mates who are about as pretty or handsome as we are. Whenever there is a PI—a Pulchritude Imbalance—and one half of a couple is far more attractive than the other, it makes the relationship unstable. Unless there is a compensating factor, which almost always is money.

From that first day on the set, I knew I was out of my league—an ugly duckling in a pond of perfection. After four weddings, a funeral, three divorces, and a voodoo cult, I'm still an outsider, but when I leave the studio in the middle of the night, it's a little late to go prowling for companionship, and besides, it's all I can do to keep my eyes open long enough to drive home.

No sense lamenting it—there's nothing to be done. For the time being, I'm a nun, and a dykey nun at that.

If that's who I am, there's no point getting really dressed to go to work. Which is just as well. It appears as if someone has detonated a clothes bomb in my bedroom. From the upper strata of the debris I unearth an only slightly rumpled French terry chocolate brown Juicy Couture track suit. After applying antiperspirant, moisturizer, lip gloss, and SPF 30, I point my dressed and lubricated self out the door to make my usual Starbucks stop before I begin my daily hurtle along the freeway.

．．．

I wave hi to the Goth behind the counter—her name is Thondra (make that Sondra) and she now loves me—order up a cappuccino and a Danish and a *New York Times,* and take a seat. With my head buried in the paper I reach to my right, locate the pastry by Braille, take a bite, then put it back down.

"Excuse me, but is that mine or yours?" I glance up, chewing, and lock eyes with an astoundingly crinkly pair of blue ones.

"Jesus!" I sputter through the large mouthful of what up until now had been someone else's breakfast. "Oh no! It's yours. Crikey, I'll buy you another. . . ."

He deftly pretend-snatches the pastry from my grasp and breaks it in two. "Never mind," he says with a smile. "It's okay. But you've already mauled that half, so you'd better finish it."

"I'm so sorry, and since you just made me use the word 'crikey,' it means I have to buy you a drink."

"Well, we've already broken bread together, so I guess that's right. The name's Matt."

"Kate," I say with more confidence than I really feel. "I'm on my way to work. I get off at eight tonight, if you really want to have that drink."

"Wow. Those are some heavy hours."

"That's okay. They pay me well. Where shall we meet?"

"How about the Magic Castle?"

"The magician's club? You're a magician?"

"Yep. I do my final set at eight thirty. I'll leave a pass at the door."

We swap info, me and my Houdini. As we stand, he pulls four quarters from behind my ear and drops them in the tip jar by the register.

Which causes my inner skeptic to give me a stern talking to. So, he's cute enough, but did you really just make a date with a complete stranger? What on earth are you doing?

As soon as I close the car door, I immediately want to call the whole thing off. Instead, I turn up the radio to quiet the itchy misgivings in my head. I'm even itchier when I realize that I've left my script at home—again.

* * *

I chug into my space on the studio parking lot on the same three and a half wheels I've been driving on for weeks—after Erwin, I never quite got around to getting a real tire put back on the car. I haul my butt into the studio and prowl the corridor till I spy my quarry: an unattended script. It's Priscilla's—no problem there. He never reads it anyway. Lightfingering it into my bag, I dash to my room and quickly dismember it. Inventing a bit of clear space on the floor, I jam a pillow down and sit cross-legged, madly turning pages, dogearing my scenes and outlining my massive speeches.

There has been a murder; there is a corpse; there are footprints; and I will be spending the day twirling my mustache (metaphorically speaking), checking out suspects, and pondering motives.

I trot into Makeup with a cheery "Hi and fuck you" to one and all, only to find that a new face unexpectedly awaits me. "Hi, I'm Christine Sinclair. I'll be doing you today."

Aaaaaiiieeee! Even as my face gets instantly huge, all the blood in it goes south, plunging pell-mell for my ankles. From within my bloated, pasty pallor I hear my breath coming in shallow wheezy soprano snorts, like an asthmatic piglet. Am I scared? You bet. This woman holds the power to make me either a princess or a troglodyte, and the difference between one and the other is the difference between Julia Roberts and Linda Tripp. JJ's no intellectual bright light, but she knows how to make me look good. More than that, she **likes** *making me look good.*

"No offense, er, ah . . ."

Whoever she is, there's no sense pissing her off. Diplomacy, Kate. Diplomacy.

"Christine."

"Christine. Yes, right. I'm sure you're very good at what you do, Christine, but I'd really prefer to work with JJ. Is she sick?"

"Didn't they tell you? She's not with the show anymore."

Nooooooooooo! I feel like a deformed toddler whose favorite stuffed bunny has just been flushed down the toilet. My cheekbones and my eyebrows are now swollen so badly that they have met up and fused together, forming a horizontal seam across the bridge of my nose, zipping up my eyeballs on the inside. Not only am I hyperventilating, I'm also blind.

"I beg your pardon? She was here yesterday and didn't say anything about leaving." *I mouth the words with great difficulty, because my lips are the last feature that's still on the outside of my head. Everything else has been swallowed up inside the face balloon.*

"Chalk up another victory for Meredith," says Trent, chiming in from the pod next to mine.

"What happened?"

"JJ couldn't make LaTrisa ugly enough," he says without a trace of irony.

"So Daphne fired her?"

"Yeah, it's the pits," he says.

"Actually no," Christine says quietly. "Daphne took care of her. She made a phone call to Murray at *Love Never Dies.*"

"She called the producer on another daytime show?" Trent is incredulous.

"Yes, and basically negotiated a swap," Christine affirms as she reclines me into dying bug mode. "JJ took my job over there and I came here."

Twenty minutes later, she tilts me back up and hands me the mirror. I'm instantly reassured—it's not that I look as good as when JJ did me, I look . . . exactly the same. "We talked last night," Christine explains as I look questioningly at her.

This might be all right after all. With the way you behaved at first, Ms. Kate, it's a wonder she didn't poke your eye out with that Laura Mercier Purple Sapphire Kohl pencil she's been wielding.

"I owe you an apology, Christine. It's just that actors—"

"Are creatures of habit," she says, picking up my sentence, "and the least change in the routine can be very upsetting. No apology necessary, Kate. My husband's in the biz. I know just how it is."

"What's his name?"

"Wyatt. Wyatt Sinclair."

"Good man!" Trent pipes up. "He plays Ian Glenullen on *Denver General.*"

"Kate," comes the disembodied voice over the paging system, "there's a chair available in Hair."

Shit! Much as I'd love to continue this conversation, the day's going to be long enough as it is without keeping Charlie waiting. I frenetically gather my deconstructed script and assemble it into something approximating working order. I realize dismally that no one else on the planet would be able to decipher my various notes, diagrams, cuts, and rewrites. But then again, I also realize, no one else *has* to. This is *my* working script, and I am a genius.

I slide onto Charlie's perch. "My, we seem to be very up this ayyem, cherub," he mumbles.

"Oh . . . you noticed! I've got a date tonight!"

"Somebody from the cast?"

"No, a magician!"

Charlie blinks. He is slowly chewing gum. He looks like a wise cow. "Oh, really!" he says with calm surprise. "You mean you're dating a civilian?"

With that, we both get to work. He focuses on a particularly troublesome spot of brunetteness; I begin running my lines. I have volumes and volumes to learn—about forty pages in all. They sit heavily in my crotch, mocking me as I attempt to memorize every ludicrous plot point and dreary expositive passage. I mumble and mutter in various tones of voice, staring off at imaginary persons both stage left and stage right, trying out inflections and hand gestures for each turn of phrase. To an observer I look like someone with a particularly virulent case of Tourette's.

Juliette Boudreaux, a rich socialite, has disappeared. Hamilton Boudreaux, her distraught husband, suspects foul play. It is a tedious C plotline that I have been roped into because as the truth emerges, characters that I am involved with are going to be implicated. I get to the final scene in the script—body falls out of the closet (how clever)—in a dead heat with Charlie, who is removing the rollers and starting to backcomb me.

•   •   •

Minutes later, the teased, sprayed, and lacquered gay goddess—*moi*—heads back to her dressing room, where Wardrobe has deposited a black polyester JC Penney pantsuit and a lived-in raincoat.

My spirits lift as I stare at the soiled and rumpled raincoat—the coat is an oasis of realism in a parallel universe, and a particular victory of mine. I had to beg and bludgeon Ruben to make it appear as if it had been worn, but in the end he got it exactly right.

I finger the material on the sleeve—it is rough and frayed at the cuffs. I love this coat—it's my talisman. I sit on my pillow, drape the coat across my lap, close my eyes, and let it transport me into my character. As I envision Devon waking up to a phone call about a possible murder, Kate recedes. Twenty minutes later, I slowly dress. Or rather, Devon dresses. At this point the transformation is complete.

I begin to improvise, now with some urgency, as I put on my cufflinks. I wedge an imaginary phone between my ear and shoulder—"Frank, do we have witnesses?" I pause and nod, listening to my imaginary cop in the field. I playact in my dressing room, leaping amid the clutter, conjuring up make-believe cops and reciting my lines.

I catch a glimpse of myself in the mirror. Staring back is a woman in a mannish suit and rumpled raincoat, but she is wearing false lashes and a ton of makeup, and her hair is tumbling about her shoulders in incongruous waves. I may be Ellen DeGeneres as Humphrey Bogart from the neck down, but I am Sam Spade as Dolly Parton from the neck up.

Note to self: When you're feeling brave, talk to Daphne about cutting your hair.

* * *

We are standing in the middle of the Hope Canyon Country Club set. This plotline is at its point of beginning, and it is still very much a work in progress. Writers have been called; scenes have been cut, rewritten, and switched. We are mired in one scene, replaying it like an endless *Groundhog Day.* I wonder what time it is, and for a brief moment Devon allows Kate to think about her date later tonight. I pick up my script, pretend to scratch the back of my hand, and in so doing deftly but furtively glance at my watch.

It feels like we have been at this all day; in point of fact, we have. It is now 5:30 P.M., hour seven on the set. We have two noncontract day players working today—a butler and a maid. Their heads are spinning with all the script changes, and they keep dropping their lines. As they flub yet another take, I stare at the ground and contemplate

1. suicide; or
2. homicide, specifically butlercide.

In lieu of bloodshed, however, I offer to run the scene with the day players yet again.

I realize my mistake as soon as the words leave my lips. Daphne, ever present, is grinding her chin. Worse yet, she is relentlessly grinding all within her hawklike sight into the ground. We are all prey, and it is gruesome. "You were horrible in that last scene!" she says by way of response, spitting through gritted teeth. "Mumbling and shuffling about . . . Who do you think you are, Columbo?"

Well yes, I do, actually, I think to myself.

At least I am wise enough to say nothing—I've said more than enough as it is. Instead I cast my eyes down at my script and turn to the scene we are all stuck in. But in the same way that you can see where a piece of the jigsaw belongs when you walk away for a while and come back to it, in a moment of clarity I realize how to fix our problem. "Perhaps we should just cut the butler from this scene entirely, and then he won't be in danger of hearing the plot points that we are all trying so hard to hide."

All activity onstage comes to a halt. There is palpable astonishment: not only did these words escape from my mouth, they were **audible.** The entire cast and crew stares at me with the same communal thought: we're all trying to keep our heads down, but the damnfool dyke is crazy enough to speak not just once, but twice! Even I am surprised at my own chutzpah; I hadn't really planned on being this brave—or foolhardy.

Daphne's head swivels on her neck like that of a barn owl. Raptor that she is, she glares at me as if I'm the lunch that got away. It's as if I'm a deranged, suicidal ground squirrel who had gone over the falls before she could eat me. "Very clever, Kate. Perhaps you would prefer **my** job," she hisses through her slit of a mouth.

There's nothing for it now but to see it through. "I can take all his dialogue," I explain, "and then he won't have to agonize over the names and places he can't remember."

More to the point, I continue to myself, **we** *won't have to agonize over what he can't remember, either.*

With one hand Daphne continues to toggle her chin; the other snap-snaps an *allegro con brio* cadence with her fingers, setting the tempo as her long-suffering assistant turns the pages of the script. Suddenly, Daphne laughs. A big masculine guffaw erupts from deep within her solar plexus. "Right!" she barks. "Let's cut the guy from the scene and put this thing to bed. Kate—take his first, middle, and last speeches.

"You sir," she continues, to the dismissed butler, "sit down until we call you again." With her index talon, Daphne indicates a chair in the corner, which he quickly takes. As the desperate rush of anxiety that had coursed through my body subsides, I breathe a sigh of relief and slump against a wall. Everyone else explodes into action.

Trailing various assistants and minions like so many tail feathers, Daphne briskly marches past me in her Ferragamos. "We're the only two around here with any brains!" she whispers, without breaking stride. I giggle. She is truly weird. I watch her exit to the booth, her legendary heels clip-clopping the floor as she goes.

* * *

I once again glance at my watch. It is now almost seven P.M. The action sans butler went smoothly, but when we got to the next part involving the maid, she couldn't get her lines right, so Daphne cut her as well. It's so hard to get good help these days. More impromptu story conferences, more rewrites. Mercifully, the next eight scenes involve just me and my detective partner and masses of snooping around, one big stunt fight, and finally the discovery of the body. I quickly do the math and am unhappy—at roughly fifteen to twenty minutes a scene, plus the stunt, plus more time for Daphne screwing with the storyline, I am not leaving the building till 10:40 at the earliest.

Daphne's voice comes over the loudspeaker. "Got a hot date, Ms. McPhee?" she asks acidly. "Do we need to be somewhere?" She must have been looking at the monitor when I checked my watch—I wasn't nearly so sneaky about it this last time. Either that or she heard me thinking, and one is as likely as the other. Big Brother has nothing on her.

Fortunately we're due for a break. Better call my magician and give him a heads-up. My fingers tingle as I punch his numbers into my cell. "Hello, you've reached Matt. Sleight of hand makes it impossible for me to answer the phone. I am currently handcuffed to the inside of a fridge at the bottom of Toluca Lake. Please leave a message." Beeeep.

Jesus. Magician humor.

"Hi, it's me, Kate. I am currently handcuffed to bad acting and won't be let out on good behavior for another three or four hours. If magicians stay awake past eleven P.M., perhaps we can meet at the Viper Room before the pumpkin arrives. Call me."

With what's left of the break I go looking for Jay. I figure we can work on the fight choreography for the scene where I tackle a mystery intruder.

I find him on the back stairs, playing Game Boy. "Yo, girlfriend! 'Sup?"

" 'Sup yourself, Sa Bum. Hey, I thought we could block out the fight scene. Who's the intruder?"

"Bill."

"Great." Bill is my favorite sparring partner. He's a pale, leathery cowboy type, and we work well together because he has no ego about having his butt kicked by a girl.

"Is it Just My Bill, or is my detective involved?"

"At first we thought it would be just you and the intruder," Jay says as he slowly stands. "But I then thought it would be better to have Carlos in on the action for the first minute or so," he continues. "I'll get Bill to take him down—"

"Better him than me," I interrupt with a grin. Carlos is stocky; his physique is the exact opposite of Jay's. I think of him as a walking fireplug—he has the lowest center of gravity of any human being I've ever seen.

"Then the two of you will really go at it."

As Jay leads me through the windowless corridors to the rehearsal room, I'm jazzed. The tomboy in me loves a good fight with the boys—and Jay stages and choreographs it to make me look like the Matrix Queen. I've come to like it that my muscles are sore the next day. God knows it's the only exercise I have a chance to get.

Bill is waiting for us in the rehearsal room, reading *Playboy*.

"Who's on the cover?" I inquire of Bill. (Well, I'm supposed to care, right?)

"Pamela—again!" Bill groans insincerely and rolls his eyes, stuffs the magazine into his duffel, then starts shaking his arms out and hopping from foot to foot to get his blood circulating.

I head for the paging system on the wall. "Carlos de la Fuente to the rehearsal studio. Carlos, rehearsal studio for fight sequence. Thanks."

I'm into my own warm-up, shadowboxing and humming the theme from *Rocky,* when Carlos bursts into the room. "I come on thee dobble," he says in a nasal, deliberately singsongy voice that mimics the old school Speedy Gonzalez stereotype of Latinos. *"A sus ordenes, mi puta marimacha."*

"¡Chinga tu madre!" I respond with mock anger. "Speak English, you fuckin' wetback. It's high time we went a few rounds."

Carlos plays Sgt. Enrique Morales, my Hope Canyon PD sidekick, and together we have a grand but politically incorrect time rewriting scenes to incorporate donut gags, coffee runs, and tons of other police stuff. He is the person solely responsible for making me seem even remotely credible as a detective. He has a knack for it because in a prior life he actually *was* a cop.

He'd been assigned as police liaison to a made-for-TV movie shooting in Pasadena when he spotted a major procedure faux pas. He mentioned it to the assistant director, saving her ass in the process. Because he was on duty at the time, the grateful AD couldn't compensate him in cash, but what she did instead was much better. She gave him a few speaking lines on her next gig, and a star was born. Carlos found he could make three times as much money playing a cop as being one, and quit the force.

Now his wife is happy—pretty much. No one is shooting at him anymore; they bought a new house in the Valley; the kids are gonna go to college; and she's a minor celebrity at the supermarket. It's almost enough to offset the fact that she ain't exactly delighted at the amount of time he spends in the company of beautiful women.

"Djou wanna a peesa me, you Eengleesh beetch?" We go into our mock combative roles and start throwing punches at each other until Jay steps between us with a get-serious-now glower. Having put an end to the horse-play between Carlos and me, he points Bill to the spot where he is to begin.

Move by move, a dance emerges among the three of us, except that Jay has to keep warning me to lock eyes with Bill before throwing a punch. "See. Think. Do," he growls. Eventually Bill tosses Carlos, who then lies on the floor smoking a cigarette, having been "knocked out."

Bill and I have a few more runs at it before we're called to the set. Carlos wraps an enormous tree trunk of an arm around my shoulder as we head for the door. "Looks good, girlfriend," Jay says by way of farewell. "Just relax, and remember: Fight in real time."

. . .

There is something strangely cold and forlorn about being in a dark TV studio late at night. We are each of us standing in our own puddle of mis-ery, and even though we are surrounded by humanity, there is a collective loneliness. We all have someplace else we'd rather be; we all have plans that are now out the window—with spouses, lovers, and kids who are sick and fucking tired of being stood up night after night. We should be tucked up cozily in our beds with people we love. It's a soap opera, after all—people watch us with one eye on their toddler and the other on their sandwich. Nevertheless, here we are. . . .

And the only person to whom it truly matters is a barking mad obsessive/compulsive in a food-fight-for-one Chanel pantsuit. Even though it is now well past midnight, Daphne's energy remains frenetic, and she demands and expects the same of all who surround her. There will be no shortcuts just because it's late and we want to go home. As she field-marshals both cast and crew, she is spraying saliva like one of those misters at an outdoor restaurant in August.

And now she has one weensy problem. Daphne is rethinking who my as-sailant is supposed to be, running plot points in her head, trying to deter-mine whether my attacker should be male or female. A much put-upon titmouse of a writer is at her side, chirping on about the merits of keeping my assailant a guy, probably because she knows it would be completely im-possible to find a stuntwoman at this hour of the night.

She's actually doing a pretty good job of selling her version of the story. "So when Devon is attacked by *a man*, it's likely that she will consider the murderer to be Hamilton Boudreaux, the husband. Therefore the story will unfold with Devon having *him* as her prime suspect. . . ."

"Yes dear," replies Daphne dismissively, "but surely the more interesting story, the more *moooving* story, is if Devon is so romantically enthralled by the **real** prime suspect—the ex-wife—Lacey Boudreaux, that she cannot help herself, even though she believes her to be the murderer."

Am I gonna get to sleep with the ex-wife? Cool! I say to myself.

"Therefore the intruder **has** to be a wooooooman," Daphne explains, "so that when the real murderer is revealed, Devon is safe in her love affair."

The director's eyes roll. I hope for his sake that Daphne didn't see him. Otherwise she'll ream him a new one, right in front of everyone. It's apparent, however, that he couldn't care if the assailant was a pair of flaming Siamese twin hermaphrodites joined at the left nostril.

I look over to Jay and Bill, who are leaning against the scenery, talking quietly. After Bill nods, Jay lopes lazily over toward Daphne. He stands quietly at her elbow, but says nothing. He understands how to work with her—it's interesting to watch the ones who do.

Eventually she acknowledges him. "What!" she snaps. Jay leans into her ear and speaks softly. Her eyes widen, then she glances over at Bill, who nods again, almost imperceptibly, in acknowledgment.

"Let me think about that," she says, tapping a staccato rhythm on her script with a ballpoint.

I look again at Jay, who returns my glance with a wink. I make a question mark of a face, but he just shushes me with his hands. Daphne briefly uses the ballpoint as a wand to vibrate her chin, then returns to tapping. It is the only sound inside the cavernous studio. The entire set is immobilized, waiting for her to do or say something—anything. She glances at her watch, a pretty diamond number hanging on a pin at her lapel, adjacent to some guacamole. Suddenly, the tapping stops, and a sharp collective intake of breath ensues.

"Right," she orders. "Shave his legs."

"Meal break. Thirty minutes. Pizza is in the prop room," Marty announces.

The worker bees spring into action, and Bill is summarily marched off to Makeup and Wardrobe. Jay smiles secretly at me and it all becomes clear—they're going to dress the poor bastard up as a girl, and he's agreed to it, probably for a whole shitload of extra pay.

· · ·

I'm not hungry, but everything is buzzing—my head, my heart, the blood in my veins. I head for my dressing room and hunker down on my pillow surrounded by my clutter. I call Matt again. This time I get a real person.

"Hi." He sounds smoky and there's low music in the background. "Am I being stood up?"

The Cliff's Notes version of the day's events pours out of me in a single sentence. "No-I'm-sorry-but-there's-been-a-murderand-no-one-could-get-their-lines-outand-our-crazy-producer-rewrote-everythingand-there's-a-stunt-scene-coming-up-for-which-she's-decided-to-turn-a-guy-into-a-girl-but-it-was-really-the-fightmaster's-idea . . . [big breath] andso-we're-now-breaking-for-dinner-while-they-shave-his-legs."

"Okaaay." He pauses, not quite sure what he's dealing with. "So . . . will they let you out any time soon, or are you in lockdown? I'm very good at es-capes."

"Do-you-know-where-the-studios-are?Why-don't-you-come-by? Ohnevermind-they-won't-let-you-on-the-lot-because-I'm-sure-the-security-guys-have-all-gone-homeAre-you-still-at-the-Viper-Room?"

"Yes," he says, keeping it short and simple. "Are you still in hyperdrive?" *Bingo.*

"RightWell-I'll-be-another-couple-of-hoursso-I'll-come-thereor-you-can-meet-me-here-at-the-gatesand-we'll-have-a-drink-or-breakfastand-we-could-go-for-a-drive-along-Mulholland-I-don't-have-to-be-at-work-for-twelve-hours-from-when-we-wrapso-we-can-hang-outWhen-do-you-work-tomorrow?"

"Lunchtime," he offers.

"PerfectI'll-probably-go-in-at-noon-myselfWe-can-chat-get-to-know-each-otherOr-I-can-collapse-in-your-lap-and-drool-over-your-Fila-sweat-pants-as-I-crashThen-you-can-wake-me-and-we-could-have-sexBut-I-don't-usually-do-that-on-a-first-dateThough-if-you-wake-me-ostensibly-it-would-be-the-second-dateSo-we-could-have-sex-if-you-wantBut-my-pad-is-reallyreally-fucking-messySo-if-your-place-is-better-we-should-probably-crash-there . . . [really big breath] don't-you-think?"

My brain is still running at Mach 2, and my mouth is laboring to keep up—or is it the other way round?

At least he has the good humor to be laughing his ass off by the time I finish. Bless him.

It occurs to me about this time that I must look like hell. With trepida-tion I glance in the mirror. I'm absolutely correct. My eye shadow is a dirty smudge, my concealer conceals nothing, having settled into the indigo crescent furrows under my eyes, like grout. My lips are cadaverously pale and dull. I head downstairs for a touch-up and arrive in the midst of the *Queer Eye for the Straight Guy* follies.

Jeremy, Ruben's scrawny queen of an assistant, is fussing and flapping. He has been given the task of dressing Bill for the scene, and he is clearly out of his depth with the assignment. He holds up one size 14 matronly outfit after another, desperately trying to find something that will disguise Bill's very broad and sexy surfing shoulders . . . but not completely. Appar-ently the latest message from Daphne is that she doesn't want a perfect transformation—she wants some of our more astute viewers to discern that the intruder is in fact a man in drag. It's a clever twist on the storyline.

Meanwhile, Charlie is hacking at a dirty-blond wig on a wig stand. Christine already has Bill in her clutches, plucking and shaving and painting him into something a little more estrogenic.

I grab a mug of coffee and nestle in on the couch next to Jay, who is eating pizza and watching the action. "That was a good call. What'd you say to her?"

"I told Daffy it was a brilliant idea to have the girly element, strangely sexual and all, and that Bill was up for a bit of drag. I knew she'd go for the sex angle, and that it would get us out of this mess, finally."

I like it that he's so relaxed around her, but I guess when you are a martial arts expert, you are always secure in the knowledge that with a sharp blow to the throat you can kill anyone who annoys you. Being this close to all that restrained power makes me feel desperately attracted to him, as usual. I love it when he holds my arms to demonstrate chopping movements, or stands behind me to show a certain death grip. I snuggle up a little closer to him. He wipes a bit of tomato sauce from the pizza off his goatee, looks at me quizzically, then stares straight ahead at Bill. He thinks I'm battin' for the other team, just like the rest of them, so he treats me like one of the guys. "You okay, sista?" This lesbian thing is proving to be extremely successful in many ways, but it also has its drawbacks.

· · ·

Thwack! Bill's shapely, freshly shaven knee wallops me right in the throat as I hit the deck. We both know it sounds loud, and the alarm in his eyes blazes through the slits in his mask. *Yeah, you're right, Bill—it hurts.* I am momentarily dizzy, but I don't want to cut now. It's two A.M. and a cut would mean a reset and an extra ten to fifteen minutes in the studio. No way—just suck it up and keep going. I look up at him and squeeze out a small nod as a signal to continue.

Bill makes himself extra light as I roll him off of me, regain my balance, and stand. I take my roundhouse kick to his head as he tries to kneel up, and he hurls himself backward. It is nicely gauged and he falls perfectly into the breakaway chair, which splinters into a hundred pieces. Excellent! It's the first time we have managed that cleanly. Bill staggers to his feet—he looks ridiculous. Jeremy got him up in a cobalt blue shiny blouse and a tweedy pleated skirt, pumps, and hose. And then of course there is the blond wig and the Richard Nixon rubber mask.

He comes at me and I throw a punch. I hit the tip of Richard's nose. Shit! I'm too close, much too close. I concentrate hard as I get into position for the last and trickiest move. Bill grabs me at my already sore throat. I twist, bend, then use his own weight to propel him over my shoulder.

*Alice drew her foot as far down the chimney as she could. . . . "This is Bill,"
said Alice, giving one sharp kick and waiting to see what would happen next.*

Bill flies.

*The first thing she heard was a general chorus of "There goes Bill!" Then the
Rabbit's voice alone—"Catch him, you by the hedge!"*

Bill lands on a table and it gives way. Terrific stuntman that he is, he falls
straight to the floor onto his back pad and lies motionless.

I stand there in character as Devon. I stare at Bill, then slowly back away
to retrieve my pistol from the floor where it had been kicked earlier in the
fight. I aim it at the intruder and walk quickly toward my partner, who is
lying unconscious.

"Morales," I yell, urgently. Carlos doesn't move.

"Morales . . . you okay?" I kneel and feel for a pulse, then pull out
my walkie-talkie. "Officer down! Officer down!" I stand and kick Bill,
who does a good head wobble. Then I turn to Carlos and yell, "Morales,
dammit!"

"Cut!" Marty bellows.

The studio erupts into applause. When cameramen clap, you know it's
a good fight. Bill stiffly rolls over and rubs his lower back.

I run to Bill, who finally sits up. "You okay? You okay?" I ask.

*"Well, I hardly know," said Bill. "I'm better now, but a deal too flustered to
tell you. Something comes at me like a jack-in-the-box, and up I goes like a
skyrocket!"*

Bill moves each of his moving parts—left arm, right arm, left leg, right
leg—then rolls his head from side to side and hunches his shoulders. "Yeah,
I'm fine," he says gruffly as he peels off his mask and wig, revealing Christine's deliberately lousy blush and gloss job. "What about you? I landed on
you pretty hard."

"I dunno." I rub the spot in my neck and sternum where his knee
landed. "Yep, you made contact." I grin.

"Lost my balance, sweetie. Sorry, babe. It was the heels." He ruffles my
hair, never mentioning how close I came to clipping him with my punch. I
don't remind him.

"Everyone's fine—nobody hurt?" Jay dashes onto the set. "That looked
amazing! Right on!" He has come straight from the booth. He knows that
all the camera angles were good and, most important, that Daphne is
happy.

"You rock, girlfriend. You my best fighter." Jay gives me a bear hug and
kisses me fraternally on the cheek before going to check on Bill.

. . .

I walk out of the set and over to a chair. As I sit down I'm shaking because adrenaline is still charging around inside my body, but even that feels good. We pulled off a great fight scene, and that makes me really happy. The applause from the crew made the whole stupid day worthwhile.

Sally Field said it all when she gave her "You like me! You really like me!" Oscar acceptance speech. We actors are needy, dammit. Maybe because we're so insecure, we hunger for positive reinforcement at every turn. That is, after all, what applause is at its most basic—nothing more than positive reinforcement. Like junkies looking for a fix, we are dependent on that pat on the back that says we've done quality work. And it's even worse for those of us who are hardest on ourselves. We are the most hopeless addicts of all—or the most insecure, depending on how you look at it—because we crave approval most from those who are the stingiest with it.

I see Daphne about fifteen feet away from me; she has the script in her hand and is intently reading. She senses me staring and looks up over her bifocals. We lock eyes—teacher and pupil. She nods and smiles ever so slightly, then goes back to reading.

Yesssssssssss! That was about as good as winning the Emmy.

I grin to myself, then wince as I realize that everything from my Adam's apple to my sternum is tender. I head to the prop room for some ice.

When I return, Carlos is still lying on the floor, pretending to be injured. We all try to ignore him, but he makes it impossible. He's such a wonderful ham. "My groin, Mees Devon, eees *mi penis,*" he says, reverting to Speedy Gonzales once again. "I know for a *machorra* like you eet's mebbe not so eenteresting, but eet hurts real bad. Djou muss loook qweek, Mees Devon."

"*¡Ay joven!* You should only hope that it's swollen—the little guy needs all the help he can get," I respond in kind. "This is all *nada mas que vergallo.* Take care of your own *reata,* Carlitos." I laugh, making a jack-off motion with my hand. Beat as we are, we are all cracking up. That's the remarkable thing about this business—sometimes the best stuff happens when you're exhausted. We can be dog-tired, but give us some pizza, a good fight scene, and someone acting the clown, and we're good to go for another few hours.

. . .

"And that, folks, is a WRAP!" Marty trumpets. "Out time: three-thirty A.M. Somebody check the scorecard to see who won the pool."

We had all put down money on what time we'd get out of here, and as the day wore on we upped the ante. There is a triumphant whoop from one of the lighting electricians—he's come into a substantial windfall, I think.

As I walk wearily back to my dressing room, I feel the cold in my bones. I just want some hot tea and a blanket. I shed the suit and raincoat, head for the ladies' room, and climb into the shower. The hot, hot water feels like warm golden honey down my back. I stand there with my eyes closed—almost but not quite asleep standing up—and just let it cascade over me. I have been here for eighteen hours, and I am raw. Jangled nerves, tangled emotions, and mangled body parts all fight for my attention, but I am deep in my subconscious, which auto-rewinds the day in review . . . Daphne's nod of approval . . . nearly clipping Bill with my punch . . . shaving Bill's legs . . . the poor butler and whether we were too tough on him . . . choreographing the fight with Jay . . . and meeting the magician this morning . . . the MAGICIAN!

I open my eyes wide, and unfortunately my mouth as well, thus gagging on a faceful of hot water. Shit! My day's not over yet. I have a date—with a complete stranger. Clad only in my towel I quickly run back to the dressing room, charging right past Carlos as he's leaving.

"*¡Caray!* Thanks for the offer, babe, but not now, sorry. Gotta go home to the wife and keeds." He grins, grabbing at a corner of the terry cloth.

"If you leave now, de la Fuente, you'll forfeit your invitation to my next girls' soccer team night!" I shout and wave as I run into my room before I hear his entire retort—something about there being more than enough to go around, Latino style.

I speed-dress and look dismally at my countenance in the mirror. I look like I have been embalmed. I snatch a pink lip gloss from the murky pile of trolley debris and smear some on my lips. It'll hafta do. Thankfully it's still dark outside. The magician has probably vanished by now anyway. I grab my keys, spray on a little lavender water, and chuck myself out the door.

. . .

The night watchman cordially waves me out as I pass under the automatic arm. Turning right out of the gateway, something catches my eye—the glimmer of a cigarette. I hit the brakes and roll down the window. Peering into the gloom I can barely make out a tall, masculine figure leaning up against a pickup truck across the street. Suddenly, the burning butt of a cig flies through the air, and the man strides purposefully over to me. I quickly put up the window and hit the door locks. I think about stepping on the gas, but look up to see that it is in fact my magician. At least I think it's him. I'd only seen him once for all of two minutes, and that was many hours ago. He taps on the window. I roll it down.

"Trying to escape, huh?" He looks really unsure of himself. I can understand why. I look like I might scare small children. "How was it?"

"Torture, brutal, and good all at once," I answer honestly. "I'm really exhausted. . . ." This last is said as the tentative offer of a cancellation clause. I'm not at all sure I want to go through with this, but I want to give him the opportunity to back out.

If you want to disappear now, it's fine by me, but it's really your call.

Instead he just smiles. He has one of those water buffalo haircuts—short in the back and long in front, parted in the center and hanging in two large S sweeps. It's kinda cool, even at four A.M. on a complete stranger.

"Um . . ." he says.

Um . . . he said um! Believe it or not, this catches my attention. I like a little insecurity in a guy—perhaps because I have so much of my own.

"Um, I figured you'd be really trashed, so I put a thermos of hot tea and a blanket in my truck. If you want to leave your car here, I'll drop you home, and pick you back up in the morning. No hassles, okay?"

Am I dreaming? Did he say tea and a blanket? Is he now going to hold up the eight of spades against my forehead and guess my birthday? I am speechless.

"Will they let you leave your car overnight?" he asks, now leaning his elbow on my door. His hair is in his eyes again, and he shakes it out. His eyes are beautiful, really sky blue. He has a strong Roman nose, and a cleft in his chin. It finally dawns on me what I saw in him: he is adorable.

"Yes. Yes. I can leave my car. Hang on a second." I back the Honda right up to the gate. The night watchman cheerily waves me through in reverse, as if I do this every morning. I wonder how he can be so jovial at this hour—drugs, perhaps? I park, check my lip gloss, and whisper, *"Careful, Kate, slowly, slowly,"* to my reflection, then walk back out. The guard once more smiles amiably and tips his cap to me as I leave, and I wonder in the back of my mind what to him would constitute odd behavior.

Probably nothing short of armed robbery.

Naked armed robbery.

By pygmies.

Matt is standing by the truck, holding the door open with one hand and cradling a steaming cup of tea with the other. "It's herbal. I figure you didn't need the caffeine at this hour." He laughs softly.

"Yeah, I've had quite enough for today." I slide into the right front seat. The truck is from the 1950s, I think, but it's beautifully restored—completely cherried out.

The California car culture is still alive and well—what is it with guys and old vehicles?

"What year is it?" I ask.

His answer doesn't matter.

"Fifty-three Chevy."

It's not that I don't care what the answer is—I'm unable to care. The dreadful truth is that I'm an automotive ignoramus—everything I know about American classic cars and trucks I learned from American Graffiti. *Still, he seems flattered that I asked.*

"That was the last year that they made a split windshield. I did most of the work myself."

*Ah, a man who's good with his hands. Now **that** matters. Maybe not tonight, but it matters.*

"So," he says. "Where to?"

I give him my address and we drive in silence. I am wrapped in a plaid blanket and as I sip my tea a warm, cozy feeling washes over me. I feel . . . taken care of. After the day I've had, this is extremely good.

"So, Kate, Steven Spielberg came to watch my set tonight—can you believe that?" Matt says. "Well, not to see *me*, exactly. He had his kid's birthday party at the Castle. He has a gorgeous family."

"Oh," I say, frantically tearing around in my brain for an interesting response. "I nearly punched a man in drag in a Richard Nixon mask."

"Well, my rabbit had babies. They're very cute."

"Do they instantly know magic tricks, just genetically?" I ask.

"Yes, absolutely," he says. "They can saw one another in half, and one has a tattoo that reads 'I ♥ David Blaine.' "

Cute.

"So, Dad," I ask, "how many bunnies?"

"Six," he says, playing it really straight. Even so, his eyes have a delightful twinkle. "I didn't realize she was pregnant till I couldn't pull her out of the hat anymore."

Cuter still.

I look out the window. We are cruising Mulholland, and the lights of LA stretch out below us for miles. The truck purrs along and I feel like I'm in a giant spaceship. Matt turns on the radio. As Joe Cocker growls out "You can leave your hat on," he cranks up the volume and steps on the gas. The vintage Chevy responds quickly and smoothly—the pickup has pickup.

I look at Matt's profile; it is strong. His skin is slightly tanned in that healthy, unforced manner that suggests he didn't work at it in the slightest. He turns to look at me. He doesn't smile, but his eyes are very kind.

"You okay?" he asks.

"Yeah. I always feel beat up at the end of days like this," I answer. I snuggle down into the blanket. "It's nice of you to take me home."

"I'm not nice," he says. "I'm courteous." An odd response to be sure, but one that I'm too tired to explore at the moment.

"Hmmmn, okay. So, where are you from?"

"Cincinnati. Grew up in a big family. Five sisters—all older—one younger brother. Mom and Dad still run a farm business—knew right away that wasn't for me. Learned my magic trade in France, then came home to marry my childhood sweetheart, only to find that she'd fallen for someone else. Then I came out here and since then it's been work, work, work. You?"

Another exiled, brokenhearted refugee who fled to Southern California.

"Well, the details of our stories are different, but in a way they're sort of the same." Before I can elaborate, I realize we're close to my house. "I live right at that corner."

Matt pulls up and turns off the engine. The music stops and now the silence is a little awkward.

"So, um, I'll come get you at eleven tomorrow morning . . . well, this morning. I'll drop you at the studio—and then maybe we can hook up later?" He is staring straight ahead, brushing his hand through his water buffalo hair.

I fumble with the teacup, the flask, the blanket. "Ah, okay, ah . . . yes, thank you. Sounds good." I reach for the door handle and he stops me.

"Allow me," he says gallantly. He quickly jumps out, runs around to open my door, and then helps me extricate myself from my blanket cocoon. We begin walking to my house.

Like he said, courteous.

"Um, Kate?" I turn to him; he is quite tall. "I, um, want to ask you something. It's a little awkward, and if I spit the words out badly, please don't take offense."

"Wow. With a preamble like that, I can't wait to hear what comes next."

He thrusts his hands into his pockets. "You're not, um, ah, ah, a . . ." He pauses for a deep breath and starts again. "Well, are you a . . . a . . . a . . . lesbian?"

He looks so uncomfortable. I'm sure they didn't talk about stuff like that back home in Cincinnati.

Before I can answer, he continues, "Shit—there's one way to find out." He closes the gap between us by pulling me to him—powerfully—then grabs my chin in one hand and lays a big, strong kiss on me.

I kiss him right back. *Fantastic. More of that, please.*

He kisses me again.

Mind reader.

"No, I didn't think so," he says huskily, breaking into an aw-shucks grin.

And starring Jimmy Stewart as Harry Houdini.

"That was straight out of a soap opera," I say weakly. My knees are shaking, and it's definitely not entirely due to the cold.

"You should know," he says, giving me a big hug. "Get some sleep and I'll see you at eleven."

Tired as I am, I almost don't have the energy to ask the question. Nevertheless, I can't resist.

". . . Matt?" I say as he's halfway back to the truck. He turns. "What made you ask the question?"

"Well, it's just that I didn't know anything about you, but I remembered seeing you say hi to the girl behind the counter at Starbucks . . . so I, um, asked her about you."

"Checking me out with Sondra, huh?" I say with a laugh.

"She told me more than I ever wanted to know about Devon Merrick, the gay detective of the Hope Canyon PD. It was hard to understand her, but after she got going, I couldn't shut her up."

"Yeah, it's crazy that she's so into it."

"She was going on and on about the show—but the funny thing was that as she was talking to me, this guy jumped right into the conversation and told me he knew the real truth. Insisted that not only was your character gay, but that you were too."

"He must have been reading the gossip mags."

"Nope. Claimed to have firsthand knowledge. Odd dude. Plaid pants."

11

I T FEELS LIKE JUST MOMENTS later that I hear beeps and honks and
music, all intermingled—my alarm is going off. As my eyes adjust to the
light, I marvel that I remembered to set it at all. I vaguely remember shuffling to my bed, pulling back the covers, and just falling in. Drusilla had
made the minimal accommodation to my presence, but permitted me to
stroke her head, and that was that. Now my mouth tastes like dry birdseed
and there is all this racket coming from the clock radio.

Strangely enough, even after I silence the beeps and the music, the
honking remains. It seems to be coming from outside. Eventually, it stops,
only to be replaced by a vigorous rattling of my front door. Obviously an
intruder is trying to get in. Grabbing a make-believe gun, I hold it between
my palms, elbows flexed and barrel pointed skyward behind my right ear,
Charlie's Angels style. Then I straighten my arms, point the gun straight
ahead, and slam up against the wall next to the door, like Angie Dickinson
about to raid a crackhouse in the old *Policewoman* series. I take a furtive
look through the window and see that there is a man on my stoop, facing
away from the door. I will have to kill him.

"Who are you?" I demand.

The would-be intruder turns, and then morphs into a very cute, water
buffalo–tressed magician, holding a dozen pink roses. It's eleven A.M.—he's
come to take me back to the studio.

Note to self: Get the order right. First wake up. **Then** *get out of bed. Make certain
you are not still in character—any character—before greeting visitors.*

It's not that I'm not a morning person, although few actors are. The fact
of the matter is that I'm not really a sentient being for at least fifteen minutes after I wake up. I do not hit the ground running—or even walking. I've
actually had to tell former boyfriends that whatever I do or say in that first
quarter hour—good or bad—doesn't count.

I fling open the front door. The glorious California sunshine bursts into
the room, bringing with it a tall man and the sharp rosy sweetness of a
dozen long-stems.

"For me?"

"Yup. Just picked 'em myself."

"Liar," I say with a smile. I charge off in quest of a vase. I know full well I don't have one, but it's my last way of pretending I live in a normal household. "I guess the maid must have put it somewhere," I offer, once it's clear my search is futile.

"Liar," Matt says with a tit-for-tat grin. "You really have a maid?" he asks incredulously.

I look around the living room—there are scripts and magazines and coffee cups and clothes strewn everywhere. Any self-respecting burglar who gained entry would have turned on his heel and left, secure in the knowledge that the place had already been tossed by somebody else in his line of work. I stand in the middle of the disaster area and smile sheepishly. "She died?" I suggest lamely.

"Well, I hope she's not under all that," he laughs, gesturing toward the debris.

"I may not have a vase, but I think I've got a bucket that I can find," I say as I dash off toward the kitchen. I am mindful to shut the door to Ground Zero—my bedroom—on the way. As bad as the living room is, the bedroom is worse—much worse.

"Ta da!" The pink roses look gorgeous sticking out of the rusty tin bucket I unearthed—faux farmhouse chic. "Let me take a quick shower. I won't be long, I promise."

I abandon Matt to Drusilla's care and surrender my body to the warm water. I giggle quietly to myself. There is something delicious about the idea that there is a gorgeous man sitting in the rubble of my living room, and being absolutely certain that he's thinking about the fact that I'm naked and less than twenty feet away.

Toweling off, I ponder what to wear. I wish to appear sexy in a casual, my-goodness-how-did-my-breasts-just-happen-upon-this-absolutely-divine-corset-dress-that-cost-nothing-at-all kind of way. I'm stumped until I remember a Zac Posen dress that I wore last week to some function—lilac jersey, kerchief-pointed hem, plunge neck. I root around in the pile of dry cleaning (outgoing)—if it's crumpled enough, it'll just do the trick. I find it. I hold it up in front of myself at the mirror and gasp. My entire décolletage is a technicolor sunset, the legacy of Bill's knee to my throat. Plan B: Catherine Malandrino knit top with a high neckline and no shoulders—no back, either—and Seven for All Mankind . . . no, make that Citizens of Humanity dark-distressed-vintage-wash jeans.

Blue jeans . . . Stanley Kowalski, Jimmy Dean, Bruce Springsteen . . . How long ago was it, I wonder, that the common man and the working-class hero lost custody of denim? When did jeans become couture, and how bizarre is it that we no longer buy them looking new and do our own distressing and vintaging, just by, you know, wearing them? And how long after that did the jeans labels and the names of rock 'n' roll groups become interchangeable?

I return to the living room to find Matt picking up coffee mugs. "Oh please don't do that," I plead.

"Wow! You clean up good!" he says appreciatively. He seems genuinely taken aback, which isn't nearly so insulting when I realize what a fright I must have been when I opened the door—not to mention last night.

"Not bad for a lezzie." I grin. "Let's go. I know you've got a gig at noon."

• • •

Whump! A gnome deposits a dingy laundry bag inside the door of my dressing room.

"I don't know whose dirty clothes those are," I say grumpily, "but they're not mine." I admit it—I'm a mite cranky.

"Mail call," he responds.

"Why didn't someone sort it first? You can't really expect me to paw through all this to pull mine out of that sack, can you?"

"These are all for you, or actually, for Devon Merrick. And there's two more bags just like this in back . . . oh, and another bag addressed to Kate McPhee."

"You've got to be kidding."

"Nope."

"I'm supposed to answer all of these letters?"

"I guess."

"I can ask Daphne, but just offhand, do you know which intern will be working with me on responding to these?"

The gnome looks blankly at me, and the realization dawns that I've asked a question he doesn't want to answer.

"Surely there's someone on staff who's assigned to help with all this . . ."

"Ms. Contini has her own assistant," he says obliquely.

"Knock knock—are ya decent?" calls a cheery male voice from the hallway.

"No, but c'mon in anyway. It's just me and Mount Mailbag."

As the door opens and a handsome, well-dressed black man in his late twenties enters, the gnome sees his opportunity to escape and takes it.

"Oh, sorry," says the new arrival with a shrug, "I was hoping to warn you that the avalanche was on its way. I can see I'm too late."

"I can see that as well," I respond, a little testily, "but who are you?"

"Me? Oh, excuse me. I'm Nigel Campbell, your publicist."

Three things strike me immediately about Nigel:

1. I must know who cuts his hair;
2. This guy works out daily; and
3. I need the name of his tailor.

A fourth conclusion follows as a direct corollary. A guy with a great haircut and an impeccably tailored suit that showcases his buff bod without clinging to it like Spandex . . . if he's not an actor, he's gotta be gay. Elementary, my dear detective.

"So Nigel . . . you should know that as a kid, I had a hard time getting around to writing thank-you notes for gifts I got for my birthday. And that was family, friends, and maiden aunties—people I knew! This is all way beyond me. I need some help with all this stuff."

"Sorry, sweetie, not in the budget, at least not in mine. The little beancounter pricks topside at network have determined that fans will watch whether you answer their letters or not. And if it doesn't goose the Nielsens, they're not payin' for it. Don't you have a maiden auntie with time on her hands who would be ever so delighted to help you deal with it?"

"Fresh out, Nigel, sorry. And besides, they're all on the wrong side of the Atlantic."

"Let's both think on it a bit and see if we can find a creative solution to this somehow. At least in the short run. But you should know that if this lezzie vampire juggernaut you're on continues to pick up speed, you're gonna want your own personal assistant anyway."

"What on earth for?"

The idea of having someone else in my world "assisting" me with normal, everyday life is repellent. I think about Meredith, who expects that when she sneezes, someone will of course be waiting at her elbow to hand her a Kleenex. In dealing with bodily fluids, one really ought to be self-sufficient.

"I hate to break this to you, my love, but those Santa baggies full of fan mail should be a clue. Congratulations, Ms. McPhee: you're the flavor of the month. You're hotter than hot right now. And when you're hot, you've got to go for it. Better than that, you've got what every Daytime actor hopes for."

"Which is what, exactly?"

"Branding."

"I thought that's what they did to cattle."

"Think ketchup, sweetie, not 'Git along, little doggies.' "

"*What?* You're making absolutely no sense, Nigel." I am truly perplexed.

"Name a brand of ketchup," he says.

"Heinz," I say. "57 varieties."

"Name another one."

"Ah . . ."

"Precisely. Ketchup/Heinz. Heinz/Ketchup. Devon Merrick/Kate McPhee. The audience has bonded with you, and they have melded you with your character. They don't always do that. I've lost count of the number of Bradleys—the number of actors who've played Nicholas Duncan—but it doesn't matter. As often as they change, it doesn't kick up any dust with the viewers. Whoever plays Nicholas has to be a handsome hunk with killer abs; other than that, he's replaceable, a cog in the machine. But you've claimed ownership of Devon Merrick. As far as the public is concerned, you *are* Devon, in the same way that Meredith *is* Regina."

"Unfortunate analogy, Nige."

"Sorry. But you see where I'm going with this. You're becoming famous, my love . . . which means that your days of picking up your own laundry are pretty much over."

"I didn't become an actor to be famous. Don't be ridiculous."

But of course, it's not ridiculous at all. This gig is already three sizes too big for me. My house is an absolute mess. As has become my custom, I picked out my clothes today not from the closet but from the heap of garments moldering on my floor. I know that by Sunday, I'll either have to do a load of wash or buy new panties (again), just to have some that are clean. I'm forced to admit that in my life now, a lot of the basic stuff isn't getting done at all. Just ask Drusilla, whose litter box is in desperate need of attention.

"Go out and get yourself some decent matched luggage, Miss Kate, because I'm setting up a series of personal appearances for you."

"Just what I need . . . to go dragging my ass all over creation. My cat barely recognizes me as it is."

"Now, don't be that way," says Nigel, chiding me. "It's really nothing to complain about. It's first class all the way, *and* you'll be making upwards of $5K per meet-and-greet. Besides, if I'd wanted to talk to someone who was going to be pissy about it, I'd have gone to see Meredith."

I chuckle. "Touché." *This guy's really okay.*

"Of course," he continues, "you're the one they're after, not her. Her I have to strong-arm them into taking . . . and that only works if they have a case of galloping amnesia about how she behaved last time."

Actually, he's a lot better than okay.

"But first, you have an interview with the *Los Angeles Times* for a piece in the Weekend section, a satellite interview session with the affiliates, and an interview/photo shoot at *Soap Opera Digest*. Seems you're going to be a cover girl, my dear."

"Don't they usually just make a composite from shots in the press kit?"

"Yes, but this is not usual. The buzz is up about this storyline—way up. In the meantime I want you to take these."

I see my 8x10 glossy self looking back at me from the stack of photographs Nigel hands me. "Publicity photos, but why?"

"Autographs, of course."

Famous. Me? How weird is that?

. . .

On my way to the rehearsal room, I run into Christine in the stairwell.

"So . . . how'd it go with the magic man last night?" she asks.

"Fi—wait a minute. How'd you hear about that?"

"If you think Charlie can keep a secret, you think again, missy."

"Ah . . ."

" 'Ah' nothing, Ms. Kate. How'd it go?"

"Well, for starting at four o'clock in the morning and for having been my first real date since—"

I stop myself, not knowing how much of the whole sordid Rafe-and-Leslie backstory I want to share. It's not that I don't trust Christine enough to confide in her; I'm just not sure whether I want to burden anyone else with the detritus from my busted romance.

"Since . . . ?" she says, inviting me to continue.

Go on, Katiegirl. You can't keep this inside forever.

"Since I broke up with my boyfriend and absconded to America."

"Did you break up with him or did he break up with you?"

Zing!! Right to the point.

"Very astute question, Christine. It was his choice, not mine. His name was Rafe, and he'd been sleeping with Leslie, my best friend, for a long time."

"Ouch! And you knew something was wrong, but it took you quite a while to figure out what it was."

"Sounds like the basis for a thousand blues or country songs, but there I was, getting on the plane and running away, a brokenhearted cliché."

I crumple down on the steps and sit, huddled in my Columbo Mac. Just the thought of stirring all this up again is bringing me down.

"So, don't stop now. Tell me more," she says with a warm, almost motherly smile.

My heart lurches as I think about how I used to share my confidences with Leslie. My mind is blank as I attempt to explain my vacuous relationship with Rafe. Slowly, a series of miniature, mundane vignettes line themselves up for examination:

- A day in March: giggling quietly with Leslie about a handsome guy she fancies.

- A day in August—hot weather for England. Bikinis. Backyard. "Am I fat?" I ask her. "Because Rafe no longer wants me."
- That same August: Leslie and Rafe playing cards alone when I return late from a commercial shoot. Sweet that they keep each other company, no?
- "Men and women can never be platonic friends," Leslie informs me in late September. Clever little spider.
- A letter from a campground, thanking Rafe for staying there. The letter sends thanks to a charming couple. He had gone alone. He explains the mistake by telling me that the owner of the campgrounds is an eighty-year-old man. I remain clueless.

I get dizzy downloading all this crap and stop talking. I hate the taste in my mouth. I hate the need to even share this melodrama and expose my stupidity.

"And you've kept this all bottled up since you've been here?"

"Pretty much yes," I admit. "Well, except for kicking the crap out of Rafe."

"What?"

"Kicking the crap out of an imaginary Rafe. When Jay Park was giving me my first tae kwon do lesson, he had me kick and punch at a hanging bag. I was kind of wimpy about it till he told me to pretend it was an old boyfriend."

"And then you became Fists of Fury?"

"Something like that. Feet, too, actually."

We sit in silence. I am done, drained. My cell phone erupts into "Twinkle, Twinkle, Little Star."

"Hello?" I say.

"Hey, it's Matt. Are you still at work?"

"Yeah," I say grumpily.

"Oh, okay. Do you still want to hook up later?"

"Yeah—yes, actually," I say, brightening somewhat, "that would be good."

"Call me when you know what time you'll be sprung. I'm at the Castle."

"It was Matt," I tell Christine. "My magician."

"See, someone loves ya!" She smiles her lovely toothy grin. "Little Miss Hard-Done-By, I have to get some work done, or else you'll be having your makeup applied by the embalmer after they fire me!"

And with that, she's gone. I slide my butt over to the outside wall of the stairwell, where there is a tiny window that overlooks the parking lot. I sit and stare at the cars for a bit, watching people depart and arrive, until Rafe and Leslie slip away and retreat into their little locked boxes in the back of my mind. I won't set them free just yet. I can't, but I long for the day when it won't be a necessary part of my being.

Stiffly I ascend the stairs to my closet in the rabbit warren of TV land. I dress. I brush myself off. I take myself out.

12

Tuesday morning . . . kinda

2:30! 2:30!! 2:30!!!

Bells go off all around me. It is indeed 2:30 A.M., so early it's practi-cally yesterday. Even though I had set two alarms at five minutes apart, un-fortunately the bell I hear now I believe to be the front door. Groggily, I peel Drusilla off my chest, as she does an impression of flattened roadkill. I perch her delicately on the terminally unused second pillow next to me and yearn yet again for a human companion. I want someone who would snuggle up understandingly and, more important, get up to make me toast and coffee at such an ungodly hour. The doorbell rings again and I bang the alarm button into silence. I switch on the light and Drusilla's pupils constrict as she stares at me with feline fury.

"Oh, sorry Droos." I quickly switch off the light and stagger out to open the door. I am up at this hour because Nigel, in his marketing genius, has arranged for a TV satellite tour. The idea is that from Los Angeles I will do a machine-gun staccato series of remote interviews with our affiliates' local morning news anchors, all in a single morning. Because many of the sta-tions are on the East Coast (and therefore ahead of LA in oh, so many ways), I have to haul my ass out of bed to be made up and camera-ready by 4:00 A.M. The progression of interviews will follow the sun as it rises, begin-ning with eastern cities and moving west.

I open the door to Christine and Charlie, who carry mugs of coffee from home and steel cases full of mysterious products to make me look pageant presentable. "Good morning!" Charlie and Christine singsong, "Ms. McPhee, this is your wake-up call!"

"Have to shower," I mumble, and stumble toward the bathroom. Left unsaid is the thought that people who can manage to be that cheerful at this hour without chemical assistance should be shot on sight. On the way,

I grab the white Helmut Lang suit, beige Sergio Rossi heels, and nude Le-jaby undies that Ruben has supplied for me—aware, as he is, of my deeply ingrained laundry phobia.

I lean under the boiling hot jets and will my grey matter to stand at attention—or at least at half mast. My brain, alas, simply refuses to comply, even though I turn the water to freezing in the hope that some distant Celtic relative had fucked a Scandinavian so that some part of my DNA might recognize that it ought to be stimulated by an icy postsauna shower. But no, only Irish potato farmers' blood in me. Clean but still comatose, I scramble for my towel and lavish creams on my face and body—courtesy of a rather nice Kiehl's basket messengered to me by the studio as a thank-you for rousing myself at this unspeakable hour:

> Dear Ms. McPhee:
> We are so happy you are joining us for our media tour.
> We'll have fun. All The Best.
>   Your Friends at Network Headquarters

You're not my friends, I think ruefully—it's too early in the morning for that. However, the coriander body lotion smells divine.

I pull on my white suit, feeling a little more human, and pad out to the makeup triage in my bare feet, unable to face heels yet. Charlie and Christine have cleared a space on the cluttered dining room table. Jesus, I had forgotten it was green. Charlie hands me a portable mug of steaming coffee.

"Brewed at home, cherub." He smiles, pulls my hair back, and starts combing through the knots and tangles. They seat me in a chair piled up with two of my couch cushions so that Christine is able to reach my sheet-crumpled face without breaking her back. They work in silence, smoothing, painting, drying, and fussing. Cold compresses are applied under my eyes. I am a performance art creation—and a forgery at that, I fear—but only the experts will know. I nod off.

Half an hour later, having worked speedily in tandem, Charlie and Christine announce that I am physically presentable for the greater Eastern Seaboard. They bundle me up and shove me into the Town Car that the network has sent to ferry us off. The driver politely informs me of his name, which I promptly forget. He hands me the *New York Times* and a bottle of water, which I clutch to my chest the entire way, staring out at the dark city and envying those still tucked away in their beds. Charlie and Christine giggle quietly about some *LFT* gossip and again I wonder how I am lucky enough to be surrounded by such great people. I nod off—again.

"We're here," Charlie chirps.

I am shunted into a tiny cubicle studio. In the center of the room is a black director's chair, an IFB and a microphone hanging from the back of the chair like menacing electrodes. (Improbably enough, IFB stands for "interruptible fold back," which is technogeek-speak for that little earphone that lets you hear the news anchors when they talk to you from 2,500 miles away.) Facing the chair is a TV monitor; on the floor is a smaller one. To the left is a large roving TV studio camera, with a cameraman peering around the side.

"Morning!" Camera Guy says, all too loud and cheery. He's in his late forties, wearing a visor that reads OPRAH. Impressive. "I'm Ted. Happy you're joining us. What ear do you want your IFB in?"

"Um," I answer.

Charlie hustles in, helps me insert the hearing device in my right ear, and arranges my hair around it. He and Ted fuss about the microphone.

"Do you want a vampire?" Ted asks.

"Um," I answer.

Charlie affixes the vampire clip containing the miniature microphone on my suit collar. It's at that moment I realize I have forgotten my shoes. I stare down at my naked feet.

"I don't have any shoes," I mumble mournfully.

"Don't worry," says Ted in a bored tone. "We're only shooting you from the waist up. Unless you do a handstand, the American public will be none the wiser."

Four A.M. humor.

Charlie claps his hands like a circus ringmaster: "What we need is coffee, gobs of it. Then eggs, bacon, toast . . . and more coffee. I'll be right back!"

Christine is painting my shiny nose. Somewhere in my infantile mind, I wonder if she will spoon-feed me herself. I hope so.

Cameraman Ted has finished fitting me up with various electronic things and has returned to his camera, fiddling with the lights on the way. I glance down at the monitor on the floor, which shows me the picture of a vacuous, well-made-up person in a designer suit without a thought in her head. Me.

Suddenly, the room fills with people. A hyperactive director, a studio PR person, and Nigel. I hate him. I glare at Nigel as Charlie hands me an egg sandwich with ketchup. He has the smarts to drape the $1,500 suit with napkins.

"No money for shoes?" inquires Nigel sarcastically.

"Not the seven-hundred-dollar Balenciagas I want, no," I reply with as much bitchiness as I can summon up.

"How about a personal appearance in Birmingham, Alabama, then? Usual fee, McPhee?"

"Okay. Done," I answer with some surprise.

"On air in five, Ms. McPhee . . ."

"Call me Kate."

"Yes, Kate. We're so happy you're joining us. We're going to have so much fun!"

Are we now?

"Did you write my card?" I ask between mouthfuls.

"What card?"

"Never mind." I gulp down coffee and listen to Nigel blather on about which plot points to hit and what to avoid. Push the sex scenes in vampire-land, and never, *ever* speak about Meredith.

Christine reapplies my lip gloss and grabs my face in her two hands as everyone else files out.

"Wake up, honey," she says as she stares kindly into my eyes. "It's show-time."

I smile vaguely back at her and watch her exit, then run my tongue over my front teeth to make sure no breakfast resides there. Nigel, Charlie, and Christine are outside, but I am alone in the cubicle with Cameraman Ted. They are the only people I'll actually see—I'll never lay eyes on the anchors I'll be speaking with from thousands of miles away. I'll just hear their disembodied voices in my IFB. My job will be to keep eye contact with Ted's camera and to do my best to pretend that I'm talking to real people.

Ted holds up a piece of paper in front of the camera that reads:

Suzie & Geoff
Pennsylvania morning show
Three-minute segment

Suzie and Geoff. Suzie and Geoff. I try to cement their names in my mind. Suzie and Geoff. Push the sex. Don't mention Meredith.

"Hello there, Pennsylvania. Today we have with us, live from Hollywood, Kate McPhee of *Live for Tomorrow.* . . ." I hear the anchors in my IFB, giving me an introduction, which, luckily, most people improvise. Nigel has sent out a frightening barrage of credits and studio piffle to the affiliates. Most of them take this stuff with a pinch of salt and mercifully skip reading it on the air.

"So, Kate . . ." A man's voice enters my ear canal. "How's that Meredith Contini in person? She's quite a handful on the show, huh?" The question is accompanied by guffaws in the background, those forced anchorish guffaws typical of morning on-air camaraderie intended to jolly along the viewership as it finds its eyeballs getting ready for work.

The laughter collides with the fog in my head.

Meredith. I'm not supposed to mention Meredith.

I sit there, staring at the camera. My mouth is doing a koi imitation.

"Hello, Kate! Can you hear us? Suzie and Geoff, *Live in Pennsylvania.* Good morning!"

Silence. An expectant pause. I blink.

"Hello there, Kate! Can you hear us? Well, folks, I guess we're having a little technical difficulty right now. We'll try to catch up with Kate McPhee from *Live for Tomorrow* shortly. Right now, the weather today across Pennsylvania is somewhat chilly, but warmer than yesterday. . . ."

Nigel bursts angrily into the room. "Hello, LA, Ms. McPhee. It's a live morning *talk* show. You're supposed to **talk!**" He snaps his hands open and closed like a crocodile puppeteer.

"But they asked me about Meredith," I whine.

"Parry!" shouts Nigel, almost savagely. "Swoop and parry, darling. You *are* an actress, are you not? 'Oh, Meredith's a lovely person, but the one you have to look out for is our evil vampire mobster.' That, darling, is how you do it. C'mon, *wake up!*" He slams the door for emphasis.

Ted silently puts another piece of paper in front of the camera:

Shirley, Isaac, and Bob in Philadelphia
Good Day Philly
Live five-minute segment

My heart sinks as I read "five-minute segment." I take a deep breath and smile into the camera.

"Hey, good morning to you, Kate! I'm a big fan of the show. Been watching for thirty years. That Meredith doesn't get a day older, does she?" A female voice I presume to be Shirley.

"Oh, she's a lovely person—never ages. Unlike our vampire mobster who is two hundred and four," I hear myself saying in a mechanical voice.

"Whoa! I bet Meredith wouldn't be happy if you announced her age on national TV!" Guffaws all around the Philly newsroom.

I blink. I open and close my mouth. *Talk!* This is a talk show. *Say something!*

"No, I'd be fired." I laugh. *What? What did I just say?*

"Oh, yeah! I'm sure you would." Shirley guffaws again. Safe Shirley, miles away. Seven A.M. Shirley. Totally awake Shirley. In bed by five P.M. Shirley.

"Shirley," I say. "Let's talk about the vampires and how hard it is going to be to round them up," I speedily read. Nigel has burst into the room again holding up signs in black Sharpie:

VAMPIRES
ROUNDING THEM UP
EXCITING
SEX SCENES

"It's going to be exciting with lots of sex scenes . . . um . . ." I search, but there are no more signs. Nigel rolls his eyes and hangs his head.

But wait! That's actually enough fodder for professional anchors. They're off and running. "Hey, sex with vampires. Isaac, I bet that's the only way you'll get a date, huh?" More guffaws.

"Oh, Shirley, you're just jealous because you've been taken out of the playing field. Shirley recently got married, Kate," says a voice sounding like Isaac.

"Congratulations," I bleat.

"So, Kate. Do you have sex with one of those vampires?" asks another male voice in my ear, which I presume to be Bob.

"Maybe. You'll have to watch," I answer weakly.

"Will it be a woman?" asks Isaac. " 'Cause I'll surely watch that!" Guffaws again.

"Sure you will, Isaac," Bob chortles with what sounds unfortunately like a back slap. I grimace.

"Well, yes, it will have to be a woman because my character is a les—"

"All right, then. Well, thanks, Kate McPhee of *Live for Tomorrow,* for talking with us. You can catch Kate and her vampires weekly at noon right here on channel 8. In other news today . . ."

And I am cut off. I guess you can't use the L word on breakfast TV.

"Ixnay on the ezzbianlay!" hisses Nigel. But he gives me a thumbs-up: "An improvement, but for God's sake don't even use the words 'age' and 'Meredith' in the same sentence, okay?"

"Okay." I take a gulp of coffee and glance at the next piece of paper Ted is waving at me:

Carmen and Toth
Burlington, Vermont
Three minutes

"How many more, Ted?" I ask quietly.

"Um." He looks behind himself and counts the pages on his chair for a rather long time, I fear. "Fourteen more, Ms. McPhee—Kate. You're doin' great!"

I don't feel as if I am and I doubt if I can make it through fourteen more. But I sit up straight, take a deep breath, and smile at the camera.

"Good morning, Kate! This is Carmen here in Burlington, Vermont. I'm a huge fan of the show and I just can't believe that Meredith. . . ."

And I get better at it.

Gayle in Boston
George and Harriet in Miami

And then . . .

Dorothy
Raleigh, North Carolina
Five-minute segment

"Hey, y'all! Gawd mornin'!" I listen to her give the preamble, when suddenly I blanch. Horror of horrors, she's reading my entire biography, as written, in a monotone drawl.

". . . studeed bah-lay from the age a three. In th' riginul Lundun cast a *Cayats*. Became the awsum detective Devon Merrick on comin' to the States and is wowin' ow-dee-yences with her 'mayzin' portrayul of a gay woman facin' obstacles that a man wun't hav tew in a similar sitchuashun."

I am staring at my bare feet, mortified by Nigel's prose, fighting off the blush I know is coming. "Hi, Dorothy."

I raise my eyes. Unfortunately I see Nigel with his back to me, his head facing into a corner of the room. He clearly has his own IFB and has heard his poetic words read back to him by the deadpan anchor. In my mind this qualifies as a much-deserved punishment for writing such drivel in the first place. With creeping dread, I realize that his shoulders are heaving up and down. A red-hot flush sweeps over me. The fucker is laughing. A huge grin breaks over my face as I try to control the heat emanating from my body, bringing with it the desire to crumple to the floor and die of embarrassment.

"Kayat, I hafta say yew really are a grand idition to *Live fer Tumorrah*. How dew yew like wurkin' with all them handsom soap actors?"

"Oh, yes, they're something. They wear more makeup than I do."

"I betcha they do. But as a gay woman, I guess yew ain't interested in them all, huh?"

I let it slide. Let them all speculate. What harm, really?

"No, I'm not." I could be answering a question about the foppish actors or about my sexuality. Innuendo, my dear Watson, innuendo.

Tom and Bob in Chicago
Paula and Stan in St. Louis
Rochelle and Steve in Denver

The media tour wends its way across the country and concludes in Los Angeles, where I finish with a roar. After speaking with seventeen media outlets, I finally have the hang of talking to myself in a small studio with an earpiece and a mike. Not as easy to do as it looks; not as hard, either.

With breaks and five-to-ten-minute segments, the Media Tour has taken around three hours. It is about 7:30 A.M.—and I still have no shoes.

Before I can catch my breath, an exuberant Nigel races in, yelling, "Photo shoot!" Now I remember: the rest of my one and only day off is going to be taken up with the ever-so-important *Soap Opera Digest* photo shoot. The only thing cheering me up is that Charlie, Christine, and Nigel will be with me and we can enjoy a catty postmortem of this morning's comedy.

"Good-bye Ted, and thank you," I say as I climb out of the chair and stretch my legs. He unpins my microphone and I hand him the warm earpiece through which so much merriment was channeled.

"Have fun," Ted grunts. "Nice workin' with you." He eyes me oddly, but smiles anyway. I suppose all this chitchat about vampires and lesbians can be hard to take this early in the morning.

"Did you work with Oprah?" I ask, pointing at his visor.

"Oh, yeah. Shot her Oscar special at the Kodak Theater," he announces proudly, taking off the visor and smoothing back his hair. He glances at the visor as if it held some magic and then replaces it.

"Wow," I say. "Was she pleasant to work with?"

"Yep. Class act, that one," he says as he busies himself folding wires and unplugging equipment. I see that my time in the studio is over, but I feel weird as I leave the room: I am overcome with neediness and anxiety. My "am I good enough?" gene kicks into turbo, and as I open the door I feel like a small girl being asked to leave the classroom for bad behavior.

"*Bad child!*" *I scold myself.* "*That was a bad media tour! Next time, read the textbook and do your homework!*"

Blinking, I step out into the pink-and-beige lobby. Odd, I hadn't noticed the lobby at all on the way in at four A.M.—perhaps because my eyes were closed. I feel all at once as though I want to cry, sleep, eat, and drink a gallon of water—or hash it all out in a long talk with Trent. On the days when I'm not on the set, I miss his handsome, cheery smirk and his biting sarcasm.

"Are you okay, cherub?" asks Charlie.

"I want to cry," I tell him.

"Why, honey? You did great, you looked great, and you said all the right things."

"I'm thirsty." I grab a Crystal Geyser from the table, nurse from the sport top till the sides of the plastic bottle start to cave in, and in a daze allow Nigel to lead me out to the car. I fall into a deep sleep.

I awaken, drooling, to find myself in the company of the nameless driver, sprawled across the back seat in a Town Car parked quietly behind Sunset with the engine running. "Good morning, ma'am. Your friends are having breakfast. I'm to pick them up in twenty minutes," he informs me. Apparently my posse had decided it was best to let me sleep in the car while they descend, famished, on IHOP for an enormous cholesterol-laden feast.

"Right," I reply.

As my getaway driver and I cruise slowly over to the IHOP, I hit Trent's number on my speed dial. "Saw you on the *Breakfast News*," I hear him say through his sly smile, as I smile back into my Catherine Zeta-Jones Direct Dialing Plan. "You looked half asleep."

"Shut up," I respond with a laugh. "No way—I'd already been at it for two and a half hours. I had to look awake by then."

"Nope."

"Asshole."

"Hair looked good, though."

Gotta love actors. "So now I have to go to a photo shoot. Wanna come?"

"I'd rather stick needles in my eyes!"

"Trent, what else have you got to do? I know you're not working."

"My dear Kate, as much as I love you, to spend my hard-earned day off watching you smile self-consciously into a camera to publicize a detective/vampire/mobster story would render me catatonic."

"I won't be self-conscious," I whine.

"I am going surfing with some buddies. I'm gonna drink beer and pick up a cool chick at Neptune's Net," he says, dripping with irony.

"Oh, that does sound better."

"So cheer up! Imagine this: by the time the photo comes out, it will put you right on the top of the game. No one ever gets a single cover on *Soap Opera Digest*, it's always couples. Have a great time!"

"Wait! Trent, Trent, Trenty, pleeese," I wheedle. "I cannot do it alone," I whine. Big-time pouting now.

"No can do."

"Trent, please," I say in a more serious, forceful voice.

"There are waves to surf, babes to surf. It's a beautiful thing!"

"I'll pay you," I say in desperation.

"How much?"

"Um, dinner. Anywhere. Your choice. I am desperate," I admit.

"L'Orangerie?" He sounds a little hesitant. I can hear wavering in his voice.

"Sure!" I am jubilant. "Please come, Trent. I need you."

"Do you know how expensive that dinner will be?" he asks.

"No." In fact, I have no idea.

"Very, very *mucho dinero*," he says threateningly.

"I don't care. I'm going to Birmingham, Alabama, for five grand so I can buy Balenciaga heels and we have to be able to have dinner on what's left, right?" How much can it be, I wonder?

"I'm going on that Birmingham junket, too!" he says with laughter. "Oh Kate, Katy-pooh, whatever will we do with you?"

"Will you come? Will ya? Will ya?" By now, I'm panting like a dog and making poodly whimpering noises. The driver is looking aghast in his rearview mirror.

"All right. Give me the address. I cannot believe that I am doing this," he says with resignation. Or is he really plotting a very expensive bottle of wine at L'Orangerie?

The driver gives me all the information for the photo shoot, which I repeat into the phone for Trent. I hang up just as my posse clambers back into the car, sated with IHOP pancakes, but thoughtfully bringing some for me as well. Naturally, they want to share the fat. I wolf down a large Styrofoam box full of Belgian waffles, oblivious to the likelihood that I have some tight-fitting outfit waiting for me at the photo studio. I don't care. I shall be a puffy lesbian heroine!

Photo shoot–9:45 A.M.

When we arrive at the chic, too-trendy-for-its-own-good photo studio, I am thrown into a state of wonder. Everything is white. White cement floors. White walls. White ceiling. White drapes. White window frames. It is breathtaking. I pad in, shoeless, licking leftover whipped cream from the waffles off my fingers and suddenly bump into a very tall, scruffily dressed individual. He has the prerequisite Los Angeles goatee, longish hair, crooked nose in a gaunt, angular face, and his body is swathed in a very expensive but purposefully worn black T-shirt and indigo jeans. He also has no shoes.

"Aha! Ze shoe thief . . . 'e 'as taken yours, too, eh?" he asks me in a supercool French accent.

I look down at my feet and whisper, "He's right outside in a getaway car. Shall we call the police?"

"I sink zo." He winks conspiratorially. "Were they expensive, ze shoes?"

"Oh, yes, very. I'm going to claim them on my insurance. In fact, I think I should go now. You see, I have to do a painfully horrible photo shoot and I'd rather go and sit in an insurance office with diabolically boring individuals." I stare up into his hooded, greenish eyes and think of how sexy he is.

"*Mais non!* Zhat is no way for a young lady to spend ze day. Ze photo shoot, it will be much better!" He is very cute.

Nigel barges in, cramping my style. "Oh, I see that you've already met Jean-Luc. . . . Jean-Luc, your subject for the day, Kate McPhee. Kate, meet Jean-Luc, your photographer."

Note to self: Please shut up.

I mumble a greeting. He throws a magnanimous arm around my shoulders and leads me into a cavernous, even whiter studio with huge lights, a large white canvas backdrop, and some scaffolding.

"We shoot 'ere, okay?" he asks me, bending down to brush my unruly hair out of my eyes. "It will be good. Don't worry."

Charlie rushes up. "We need touch-up time, both hair and makeup. And Wardrobe is here to dress her." He is fussing around me. I expect he thinks Jean-Luc is cute, too.

"*Non. Non.* I like 'er as she is . . . messy 'air, crumpled suit, no shoes. We shoot some like this. Come!" He leads me to the set. "Polaroid!" he snaps toward a young assistant, a punk teenager named Jared with short cropped black hair and a T-shirt that reads GOD SAVE THE QUEEN—SEX PISTOLS.

"I like your T-shirt," I say as Jean-Luc deposits me in the center of the white backdrop. Jared glances up, nods, and then busies himself checking the cameras. Jean-Luc fiddles around behind me with the backdrop, exposing some scaffolding on one side, making it look unfinished.

"We shoot!" he announces to the assembly. He goes to the front of the canvas backdrop and stands on a ladder pointing the camera down at me.

I stand in my bare feet, hair hanging in my face, one button undone, exposing a bit of boob. Charlie, Christine, Nigel, and the myopic Uta, who has been sent over by Ruben with my wardrobe, watch, clearly appalled. I stare back at them, beseechingly.

"Don't look at them! Look at me!" Jean-Luc barks. "I want to take a Polaroid. Look in 'ere!" He points right at the lens. *Blam!* He takes a photo and the whole room explodes in a flood of light. I stand there dazed and momentarily blind. ***BLAM!*** He takes another. Jared removes his shoes so as not to dirty the pristine whiteness all around me. He walks up to me with a black light meter, which he holds up to my nose. He calls the number back to Jean-Luc, who is holding the two Polaroids under his armpits to hurry the exposure. Jean-Luc adjusts a light, and then peels apart the Polaroids.

"*Très jolie.*" He looks at the pictures through a small loupe handed to him by his assistant and then shows the photos to my assembled posse. Murmurs of approval.

"May I see?" I ask.

"*Bien sûr!*" Jean-Luc brings the Polaroids over to me.

I look at myself with a strange sense of detachment. The photos show an image of an unsure woman in bare feet with messy hair. She is lit perfectly, her skin glows, her hair shines, and she looks completely in place—her messy self in front of the unfinished backdrop and scaffolding. I don't look half bad.

"It's me," I say stupidly.

"*Oui,* it's you. *This* you!" Jean-Luc touches his hand to my chest, as if to say that it is a photo of the core of me. "It's sexy, *non?*" He grins at me and winks. Then he prances back to the ladder.

Christine and Charlie can't help running up to fiddle with me. Christine throws a little gloss on my lips while Charlie fluffs my hair.

"Don't touch 'er!" Jean-Luc yells. *"Merde!"*

Everyone scampers back in alarm. Jared puts a CD in the player, and the studio suddenly comes alive as Limp Biskit blasts through the speakers.

"We shoot!" Jean-Luc roars over the music, and begins to wiggle his hips as he is balanced precariously on the swaying ladder.

"We dance!"

Charlie needs no further invitation and starts jiggling around the floor like the darling hairdresser queen that he is. He's soon joined by Nigel, who doffs his jacket and rolls up his sleeves to show he means business. The pair of them wiggle about as though they are at the Mother Lode on Santa Monica Boulevard.

Not one to spoil a party, I join in. I begin to tentatively wave my arms about, like a white girl trying desperately to forget decades of ballet training. Jared starts pogoing like a maniac, while Christine and Uta adopt a gentle form of hip-hop so as not to injure any internal organs.

Blam! Jean-Luc shoots and the room explodes once more. ***BLAM! BLAM!*** Even as I am into it, I can feel how the camera catches me at various points of expression. Serious. ***BLAM!*** Smiling. ***BLAM!*** Wary. ***BLAM!*** I'm having a ball!

"And for this, I missed surfing and a shag?" Trent announces loudly as he arrives to survey the astonishing melee. Trust Trent to make a grand entrance.

"Who says you've missed a shag?" answers Nigel, who grabs him, whirls him off, and pushes him into a Charlie/Nigel sandwich.

Will you, won't you, will you, won't you? Will you join the dance?
Will you, won't you, will you, won't you? Won't you join the dance?

●　●　●

Several hours later, we are all in the trough of an MSG slump from the Thai food consumed during our one-hour lunch break. Christine, Charlie, and Nigel are cleaning up the Chan Dara takeout containers. Trent is in the corner on his cell phone—no doubt trying to hustle up a date for tonight. Jean-Luc has disappeared and Jared is tidying up the set. Janis Joplin is wailing through the Bang & Olufsens.

In another corner, I am trying to be witty whilst babbling away to the writer from *Soap Opera Digest.* The "clients"—*SOD* photo editors and executives—have been arriving on the scene in a steady trickle since eleven A.M. There are now approximately a dozen women, whose names and jobs I cannot begin to recall, milling about the studio, sipping white wine and seeming impressed. They are all pleasant enough, happy to meet me, and excited about the photo shoot. They *ooh*ed and *aah*ed when Jean-Luc showed them the photos in the crumpled white suit and no shoes. That seems to be a strong contender for the cover.

". . . And pigs will fly," Trent had remarked at the cover suggestion, assuring me that one of the safer, smiling, well-coiffed close-ups would be peering out from newsstands.

"So Kate, what do you see in the future for Devon?" The slight, fawnlike journalist presents her tape recorder under my chin in the hope that I will utter something delectable, fascinating, outrageous—and, above all, printworthy.

"Happiness," I say dreamily, staring over my Thai iced tea and trying to conjure up what that might mean for my gay counterpart.

"What might that entail for Devon?" She is obviously reading my mind.

"Uuumm . . ." Just then, Jean-Luc enters the room, extinguishing the remains of a Gauloise into a paper cup, which he tosses absentmindedly into a trash can. Following hot on his heels is an adorable blonde curlylocked girl, about three years old. He turns back, picks up the toddler, then swings her nonchalantly around his slight hips. She babbles nonstop and waves her arms with excitement. The doors open again and a stunning woman enters. She is wearing a vintage patterned silk dress, across which a canvas sling holds the tiniest of babies.

"How darling!" "How cute!" The room erupts in a coo-chorus of high-pitched baby-shower voices, as the entire *SOD* contingent converges on the beautiful mother and child.

I remain seated and watch silently. The mother extracts the tiny infant from the sling and holds the child up for admiration. She seems very proud, and a delicate blue vein pops up on her smooth forehead as she smiles. Jean-Luc hurries back to the woman and takes the baby. He gestures toward the table where he has fixed a plate of chicken satay, rice, and curry. The little girl is already spooning rice into her mouth, onto her dress, and onto the floor. Charlie is flapping about with napkins.

The woman floats over to the table and sits slowly, gingerly, picking up some chopsticks and speaking in French to the little girl. I watch the woman elegantly handle her food. She turns to Jean-Luc and says something I do not understand. He nods and brings the baby to her, whereupon she unbuttons the top of her dress and proceeds to nurse the infant, covering herself modestly with the sling.

I marvel at the tableau unfolding before me. Jean-Luc perched on the edge of the table, the little girl chasing rice around a paper plate, and the woman with the infant. So perfect. So beautiful.

"That!" I suddenly say, somewhat surprised to hear myself speaking at all. "That's what I see in the future." I look around me to where the writer was sitting, but she has gone. Perhaps she, too, was smitten by the baby when it entered, and she has not returned.

But whose future? I wonder to myself. Surely not Devon's. Mine?

"Ah, domestic bliss," says Trent with a wry, even cynical tone, as he slides into the seat vacated by the journalist and takes a sip of my tea.

"God, Trent. They look so happy." I snatch my tea back.

"Don't let that fool you. It's a clever façade, behind which is nothing but wet diapers, sleepless nights, puke, and poop." He tosses his cell phone from hand to hand.

"Oh, come off it, Trent. If it is so bad, how come the whole world does it?"

"They fall into the trap. It's one of Mother Nature's cruelest hoaxes, designed to produce these little rug rats and perpetuate the species. Thanks, but no thanks."

"I had no idea you were one of the militant childless," I reply. "I don't suppose you believe in marriage and happily-ever-after, either."

"Monogamy . . . monotony. It's no coincidence that they sound the same," he snorts in derision. "How many people do you know who that's really worked for?"

"Aah . . ."

"My point exactly. Love—romantic love—withers away."

"Romeo and Juliet?" I ask.

"An affair—a one-night stand. Shakespeare was smart—he killed them off before the glow faded. Even the Bard wouldn't have been able to make what happened after that interesting."

"Ouch!"

"Wanna come to Neptune's Net?" he asks, tapping me on the nose with his finger.

"When?"

"Now . . . when are you finished?"

"Okay." I feel weary. The early morning, the media tour, the photo shoot. "I'll be done in an hour. Will you wait?"

"Always." He jumps up as his phone rings. "Yup . . . Hey, how the hell are you?" And he's gone, back into his corner.

I continue to gaze enviously at Jean-Luc, his lady, and his family. What strikes me most is their ease. They seem so relaxed, casual, bordering on serene, comfortable with what they have attained. Jean-Luc catches my eye.

"We shoot!" he bellows, jumping up from the table. His little girl jumps up, too, yelling, "Papa, Papa." He throws her up onto his shoulders and carries her to the white backdrop. He puts her down, grabs his camera, and pretends to shoot her picture. She runs about giggling, posing, and sticking out her tongue.

"She's quite a handful," a woman behind me says. I turn, and see that it is Jean-Luc's lady.

"She's gorgeous," I say in reply.

"Thank you." She holds the baby over her shoulder, rubbing its back. She smells faintly of lilacs and milk.

We stand like this, side by side, watching Jean-Luc and his little girl until it is time for me to be the actress again and her to be the mother. Trent's sarcasm notwithstanding, I go back before the camera wondering whether she's got the better deal.

13

Two weeks later

AS I DAWDLE UP TO THE SET sans rehearsal, I find I have an itchy soul. Days like these are troublesome, and not just because I am once again working with Meredith. Meandering through the extensive warren of hallways, I come to my friend Rhonda's office. Keenly competent, she is a production assistant, but one who is clearly destined for bigger and better things. Rhonda is one of many such women who work here—indeed, the entire building seems to be peppered with young women with expensively blown-out straight hair who do all of the heavy lifting that keeps the place running. In fact, I had noticed that the real work in Hollywood is done almost exclusively by women just like Rhonda—brainy women with fierce college educations, Calvin Klein wardrobes, naturally curly hair, and flat irons. Rhonda has been extraordinarily kind to me since I started, spreading her fantastic sense of humor over me like liniment as she talked me through bad storylines, Meredith's tantrums, and snarky jibes from the three witches (Amber, Alison, and Tiffany)—four, if you count Priscilla. I had taken to spending my free time between scenes visiting with her in her office.

"Hey Rhonda, what's up?" I ask.

"Hey, great lesbo article!" She waves the *LA Times* Weekend page at me. We bullshit together until I'm called to the set.

"We still on for Friday?" she asks as I head out the door. We'd already arranged to get drunk on Friday with a few of her girlfriends who likewise avoid humidity and worship at the flat-iron altar.

"Absolutely." I haven't had many nights off, at least not many where I didn't collapse into bed early, exhausted from too many hours on the set or from satisfying Nigel's relentless publicity needs. "A girls' night out is just what I need."

Once on the set, I'm staring into the eyes of an XXL horse. With the vampire threat looming larger than ever, Regina has arranged for mounted police to stand guard around her estate. In today's segment, Devon is to walk the grounds at night—with a half-ton stallion breathing down her/my neck. Even though I knew there would be a horse on the set, I hadn't really appreciated the idea that he was going to be so huge. And the set looks great; the designers have done their job well, hiding the fact that the working space is scarcely bigger than a commemorative stamp. Dimly lit, it's all very eerie and very Gothic, with owl noises, bats, and an anemic sliver of a moon. The equestrian cop has been tasked with spewing out most of the expository drivel (sparing me from having to do that) and is delivering backstory about dead cows sucked dry of blood and other strange goings-on while I nod warily.

Regina wafts into the scene. Even I am astonished by how she is dressed. Outrageously tricked out in an orchid peignoir, fluffy mules, chandelier earrings, and a double set of false eyelashes, Meredith is also wearing about three gallons of industrial strength foundation-cum-Spackle on her face. I marvel again at how short she is.

EXT.—ABELL ESTATE—NIGHT

                    DEVON
    Ms. Abell . . . all seems to be in order.

I try not to look bored as I deliver my lines, but I am unsuccessful. This has no effect on Meredith, since she never listens anyway. Instead she plows straight on with the speech she glanced at for the first time during a lip gloss application two minutes ago.

                    REGINA
    I'm terrified, Officer Merrick, terrified I tell you . . .
    terrified.

Without a TelePrompTer, she'd be toast.

                REGINA (CONT'D)
    I feel terrified that someone is going . . . to at-
    tack . . . Mallory. She means all the . . . world to
    me. She's terrified . . . I'm terrified, Officer Merrick.

"Detective Merrick," I hiss through clenched teeth. It's not my character's demotion that bothers me, but her atrocious phrasing. I lean in, ticking off the number of *terrifieds* in her dialogue.

                    DEVON
    No one is coming anywhere near you, Regina. You have

```
twelve  mounted  police,  three  security  guards,  an
electric gate, an alarm, and bad breath.
```

Her character has supposedly been living on a diet of garlic to ward off the vampires, so I added that last bit about the halitosis. Well, no . . . I added it because I knew it would piss her off. I see her eyes flash for an instant and I wonder if she's going to bring the scene to a halt, but she knows Daphne will skin her without an anesthetic if she does.

```
                    DEVON (CONT'D)
What about your daughter?
```

```
                    REGINA
Mallory is in her bedroom studying. . . . Officer . . .
Detective Merrick. Please come and . . . check her win-
dows.
```

Meredith purses her lips and flicks her head toward me seductively, but the signal reaches another, entirely unintended recipient. Recognizing the sign, the stallion's eyes widen. He flicks his head twice, flares his nostrils, and blows a raspberry. I glance at him.

```
                    DEVON
See, he agrees. You are perfectly safe. I will be
happy to come check on your daughter and reassure her.
Head up to the house. As soon as I brief my men, I'll
be right behind you.
```

```
                    REGINA
No, no, Detective. I am terrified—terrified—to walk the
woods alone.
```

Okay, that's eight *terrifieds*. She interweaves her arm with mine seductively and presses herself to my side, peering at me trustingly. I summon up all my butchness and extricate my arm from her soft, dimpled one. She flicks her head and stares, beseeching me to lead her through the treacherous un-dergrowth. The horse whinnies and nods twice. It's become a courtship now.

```
                    DEVON
Ms. Abell, you called me out here to organize my men,
so organize my men I will.
```

I bite the words out fast, hoping to inject at least some rhythm into the scene. Meredith lowers her eyes and shakes her hair. The stallion snorts and tosses his huge mane in response—with all her flicking and shaking,

it now seems apparent that she has stumbled on Horsey Morse Code
for "Let's get jiggy wid it." I glance up at the rider, who is struggling for
control.

> REGINA
> (uncertainly)
> Yes . . . Of course.

As Regina coquettishly shakes her head yet again, I find it hard to watch.
The air is heavy with seduction. It's not that she's actively trying to seduce
the horse; it's just that she doesn't know any other way to comport herself—on camera or off. To avoid making eye contact, I talk to the orchid
negligee.

> DEVON
> Give me just a few minutes here. I will come up to the
> house directly.

> REGINA
> I am terrified.

Nine.

> POLICEMAN
> I've got it covered here, boss.

> DEVON
> Ms. Abell . . . If Mallory is afraid—terrified—to be by
> herself, who's with her at the moment?

Ten. Why should she have all the fun?

> REGINA
> Magda, her new math tutor.

> DEVON
> What's her last name?

> REGINA
> (hesitating)
> Why, I'm not sure. . . .

Meredith's fingers flutter in midair.

> DEVON
> (instantly suspicious)
> You let a stranger into your home? What do you know
> about her?

REGINA
Laszlo recommended her. She just arrived from Budapest. I believe she's an old friend of the family. . . .

DEVON
And let me guess. Because Laszlo vouched for her, you
didn't check her references.

Meredith gasps, melodramatically.

REGINA
Detective Merrick, what if . . . ?

As Meredith's words hang leadenly in the air, she shakes her head and
flicks her titian tresses yet again, causing the horse to toss his mane,
whinny, nod, neigh, and stamp in response.

POLICEMAN
Easy there, Thor.

His nostrils are flaring widely now, and his eyes are focused only on Meredith. She is oblivious (no surprise there), but the stallion is really getting the
"Come and get me, big boy" message. I see the guy on Camera 1 make an
uncharacteristically abrupt adjustment in his shot. The reason quickly becomes apparent.

POLICEMAN (CONT'D)
Settle down now, Thor. Easy boy.

What we have here is a horse with a hard-on. Big-time—it looks like he's
standing on five legs. The rider, an accomplished equestrian, attempts to
gain control of his mount, but the steed sidles over to Meredith and tries
to nibble her hair.

POLICEMAN (CONT'D)
Easy there now, big fella. Steady.

Or is he trying to blow in her ear? Are we about to explore an alternative de-
finition of "mount"? I hope not, at least not on camera, and certainly not
without a precoital glass of merlot.

POLICEMAN (CONT'D)
(to Thor) Easy there. Easy.
(to Regina) My apologies, Ms. Abell.
(to Devon) He's not usually like this. I don't know
what's gotten into him, boss.

I pause. A sweat breaks out on my brow. I look straight into the ground because I am on the verge of cracking up. I tell myself terrible things. I'm enlisting every actor's trick I know in an attempt to dampen an enormous urge to lose it right about now. I conjure up horrific images—the slavering orcs from *Lord of the Rings,* Anthony Hopkins as Hannibal Lecter, Amber as Lady Macbeth—anything to erase the picture of Meredith and Thor, cantering away through a field of wildflowers to perpetual bliss in a land of mirrors.

Eventually the rider settles Thor down, but the big Thoroughbred continues to stare longingly at Meredith's back, awaiting her next signal. Meanwhile, I suppress the giggles, and as the purple-and-pink *My Little Pony* image recedes, I raise my head. Slowly.

DEVON
Very well, we will walk together, Ms. Abell.

I offer her my arm and as we pass the great animal, Meredith flutters her eyes up toward him. She just never quits. The horse flares his nostrils once more and arches his neck. I choke off another rising wave of hysterics. He is smitten. Meredith does it again—another actor eating out of her hand.

"And cut!"

Relieved that it's over, I throw myself down on a metal chair next to the woodland scenery and allow myself to grin at the absurdity of it. Meredith swans over to her makeup triage and is set upon by three worker bees. The cop dismounts, and he and the horse wrangler attempt to lead the lovestruck creature to his trailer for the road trip back up the 101 to Thousand Oaks. "Shit," says the cameraman. "When he gets back to the barn, the first mare he sees ain't gonna know what hit her."

As the stagehands gear up for the next shot, I spy a mini-gaggle of visitors headed for the set. All visitors are something of a mixed blessing. Even if they try to be unobtrusive, they're still there, and they inevitably slow things down. My radar goes up. Network types? Itinerant dignitaries? In a way, it doesn't matter. Whoever they are, they always want the same things: a candid shot with a star and an autograph on whatever piece of paper is handy, be it a script, an 8x10 glossy, or a cocktail napkin.

This group is clearly a bunch of civilians—fans—and some of our most loyal viewers at that. If you're not in the biz and you've got enough juice to get through the door, it follows that you're a true devotee of *Live for Tomorrow.* They're headed straight for Meredith, her perfection now restored after the stress of being *terrified* and flirting with Thor. "Oh, Ms. Contini!" gushes one girl in her late teens. "I am so thrilled to be here. My mother bought this tour for all of us at a charity auction, but she couldn't come with us. I wonder, would you please be kind enough to sign this for her? It would mean so much to her." The girl proffers the bill of a pale blue *LFT* baseball cap toward Meredith—the group has obviously buzzed the network gift shop before coming on set.

"This is so difficult for me," Meredith replies with yet another shake of her hair. "I've had a lot of very emotional scenes today. And I've tried on clothes." And with that she turns her back and glides grandly off down the corridor. I'm dumbstruck, but no more so than the fans and the young page who is shepherding them. What the hell would it have cost her to at least be amiable?

"She really needs the cap . . ." the crestfallen girl calls desperately after the retreating figure, her voice falling away, "until her hair grows back after she's done with chemo." I'm already out of my chair and headed over there to make amends, but Lauren Elizabeth Fielding beats me by half a step. Lauren, age not-quite-eighteen, plays Meredith's daughter, Mallory Abell, age just-over-thirteen.

"Here . . . let me get that," she says warmly to the fan, grabbing the cap and a pen. "Tell me now, what is your mom's name?"

"Crystal. I'm Jasmine."

"When you get home, Jasmine, you be sure to tell Crystal what a thoughtful daughter she has."

"And that," whispers Nigel, who has come up behind me, "is how it's done. You're watching a master at work. Lauren has a poise and a sophistication well beyond her seventeen years, in part because she grew up in front of the camera."

"It's always great for us to meet people who love the show," Lauren continues, "but you'll have to excuse my 'mother.' She's having a tough day—those vampires can really be so tedious. She's worried about keeping them out of the mansion, but I'll let you in on a little secret: she let one in herself—right through the front door. My tutor Magda is not what she seems, but don't worry, Detective Merrick will get to the bottom of things. Now, let me tell you about how we do what we do here." And with that, Lauren begins explaining a bit of the stagecraft behind the scene we just finished, then poses for photos with everyone in the group. All is redeemed and fifteen minutes later the group leaves happy.

"Jesus H. Christ!" Lauren says harshly once they are out of earshot. "I'm used to saving Meredith's ass and cleaning up after her fuck-ups on-camera. Now I have to do it off-camera too?"

"So, Nigel," I say, "what brings you up here?"

"You, Ms. Kate, and you, too, Ms. Lauren. I hope you didn't have plans this weekend."

My plans are to veg out, see Matt, and grab some much-needed me-time, but he doesn't have to know that.

"I most certainly did—do. Your use of the past tense troubles me."

"I'm good, Nigel," says Lauren. "What's up?"

"Get thee to Anaheim, fair ladies. Both of you. Tonight. Your presence is most urgently requested at Fan-Tastic, a soap convention."

. . .

On my way to meet up with Matt, singing "I'm gonna soak up the sun" along with Sheryl Crow, oblivious to the world. Oblivious, that is, until I see the twirling bubble-gum lights on top of the cop car, and that one piercing white light reflecting off my rearview mirror . . . the one that means "Bad news. You're busted."

This is going to be a problem. I've got my UK license, but I never got around to getting one from the state of California. I roll down the window of the Honda as the woman cop comes to the side of the car.

"Good evening, Officer."

"Good evening. License and vehicle registration, please."

I fumble in my purse to produce the license, then open the glove box in search of the registration. This is most unfortunate. A veritable rat's nest of papers explodes out of the compartment when it opens, many of which are parking tickets from the City of Los Angeles. Tickets gleaned from leaving the Honda overnight in front of my house. Unpaid, overdue parking tickets.

"Do you know how fast you were going?" the cop asks as I fumble-sort my way through the wad of citations.

"Why no, Officer—" I glance at the badge. "Officer Martinez."

"You were doing fifty-seven miles per hour in a thirty-five mph zone, Ms. ah, McPhee. That's more than twenty miles per hour over the limit."

"Sorry, Officer. I guess I was on autopilot."

"Indeed."

Officer Martinez walks back to her squad car, I assume to run my data through the system to see if I'm a serial killer. Which means I'm toast— those parking tickets are bound to show up. I watch in my rearview mirror with dread as she walks back toward me. Shit. I'll be lucky if she doesn't haul my ass off to jail.

"Say, you aren't Kate McPhee from *Live for Tomorrow,* are you?"

"Actually, I am."

"Watch you all the time, Detective Merrick."

"Thank you."

"And I just want to say how much I appreciate the fact that you're, ah, walking point for all us gay women on the force."

The good news is that she's a gay cop.

"Happy to help," I say.

"And as one sister and fellow officer to another, I'm going to let you off with just a warning, but I was wondering if you could do something for me."

The bad news is that she's a gay cop.

"If I can," I say.

Oh please, God, don't let her come on to me. Pleasepleaseplease let this be something I can handle.

"Do you think you could get me an autographed picture, just so I can prove to everyone back at the precinct that it really was you?"

"Absolutely," I say with a very relieved smile. "I'd be delighted. I don't even have to send it to you. I have some right here."

Bless you, Nigel. Bless you. And bless you too, Lauren, for my first lesson in how to do this.

I reach into the back seat and grab the stack of photos. "What is your first name, Officer?"

"Elena. E-L-E-N-A."

"That's a lovely name," I say, writing *Dear Elena—warmest wishes from one cop to another. Devon Merrick/Kate McPhee.* "Perhaps you'd like some for your friends?"

Nine more autographs later, me and Sheryl Crow are back on the road.

Note to self: a California driver's license—embrace the concept.

* * *

Thanks to Matt's directions I find the slightly ostentatious house in Sherman Oaks without much difficulty. Matt is doing close-up magic during the cocktail hour at an intimate but expensive gala for a couple's fiftieth wedding anniversary. He looks good dressed up! When he sees me he gives me a tiny smile to acknowledge my presence, but I hover near the door—I don't want to intrude on the scene. No one has to point out the celebrating couple to me—the bride and groom are decked out with corsage and boutonniere (respectively), and the room has gathered around them in rapt attention. "Here," Matt says, deftly arraying a deck of cards face-up before the Barbara-Bushy bride, a vision in ivory taffeta (with a teased and lacquered helmet of hair to match). "Lucille, I want you to pick a card—any card." The woman selects the ace of diamonds.

"Is this okay?" she inquires, looking uncertainly at Matt.

"It's fine with me, Lucille," he coos. "Do you think it's a good card, Saul?" he asks the groom, showing him the card. Saul nods his concurrence—and one gets the impression that's pretty much how it's gone in this household for the past half century.

Matt then shows the card to the rest of the room. "The bride has chosen the ace of diamonds," he announces, pulling a pen from the breast pocket of his jacket.

"Now, Lucille," he continues, "I want you to take this Sharpie and write your name and today's date on your card, along with any message you like."

Lucille raises her painted eyebrows and looks a little uncomfortable. Matt has given her permission to do something a bit wicked. Autographing a playing card is obviously a violation of what had hitherto been "the rules": Don't bend the cards; don't get them sticky; and for goodness' sake, don't mark them up. "Write?" she asks dubiously. "On the card?"

"Absolutely," Matt says reassuringly, shuffling the rest of the deck as she inscribes her name and begins making a few doodles. "That's fantastic, Lucille."

Matt shows the card to the assembled children, grandchildren, and lifelong friends of the couple. "See what a great job she did?" Although a bit self-conscious at being made much of, she now beams at his approval.

"Okay, Saul, I'm going to put you to work," Matt says, turning once again to the groom. "I want you to take that ace of diamonds that Lucille has decorated so beautifully, and put it back into the deck."

"Anywhere in the deck?" he asks.

"Anywhere you like," Matt says. It's clear that Saul's a skeptic. Not only does he believe he can puzzle out the trick if he watches Matt intently; he also thinks he can make it tough on him by inserting the card someplace other than the middle. As he holds the deck on edge, Saul wiggles the card into place, as close to the top card as he can get. "That's just fine, Saul. Couldn't have done it better myself."

Matt then produces a rubber band—seemingly out of nowhere—and wraps it around the deck. I marvel at how smooth his movements are, how effortless it all looks. "Watch carefully, everyone," he announces. "May I direct your attention to the ceiling," he says as he tosses the deck skyward. When it makes contact with the ceiling, the rubber band releases, and all of the cards cascade downward, showering the guests. All of the cards, that is, except one.

"That's my card up there!" exclaims Lucille, clearly thrilled. "Look, Saul, it's stuck to the ceiling! That's my ace of diamonds!" The rest of the party oohs and aahs appreciatively.

"Grampa! How'd he do that?" asks a nine-year-old grandson.

Poor Saul. He was so sure he could figure it out. But there he sits, without a clue. "I'm afraid I don't know, David," he answers ruefully.

"Ladies and gentlemen," says Matt as he goes into his final speech, "my time's about up. Saul and Lucille . . . thank you for inviting me into your home. It's been a pleasure helping you celebrate your golden anniversary. I hope you've enjoyed it as much as I have." Lucille is glowing and leads the applause. "And if I'm lucky, you'll invite me back when you celebrate your hundredth." Saul laughs in spite of himself. "I hope all of you are hungry—

the caterers tell me that your wonderful dinner is about to be served."
More applause. "And Lucille, that ace of diamonds up there on the ceiling
is your keepsake from this very special evening. One of the wait staff will be
along shortly to retrieve it for you. Thank you all, and enjoy the rest of your
night." Lots more applause—hearty and enthusiastic applause. The boy is a
big hit.

Matt and I are two steps from the door when I hear, "Devv-onn! Look!
It's Devon Merrick!"

Instinctively I turn around. Wrong move. I should have just waited for
Matt outside. One of the women waves vigorously and yodels to me en
route across the room. "*Devv-onn!* I can't believe it's you. I've been watching
Live for Tomorrow for so many years. You're the best thing that's happened
to the show. May I have your autograph?"

I grimace when I see what she wants me to sign; she's holding out one
of Matt's playing cards, which she's picked up from the floor. She is soon
joined by half a dozen more fans, and eventually by a mini-stampede, all
headed my way with the same idea in mind.

Ouch. The last thing I wanted was to draw attention to myself in a gathering like this.

Note to self: Fame hurts sometimes, Katiegirl, and not just you, but other people
as well.

Without intending to in the slightest, I've rained on two parades. First,
the hubbub and interruption over my presence has made Lucille and Saul
feel less special. Second (and perhaps worse), it's diminished Matt's triumph as performer. I've upstaged him just by showing up.

There's no way I can bring myself to sign the playing cards, so I head
back to the Honda to fetch Nigel's stack of glossies. By the time I'm finished, I'm guessing the caterer is mad at me, too, since the whole process
has delayed the serving of the anniversary dinner. I feel like I should run
around apologizing to everyone, but I settle for apologizing to Matt over
lemon-rosemary roasted chicken and garlic mashed potatoes at a little
French bistro on Ventura Boulevard.

"It's okay, Kate, really," he says with his most beguiling Jimmy Stewart
smile. "After I'm done at the Voodoo Lounge, how 'bout we just go climb
in bed . . ." As he brushes the water buffalo curls away from his forehead,
the smile turns into a broad grin, with just a hint of leer. ". . . and not come
out till dinner tomorrow?"

My face clouds instantly. "What's the matter?" he asks awkwardly, as if
embarrassed. "I thought . . ."

Oh God! Now he thinks I don't want to sleep with him!

"No! No! It's not that. But . . ."

"But what?"

"But I can't." I was hoping to break the news of the trip a little more gently, but now I just have to blurt it out.

"I see," he says, with just a touch of frost.

"Fantastic."

"Excuse me?"

"Fan-Tastic. Soap convention. I'm supposed to check in at the hotel in Anaheim tonight so I can be there for breakfast early in the morning. I'm sorry. I was going to mention it earlier, but I didn't want to stop you with Saul and Lucille—you were wonderful, by the way—and then there was that whole dreadful thing with the autographs. I feel like I've made a mess of everything this evening . . . or rather, Devon Merrick has."

"And let me guess—you'd like me to feed Drusilla while you're gone?"

Shit! I hadn't even thought about that. Nigel's idea about a personal assistant is looking better all the time.

"I suppose so," I say awkwardly, "if you don't mind."

"I don't mind," he says. "Now go home and pack—it'll take you a while to excavate what you need out of that pile of clothes on your floor."

14

IT TAKES ME ROUGHLY TEN MINUTES to pack: a day outfit and an evening outfit. For the day outfit, I decide to play up a safari theme, since I'm going outdoors and I'm traveling into the unknown area of greater Anaheim. I choose white linen Ralph Lauren pants and a khaki Yoji top with complicated straps and buckles. They both need ironing, but perhaps there will be a helpful maid I can butter up at Disneyland. For the evening fanathon I pick out black cigarette pants, a LAMB T-shirt, and a cranberry three-quarter-sleeve cardigan from Banana Republic. They're new, with tags on, so I'll look relatively well put together. Except for my lack of a manicure.

These I hang up in the back of the Honda. The rest—shoes, undies, toothbrush, sunblock, and so forth—I plonk into my Stella McCartney overnight bag, which I hurl into the trunk next to Meredith's gift basket.

I give Drusilla a hug and leave a note with feeding instructions for Matt, sealed with a kiss. Then I hit the road.

Driving at night in Los Angeles, the CD player blaring, windows down, and munching a bag of M&M's, I feel as if I am on top of the world. I hold the speed to an approximate sixty-five and keep on eye on my rearview mirror.

Lil' Kim is yelling expletives at me and making me laugh as I sing along. There is, of course, nothing worse than an English person trying to rap, and I am grateful there is no one here to witness it. Nonetheless, I "yo' mutherfucker" all the way to Anaheim.

We are set up at Disney's Grand Californian, and a porter dressed like Pinocchio carries my bag through the lobby and opens the door to an unbelievably enormous suite.

"Uh, there must be some mistake," I say, fiddling in my purse for a suitable $100 tip. But he assures me this is my room and takes the three bucks that I hastily jam into his hand as he closes the door.

Wow! I survey my castle. There are huge French doors opening onto a patio that overlooks a large swimming pool. Damn, no bikini. I do a quick mental sort through the undies I've brought and decide that a pair of black boy shorts and a Calvin Klein stretchy tank could easily pass for a tankini. Excellent! I look forward to a midnight swim. I bounce up and down on the sofa and then mosey into the bedroom. White sheets, luxurious coverlets, and the softest of soft feather pillows. I throw myself down and snuggle in, kicking off my shoes. To my left is a beautiful marble bathroom, and I imagine my Barbie battery-operated toothbrush and my five-year-old vanity bag are going to look mighty stupid in there.

Note to self: Buy some lovely bathroom things for travel.

I know I won't. I close my eyes and savor the softness of the cool sheets. When I open my eyes, the sun is glaring down at me through the bedroom window. Missed the midnight plunge—it's morning! I jump up in a panic and look for the clock. Whew! It is seven A.M. and I don't have to be ready until nine. I have time for a quick dip.

I climb into my makeshift bathing suit and throw on the complimentary white terry robe that apparently you can buy for a mere $100. Why should you, when you can steal it? I grab my towel and my flip-flops and run down to the pool.

Just as I stick my big toe in to test the water, a flashbulb goes off in my face.

"It's her! It's HER!" a voice screams.

"OmyGod . . . omyGod! Quick! Quick! Take my photo!"

I stand there. Nonplussed, frozen in an odd tableau, toe still in the water. Flashing from several angles, more throwaway cameras fire away at me.

Note to self: If you're out in public, you're on. The times when fans are most likely to recognize you are the times when you're trying hardest to be anonymous.

"Oh, please . . . Devon, Devon . . . Look here, over here!"

"Here, Miss McPhee, over here!"

"Oh my God! You're soooo tiny! Isn't she tiny? She's so tiny, isn't she? Isn't she tiny, everyone?"

Not only tiny, but deaf and soon to be blind, as my retinas curl up against the back of my orbital cavities in an attempt to rescue themselves from the morning sun and a dozen instant camera flashes.

I stand upright and yank the tie to my robe fiercely around my waist and try to organize my hair into something resembling me. An impossible task, of course, with no makeup paramedics. So I smile and try to remember Nigel's instructions. I search my memory, but that has gone into hiding with my retinas and my dignity. However, I do hear a small voice that sounds remarkably like Nigel saying: "Always be civil and don't give away plotlines."

A bevy of women attired in DISNEY FAN-TASTIC orange T-shirts, Gap shorts, and tennis shoes are clustered around me—putting arms around me, posing, squealing, and jostling. One of them thrusts a large banner in my hand, which reads:

Daring Detective Devon
Deals Daily at Noon

These women breathlessly inform me that they've just had breakfast with Gore Ivanov, a hunk from another soap, and they are all swooning about his charm, intelligence, and hairy chest—which he obligingly displayed for them. I am thinking that they should be grateful I haven't inflicted my dimpled white thighs on them in the morning glare, but I become sidetracked with questions about my tinyness, general shortness, and shocking difference from the way I appear on TV. I feel like telling them that someone else plays me on TV, but I try to remember that I am civil and I represent the show. So I decide to tell them some of the plot secrets instead.

I am halfway through divulging the switched-at-birth real mother saga, when Nigel swoops down on me from a balcony somewhere and clasps his hand firmly over my mouth.

"Ah, sweetness, here you are," he purrs. "I see your fans have found you!" He is all smiles in khakis with a razor crease in them and a whiter-than-white T-shirt that looks as if it has been both starched and ironed. Fastidious gay guy grooming—nothing like it. "Ms. McPhee is going to get ready to join all of you out in the park shortly. Please have a pleasant morning." And I am whisked away in silence.

I turn to wave farewell to the group of women with their homemade banner, and they all wave enthusiastically back at me. "She's so tiny," I hear again as I round a corner. And all this time I thought I was average height. Oh well.

Nigel shoves me into my suite and barks orders about always needing an escort around the park and other nonsense along the same lines, as though I was an important visiting dignitary, or completely stupid. We order breakfast and a housekeeper removes my safari wear for ironing.

Shortly, a locally hired "wedding makeup-and-hair artist" sets about turning me into a bride. Lovely Lauren arrives and gets her hair blown out, as I attempt to unfuss the curly mess I have been teased into by our local professional. I end up throwing my hair back in a ponytail and wiping off the pink lipstick. Me in my safari gear and Lauren in her sundress are quite an odd couple as we set off on our adventure at Disneyland.

We walk past shops selling silly plastic objects and enormous suckers shaped like the Seven Dwarfs. I have entered a world that smells like cotton candy and sunscreen, full of supersized people with cameras, people who are on a mission to extract enjoyment-plus-tax from every conceivable situation. I admire their optimism and pluck.

It's unusually hot for this time of year as I struggle along on my Miu Miu mules and stare out through my ill-gotten Chanel sunglasses, lifted from the *Soap Opera Digest* shoot. Some people who recognize Lauren and me try to get us to stop for a picture or smile for the camera, but Nigel has us on a full boot camp march. Hut-two-three-four. Left-right. Left-right. We're not stopping, no way, no how.

We approach an oasis—two large blue umbrellas, side by side. Under each umbrella is a tall table, a director's chair, a stack of 8x10s, some black Sharpies, and a glass of cool water with major condensation puddling at the base. Winding in a long, irregular line away from each station are hundreds of enthusiastic-looking people.

"Now you two are all set," says Nigel as we near the end of our hike. "You're both clear on the ground rules?"

"Yeah yeah yeah," says Lauren, to whom all of this is surely old hat. "Be nice to everyone and don't give away the plot."

"And if they start talking about Meredith?" I ask.

"Just like on the satellite interviews: Don't go there," Nigel says firmly. "And one more thing—and this is for both of you—I know it's tempting, but stay away from smartass answers to dumb questions. If the question is important enough to be asked, they won't appreciate satire in a reply."

I stop, frozen, and take in what I see before me. Men and women are standing in the heat, laughing, talking, and fanning themselves. A few are rocking children in strollers. Many are waving and snapping pictures. They are all subjecting themselves to this in order to visit . . . me, or—forgive me, Lauren—us. I think briefly of faking a sunstroke, but it is too late: Nigel grabs me by the hand and insists that I get to work.

I glance over at Lauren, who is already signing and chatting away with a gaggle of fans. She looks up at me and winks. I take heart. I can do this, I think, and I step up onto the platform. Again, I look at the long, hot line. I want to say something to break the ice in this boiling temperature, so I step to the front and everyone yells, "Kate, Kate! Devon! Kate!"

I start laughing and hold up both of my arms. "Are you mad?" I bellow through cupped hands. "Go home! You are nuts!"

Everyone giggles as though they have been caught doing something silly and childish. But no one leaves. "You are going to die of heatstroke! You must have something better to do on a Saturday!" I yell with sincere disbelief.

There's no hope. "We love you, Devon!" They take up a chant and applaud louder than ever.

As Nigel grabs me again and firmly guides me to my chair, I shout, "Well, if you insist. But you can't say I didn't warn you! Thank you for coming, you're all crazy! Have a fantastic time!"

Another yell erupts from the line, and I sit down to start autographing. A sunburnt woman with a Mickey Mouse hat that has a built-in fan steps up. Around her neck are several silver chain charm necklaces.

"These are pretty," I say, pointing to them, and grabbing another 8x10 glossy to sign.

"Oh, thank you. I bought them on QVC from Contini's Catalogue. I love them!" She has a very California accent and her name is Jenna. I sign my photo with *Best Wishes*.

"Hello! It's so good to see you!" I say to a pleasant-looking woman, age forty-five or so, in electric blue who is next in line. "You must have gotten here really early!"

"I just want you to know, Ms. McPhee—May I call you Kate?"

"Of course . . . Rosemary," I say, reading her name tag quickly, "but it's very considerate of you to ask."

"I just want you to know, Kate, that I know someone at home who is exactly like Devon Merrick."

Before I can say, *You know a lesbian detective?* I see Nigel in the corner of my field of vision. In my mind's eye he is waggling his finger at me, as if to remind me, Nyetsky on the smart mouth, Kate.

"She has the same accent, same intelligence, same haircut. . . ."

"Oh, Rosemary, I do hope this is someone you like!"

"Absolutely. She's my mother . . ."

Ow. That one stings a bit.

". . . And she still watches the show every day."

"What is your mother's name?"

"Adelaide."

"Well then, shall we have them take our picture together, for Adelaide?"

"Could we? Really?"

"Of course. It's my pleasure."

"Hello, Kate, I'm Gillian."

"It's a pleasure to meet you, Gillian. Thanks for being so patient." Gillian is about thirty-seven, with honey blonde hair.

"I've been watching this show since I was a teenager, Kate, and don't you think Regina has gotten totally out of control? I mean, what kind of woman would still be seeing a man like Laszlo, who may have gotten her daughter pregnant? Her behavior has been just terrible lately, and I'm losing patience with her."

"I know exactly what you mean, Gillian. Regina can be difficult." *You don't know the half of it, my dear.*

"She's behaving like a spoiled, petulant, obnoxious child. A lot of times she's charming and fun, but right now, she's a horror."

Okay, Katie, Nigel wants you to bite your tongue. It's time to be a team player. Every bone in your body may want to dump on Meredith; that's not what this event is about. But how to deal with the question? Nigel said not to talk about Meredith, I tell myself. He didn't say anything about not talking about Regina.

"Well, Gillian, I think we have to cut her a little slack right now, okay? Regina is almost always strong enough to maintain her feisty spirit, no matter how powerful the dark forces are in her life. And that's what women do, isn't it? We carry on in spite of everything. Don't forget that Regina is the way she is because of a tragedy in her early life, one that she'll never really get over."

"Yeah, I guess you're right," she says reluctantly.

Next.

A blonde, smiling face with three small children appears. All four are clad in various Disney character T-shirts. The mother holds out a *Soap Opera Digest* for me to sign. This is the first time I've seen it. My cover.

"I think that's a great shot," the woman says. There is a seasoned, judgmental quality to the way she speaks, as if she is an expert on soap operas. She wants me to sign it to Mandy, spelled M-A-N-D-E-E.

I comply. I sign across the photo of me wearing the crumpled white suit. My hair is messy and I look sullen. The headline reads: THE ANTI-HEROINE OF *LIVE FOR TOMORROW* SPEAKS OUT.

A thrill runs through my body. They chose that shot! It's really me! Messy and unglamorous! They went with the Real Me. Cool. Then, another thrill runs through me—one of apprehension. What the hell did I say when I "spoke out"? I can hardly wait to read it.

Mandee steps down with her three children, each sucking on a strawberry Dopey, Grumpy, or Sneezy dwarf.

The next fan steps up. He is an older man, grey hair, thick Coke-bottle lenses in his glasses, sweaty upper lip, pallid complexion.

"Devon, I watch the show religiously," he whispers in an urgent, confidential tone. He's also a bit of a space invader; I feel him intruding on my bubble and I move my chair back an inch or so.

"I think you need to get better technical advice on police issues, because some of the procedures you follow are not strictly ethical," he says, looking at me intently. "You need to watch yourself. I notice that there has been no talk about silver bullets yet, but you should be aware that technique has never proven one hundred percent effective." He is trying to look stern but is striking me as bug-eyed looney instead.

Just what I need: lectures on the technique of pursuing and capturing vampires. He has a copy of the *Soap Opera Digest*, too, and his hand shakes as he holds it out for me to sign.

"Best to use 'Albert Green III,' in case any of . . . *them* . . . are watching," he whispers. I sign it and thank him for the advice. Then, he hands me his ALBERT GREEN III card and a sweaty, long-stemmed rose.

"In case you ever need more advice, I know all about vampires," he offers in a conspiratorial tone. He wraps his clammy hand around mine and pulls me off the director's chair to take a photo. One of the Disneyland cast members holds up Albert's camera and we pose for a shot. Albert's arm is shaking as it snakes around my waist. We smile, the camera flashes, and he is off, wobbling back into his world of X Files and conspiracy theories. In Albert's case the truth is not only out there, it's *way* out there.

I watch his hunched back recede as he adjusts the angle of his fishing hat after looping the camera strap back over his neck. As if he can sense that I am looking at him, he turns and puts his finger up to his lips, as if we share a secret. Then, he disappears into the crowds of children and Disney characters. We could use him as a writer, I muse.

Next.

A husband and wife from New Jersey. Him: all gold jewelry and slicked-back hair. Her: all gold jewelry, manicures, pedicures, Louis Vuitton, and slicked-back hair.

"I never watched soaps," he says with a Jersey accent. "Then, one day I'm laid up with the flu and the wife has *Live for Tomorrow* on and I'm hooked. I got TiVo, just to make sure I never miss it. Now, we watch you every night when we're havin' dinner together." They smile at each other.

For Tony and Deena. See you for dinner.

Next.

An African American lady with a teeny baby. "You're the best," she says to me with a hearty laugh. She hands me the little girl to hold for a photo. The baby smells good and her head is covered with sweet little braids. I don't want to give her back. I cuddle her while I sign my photo to Desiree.

The hot day begins to blur:

Jane, spelled J-A-Y-N-E.

Ashley, spelled A-S-H-L-E-I-G-H.

Lisa, spelled L-E-E-Z-A-H.

Next!

"Hello, Kate! I'm Kaitlyn and these are my sorority sisters Mackenzie, Chelsea, Danielle, and Samantha."

Standing before me are four young women with unblemished faces, snow white teeth, and Mickey Mouse ears. "It's a pleasure. Where do you all go to school?"

"USC, Kappa Kappa Gamma," says Kaitlyn.

"What are you majoring in?" I ask.

"Broadcast journalism," says Kaitlyn.

"Religion," says Mackenzie.

"Kinesiology," says Chelsea.

"French," says Danielle.

"Biomedical engineering," says Samantha. "We should be studying, but we wouldn't have missed this for the world. We so love the show!"

I pose for photos with the ladies of KKG and check in with Nigel, who gives me the universal index finger-across-the-throat high sign for "Cut this off—we're done here."

After the fan signing, I go for a couple of Disney-themed rides with Nigel and Lauren, then back to crash in the suite. With the A/C blasting, it's superfreezing in the room. On the coffee table are two gift baskets. One is from the Fan-Tastic PR team. I open it, always hoping for something fabulous. It contains the orange T-shirt in size XL, which could double as a search-and-rescue jumpsuit; a Goofy mug; a large packet of popcorn; a wired, battery-operated twirling Tinker Bell thingy that I couldn't imagine a use for; some notecards, and a cuddly Winnie-the-Pooh. The card reads: WELCOME TO THE LAND OF SMILES.

I go to the minibar. Armed with a stiff vodka and cranberry, I feel brave enough to open the second basket. It is tied with a thick washed-linen ribbon; the basket is crammed with natural wood shavings that smell of lavender. Nestled among the wood chips are soap, body lotion, and three large fizzy bath bombs that smell of roses and lemon verbena. The note reads:

> Dear Kate,
>   Have a relaxing bath on me, and thank you.
>   The fans really appreciate it.
>   Remember, without them, we are nothing.
>   With gratitude, Daphne

I sink to the floor. I down the vodka. My God, how unpredictable is that? Daphne sending me a gift basket? Well, not her, her assistant. But still, it's the idea that Daphne would even remember I was in Anaheim at all. I reach for the notecards from the Fan-Tastic basket and select a Grumpy dwarf card. I write:

> Dear Daphne,
>   I am happy to be a part of it. Thanks for the basket. I'm sleepy now, so I'm going to have a bath.
>   Kate

Stupid. But I don't care. Maybe I'll give it to her on Monday. Maybe I'll leave it in my bag and discover it two months from now. I fill a bath, plop in a fizzy bomb, pour myself another vodka, and marinate in the delish rose vapors. I have one hour before the fan dinner, so I veg in front of some reality TV. Wrapped in my toweling robe, sipping my cocktail, I watch some folks grabbing their fifteen minutes.

All too soon it's time for the evening session of the fan extravaganza. Strangely enough, however, this time it's a bit easier. Maybe it's the bath, or maybe—just maybe—I'm getting used to it.

* * *

Seated on a banquet dais facing an audience of a thousand fans sitting at tables in a large, bland conference room, I feel as though we are doing a soap tableau of the Last Supper. We Soap Disciples are posturing and gesturing and trying to eat pieces of rubber chicken as pocket cameras flash. A couple of buff actors stand up. They holler and wave and do the lounge singer point a half dozen times until the fans are really whipped up.

They scream for flesh: "Take it off! Take it off!" I sip my martini and smile with the supreme confidence that there will be no stripping in a place like Disneyland. I am mistaken. *Snap, snap, whoosh.* Both actors have torn off their shirts in a tribal display of virility and are whirling them around their heads. Of course, they do not hurl them into the audience, despite pleas. I know for a fact that one is a Prada and the other a Dolce. One can only go so far to appease the fans.

Oblivious to the Chippendales show on the dais, an unseen announcer begins to introduce each actor. The audience responds with applause and catcalls as they each stand to take a bow. I worry about my own status and am suddenly nervous. What if no one cheers? I notice that degrees of popularity can be measured by the audience's response, rather like a clapometer. A waiter quietly delivers another martini, unbidden, and I eat the two olives and pick my teeth with the orange palm tree stirrer. Suddenly, my name is called and I almost choke on the drink, while trying to smile.

"I'd better go in at once," said Alice. And in she went, and there was a dead silence the moment she appeared.

I can hear nothing. I am deaf. I stand. I smile and wave, and then notice that everyone in the audience is waving their arms, mouthing my name and—yes—cheering and clapping. As if my ears have popped while coming in for a landing, I can suddenly hear the whistling and applause. People are cheering, and in an instant I am redeemed. After a day of signing my name 640 times, I can finally take my place with the other Apostles at a $149-a-plate dinner at Disneyland. I've arrived!

Alice glanced nervously along the table as she walked up the large hall and noticed that there were fifty guests, of all kinds: some were animals, some birds, and there were even a few flowers among them.

Tellingly, I occupy the Judas seat in the tableau. I am between Gore Ivanov, one of the erstwhile strippers (who has since rebuttoned his Dolce), and his onscreen mother, a popular actress of a certain age who recounts all of her recent plastic surgeries throughout the hors d'oeuvres. I feign interest and make a mental note of her doctor's name for the day when my own face crumbles into my soup plate.

Staring out over the room, I try to analyze these people—our fans, our audience . . . without whom, as Daphne reminded me, we are indeed nothing. They appear to be fairly normal, mostly women of varying ages, some with teenage daughters, and a handful of men. Somehow it is oddly comforting to be in a room filled with people who watch the show. It makes soap opera feel like theatre for a moment, as if there is an intimacy to sharing your performance—even though we are not acting now. Well, some of us are not. I wonder if I will think about these people when I go back to work on Monday? Jenna, Mandee, Adelaide, Kaitlyn, Tony and Deena, Albert Green III. I doubt that I will remember them as individuals, but perhaps some sense of their collective warmth and friendliness may stay with me. As I gaze down into the bottom of yet another empty martini glass, it occurs to me that it is unlikely anything from tonight will stay with me other than a massive hangover.

Looking up, I catch the eye of a woman sitting at one of the front tables wearing a red sweatshirt across which a felt Rudolph the Red-Nosed Reindeer leaps, and the message HO HO HO is emblazoned. She raises her glass to me. I smile back. I wonder where she is from, what brought her here, and what is the story of her life. I also wonder where she keeps her Rudolph sweatshirt all year around. Under the bed in a box? Holiday clothing. An odd concept. The woman grins knowingly, as if the absurdity of our situation at this fan dinner is also apparent to her. She points to something on her sweatshirt. A button I had not noticed. I squint my eyes. My jaw drops. It is a button with my face on it. My face is smiling back at me from a homemade badge on a stranger's HO HO HO holiday sweatshirt. My face!

I look around the room for someone—the authorities, the Fashion Police, a governing soap opera body—that would remove the offending object. But there is no one. And even if I explained my predicament—the odd fact that a complete stranger has a photo of me pinned to her breast, across which also stampedes a large jolly subarctic deer—what would anyone do? We soap stars are here to be admired as we chew our food, and admired we shall be. Fair enough. I cradle my empty martini glass in my hands and contemplate what might have motivated this lady to compress my likeness between two plastic discs and affix them to her happy sweatshirt. O-ka-ay. I am not Bono, not Bowie, certainly not our beloved Madonna—not even Clay Aiken, for God's sake. Do you suppose that if I pointed this out, she might reconsider her misdemeanor and remove the pin with a toss of her head, braying loudly, "What was I thinking?" Then her mistake would be rectified, all would be balanced once more, and she would not, in fact, be crazy.

None of this is likely to occur. I am seated on an altar, breaking bread with two soap queens: one a quasi-male stripper, the other a well-preserved, perhaps mummified, veteran, and I am delivering the goods, smiling, and not giving away plot points . . . yet.

I look back at the lady with Rudolph. She is eating cake, intent upon a conversation with her neighbor. I am forgotten at the moment, even though this small image of me hovers inches from her chewing chin. What would I think if I was that button sitting on her breast? Probably that the actress impersonating me up on the dais should stop drinking. Point taken. I order another martini.

> "O Looking Glass Creatures," quoth Alice, "draw near.
> " 'Tis an honor to see me, a favor to hear.
> 'Tis a privilege high to have dinner and tea
> Along with the Red Queen, the White Queen and me."

During dessert, an actor from *The Young and the Restless* grabs the microphone and conducts a Q&A, à la Oprah. Surprisingly, this turns out to be my favorite portion of the entire day. Various fans stand and ask questions directly to the actor of their choice. By this time, I have lost track of how many martinis I have consumed, so I'm not sure whether the questions are genuinely funny or I am just lubed enough to think that everything is hilarious. The fans seem to be on target, masters of each and every soap storyline, and they do not miss a chance to pin down their favorite characters. They ask why certain characters begin affairs even before their ex's coffin has been nailed shut, or who the real birth mothers are, or where all the money is, or—to me—how I intend to catch the vampires.

It's pretty funny to watch the actors bob and weave. Most of us let loose and make jocular comments about the current storylines of our show. A few actually complain about the direction that their character is taking, others seem thankful to have a job, and a minority, like me, are glib. I dodge the predictable silver bullet questions by laying little red herring tidbits about mobsters and aliens. I know there is a story in the pipeline that's borrowed from *Starman,* and I drop a few hints. Nigel is down front, giving me an obvious slash-to-the-throat sign when he sees where I'm heading. I promptly shut up and leave everyone hanging—which seems to work out. The room erupts just as the MC wishes everyone a fond good night.

We depart the dais like gods departing Mount Olympus, with excessive adoration and applause showering down. I'm starting to like being a rock

star, and I wave and blow kisses along with the best of them, with my latest martini clutched to my chest. I'm still waving and kissing when I walk
right into Nigel, who is standing just offstage, glowering.

"You, Miss Glamour, are on my shit list. Do not toy with future storylines in front of the fans, and never guzzle countless cocktails in public.
You'll be the Lush of the Week in *SOD* if you're not more careful."

"Who giz a sheet?" I slur purposely and hand him my drink.

He walks Lauren and me to our rooms, and gives us each a peck on the
cheek. Eventually, I fall asleep to David Letterman's musical guest, Phil
Collins.

Monday morning

"THERE!" SAYS RUBEN PROUDLY and with finality. "Dressing you gives me fits, Kate, but we've finally got it right! It's not girlie, but it's not über-butch, either."

What it is is Rifat Ozbek for Pollini, and the warm taupe dress has a fit to die for. "There's a jacket that goes over it," he continues, "but leave it off for the wedding. The cut of the neckline really sets off your shoulders. You look fantastic, Kate, at least I think so."

Ruben's right—I look good, which takes some of the sting out of having to participate in another benighted wedding, even though this one has some redeeming qualities in terms of delicious plot ramifications. This time it's Burke Chaney and Jennifer Abell (Kirk and Amber) tying the knot, but mercifully, I'm just a guest, not a bridesmaid. Burke was Devon's one-time true love, the man who was driving at the time of the catastrophic car crash, when I took over the role. Because she's now come out as a lesbian, Devon is merely wistful, not devastated over losing him to Jennifer. More-over, detective that she is, Devon suspects that the marriage may be a sham. Amber is pregnant with Trent's baby (make that Jennifer is pregnant with Philip Salisbury's baby) and Trent, playing Philip as a cad, refuses to marry her. Then there is the question of what Regina thinks about Burke marrying her younger sister, even though she's now involved with Laszlo. After all, if she slipped Burke a mickey because she was jealous of his rela-tionship with Devon, is it better or worse for her now that he's about to become her brother-in-law?

Who keeps all this straight? Pretty much everyone who watches. For regular viewers, an emotional involvement in the lives of the characters and an intimate knowledge of their past triumphs and peccadillos is what soaps are all about. If I hadn't realized it before, the session in Anaheim really brought the point home. When fans watch a confrontation between longtime characters, they see it through the filter of all the knowledge and emotion they've already invested in the show. It's all there in the room with them, and part of Daphne's genius is that she pushes all of us—writers and actors both—to tap into that understanding to deepen the experience for the viewer.

"Goin' to the chap-pel and we're gonna get ma-a-ar-ried . . ." Marty croons over the PA, badly. "Goin' to the chap-pel of love. I need everyone goin' to the chap-pel set for the wedding scene, please. Ladies and gentlemen, this is an All-Skate. Let's book it, people."

"Gotta go. Am I done, Charlie?"

"Absotively posilutely, cherub!" he says. "Here—take a look."

"Yeah. Oh yeah!" I smile as he twirls me in the chair. I look sleek. Charlie has corralled my thick hair into a chignon and given my forehead a trendy diagonal sweep of bangs, liberating me from the Shirley Temple curls, at least temporarily.

In the corridor on my way to the "church," I pass Meredith, who is proceeding with all deliberate speed toward the same destination. Marty will be having a hairy canary before she gets there. She is taking tiny baby steps, as if someone has bound her feet. A vision in lavender, she is wearing a huge Shall-We-Dance? ball gown worthy of Deborah Kerr as Anna Leonowens, waltzing with Yul Brynner in *The King and I.* She is also sporting a matching floor-length lace mantilla, even though she is to be the matron of honor, not the bride.

And now I'm puzzled. The dress is voluminous enough to conceal a platoon of Munchkins, so why is she mincing along rather than striding out fully? As always, of course, it's important to her to be the last one on the set, but she could solve that problem just by leaving her dressing room late. The real reason, I deduce, is that she's once again teetering on four-inch stilettos.

"Hey, Meredith," I say as I go by, "you must be wearing the hottest new Tüblöks under there. I've heard they're all the rage."

Meredith looks me up and down and crinkles up her nose. "Tüblök . . . that must be a new designer. I don't recognize the name, Kate, but these . . ." It takes considerable effort, but she manages to extend a well-turned ankle past the hem of her dress in order to expose her to-die-for jeweled ankle-wrap sandals, then shakes her hair at me and continues, ". . . these are René Caovilla."

"Tüblöks as in 'two blocks,' Meredith. Because that's about as far as you can walk in 'em. Unfortunately, the set is another thousand meters farther than that. The truth of the matter is that you might as well be wearing Doc Martens—your feet are entirely invisible. If the Tüblöks hurt that much, just take 'em off and walk barefoot. Otherwise you'll never get there."

Even though I know she's launching daggers out her eyeballs toward my spine I continue walking. That one was worth it.

"Hey now, aren't we stylin'!" says LaTrisa, giving me the once-over as I arrive on the set.

"You like, Tri?" I inquire.

"I do!" she responds with enthusiasm.

"Hey, that's my line!" says Amber in her bridal finery, only half in jest.

"No kidding, Kate, you should steal that look for your own self, girlfriend," LaTrisa adds with a twinkle.

"Awesome! Two thumbs up!" says Kirk approvingly. "I know I'm about to be a married man—"

"Not that that would ever stop you," I interrupt.

"But you look good enough that we could pick up where we left off."

Leave it, Kate, I tell myself. Don't even go there.

As Kirk leans over toward me, I become painfully aware that with my hair in an up-do, my ears are exposed. "Kate," he says in a whisper that threatens to become a nibble, "you're not fooling anyone with that gay act—at least you're not fooling me."

Just let that sleeping dog lie, I remind myself. You say, "No thank you."

"No thank you," I say out loud, startling myself. "Sorry, but I'm allergic to raspberry tart."

"What?" LaTrisa, Kirk, and Amber respond in unison.

"Oh, never mind."

Meredith is still inching down the hall on tippy-toes, and although she was too far away to hear the conversation between Kirk and me, she must have seen him lean over and whisper in my ear. Behind her I see a group of visitors on a guided tour, headed for the set. To my surprise, they thunder right past her and come up to me. "Devon . . . Ms. McPhee . . . Kate . . . could you . . . would you . . . ?"

"Of course. I'd be delighted." By the time I'm done with photos and autographs, both Charlie and Ruben are waiting for me, as is Maggie, Daphne's current lieutenant.

We've all decided that it's useless trying to keep up with Daphne's assistants; she chews them up and spits them out way too fast. The bad ones are summarily fired, often in front of cast and crew. The good ones, much as she might like to keep them, quickly leave for greener pastures and a less authoritarian employer-employee relationship. Because of the churn, there's no point learning their names, but Daphne long ago solved that problem. She addresses all of them as Maggie. So do we—it's just easier. This, apparently, was the name of her first assistant back when she began in television. To hear Daphne tell it, Maggie the First, aka Saint Maggie, was a paragon of virtue who could practically divine whatever her great leader needed at any given moment. She stayed with Daphne for many years. Clearly she had no life, until early one bright Tuesday morning she drove her car off a bridge into a lake.

But I digress. Hair, Wardrobe, and Maggie the XXIII await me—it can't be good news. "What's going on?" I ask.

"Is this what you're wearing?" Maggie asks.

Of course it is. What kind of question is that? Why would I come on set in anything other than what I'm wearing?

"Why yes, it is."

"Do you have a jacket that goes with that?" Maggie asks. I throw Ruben a look, but he is striving mightily to avoid making eye contact.

"Well, yes."

"Ah, we think you should wear a jacket," Maggie opines, as Ruben assiduously studies the tassel of the loafer on his left foot.

We do, do we? I wonder just who the fuck we *might be.*

"Well, certainly. That's fine. I'll wear the jacket if you like."

"I'll go back down and get it for you, Kate," Ruben volunteers, retreating down the corridor. Anything to escape.

"And your hair," Maggie continues.

"Is there a problem?" I ask.

"We think that it probably looks a bit too . . . messy," she replies.

"Messy?" I echo, incredulously.

"You know, messy . . ." says Charlie, pawing at his forehead.

"Aha," I say, mimicking his gesture and stroking my bangs.

"Perhaps a hat?" Maggie suggests, a bit too eagerly.

"Over a chignon?" I respond. "How about we just push them back?"

"Oh yes!" says Maggie with a sigh of relief. "Great idea. I'm so glad you thought of it, Kate. That would solve the problem."

"I'll go get a brush and some spray," Charlie offers, departing at a trot— like Ruben he can't leave fast enough.

Meredith floats up to Maggie and me, glances at the diagonal fringe on my forehead, stares hard at my naked shoulders, then scowls at Maggie with a why-hasn't-this-been-taken-care-of glower. She grasps the edges of her mantilla and flutters them delicately, like butterfly wings. As she does so, her dragon shadow reveals itself on the wall behind her, but by the time she opens her mouth to speak, the shadow has disappeared and she looks like a sugar cookie. "You know, Kate," she says affably, making a concerted effort to sound helpful, "you really should be wearing a jacket and a hat. For a church wedding, the head and the shoulders should be covered. Otherwise it's disrespectful."

Of course. It's all clear now. Kirk has nothing to do with this. Even before she saw him whisper in my ear, the Queen was having bang issues. Shoulder issues, too. I'm sure the tirade Meredith launched in private about my dress and my hair must have been a real barn burner. It's twisted, it's ridiculous, but who else would have such a meltdown about bangs and a jacket?

I look back and forth between Maggie and Meredith. Now it's Maggie who is passionately interested in her left shoe. I spend about three seconds trying to figure out how I want to respond—do I want to let it go, or am I ready to have it out? Quickly I decide enough is enough. I've been letting Meredith get away with her crap for entirely too long. We all have. If I cave on this one, there will be no end to it. I'm ready to rumble.

"It's fine, Meredith, really. Unlike you I don't act with my hair," I declare casually, trying to match her falsely chummy, passive-aggressive tone. "If you find that forcing me to get rid of my bangs and cover my shoulders makes me less threatening—and you a better actor . . ." I say, ". . . then fine. Peachy. As for the jacket on the dress, maybe that's not sufficient. Are you quite sure you wouldn't like me to change my outfit entirely?"

"No . . . no . . ." Maggie tries to intercede, but the fact that she is now blushing bright scarlet gives away the show.

"If it makes you feel better, I'll climb back into my black detective's pantsuit," I continue, my voice now rising. "Silly me. Of course not. Surely you'd prefer to select my outfit personally—something from the Janet Reno Collection, perhaps?"

"Here's the Ozbek jacket, Kate," says Ruben sheepishly as he returns.

"When you have a meltdown, don't browbeat others into doing your dirty work for you. If have a problem with me, Meredith, bring it to me," I scold. "At least have the guts to do it yourself."

"What the fuck is going on here?" Daphne demands sternly as she joins the discussion. Even more than usual, her face is askew. Half of it looks saggy, and her lipstick covers not just her mouth, but most of her philtrum—the space between her upper lip and her nose. She looks like I did when I was playing with Mom's lipstick when I was four.

Psst. Psst. Charlie heralds his return with two spritzes of Aqua Net. "C'mon, cherub, I'll pull those bangs back. It'll be okay, I promise," he says with a wink.

"Remind me never to eat another olive, even if everyone swears they're pitted," Daphne says.

"Excuse me?" says Maggie.

"There's always an unpitted one in the batch." Sure enough, the pale grey suit has an added black accessory: a bit of olive—probably kalamata, but maybe picholine—right above the breast pocket.

"Daphne," Maggie continues tentatively, "your lipstick is a little, um, smeared."

"It would appear that I can't even go to the dentist to replace a broken filling without this place going to hell in a handbag," Daphne resumes with an off-kilter scowl. She rubs her jaw. "Give me a mirror."

Charlie hands her the one he has brought with him. She frowns, but with only half of her face. "Shit. I put the lipstick on in the car on the way back, and until this fucking novocaine wears off I can't feel a thing. Maggie, why isn't this scene rolling?"

"Well," says Maggie, walking on eggshells, "we've had a little problem here with Kate's hair and wardrobe."

"You mean Meredith had a little problem here with Kate's hair and wardrobe," I say.

"Well, I merely made a suggestion—" Meredith begins, fluttering her mantilla once more and trying to sound innocuous.

"Yeah, right—talk to Maggie about how this went down," I say toughly, with as much testosterone in my voice as I can muster. "Daphne, I want to cut my hair. It would be more in character anyway; this is absurd."

"Give me a memo. I'll consider it," she responds coldly. "Meanwhile, I refuse to burn another minute dealing with this. Kate, you will wear the jacket. Charlie, let the viewers see Ms. McPhee's forehead. Meredith, are you under the misapprehension that Regina, not Jennifer, is marrying Kirk?"

"No, Daphne."

"Then stop trying to upstage the bride. Lose the mantilla. Oh, and Ruben . . ."

"Yes, Daphne?"

"Next time Ms. Contini decides to garb herself like the Bride of Zorro, check with me first. Maggie—in my office, now!"

"Can we try to block this scene, please? Places, everyone. Smiles!" says Marty in his best Ricardo Montalban imitation.

"Zee plane! Zee plane!" chirps Trent from the sidelines as we all begin filling the pews.

"What?" says Amber. She looks lovely, as is her custom, but clueless, as is also her custom.

"Never mind. You're too young to remember, Amber."

• • •

INT. SAN CRISTOBAL CHURCH—NIGHT

MINISTER
Dearly beloved, we are gathered here together . . .

Boy, are we gathered—the gang's all here for the wedding of Burke and Jennifer. Except for perfunctory congratulations to the newlyweds, I don't have a lot of lines, but I'm gonna have fun in this scene anyway. What I get to do is flirt shamelessly during the ceremony. The object of my affection is Lacey Boudreaux, who will eventually become my vampire lover. She arrives in the company of Magda, Mallory's tutor, and is seated way across the church from me. Lacey is portrayed by Charlotte Landry, who is new to the cast. Very striking, with chestnut hair and pale, delicate skin, she has the rounded, cherubic face of a Victorian porcelain bisque doll. Visually, she's an inspired choice for the part, because she looks so very different from all of our oh-so-California blondes. The camera finds her, even in a crowd of wedding guests.

The two of us have a grand time exchanging furtive glances until we get to

MINISTER
I now pronounce you man and wife. You may kiss the bride.

"Cut! Let's set up the receiving line, pronto! Kate, you must be directly behind Charlotte and Selena."

JENNIFER
(to Burke)
Honey, I want you to meet Magda . . . Magda . . . I'm sorry, I'm blanking on your last name.

MAGDA
Janos [pronounced Yah-nosh].

JENNIFER
Magda is your niece's new tutor.

BURKE
I don't have a niece.

JENNIFER
Sure you do. Mallory is Regina's daughter.

BURKE
Of course. I'm still getting used to all this.

MAGDA
And this is my friend, Lacey Boudreaux.

DEVON
(coming right on Magda's heels)
Jennifer, take good care of this guy—he's a keeper. I wish you both many years of happiness.

> JENNIFER

Thank you, Devon.

Amber starts to give me a hug, then steps back and shakes hands instead.

> DEVON

And congratulations, Burke.

Kirk has no trouble giving me a full-body contact embrace, much to the quizzical stares of Amber and assorted other wedding guests.

> DEVON (CONT'D)
> (looking somewhat lasciviously at Lacey)

Jennifer's a lovely girl, but tell me . . . who are these wonderful ladies in front of me?

> BURKE

Just met them myself. Devon, this is Magda Janos, who tutors Mallory Abell in . . . in . . . in what subject?

> MAGDA

Math and science. It's a pleasure, Ms. . . . ?

> BURKE

Merrick. Devon Merrick. Devon is the ace investigator on the Hope Canyon Police Department.

> MAGDA

How do you do, Ms. Merrick. I'd like you to meet my friend, Lacey Boudreaux.

> DEVON

I feel like I know you already, Ms. Boudreaux.

December Saturday

1:53! 1:53!! 1:53!!!

It's a Saturday afternoon and I am in bed. A free weekend—finally. After weeks of heavy soap drama and fan shindigs, I don't need beauty sleep; I need a beauty coma. I begged off a date with Matt last night because I needed to crash at my pad. Alone. Well, alone except for Drusilla.

She wakes me at just before two in the afternoon to explain her starvation issues to me. I feel refreshed. I really needed the downtime. I open the shades and luxuriate in the warm winter sun while she sits on my chest, purring loudly and kneading my sternum. Her purrs are particularly loud, and when I realize they are being augmented by growls from my own stomach, I rouse myself to attend to both our hungers. As I fill her dish and contemplate what to do about feeding myself, I spy a BAFTA invite inside the empty cookie jar. BAFTA, the British Academy of Film and Television Arts, is holding its annual Christmas tea somewhere in Hancock Park. Unlike the huge BAFTA do in January, a see-and-be-seen showcase for those Brits (and Scots and Aussies and Kiwis) who are in the Oscar hunt, this is just expatriate actors drinking tea. Today, four to seven. That much I think I can handle.

When I talked to Matt last night, he'd said he'd probably come by this evening so we could go grab some dinner. I leave him a note:

Off to join my fellow countrymen—and women—
bonding over unhealthy sweets and caffeinated beverages.
Back by 7:30+/− Dinner at 8:00? Or call me.

K

I peer suspiciously outside at the weather. Pale sun; bright sky; probably about 65 to 68 degrees—typical December day. I ponder what to wear and search the invite for information. "Festive attire," it reads. What the fuck is that? Whatever it is, I'm sure I possess none of it. Drusilla noisily smacks her lips around the tinned tuna whilst I discuss various clothing options with her and eat my own culinary masterpiece of Trader Joe's peanut butter pretzels and black coffee. Shower, shave, and mascara later, I climb into a black Helmut Lang skinny suit with a Mickey Mouse T-shirt and strappy heels, and throw my still-long hair into a ponytail. I look fairly severe. Good. I dig around in my jewelry box for my mom's old diamond studs, but I can find only one. Emergency. I look in the bed, under the bed, in the shower, the sink, the cookie jar, and finally . . . victory! In the soap dish, where else? I bid adieu to Drusilla and wend my way to a civil cup of tea.

If this house had been located in England, we would have called it a stately home. It's immense. After dropping my car with the valet, I walk toward the grand entrance, passing en route the strolling carolers in Victorian costume. Once inside, I have to stand in line in the marble vestibule, give my name, and be formally introduced to a quite-proper-verging-on-stuffy older couple, who I believe must be ambassadors—or something. Or maybe just filthy rich. I tell them who I am and what I do, then watch as their eyes glaze over and flicker to the left of me to greet Colin Firth.

How cute is he? I think to myself. *If he were standing in my foyer, I wouldn't be spending much time chatting up a soap actress either.*

I saunter into an enormous, sparkling ballroom with a coffered ceiling. The cavernous room is painted linen cream; the floor is black-and-white marble squares, like a life-size chessboard. There's a twenty-foot Christmas tree, lights, holly, elves, fairies. Everything is perfect, a Dickensian wonderland, and I feel a giddy rush of childhood happiness as I stare open-mouthed at the sheer beauty of it all. Twinkly lights and evergreen garlands punctuated by tartan ribbons swathe all the archways and French doors, and an enormous fire crackles in the massive stone fireplace. Everything smells of pine and cinnamon. People are standing around laughing, with bone china cups in their hands and slabs of Christmas cake and miniature sandwiches balanced delicately on tiny plates. I hear but can't quite see a quartet playing in the corner; they are blocked by the huge Douglas fir. Wrapped gifts are stacked around the tree, which drips heirloom ornaments. I giggle at the sheer gorgeousness of it all and grab a teacup from a butler in full drag as he passes me. Holding a tray of clean cups, he nods toward a gigantic table laden with goodies and informs me, "China tea, Indian, and Typhoo are labeled in the three large teapots on the left, madam. Please let me know if you desire anything other." He retreats.

"Take some more tea," the March Hare said to Alice.

"I've had nothing yet," Alice replied, "so I can't take more."

"You mean you can't take less, said the Hatter: "it's very easy to take more than nothing."

Alice did not quite know what to say to this, so she helped herself to some tea and bread and butter.

I stand in the middle of the throng, sipping my hot, sweet Typhoo and staring out at the masses. I recognize some famous English actors: Saffron Burrows, Alan Cumming (who's Scottish, really), Jeremy Irons (beyond sexy), Brian Cox; and some others whose faces I know but whose names escape me. From the tastefully befuddled glances I get in return, I suspect I strike many others the same way—nameless but vaguely familiar. I wonder if Emma Thompson's here. I don't see her. Just as well. I would have hugged her around the knees, and that would have been embarrassing, even for me. What a good crowd, though. I walk back to the table, grab three cheese-and-pickle sandwiches, and glance out through the open windows. The wonderland continues outside—the rolling lawn is studded with several large oak trees strung with thousands of little paper lanterns. I let out a gasp.

"Pretty, isn't it?" says a voice nearby. I turn. It is the hostess. She smiles. "I get a bit overwhelmed at these functions, but I do my best," she says.

"I must say that your best is pretty good! It's a truly lovely party," I reply. She thanks me kindly, absentmindedly flicks her white hair out of her eyes, and glides away. My guess is that she was not yet out of her teens when she internalized the precept that the hostess must work the room and make a point of conversing pleasantly with each and every guest, and that she has now checked me off the to do list as having been spoken with. Next! I wander toward the lovely garden, enveloped in cool dusk air, passing the enormous tree on the way.

I know who it is immediately. I don't even look at him fully; I just glimpse a familiar profile out of the corner of my eye. The hairs on my neck bristle. A man—long dark locks, skinny—hunches over the grand piano in the corner. I know instantly it is Rafe. He is playing expansively, moving up and down the keyboard, exactly as I remember him. There are surely other members of the quartet, but I can no longer see them or hear them. My teacup rattles violently in my hand. Rafe. What is he doing here? I thought we had split the continents in a game of Risk. I take greater America and he keeps Europe. Not fair.

A panic attack of epic proportions begins in my toes and surfs its way up my legs and through my bowels. I feel myself growing at a very swift pace.

"Now I'm opening out like the largest telescope that ever was!" cried Alice. Just at this moment her head struck against the roof of the hall: in fact she was now rather more than nine feet high.

The wave of panic finally breaks like an enormous Hawaiian wave over the top of my dizzy head. As my breath catches in my throat, I go under. I flounder inside the heavy tunnel of water, gasping for air, drowning and swelling simultaneously. I burst to the surface; I splutter and cough, swimming nowhere, bobbing outrageously, an enormous hovercraft crashing through waves of humanity.

I gasp again. Cold air. I can breathe. I have somehow made it outside into the garden.

I heave to, docking next to an oak tree, my huge body mass leaning against the rough bark of the trunk. I am wheezing, trembling, mouthing words attached to no sentences. My teacup, full when I left the house, is empty—I have shaken all the liquid out of it. I search frantically with my eyes for something, what I don't know. Escape, I imagine. Perhaps in the form of a huge white steed, upon which sits Colin Firth with a kind smile. Or a gate. A gate would do nicely. I stammer the words "Gate, gate," and furtively peer around the large tree trunk. I am hidden from view of the house. Maybe no one saw the inflated woman masquerading as the QE2 ram her way out of the festivities.

As I turn, my eyes adjust to the bright lights of the party continuing on in the house. I see the unmistakably familiar silhouette of my ex-lover emerge from the shadows to stand under a Chinese lantern. I shudder. Maybe under cover of dusk I can make my escape over the garden wall. Stealing only a cup and the last smatterings of dignity, I push myself away from the tree and lumber toward the tall, vine-covered garden wall.

"Kate." The voice is so recognizable as to come directly from my subconscious. Still, I fight to believe I'm imagining it.

"Kate. I thought that was you." There it is again. The voice. I turn. Slowly. It is impossible to do anything else, I have grown so enormous.

Rafe appears oddly normal. Harmless, almost. Weak. He smiles his actor's smile, unnerving because it has been cultivated for the enjoyment of thousands yet is also for intimate use. A portmanteau smile. I shudder again.

"Hello, Kate . . ." Rafe speaks, his very British public school accent gratingly condescending. "How are you?"

"Fine. You?" I speak. I am amazed I am able. "I was just leaving." *Except that I cannot move. Jammed between the tree and the wall, I've become a hulking, inflatable garden ornament.*

"I'm all right, Kate." Rafe shifts his slender frame, his tuxedo raven black in the lantern light. "I came over to play this gig for the consul general. Went to college with his son, so I snagged a little holiday for Christmas to boot."

You always were a freeloader, I think maliciously, then chide myself instantly. Never mind that. Concentrate, Kate, concentrate. Escape is a necessity. My eyes rake the house for the closest doorway. How far? Ten feet, twenty feet tops. Two giant strides and I should be able to make it.

Rafe is speaking again. What he says now catches my complete attention. Everything becomes slow motion. . . .

"Leslie's here."

"Come, my head's free at last," said Alice in a tone of delight, which changed into alarm in another moment, when she found that her shoulders were nowhere to be found. All she could see, when she looked down, was an immense length of neck, which seemed to rise like a stalk out of a sea of green leaves that lay far below her.

The words leave his lips and fly to my ears, huge dragons of evil. They flap around me, slowly, heavily, mocking my wide-eyed stare. The wind rustles the trees. I am level now with the tallest oak in the garden, such is my panic. My enormous feet are rooted firmly in the lawn, and there is no escape from my fate.

"Where?" I whisper, rustling the leaves. "Where is she?"

"I heard you're on a soap?" he says.

"Where's Leslie?"

Slowly, as if in a dream, a long dress floats toward us, a beautiful face, glowing ivory skin, jet black hair, slender hands extended toward Rafe, who protectively reaches out his own bony pianist fingers and draws the goddess that is Leslie toward him. His arms encircle her. In contrast to Rafe, she is extraordinary. She is Helen of Troy.

"Kate . . ." Her beauty is momentarily betrayed by her cheap Essex accent. "What a surprise!" She snuggles voluptuously against Rafe's body. Leslie wears her stolen crown of girlfriend comfortably and proudly. And stranger still, without question as to her entitlement. I feel . . . inconvenient, as I guess I always was. I blink at both of them from my weighty position of fallen ex, even as something stirs in the pit of my stomach. A rallying spark of anger fires through my body. I am surprised to find that a glimmer of courage is flickering around my ankles. I am shrinking. Merciful God. I take a deep breath.

"Hello, Leslie." I address the woman responsible for so many of my sleepless nights. I notice I am almost level with her haunting periwinkle eyes by now. "How are you?"

"Oh, I'm so well, Kate!" she enthuses. I detect a change in her. A plumpness around her chin and chest. It succeeds only in making her even more exquisite.

My breathing is returning to normal; I am recovering somewhat, and the teacup has ceased to rattle in its saucer. I gently stoop to lay it on the stone path. As I rise, I glimpse something that promises to suck my body dry of its last drop of blood. Snug beneath the folds of Leslie's diaphanous dress is a gentle bulge. A fruitful bulge that is unmistakable. She's pregnant.

If escape was desperate before, it has now become mandatory. I simply make a move to leave. Murmuring an uncivil, "Excuse me," I brush close to Leslie. Not so close as to actually touch her, but close enough to feel the gloating rays emanating from her satisfyingly bountiful body. My panic is returning. Another wave of frantic anxiety threatens to engulf me.

A small sane part of my brain, the little nugget that remains protected somewhere, keeper perhaps of my true personality, calmly tries to gain control of a situation that is careening toward certain calamity.

"Kate," my little nugget speaks—slowly, as to an idiot, "Kate, this is all in your imagination. You are not a gargantuan iceberg afloat at a BAFTA tea party. You are an ordinary girl of ordinary size, facing a couple of demons from the past. Pull yourself together."

The tiny, decidedly military voice reaches me somehow, and I turn to face Rafe and Leslie. I am shaking again, but I attempt to stand straight. In a dignified voice I say, "Congratulations, Leslie. Congratulations." I let the words hang in the air, mindful that I do not specify that which I congratulate her for. I could just as easily be saying a big, "Fuck you very much for stealing my man." But I smile.

"Oh, thanks Kate. Thanks ever so. Yes, we're happy," Rafe answers, uncertainly.

"The baby is due in the spring." This time it's Leslie's syrupy voice. She smiles a small Mona Lisa smile of triumph.

This is my cue to exit. I turn on my heel and walk steadily toward the lights and noise of the party. Why did she want to win so completely? Had we been at war? Had I been living in a game whose rule book I had never read?

For a time I allow the party to swallow me up, golden lights and holiday gaiety drowning out the scary darkness of the encounter with my past, but I can't bring myself to talk to another soul. Finally, I mumble an adieu to the hostess, and somnambulate my way out the door. I fish out a crumpled valet ticket and wait for my car with a small clump of other departing guests.

The carolers serenade us, and what vicious singers they turn out to be. With cruel and bitter irony they segue from "What Child Is This?" to "Have Yourself a Merry Little Christmas." The valet brings the Honda around just in time. I fire it up and drive. And drive and drive.

"At any rate I'll never go there again!" said Alice as she picked her way through the wood. "It's the stupidest tea-party I ever was at in all my life."

I drive so far along Pacific Coast Highway that it is well past sunset by the time I reach Neptune's Net on the fringe of Malibu. It's not as if I drove here on purpose—this is just what showed up when I had to stop driving. I pull the car into the gravelly parking lot and wait my turn behind a surfer and a biker to buy a Corona. I cross over the highway, my beer hidden beneath my jacket, and perch on a rock. The tide is out. I sip the beer. I reach into my breast pocket, hoping to find an old packet of cigs—I so desperately need one to complete this picture of the destroyed heroine staring out to sea. Nada. Virginia Woolf, I recall, could roll her own, and carried papers and loose tobacco for just such a desperate occasion. The last die-hard surfer slowly walks to his truck, glancing curiously at the woman in the suit with a beer and no cigarette. The sobs arrive before I notice them. I cry uncontrollably as the dark blanket of night covers the beach.

That night I cuddle Drusilla so fiercely that she hisses and spits and re-moves herself to the club chair, which is covered in clothes. I need comfort. I can find none. I ache.

She sat down and began to cry again. "You ought to be ashamed of yourself," said Alice, "to go on crying in this way! Stop this moment, I tell you!" But she went on all the same, shedding gallons of tears, until there was a large pool all round her, about four inches deep and reaching half down the hall.

Monday morning / two days later

WELL, I'M NOT SURE what we can do about these." Christine is holding wet tea bags and a big bag of ice over my swollen eyes. On the way in to the studio I had called her from the car in a frenzy—I look like Rocky Balboa. I cried so much yesterday that my eyes were swollen shut when I woke up this morning.

"I wish I hadn't cried so much!" said Alice. "I shall be punished for it now, I suppose, by being drowned in my own tears!"

"Just get me through today," I plead. "I have a light day in Hope Canyon, little scenes with no content and of no consequence. I can be out by four and home in bed by five. I want to hide."

"Whatever you say." Christine sighs, and rewets the tea bags in the sink.

"My life revolves around tea," I growl ruefully.

Christine looks puzzled. She puts the bags back on my eyes and I hear her sit in a chair. "What happened, missy?" she asks.

"I saw Rafe."

I hear her gasp. "Where?"

"A BAFTA tea party. The fucker was playing the piano."

"Shit."

"And Leslie's pregnant."

"Oh my God." Christine sounds appropriately horrified. "My God," she repeats. "And neither one of them said anything like 'I'm sorry'?"

"As in, 'Sorry I was fucking your best friend,' or, 'Sorry I was fucking your boyfriend?' or, 'Sorry we never told you'?" I shake my head no.

"Any of those would have been insufficient, but would have at least acknowledged hurting you," she says.

"Rafe never was any good at conflict at all," I explain. "We never had an argument in seven years—ever—because he never would state his case. He's very, very English that way."

"Very, very my ass," says Christine.

"Like Prince Charles." We fall silent. There is nothing left to say. Both of us ponder my position on the shitty birdcage bottom tray of romance.

They call the scenes directly ahead of me. I have to get ready.

"C'mon, sister." Christine puts her arms around me and helps me up. She has her makeup kit with her—I cannot face the bustle of Gossip Central. Slowly I begin to look functional. I drink some hot coffee and eat a bagel, the first thing to pass my lips since the beer on Saturday night. Between sips and nibbles I tell Christine what happened—my panic attack, Rafe and the triumphant Leslie, the baby, the carolers, the sobs on the beach, the ocean of tears at home. Tears prick my eyes as I come to the end of the miserable tale.

"Kate, that's about all the excess humidity around your eyeballs I'm going to put up with," says Christine with mock tough-love sternness as she soaks up the wetness with a Kleenex. "Ruin your mascara and die—I'm only doin' this once today, okay?"

Soon enough I am called to set and I numbly go through the motions as Devon Merrick. It is truly a day when I'm phoning it in. Afterward I flee down the back stairwell, where I collapse in a pile of sobs, and where Christine finds me. She hands me a mug of hot, sweet tea.

I drink it scalding hot and blubber between sobs, "It's final, isn't it." It's a statement, not a question.

Christine puts her arm around me and she talks—good, strong, down-to-earth Wisconsin sense. "It is final, and it's the pits. The hardest thing in the world to do is watch someone you love love someone else."

"You got that right. Why did she have to take him away from me like that?"

"Whoa there, Miss Kate. Don't hang this all on Leslie. Aren't you the girl who punched the lights out of the kick bag at the Dojang when Jay Park told you to pretend it was Rafe? What happened to make you let him off the hook?"

"She's pregnant. I told you that."

"Did I miss something—was this an immaculate conception? This may not be what you want to hear, but Leslie didn't get pregnant by herself. She couldn't have stolen him if he wasn't a willing participant. He's got just as much culpability as she does. And you know what? I don't hear any fat lady singing yet. This whole mess isn't over."

"I thought you agreed with me that it was final."

"No. As far as you're concerned, it's final. My God, I hope so—for your sake."

"I guess even after all this time I held out hope he'd come back to me," I confess, "but the baby changes everything."

"It changes everything and it changes nothing. What I think is that a player's a player, baby or no baby."

"Uh-huh."

"It's a pattern of behavior. He did it to you," she says, looking me straight in the eyes. "What makes you think he won't do it to her? And is that really the kind of man you want?"

I look at her as I listen. Where do guardian angels come from? Here one sits beside me in human form. An average-looking lady, unruly wavy hair, lumpy sweater, normal jeans. But she glows from within, her absolute human essence transforming her into one of heaven's messengers. I wonder at my luck to have met Christine, and I see that Leslie hasn't won. To win she would have destroyed my ability to ever trust another woman again. She didn't succeed in that. I hug Christine.

"What's that for? Don't you get all sloppy on me!" She smiles kindly, her eyes gentle in her polished, clean face.

"Thank you for talking," I whisper, not trusting myself not to get emotional again.

"I'll get you another cup of tea," she says as she squeezes my hand and runs up the stairs.

The door slams and echoes down the concrete stairwell. I feel more alone than ever in my whole life. I want to call Daniel, my brother. I resolve to get up early in the morning and call London. He'll probably be at the clinic. He never liked Rafe, and he was the first to accuse Leslie of going behind my back. I want a cigarette. I pick the pale polish off my nails instead.

I head for home, throw some cat food into a bowl, leap out of my clothes, and dive into the bed at an hour when most people haven't had dinner yet. I set the alarm for a little after four A.M. so I can get up and call Daniel during his lunch hour. I'm a little more gentle with Drusilla this time, and she nestles in the crook of my arm. Nevertheless, I cry myself to sleep once again.

Tuesday Morning

4:06! 4:06!! 4:06!!!

The alarm goes off just as I'd set it. The fact that I did this to myself doesn't make me any more cheerful about being roused at this ungodly hour, and I stare at the ceiling as the minutes go by. 4:06—4:06—4:06—4:06—4:06—4:06—4:07—4:07 flashes above me at maddeningly regular intervals.

But wait a minute—what else is up there? Something just barely visible at the corner of the 7 in 4:07, well, now the 8 in 4:08. There's definitely something up there—animal, vegetable, or mineral? I watch it long enough to assure myself that it's definitely not animal, then stagger unsteadily to my feet on the mattress. Extending both arms over my head, I walk my hands along the ceiling till I get to my quarry. I feel a hard, smooth edge, like stiff paper, and peel it off the ceiling.

My heart sinks when I turn on the light and realize that it's the ace of hearts. On it is a brief message:

Whoever he is, you're not over him yet.

Matt

Later the same day

CHRISTINE KNOCKS ON THE DOOR to my dressing room and enters bearing tea for my insides, tea bags for my eyelids, and a sturdy shoulder. Why do the British feel tea is the answer to all tragedies? For the second day in a row I called her on the way in to the studio. I am a basket case.

"Matt put the card up there yesterday," I explain between sniffles. "Sunday I was such a mess that I completely forgot to call him after not seeing him Saturday night. I didn't even realize I'd forgotten about him till I found the ace. When I finally talked to him this morning, he told me he'd snuck into the house twice—Saturday night and Sunday—thinking he'd try to come join me in bed. Not a bad plan, except that both times he got as far as the door to the bedroom and heard me crying."

"And now rightly enough, he wants to give you some space?"

"A whole continent's worth of space, actually—from sea to shining sea. He was offered a gig doing close-up magic in the lounge at a casino in Atlantic City. It's not great, but it's a foot in the door and it's certainly a step up from the anniversary and bar mitzvah circuit he's been working. He's already gone."

"Oh sweetie, he had potential, didn't he, but you just weren't ready for another guy yet—even if you thought you were, for a while. And shit, here comes Christmas, which can be especially brutal if you're trying to get over someone. What you need now, Kate, is a strategy to deal with the holidays," she says as she gives me a big maternal hug. "We need to head this one off at the pass because I can see it coming—left to your own devices you'll just wander around the Third Street Promenade, looking at all the nuclear families spending money on each other and crying whenever you see a pregnant lady. If it was up to you, I'm sure that you'd let December 25 come and go with no acknowledgment whatsoever."

She has me dead to rights. "So what do you recommend?"

"What you have to do is reclaim Christmas. Define it for yourself. Go out and get a tree. Put lights on it. Maybe have a party."

"Sounds like hair of the dog for an emotional hangover," I say, trying to keep my inner cynic at bay.

"Because that's exactly what it is."

* * *

"Hey, Mzee!" I say as cheerfully as I can manage. The truth is that I'd been hoping he wasn't there. I don't have a lot of scenes again today, but there's a huge gap between them, and I'd wanted just to climb up his ladder and hide out till I was needed again. Christine's words are ricocheting around inside my head, but there's so much other noise in there that I'm having trouble trying to sort it all out.

"Hello, Kate," he says warmly. "You okay?" He furrows his bushy brows. "You look like you maybe have something in your eye."

I decide not to go into it with him. Someday, perhaps, but not now. There is a corresponding flicker in his eyes that suggests he understands and has the same thought—Eventually she'll tell me, his sympathetic eyes seem to be saying, but not today.

I hang out up in the rigging till I'm called for the last scene of the day.

"Mzee," I say as I'm climbing down, "let me ask you . . . do you think I should get a Christmas tree? It's just me this year, well, me and my cat. Do you think it's worth it?"

"If you do something, something happens," he responds enigmatically, with a half smile. "If you don't, nothing happens."

19

The next Saturday

"CAN I HELP YOU?" says the man with the faint aroma of snake oil about him.

"Er, yes, I'm looking for a tree," I say uncertainly.

I'm not at all sure I should be here, except that everyone has been telling me what a good idea it is. *Here* is Santa's Forest, a Christmas tree lot that sits on a vacant commercial property in the lower east side of Hollywood. I vaguely remember its immediate past incarnation: the lot was a pumpkin emporium just eight weeks ago.

"Well, you've come to the right place, little lady. How big a tree would you like?"

Shit. How the hell should I know?

I put my hand straight up over my head. "About this tall, maybe a little taller. It has to fit in my living room."

"So, nine to ten feet then. Let's have a look over here."

The salesman leads me to an aisle in his rootless forest and holds out one specimen for my inspection.

"Now this one's a beauty."

"Ah . . ." His "beauty" has two tops and a gaping hole in the middle of the side he presents to me.

"Don't worry about that little gap, miss. We can wire in a branch to fill it."

"Ah, I think I'd rather not have to do that, thank you."

"Okay then, how about this one?"

"Not too bad . . ." The shape is about right. It has one and only one top.

"You don't want that one," interjects a male voice next to me.

"I don't?"

"That's the one they tried to sell me just a couple of minutes ago. Feel it—it's way too dry." I do. He's right.

The salesman tries to hide his irritation. "Well then," he says, "what about this one?"

"Okay," I say, "the shape is good, but I think we'd have to lop off the bottom foot or so. Too tall."

"No problem. Easy to do," says the salesman with a large smile. "I'll have the guys get right on it."

I don't doubt him for a moment. Santa's Forest is a noisy place, filled with young Latino men in red plush Santa hats, white pompoms bobbing absurdly as they perform surgery on the trees, wielding chain saws and hammers to level the bottoms and affix them to tree stands.

"Well then, are you going to give it to her for the eight-foot price?" It's the same guy. I look at the salesman, who remains silent. "These babies are priced by the foot," he continues, "and at these prices, when you lop off that much you're tossing away thirty dollars' worth of tree, easy, maybe more."

"Wait a minute," I say. "How much is this tree?" The salesman is now looking mighty unhappy.

"Sorry to butt in," the fellow shopper says to me apologetically, "but there's no sense paying for something they're just going to cut off."

"I can let you have this one for twenty-five dollars off, call it a hundred seventy-five," says the salesman, recovering his air of bravado.

"What??" I am flabbergasted.

"That's way too much," concurs my advocate.

"Perhaps you two would just like to select a tree together and then I'll give you a special price," says the salesman, the last of his counterfeit good nature wearing thin.

"Fine. I think what we're gonna do is go pick out a tree together—someplace else," says the guy.

"Ah . . ."

"Let me introduce myself. I'm Mark van Gelder. I'm not an ax murderer, and I don't usually make myself a participant in other people's Christmas tree transactions, but I could see you were about to get ripped off."

He's about thirty-five. Brown hair, tousled. Brown eyes, rimless glasses that seem to have found a permanent home halfway down his nose. Long charcoal grey coat that almost brushes the ground. Clumpy boots. Scruffy, but not weekend scruffy, like those guys who let their beards go for two days, then clean up Monday morning and put on a three-piece suit. Genuine scruffy—Mark strikes me as a guy whose idea of getting dressed for work is putting on a sweatshirt and long pants. Still, he seems kind, and I believe him about not being an ax murderer.

"Kate. Kate McPhee. And don't apologize. This is the first time I've bought a tree in this country. The prices are staggering."

"Let's go, Kate. I think I saw another lot down the street."

Sure enough. I follow his big Expedition a couple of blocks till we see a sweetly hand-lettered sign reading KRYPTONITE HIPPOS KRYSTMAS TREES. We pull in, park, and see a guy out front, some dads and moms, and a dozen or so fourteen-year-old boys working the lot, all of whom are wearing green T-shirts emblazoned with KH.

"Hi, I'm Coach Farooz," says the guy who greets us. "Help yourself to a cup of coffee; cream and sugar are over there next to my wife, Zenobia. As far as trees go, just look around. Take all the time you want. If and when you need help, ask a Hippo."

"Excuse me?"

"These guys are my Kryptonite Hippos, AYSO Region 78. We're raising money to go to a soccer tournament in Hawaii this summer, and one of the ways we're doing it is with this tree lot."

Deshondré, one of the Hippos, helps us find a tree, after which other members of the team fit it to a water bucket stand and tie it up for the trip home. Zenobia, who is working the cash register, throws in a free wreath and a nickel bag of mistletoe. Grand total: $58. "I have to ask," I say to Deshondré, who turns out to be a midfielder. "How did you guys come up with the name 'Kryptonite Hippos'?"

"Kryptonite's green and hippos are, well . . . Uniforms are green and silver—light grey, anyway," he replies. "Had to have a name that went with the colors. Not as good as we did last year, but it was the best we could come up with."

"What was last year?" Mark asks.

"Last year we were orange and black," he says, "so we were the Carrots of Death."

By the time we get out to the parking lot, a dad-and-Hippo duo has already hoisted the tree onto the roof rack of Mark's Expedition and is in the process of tying it down. "Ah, that's the wrong . . ."

"No, actually it's okay," says Mark. "You're gonna need help getting it into your house anyway, Kate. It doesn't matter if I follow you home with the tree on top of my car or on top of yours. But first, food!"

I follow him to a little organic soup-and-sandwich place on Melrose Avenue. "Wait a minute, Kate. Before we go in, I have to let Nietzsche out of the car."

"Nietzsche?"

"Nietzsche. My dachshund. I don't leave him for long because he has a weak bladder. C'mon, Nietzsche," he says, opening the tailgate. "Come to Daddy."

Nietzsche does a flying leap into Mark's arms, and is thereafter deposited on a strip of parkway grass, where he pees enough for a dog three times his size.

"Ready?"

"Oh sure," I say, "let's." But Mark is talking to his dog, not to me. Nietzsche runs back into his father's embrace.

"You're lucky he's not a Great Dane," I say as he lifts the dog back into the SUV.

"Oh no, that's Kierkegaard. His bladder's made of cast iron. I hope you're hungry—I'm starving. Hey! What happened to your car?"

"Oh . . . the tire? That's just the little miniature spare from when I had a flat. Isn't it strange having two dogs of such vastly different sizes?"

"Four," he says. "Actually, there are four philosophers."

"Philosophers?"

"Well, dogs. There's Nietzsche, who you've already met, and Kierkegaard the Dane, and Sartre—"

"Let me guess—a poodle, right?"

"How'd you know?"

"I think I get the pattern. The fourth one's . . . lemme see . . ."

"Hobbes, a bulldog. He may look nasty, brutish, and short, but he's really a sweetie."

"So . . . you're an actor," he says once we're seated.

"Yeah. Right now I'm on a soap, *Live for Tomorrow*. So . . . you're a screenwriter," I reply.

"Yeah, well, no."

"Which is it?"

"So far my body of work has been in television, not film, even though that's eventually what I'd like to do."

"What kind of stuff?"

"Comedy. I wrote for MAWWAM."

"Okay, you've got me there. I haven't been able to spend as much time watching nighttime TV as I should to keep up."

"Sorry about the acronym. The full name was *Men and Women/Women and Men/It'll Never Work Out*. It was a new sitcom this season."

"You're using the past tense—there's a story to that, I suspect."

"With an unhappy ending, but I suppose I can't be surprised. We were the sacrificial lamb on the fall schedule—they put us up against *Monday Night Football*. We were invisible at first, but eventually our numbers started coming up. We were just starting to find our audience, but the network was impatient. They dropped us last week."

"I'm beginning to suspect that the holidays bring out the worst in network executives. That kind of bad news always seems to show up in December. I'm sorry it didn't work out for you, Mark."

"It's the nature of the business. The one thing all writers know when they get hired is that eventually they'll get let go, one way or another. I'm pretty good at not letting it get to me, in part because I've learned it has absolutely nothing to do with whether you're any good or not. Besides, now I have more time to work on my own stuff."

"What kind of stuff?"

"The screenwriter's stock in trade—treatments and spec scripts. I gotta have some ideas to pitch when I start knocking on doors. Which reminds me. . . . Excuse me for a moment." I expect him to get up and head for the men's room, but instead he turns himself slightly to the side, whips out a pad and pencil, and starts scribbling furiously. He writes for a good five minutes or so, then looks back up at me and resumes the conversation.

"Okay, I'm back," he says with a smile.

"You didn't go anywhere, and if you don't mind my asking, what were you doing?" I ask.

"Just making some notes about the Kryptonite Hippos," he says.

"What about 'em?"

"The kids were terrific, well-mannered but goofy. They've got a lot of comic potential. They've got soccer moms. . . . They've got annoying kid sisters. . . . And just the Hippos lineup is a hoot! Talk about your Rainbow Coalition! Remember all those World War II movies—the ones where the platoon sergeant hollers 'mail call,' and then starts flinging letters at the guys as he reads off their names: 'Greenbaum—yo!, Lincoln—yo!, O'Shaunessy—yo!, Rizzo—yo! . . .'"

"Gomez, Schmidt, Lindquist, Kowalski, MacGregor . . ." I pick up his thread, laughing.

All right! I think to myself. He's at least interesting. It's tough to tell, but under all that hair and shrubbery I suspect he's not bad looking. A little long in the face, maybe, but he makes me laugh. It's a beginning. I could do worse, and actually, as I think about it, I have.

We talk most of the afternoon till the sun starts to fade.

"Okay, here's my plan," he says as the waitress clears the plates. "Your assignment, Ms. McPhee, whether you decide to accept it or not, is to give me directions to your house, then go home and make a place for the tree in your living room."

Oh Gawd. He has no idea what a huge assignment that is. The living room is chaotic. My first job is to find the floor.

"So what's your job, then, Mr. van Gelder?"

"My assignment," he says, "is to go home and feed Nietzsche, Sartre, Hobbes, and Kierkegaard, then deliver the tree to your house, together with a nice bottle of wine. I assume you have lights, ornaments, extension cord, all that stuff."

"Nope."

"Then allow me to amend your assignment. Your assignment, Ms. McPhee, is to give me directions to your house, stop at Tarzhay on your way home for lights, ornaments, extension cord, and all that stuff, then make a place for the tree in your living room."

"I accept full responsibility for my assignment," I say as I write out my address and directions. "I'll even throw in some cheese and crackers, but I don't know you well enough yet for chestnuts roasting on an open fire. See you in what—about an hour and a half?"

"More like two hours, with the holiday traffic."

Notes to self:

1. *Never go Christmas shopping at Christmastime. Target on a weekend in December greatly explains the appeal of Buddhism.*
2. *Either find a housekeeper or take two weeks off and clean up the house yourself.*

Because Target was hell and cleaning up was worse, Jack Frost and Jack Daniel's are both nipping at my nose by the time I open the door to Mark, who is resplendent in a pair of fuzzy red felt reindeer antlers, from which dangle some mini-ornaments and blinking lights. He is also brandishing a bottle of Matanzas Creek merlot.

"Tree delivery, ma'am," he announces as he comes into the house. "Before we bring it inside, let me take a look at where you want it to go."

Mark cases the corner of the living room where I would like to place the tree and nods his approval. "Okay . . . just so I don't have to crawl under the tree later, let's plug the extension cord into the outlet now."

Leaving my front door ajar to bring in the tree, we head out to the street. I open the left rear door of the Expedition and am about to hop up and untie the tree when I am knocked backward by a canine stampede. A harlequin Dane, a bulldog, and a silver grey poodle explode from the vehicle and head straight into the house; Nietzsche brings up the rear.

"Mark?" I note sardonically that in this instance the doxie needed no assistance whatever in jumping from the SUV.

"They'll be fine once they settle down, honest."

By the time we walk the tree in, they're settled just fine. Kierkegaard has made himself at home on the couch, and Hobbes and Sartre are sprawled on the bed. Nietzsche runs circles around Mark's ankles while I go looking for Drusilla. I find her, safe but disgruntled, on top of the refrigerator. It's perfectly obvious to me that she's plotting her revenge, but whether it's on me or on the dogs is unclear.

The merlot does much to assuage my aggravation as I put some Johnny Cash Christmas music on the CD player and Mark sets about wrestling with the tree lights. "How many strings did you buy?" he asks.

"A dozen," I reply. "They were on special."

"What the hell—I'll use 'em all."

As we hang the last of the ornaments, I step back and say, "It's lovely, but it's missing something."

"Something on top, I think," he replies. "When I was a kid, we always had a star on top of the tree."

"In my house it was an angel," I say. "Damn, I should have bought one today. . . ."

"Too bad."

An idea dawns. "But I know what I can use instead. Your assignment, Mr. van Gelder, is to pour each of us a brandy while I go out to my car."

"I humbly accept my assignment, Ms. McPhee, provided you tell me where the glasses are."

I head out to the Honda, ransack the trunk, and exhume Meredith's gift basket. I loosen the red-clad Meredith doll from its ribbon moorings and bring it back in the house. "Ta da!" I exclaim triumphantly.

"Yeah, that'll work," he says with a nod, causing his antler headgear to quiver ridiculously on his head.

"But it doesn't have any lights—the top of the tree should light up."

"No problemo," he says, cradling the brandy snifter in his hand. "What I can do is wire her legs shut and coil a bunch of lights around them. She won't be able to walk, but her skirt will glow red."

"You have no idea how apropos that is," I say, giggling.

Mark moves over to put his arms around me. "Kate . . ." He is cute, and it's a really good hug, but I'm not sure.

"It's not you," I say as a brief vision of Rafe trots through my brain.

Mark senses my ambivalence and looks at me questioningly, but does not drop his arms or move away. I give him the short form of the Rafe-and-Leslie debacle, up to the BAFTA tea party and the "What Child Is This?" departing serenade from the carolers. "From a relationship standpoint, I guess you could consider me 'walking wounded,' " I say.

"What a blackguard!" he exclaims. "It's enough to wreck the Christmas spirit."

"That's certainly the way it was headed. It was always my favorite holiday, but after the tea party I was perfectly prepared to hide under a rock till January. As my friends started to put me back together, they gave me the job of reclaiming Christmas for myself."

"And you went looking for a Christmas tree as part of your therapy?" he asks.

"Yeah," I admit, "I guess that's basically it. They didn't even trust me to show up at somebody else's house for holiday dinner, so they've made me host Christmas for a bunch of them. Which is courting disaster since I don't know anything about cooking."

"It's not that tough to learn. What did you do after you left the tea party?"

"I drove forever. I finally got to this biker/surfer seafood shack in Malibu called Neptune's Net. I bought a beer and went and sat on the shore and cried my eyes out."

"That does it!" he exclaims. "In the morning, Good Miss Kate, your therapy continues. You are well begun on the effort to reclaim Christmas. Now, if you would allow me, it would be an honor and my great pleasure to help you take back the beach and the ocean. It would be a shame for you to continue thinking of them as places for tears and sorrow. Tomorrow we are going to load up the Expedition with balls and Frisbees and dogs; we will stop to have a sumptuous yet casual seafood repast at Neptune's Net, then head for Dog Beach."

"Dog Beach?"

"At Leo Carrillo right near Neptune's Net, people bring their dogs to romp in the surf."

"Don't they fight?"

"Actually, they all seem to do fine. There's probably a lesson for world peace in there somewhere, but I've had too much brandy to be eloquent about it. Just a thought, but it seems to me that to get over Rafe you need to spend some time having fun with a nice guy. I think I qualify. No strings attached."

"If you rummage through the CDs over there, I think you'll find Elvis's version of 'Help Me Make It Through the Night,'" I say, only half in jest.

He kisses me instead as Nietzsche tries to insinuate himself between us.

"You're sure I'm not just fodder for some screenplay or other?"

"Positive," he says, kissing me again and taking my hand.

. . .

A stab of nervousness catches me off guard as Mark leads me toward the bedroom. En route I guzzle the last of my brandy for Dutch courage. When first-time sex is about to transpire, there is a moment for me where I hold my breath in anticipation of two things:

1. He is proficient—no pawing or dithering allowed; and
2. Everything is shipshape down there.

That's because the last thing we girls ever talk about is size (liar, liar, pants on fire).

Tonight, however, I need not worry. Behind the spectacles lies a very healthy American male in sheep's clothing. He has jammed me up against the closet and is peeling off layers of our clothing when I surface to gulp air.

"Have you got something?" he asks hoarsely, while masterfully unhooking my bra with one flick of his finger. For a second I consider confessing that I have the beginnings of a cold, but then realize he means a prophylactic.

"Ah, bedside table."

Brilliantly he steers us toward the bed and gently lowers both our bodies whilst searching in the drawer for a slim foil envelope. Good multitasker. I'm impressed. "Where?" he asks with a sense of urgency.

"Okay, hang on." He rolls off me and I start my search. This does not deter Mark, however, and he continues his mission for total nudity. I rum-mage about in the drawer, but it's getting very hard to concentrate.

"I can't find them. Crap." Breathlessly I sit up on the bed. As Mark turns to face me, an enormous Scooby Doo head rises over his shoulder.

"What's he doing in here?" I shriek. Mark, dressed only in his Calvin Kleins, turns around to stare at the Great Dane.

"Fuck off, Kierkegaard." He tosses a shoe at him, which hits Hobbes right on the nose. He yelps.

"Do you sell tickets?" I ask, fishing around in the second drawer now, whilst his four dogs file in and take their places in the peanut gallery.

"Oh Jesus, let me get rid of them." He stands, which is admittedly a tri-fle difficult for him in his current state.

"Fuck off and fuck off." He is herding them out of the bedroom when I tell him the bad news.

"We have to go to the market."

After a feverish struggle to dress again, we find ourselves outside Ralphs. "You better go in by yourself," I inform him sheepishly. "I don't want any tabloids reporting that I was buying the special ribbed kind, you know."

He leans back in the Expedition driver's seat, running his hands over his face and hair as if to shake himself out of his amatory state. I giggle.

"You owe me big-time, madam," he says as he peers sexily over his glasses. *Yes, I do, I think to myself.*

He climbs out of the car and gallantly strides over to the store, gathering his long wool coat around him. He looks very desirable and erudite as he enters Ralphs to hunt down a latex shield. It is oddly seedy, but necessary.

He returns with a bouquet of supermarket flowers anchored by a helium balloon in the shape of a Christmas angel. Taped to her halo is a packet of Trojans.

"Your knight has returned." He slides into the car, grabs me, and kisses me. He drives back at about eighty miles per hour.

"Where were we?"

The dogs have settled once again around the bedroom in anticipation of our return, and sit up eagerly, panting, waiting for the show to start.

"Um, Mark, I don't think I can do this with them watching." I'm step-ping out of my jeans as Mark is dimming the lights.

"You're an actress, aren't you?"

"But it's weird."

"I know." He has the look of a man about to explode as he strides pur-posefully toward me, removing his glasses and setting them next to the bed. I'm suddenly feeling a bit self-conscious and, alas, all too sober.

"Do you want a drink?"

"No."

"Can we put them outside?"

"They'll bark."

"But—"

"Jesus. Stop talking." We are back to second base and I'm gazing up at a really cute man when I feel a cold canine nose on my toe.

I leap out of bed. "That's just gross!" I yell, stepping on Nietzsche, who yelps also, setting up a domino effect of barks and howls.

Then all hell breaks loose. Mark jumps up, crashing around, booting dogs in all directions and yelling obscenities. In his cotton Y-fronts and with the sound turned down, he could be one of those funny "Fruit of the Loom" commercials. I jump back into the bed and huddle down, watching a stranger flap about in my bedroom. Finally all the dogs are in the other room and the door firmly locked, but not before Mark has grabbed another bottle of wine and the remote control.

"Wanna watch Letterman?" he asks, climbing into bed and putting on his glasses.

"Oh, okay." I'm nonplussed.

I figure perhaps he feels embarrassed by his display of irritation at the dogs and wants to cool off. . . . Or perhaps he is sensitive to my discomfort over his display of irritation at the dogs, or perhaps his irritation over the dogs has put him off the whole idea. It feels strange, yet not uncomfortable, lying close to this man I met today buying a Christmas tree. This almost naked man. I am puzzled by his sudden inertia, but he does know exactly what he's doing. We lie under the sheets, side by side, watching Dave and sipping merlot, laughing at the same jokes.

Then he moves in for the kill.

* * *

6:34! 6:34!! 6:34!!!

It's 6:34 A.M., Pacific Ceiling Time. I didn't set the alarm, but I know exactly what time it is because I'm lying on the floor looking up at the ceiling, having fallen out of my bed. Even without me, there's a population of four still in it. Make that a dogulation—everyone remaining on the mattress has four legs and a tail. Of the group it's Hobbes who's the real bed hog. And he's frightfully good at it. He's now sprawled on my side of the bed, because every time I moved, he moved, altering his sleeping position to conform to my body. He kept nudging me farther to the edge until he finally pushed me off.

Mark is already up. He's in the living room, writing more notes.

"Good morning," I say softly.

"Morning," he says, with a soft smile. "You're up early."

"Hobbes pushed me out of bed," I say.

"Oh yes, well, he does that," Mark replies calmly but kindly, finally looking over the top of his glasses. "Coffee's ready—I hope you like it strong. I went out for bagels and cream cheese. Your fridge was empty. Bought some extra cat food and toilet paper as well."

A man who made coffee and brought breakfast. I could get used to that.

"I hope you slept well till he misbehaved."

"Sort of, or at least I did, but Kierkegaard started running in his sleep and bumping me in the back with his ankles."

"Actually, those are his knees."

"Have you seen Drusilla?"

"Sorry."

I go to the kitchen in search of the promised coffee and find a small poinsettia on the counter, to which the helium angel is now attached. Not seeing Drusilla, I shake the box of Friskies, which usually gets her attention. Unfortunately the noise attracts four yapping dogs, but zero cats. "Incoming! Incoming! Mark—do you have any food for these guys with you?" I holler toward the living room from my beleaguered position in the kitchen.

"In the Expedition," he calls over his shoulder, scurrying out. "Be right back."

Mark returns with a large sack of Science Diet. Moments later, peace is restored and all is quiet, save for heavy-duty sounds of munching and chomping.

Meanwhile, Drusilla enters the kitchen from parts unknown. Sartre looks at her as a curiosity. Kierkegaard looks at her as a potential hors d'oeuvre. Hobbes comes over to her and gives her rear end a sniff—in the manner of the tried-and-true doggie greeting—and gets a hiss and a swat to his nose for his pains.

"Okay, guys," Mark says, addressing the dogs with mock seriousness. "Listen up. The cat is off-limits. There will be no—and I mean absolutely *no*—kitty harassment." The four of them look suitably chastened. "Now, we're going to have an outing. You must be on your very best behavior. Your job—all of you—is to make sure Kate has a good time." As if in response, Sartre comes over and gives me an affectionate nuzzle.

"Kate, dress in layers," Mark advises. "It will get warm in the middle of the day, but if the wind picks up or you get damp from the salt spray, you'll want something to keep the chill off."

I head into the bathroom as Mark takes the dogs out back to make sure they have emptied their bladders for the car ride. He returns to find me fiddling with my eyelash curler. "Oh no you don't!" he exclaims, coming up behind me. I back up into his encircling arms and contemplate the vision of the two of us in the bathroom mirror. "This isn't supposed to be work, remember?" he says, chiding me gently. "Besides, you look lovely in just your naked face . . ." A small wispy smile flashes across his face, wrinkling the corners of his eyes. ". . . and naked other things, too."

We pile in the SUV and haul it for the ocean. It is indeed a glorious

Southern California winter day, or at least what passes for winter here. It is crystal clear and 73 degrees as we drive up PCH through Malibu. We leave the four philosophers in the Expedition while Mark and I gorge ourselves on mountains of fresh shrimp, clams, and crab. "You see people here eating nachos and chili dogs—I think they're nuts," Mark confides as he dismembers a crab and dunks the succulent red-and-white flesh into a vat of lemon butter. It seems that we consume a pint of melted butter and a quart of tartar sauce between us; we wash it all down with icy cold beer. Surrounded by paper plates and plastic forks and empty shells—the detritus of a great meal—we sit on the funky patio, looking out on the Pacific's perfect rollers just across the highway. Life is good.

It's a short trip from the restaurant to the beach parking lot, which despite the clear day is almost empty. Mark opens the doors and the four dogs spill out and head for the sand. "Technically they're supposed to be on six-foot leashes," he informs me, "but in the winter nobody much cares." Mark throws his arm around my shoulder as we walk along the water. Nietzsche is by his side. Kierkegaard is running ahead of us, playing tag with the incoming tide. Sartre is in frolic mode, joyously porpoising through the spume in a most unpoodleish manner. "The saltwater helps fight off the fleas, but I think it's bathtime for all of them when we're done here," Mark says, just as Hobbes streaks by in the company of a golden retriever. He hands me a Frisbee to fling, and Kierkegaard takes off after it. The Dane returns crestfallen and empty-handed, or rather empty-mouthed. Shortly thereafter, a Chihuahua materializes, proudly bearing the Frisbee like the trophy that it is. He sets it down at Mark's feet as if to say, "Throw it again! Throw it again!" Kierkegaard picks it up instead, and starts racing down the beach, with the Chihuahua in hot pursuit.

We stay long enough to watch the sun start to go down, adding layers of clothing as the afternoon breeze kicks up and the temperature drops. "You doin' okay?" he asks.

"Yeah, absolutely," I reply.

"Stay here a second, okay?"

Mark heads for the car and returns with a bottle of Schramsberg *blanc de noirs* champagne and two Styrofoam cups. "I hid this away in the cooler after lunch," he confesses. "I hope you don't mind. We should celebrate the setting sun."

"Very sneaky of you," I say with a smile, "but Styrofoam?"

"The most important attribute of a wineglass, dear Ms. Kate, is that it not leak."

"Quite so."

"Here's lookin' at you, kid," he says in a Bogey voice as the red ball starts to sink below the horizon off to our right.

"Thank you for today," I say simply.

"Thank you nothing," he replies, gathering me in his arms. "This was at least as much fun for me as it was for you. I had a great day—and so did they. It's only fair to warn you, however, that the car is going to smell like *eau de wet dog* all the way back."

When we get to the house, Mark heads into the bathroom with Kierkegaard, a bottle of flea shampoo, and a pile of towels.

An hour or so later, having decided to do a little work, I start looking for my script. "Mark, I can't find my script—I'm sure it was in the living room."

"Ah, Kate . . ." he says somewhat ominously.

"That doesn't sound good."

"Was this it?"

"What do you mean 'was'?"

Mark is dangling the shredded sheaf of paper, which is all that remains of my script for tomorrow. He scrooches up his face, faces the canine quartet, and waves the tatters in the air. Kierkegaard, damp from his bath, is the only one who looks contrite.

"I know he looks guilty, Kate, but don't believe it. He's a compulsive confessor. He's probably covering for one of the others."

"I see."

"Sartre's usually the critic in the group—he's the only one with literary pretensions."

"Are you telling me that he chewed it up because he thought it was a crappy script? If that's the reason, Sartre should have no trouble coming forward. How do you know it wasn't Nietzsche?"

"All right. Whooo did it? Whooooooo did it?" Mark says, in a pretty good imitation of Jimmy Cagney as the captain in *Mr. Roberts*.

. . . So good I can't resist. "Captain, it is I, Ensign Pulver," I say, summoning up as much of Jack Lemmon's swaggering irate lunacy as I can muster, "and I just threw your stinkin' script overboard. Now what's all this crud about no movie tonight?"

"Movie? Shall we?" says Mark.

"Might as well," I say. "Why should Meredith be the only one who never learns her lines?"

We head out to the local multiplex but return to absolute chaos. All in all, it looks rather like it did before I cleaned up.

I take a look at the chaos and sigh. "The dogs, Mark, I don't know if I can deal with—" I begin.

"Hush now, pretty lady," he says, running his hand gently over my neck, then kissing me repeatedly to make me stop speaking. "This sounds like something we should talk about, but let's do that tomorrow. For now let's just jump in bed—we might even get some sleep."

Next morning

7:46! 7:46!! 7:46!!!
I had let myself be persuaded, but in truth I didn't get much sleep—not with seven mammals in the bed. And now, of course, I need to be off before I have a chance to do much of anything except feed Drusilla. And it does dawn on me that I really ought to learn my lines.

Drusilla and I sneak out of bed while everyone else is still snoring. I move her dish up onto the kitchen counter, out of the reach of all but Kierkegaard, who's so big he could get to it easily but hasn't figured that out—yet.

"Yeah, I know, pretty crowded, huh?" I say to her as I replenish her food. "They're sort of a mixed blessing, aren't they?" It occurs to me that if Kierkegaard ever realizes how tall he is, I may have to start feeding her on the roof. "On the one hand we've got companionship, and on the other hand, a lot of the time it seems like too much companionship."

I head into Gossip Central and settle into Christine's station. She takes one look at me, throws both hands in the air, and tremble-shakes them as if in the midst of religious rapture. "Well, hallelujah! I can put the tea bags away!" she says by way of greeting. "You look a damn sight better than you did the last time I saw you—actually the last two times I saw you."

"And good morning to you, too," I say, laughing.

"So . . . did you get a Christmas tree?"

"Yes. Yes I did. I got a tree, lights, ornaments, a guy, and four dogs, all of whom have been in my house ever since."

"*What?* Tell me everything."

"His name's Mark van Gelder. Screenwriter. Well, TV writer with feature-length aspirations. Met him on the tree lot. The Kryptonite Hippos put the tree on top of his car instead of mine, so he followed me home."

"And you kept him."

I shrug my shoulders. "Yeah, that's sort of it."

"Tempted as I am to ask about the Kryptonite Hippos, now is not the time. Kate, maybe you haven't noticed, but you're still bleeding from a broken heart. Bleeding as in major hemorrhage. Are you sure this is wise?"

"Maybe it is. Maybe it isn't. But he's warm and he's funny and he makes me drink champagne on the beach at sunset out of Styrofoam cups. It's part of his contribution to helping me get over Rafe. He'll be at my house for Christmas dinner."

"You just met him. Isn't it a little soon to be spending Christmas together?"

"Well, which is it, Christine?" I say in exasperation. "First you tell me to reclaim Christmas for myself. Now you seem to be telling me that I'm supposed to spend it alone."

"Easy there," Christine replies, trying to soothe my ruffled feathers. "Don't get all huffy on me. I'm on your side—honest. But it sounds like this relationship seems to be moving pretty fast, and I just don't want you to get hurt any worse than you already are, Kate."

"He's not an ogre, honest. Come to dinner and judge for yourself."

"Love to, but we're going to Wyatt's mother's house."

"Drop by in the evening for dessert, then."

"Ordinarily we'd love to, but this Christmas is carrying a lot of emotional baggage. This is Wyatt's mom's first Christmas as a widow; we pretty much have to stay put."

Priscilla arrives at the pod next to mine and insinuates himself into the seat. " 'Lo, Kate, Christine."

I wave a half-assed greeting from my reclining position. "You seem to have forgotten to get dressed this morning, Pris," says Christine. I begin the struggle to get up to have a peek, but Christine digs her elbow firmly into my sternum, pinning me down in dying bug mode as she continues to work on me.

"Kate!" she whisper-hisses in my ear as she plucks at my recalcitrant eyebrows. "Save yourself some indigestion and stay down there, will ya? It's Priscilla in a loincloth—well, more of a hand towel, actually, and it's gah-ross. This is *not* something you want to see."

"Got a hot-and-heavy scene with Tiffany this morning, ladies. Oh, Debra . . . extra heavy on the eye stuff today, okay? And like this on the chest, okay? Do you need to spray it to make it stay that way?"

"I don't believe this," Christine murmurs. "He's a flaming heterosexual, is what he is. He wants poor Deb to part the straw thatch that is his chest hair in the middle, comb it to each side, and then spray it in place." Very softly she then begins to sing:

I'm too sexy for my shirt too sexy for my shirt
So sexy it hurts.

I try very hard not to splutter, and pretty much fail. Christine covers for me by grabbing a tissue, holding it over my nose and mouth, and loudly saying, "Gesundheit!"

Priscilla begins admiring himself in the hand mirror just as Marty calls his scene over the PA. "That's for me, Deb," he says. "Gotta go, but pretty-please can you get me a glass of wa-wa?" As soon as Debra complies, Priscilla takes a swig and pops a couple of pills.

"I thought it was the woman who was supposed to have the headache," says Christine acerbically.

"Right Said Fred!" I pipe up, laughing.

"Tiffany never has a headache, and besides, these aren't aspirin—they're vitamins," he sniffs. "Niacin, if you must know. Gives you a rosy glow."

"I need Fallon Salisbury and Gallagher Molloy," Marty repeats. "Fallon and Gallagher only. Tiffany and Priscilla. Everyone else, clear the set!"

Scraping, shuffling, and thumping noises continue to emanate from the ceiling after Marty finishes speaking—it sounds as if the intercom mike has accidentally been left open. Soon, we in Gossip Central hear muffled voices in the background over the PA.

"Hey Marty . . ."

"Yeah, Pris?"

"You got anything for itching?"

"Depends on where you itch, Pris. If it's *down there,* I can't help you. Or rather, I won't."

"No, Marty, it's mostly my face and neck . . . well, and my chest, too . . . Actually, now it's kind of all over, like a cross between itchy and tingly."

"Hmmn. You're getting blotchy, too. Are you allergic to anything?"

"Nope. Not that I know of. Shit! It's getting worse!"

"Looks like it, too. I hate to say it, Priscilla, but if we turned out the lights, you'd glow red and violet in the dark."

"Now it feels like I'm on fire! I must have a fever of 105—and I'm starting to sweat like crazy. Marty, call the doctor."

"I doubt that will be necessary, Marty." Even though it's muted, Daphne's voice is unmistakable.

"But Daphne, this could be serious!"

"Priscilla, did you take anything before you came up here?"

"Well, yes."

"What and how much?"

"It was just niacin, Daphne, honest. Five pills."

"I don't care how many pills. How many milligrams of niacin?"

"A hundred milligrams."

"That's not so bad."

"No, per pill."

"*Each?*"

"Well, yeah."

"Did you have pellagra, Priscilla?"

"For lunch? No, I didn't have any fish for lunch. Didn't have lunch at all, actually. Trying to watch my diet, you know."

By this time, all painting and curling in Gossip Central has ceased. All conversation as well. We are each and every one of us paused in midtask, staring at the speaker box in the ceiling and hanging on every barely audible word as this melodrama unfolds.

"Let me see if I understand this correctly," Daphne continues. "You took five hundred milligrams of niacin on an empty stomach?"

"I guess so, yeah."

"Priscilla, you are an idiot. Your mother should have thrown you away and kept the stork. What you have is a world-class niacin flush, and you'll be glowing like a red-hot rivet for the rest of the afternoon. Go back down to Makeup and get them to tone you down a little. I have no sympathy for you because you did this to yourself."

"Sorry, Daphne."

"And for the record, 'pellagra' is the name of the disease caused by niacin deficiency. It is characterized by the three Ds—diarrhea, dermatitis, and dementia. I don't know—and don't care to know—whether you suffer from the first two, but your behavior would certainly be consistent with the last."

"Yes, Daphne."

As the entirety of Gossip Central is laughing its collective ass off, Christine leads us in a rousing chorus of:

> I'm too sexy for my shirt too sexy for my shirt
> So sexy it hurts.

LaTrisa finally brings us all back to earth. "Okay, okay," she says. "Simma down now, people, simma down. It's gonna be real tough, but we have to control ourselves before Pris gets back here."

Debra sighs, picking up a liter of Suntan 4. "I'm going to his room to paint him top to toe. I may be some time." She shuffles out, laden down with sponges and towels, a protective nurse preparing to minister to her patient.

December 24

1*0:07! 10:07!! 10:07!!!*

Yay! It's after ten in the morning and I'm still in the bed. The dogs haven't pushed me out, and I don't have to go to work. Best of all, it's Christmastime. I don't care what the Scrooges may say, you gotta be in desperate need of Paxil and all its severe side effects to not get a thrill when school's out and it's party time.

LFT is dark for ten days around Christmas. Ten whole lumbering free days to sleep in, drink, and forget who you are. I wake up on Christmas Eve morning and stare out the admittedly grubby window at yet another crisp sunny day outside. I roll over Nietzsche and gaze somewhat lovingly into the large floppy ear of Kierkegaard. I peer over the Dane's enormous head and spy Mark balanced treacherously on the edge of the bed, devoid of sheets and pillows. Lousy philosophers. I tap him on the shoulder.

I adopt my best gravelly Scarlett Johansson voice: "Wanna fool around?" Mark stirs and efficiently jettisons the four-leggeds from the bedroom. It's surprising how quickly one can rid a bedroom of several hundred pounds of dog- and catness when one needs to. He's back in bed before I can wriggle out of my La Perla teddy.

After lazy morning sex, we shower and dress, feed the menagerie, and head out for Starbucks, the *New York Times,* and last-minute Christmas shopping at Barney's. In my excitement I am practically jumping around in the passenger seat as the Barney's valet opens the door of the Expedition.

"Happy holidays," he says for probably the zillionth time this season.

"Oh thanks, yeah, merry Christmas." I urgently grab Mark's hand and dance through the door. We are thrust into a bustle of riches. Mark is resplendent in his fuzzy reindeer antlers and I'm wearing a Santa hat. Otherwise we are dressed quite respectably, for I had feared we would be thrown out on our ear from the swanky store. I'm wearing a vintage Azzedine Alaia black dress and green mock-croc knee boots, and Mark is in his usual faux fatigues, which is somewhat rock 'n' roll, I hope. My dark green Balenciaga bag is weighted down with filthy lucre, itching to be spent on just about everything I spy.

"I desire to purchase you perfume, milady," Mark informs me with a swooping bow and a kiss to my hand.

"Excellent," I reply. We sashay over to the delicious-smelling parfumerie and start playing around with different scents. Some make my nose ache; others are too fresh or soapy. We narrow it down to two choices: Kai, with overtones of gardenia, jasmine, tuberose, and lily, which is apparently leaping off the shelves, or so we are informed, and a tea rose concoction that Mark really likes. It's a toss-up. I walk away and leave the final decision to Mark, so I can be at least a little surprised in the morning.

I meander around, feeling cool and hip, part of the LA scene, just hangin' out at Barney's. We have set this time aside for secret shopping— things we want to hide from each other till the morning. I slap down my exhausted Amex for some Burberry collars for the canines and feline, grab Da-Nang pants for Mark, and drool inelegantly at the vintage jewelry. A few people smile and assure me that they love the show, so I try to act detached, yet grateful, emulating Sally Fields at the mall in *Soapdish*.

I call Mark on the cell. We meet upstairs at Barney's Green Grass for a late lunch, grinning sheepishly at each other and staring at the black bags in spite of ourselves. He has one very small Barney's bag and I hope he got a little trinket for moi. We order a bottle of Bolli.

Next stop: the Beverly Hills Cheese Shop. We get some Stilton for after dinner tomorrow, and I spy a really cool present for the house. It's a wooden girolle, a circular slicer/shaver that grates cheese in thin slivers. It can also be used on chocolate. I buy a huge round block of marbled chocolate, and the grater to go with it. My plan is to wrap it up so we can open it after dinner and gorge ourselves on Swiss chocolate. Mark buys some fab wine. We drive home, make a fire, and silently wrap our presents in different rooms, while Bing Crosby promises us that it's going to be a white Christmas.

We watch black-and-white movies that we have been hoarding from Blockbuster for just this night, finishing up with *It's a Wonderful Life*. In the end we're both crying, Mark because he's a normal human being, me because I want to marry Jimmy Stewart and live with him in that house happily ever after.

"I'm going to prep the bird," Mark announces, wiping away his tears.

"Okay, I'll watch." I pour us each a glass of red wine. Mark does lots of clever gynecological things to the turkey, and I chop a salad for our Christ-

mas Eve dinner. The dogs are extremely interested in the kitchen goings-
on, and it gets very crowded and dangerous, as Kierkegaard's nose could
easily be mistaken for a potato when he props it up on the kitchen island.

"Bugger off!" I tell him for the umpteenth time, and nudge him with my
hip, which only serves to almost dislocate my back. He won't budge.

"So tomorrow, what time do you want to eat?" asks Mark.

"Um, when are Charlie and Don coming over?" I've invited Charlie and
his partner for Christmas dinner. They're going to help cook it and then
Richard, Trent, LaTrisa, Mzee, and Nigel will be coming around at three,
after visiting their respective families.

"You don't remember?" he asks.

"Right." I blink. "I'd better call them."

I stagger over the many animals and locate the phone, reminding myself
that I must do a little tidying up in the morning. The tree looks beautiful
all lit up, Meredith the Barbie doll perched high, a branch up her ass, and
all the presents wrapped and scattered around the base. I hug myself. I love
Christmas.

"Hey, cherub!" Charlie's voice crackles on his cell phone, lots of background noise, a party probably.

"What time tomorrow?" I ask him.

We agree on one P.M. for drinks and canapés and bird prep.

"Canapés! Oooh Charlie, I haven't got any of those!" I wail, alarmed.

"Darling, the fags always bring the canapés. Worry not. Cherub, do you
have vodka? Don drinks vodka."

"No," I wail.

"Don't worry. We'll bring that, too. Tomato juice?"

"No," I wail again.

"Darling, do you know how to shop at all?"

"I guess not."

"Don't worry, cherub. We will come armed and ready to fight. What
time are the guests arriving?"

"Three P.M." That, at least, I know.

"All right. Sweetheart, do you have silverware and napkins and everything?"

"Yes. Mark and I went to Tarzhay and we have everything, even enough
chairs." I sound a little surprised.

"Cherub, we shall make a woman out of you yet."

"I do hope so."

We hang up, wishing each other a happy holiday, and I go over to touch
the presents. Wrapping paper is magical, concealing parcels filled with
promise. I know what some of them are. I touch a small soft package with
LaTrisa's name on it. It is a pink Raw 7 cashmere sweater that she'll look so

pretty in. I glide my hand over to Charlie and Don's gift—hand-blown glass veggies and fruits that will be beautiful piled in a bowl. A bio of Churchill and one of Eisenhower for Richard, Arabic sandalwood oil in a beautiful Egyptian decanter for Mzee, a slick Gucci wallet for Nigel, and Laker tickets for Trent in a red envelope. I pass my hand over a square box that contains the chocolate and the girolle slicer, then over to my gifts for Mark. We have hung two woolen socks of his above the fireplace; later tonight we'll stuff them with candy canes and little treats. Excitement creeps through me; I am a small child again.

"Penny for them." Mark has crept in behind me. He puts his arms around me and we kneel there, gazing up at the tree in wonder. He kisses my neck and we lay back on the rug in front of the Christmas tree. When we wake up, it's about two A.M. and the fire is all but extinguished. Groggily we make our way to bed, which is already inhabited by thunderous snores from the fur quintet. We shoo them off and climb in.

"This feels good, but we never ate dinner," I mention.

"Mmmm," Mark says. "Too late now." He kisses me on the forehead and we snuggle down.

I contentedly wrap his arms around me. "If you do something, something happens. If you don't, nothing happens."

"What?"

I don't answer. I'm drifting off to my childhood dreams. 'Twas the night before Christmas. . . .

December 25

6:43! 6:43!! 6:43!!!

I wake up early. I cannot help it. It's CHRISTMAS! All the boys are back on the bed and Drusilla is curled up in the armchair in a huff.

"Happy Christmas," I whisper to her, and stealthily climb out of bed. I grab a sweater and put it over my silky nightgown and pick up the phone. Curling up with Drusilla on the armchair, I call my brother in London.

"Fun Central," Daniel answers when he picks up. In the background I hear my nephews pounding around, screaming maniacally.

"Hello, gorgeous. Happy happy," I whisper.

"Bloody hell! Don't pull the drapes down, Maxwell. And I swear I will garotte you with your own intestines if you hit Freddy again. Hello, darling . . . Jane, take the baby, will you? It's Katie. . . . Jesus, Maxwell . . . Jane, JANE. Hang on, Katie. . . . Jesus . . . *JANE!!!!!*"

I hear pattering and clicking and more hollering from my two crazy nephews, and I giggle to myself. Christmas at Daniel's is ridiculous and always ends in tears, but I love it and miss it and get a pang of homesickness. It takes me back to my childhood. As kids on Christmas morning, Daniel and I used to wake up together, dash madly downstairs, then start feeling and shaking all the gifts. We were allowed to empty our stockings, but we had to wait till lunchtime for our main presents, a rule we resent to this day. Now, whenever we are together for Christmas, we rip open all our gifts at breakfast.

"Hello, darling. Sorry about that." Daniel sounds breathless, as if he has been wrestling. "Some idiot gave the little fuckers swords for Christmas, and now they are intent on murdering each other. I'm almost ready to let them."

"Oh good. They like the swords, then," I answer.

"Sorry, that was you? Thanks a bloody lot, Aunt Katie. How are you, dear?"

"Good. I miss you. Did Jane like her bag?"

"Yes, but talk to her about it later. I want to know how you are."

"I'm okay. I've got four dogs, a cat, a man, and a tree."

"What, no partridge?"

"Well, a turkey. I s'pose that counts."

"We had a goose; it was scrummy."

"Lucky you. I wish I was there."

"Me, too. Next year, maybe, or we'll trek out there."

"God forbid. Maxwell and Freddy will destroy this place. I'll come to you. How's the baby?"

"Mr. Gideon is gorgeous. Jane is still crying that it wasn't a girl. She feels overcome with penises in this house. I think she's postpartum. I've promised her we'll try again, but I think I'll go in for the old snip-snip once she gets out of the blues. Is that wrong?"

"Yes."

"Well, we'll get her a girl kitten or something. Anyway, who's the man?"

"A writer. Sssh. Can't talk—he's in my bed."

"Ah."

"He's nice."

"Are you better about dickwad Rafe now?"

"I guess. Yes, yes, I am. Especially today. It's CHRISTMAS."

"Yes, darling. Happy Christmas, my love."

And we go on talking for an hour and a half. Daniel takes turns with Jane, who loves the bag, and the boys, who are still bouncing off the walls. They even put baby Gideon on, so I can hear his gurgles and giggles. So sweet. By the time I hang up, I'm sniveling like a crybaby. I love my bro and miss him, so I hug Drusilla and wipe my nose on her.

"Merry Christmas, Kate."

I squint over Drusilla to see that Mark is awake. He is propped up on a pillow with his arms behind his head. "I've been watching you talk to your brother," he says.

"Oh," I sniff.

"Yes, very touching."

"Shut up."

"No. Really. You guys are cute."

"Oh shut up!" I throw a pillow at him, and all the dogs bark and scramble around. All except Kierkegaard, who just lays there and lets us dance about him on the bed. Odd.

"Let's get this party started," I shout, and put the Black-Eyed Peas on the CD player. We dance around some more and crash out into the front room and stop dead.

Someone has opened all the presents. And eaten them.

"Christ, what the hell . . . ?"

Mark dashes over to the tree and stands there amid the debris. LaTrisa's sweater is out of the paper and mildly gummed. There are torn bits of Laker tickets as well as glass vegetables scattered everywhere. The Egyptian decanter is on its side. Mark's clothes are strewn about. The wooden girolle has been lovingly chewed through the middle. The block of chocolate is missing.

"What the hell happened here?" Mark raises his arms to the room and we all gape expectantly back at him. Me and the culprits.

"You stupid idiots! What did you go and do?" He marches fiercely over to the dogs.

"It's okay, Mark. It's just stuff."

"No, no. They ruined everything. It looked so nice, Kate." Mark is standing among his dogs . . . well, Nietzsche, Sartre, and Hobbes. Kierkegaard is still lying on the bed.

"Come here, you lazy mutt!" he shouts to the Dane, but he doesn't stir. All I can see are his slender white thighs disobediently staring back at us from the bed.

"Kierkegaard. KIERKEGAARD!" The name sounds absurd when shouted in anger. Mark should have taken that into consideration when choosing it.

"Is he all right?" I ask. I'm suddenly concerned. This is so unlike him. We walk over to him and he looks up at us morosely.

"Are you okay?" I ask him, stroking his brow. "He's breathing heavy," I say to Mark.

"Bah. The idiot, he just feels bad because he destroyed all the gifts." Mark marches back into the front room and starts picking up the wrapping paper.

"Mzee's oil didn't leak out; that's good." He picks it up and puts it on the mantel, out of harm's way.

It suddenly dawns on me. "Oh my God, Mark, I think he ate all the chocolate."

"What?" Mark looks startled.

"Chocolate is really poisonous to dogs. We have to get him to Emergency."

"You're right, Kate. That's what he did. He found the chocolate, and then started ripping through the other gifts looking for more. Shit."

"Maybe we should take them all to the vet, in case they had some, too."

We call the emergency animal clinic, and they confirm that chocolate is highly dangerous, especially when we tell them that it was about two pounds' worth. We hurriedly dress and bundle all the dogs into the Expedition. It's especially hard with the Dane. As we leave I glance back at Drusilla, who is delicately picking her way across the wreckage on the floor. She slides her gaze over to the door and gives me a dismissive look.

"Sorry," I whisper.

* * *

"You'll have to watch the Dane closely," the vet, a sturdy, white-haired woman, says. "I have a hunch he ate the majority of the chocolate, being the dominant canine." She struggles getting Hobbes's bulldog bulk off the examination table, and Mark clumsily assists.

I sigh and glance at my watch. It's 1:30 P.M. We had to wait ages while they wrestled with Kierkegaard in the back room. It had taken two grown lab assistants and Mark to get him in the door at all, and then to administer the puking agent—fuhgeddaboutit.

An icy realization creeps down my back. It is 1:30 and there are two people waiting at my house with canapés and vodka. "Shit! Charlie and Don."

I excuse myself and exit the room, as Mark tries to catch Nietzsche, who is attempting to escape through my ankles. I grab my cell and dial Charlie's number. "Charlie?"

"Where are you, cherub?"

"We're at the emergency vet. Kierkegaard, one of Mark's dogs, ate two pounds of chocolate," I explain.

"Oh darling! Well, as long as he didn't eat the turkey. Where is it, by the way?"

"In the fridge."

"We let ourselves in. The door was unlocked and we were terribly afraid. It looked like you were burgled, even more so than usual."

"The dogs ransacked the gifts. . . . I'm so sorry."

"Oh cherub, I love the glass fruit and veggies. I know those are ours, 'cause everything else is so butch, except for the pink sweater."

Bless him.

"Once we were sure that there were no dead bodies or blood, we poured ourselves a vodka and waited for your call. Don's cleaning up now and I'll start the bird, all right?"

It's four in the afternoon by the time Mark pulls the car up by the house. The Expedition is truly toxic. Mark and I hurl ourselves out as soon as the car stops moving.

"Jesus!" I gasp for air. "We're putting them all in the back yard. They aren't allowed in the house."

"It's a bit chilly, but the least they could do is die from hypothermia, with the money I've just spent on them," he mutters grumpily, and drags the dogs out of the hatchback. They all seem a bit wobbly, Kierkegaard most of all.

I gently coax him through the gate and the four of them patter off in various directions.

Mark is a wreck. Unshaven and unkempt. I don't look much better, except for the shaving part. "Merry Christmas!" I put my arms around his neck and he grudgingly smiles.

"It's okay—really. Let's have showers and mingle. Everyone's here." I don't think he'd noticed all the cars parked outside the house.

When we enter, the party is quietly in full swing. Don and Charlie have not only restored order, they've also rearranged my furniture. The gifts are neatly stacked under the tree; the floor has been vacuumed; there's a hearty fire; canapés are laid out; the tree is lit; and all my friends are there.

"SURPRISE!" they shout.

I introduce Mark to everyone; we tell them about our day and we hear about their Christmas mornings. Charlie and Don are cooking a perfect crisp turkey, and delicious smells are filling the kitchen.

Mark and I excuse ourselves to shower and dress. By the time we're back, all the food is on the beautifully decorated table and Nat King Cole is singing away.

I get out the Christmas crackers, and we all pull them and put on silly hats. Everyone laughs and claps, and I go into the kitchen and check the water level on the Christmas pudding boiling away on the stove. Daniel sent me one from London, and I'm going to treat my American cousins to the British sweet delicacy. Trent follows me in. "He's okay, you know," he tells me as I peer into the pot.

I peek through the door—Mark has put the disaster with the chocolate and the trip to the vet behind him and is having a great time with all my friends from the show. Everyone is laughing and joking.

"Thank you for giving us your blessing, Father Winterfield," I say merrily.

"Seriously, Kate, if he wasn't, I would have told you," he says.

"Thanks. I know that, Trent, really."

Drusilla chooses that moment to wrap herself around my legs.

"Hey Droos, happy Christmas." I pick her up. "I've got a very stylish Burberry present for you, if Kierkegaard didn't eat it."

She freezes at the mention of his name—or maybe she fears that I'll add her to the pot where the pudding is boiling—and in any event wriggles to get down.

The turkey is delicious. We follow it with Stilton—not surprisingly, Richard has brought some vintage port to go with it. LaTrisa offers up some chocolates as we all watch *It's a Wonderful Life* again.

The Christmas pudding is ready. I turn it upside down on the serving platter. It sits there all brown and steaming. I put a holly sprig on top and pour brandy over the whole thing.

"Turn down the lights!" I shout, then put a match to it. Blam! It flames up and I walk out to thunderous applause.

"What Impertinence!" said the Pudding. "I wonder how you'd like it, if I were to cut a slice out of you, you creature."

"What the fuck is that, honey?" shouts Nigel.

"Plum pudding, traditional British fare at Christmastime."

I set it down, and serve the brandy butter and cream. Everyone takes a slice. Mark excuses himself briefly to go check on the philosophers. I lean back in my chair, full and happily tipsy. The day has turned out all right in the end—more than all right.

Nigel is leaning back, smoking a cigarette. Mzee is handing around a fat spliff. Trent and Mark are chatting, and Richard is slurring along with Nat King Cole. LaTrisa, Charlie, and Don are giggling about something and I just sit. With my friends. My new American family.

Early February/Wednesday

I STUMBLE INTO THE REHEARSAL ROOM, where Jay has had them hang a cadaver-size practice bag for me to kick at. As I get into my routine, I can see that I'm making a bit of progress. I'd painted a little white line on the bag to indicate the highest point where my right toe could reach; today I'm routinely striking above it. I'm now within range of the solar plexus of the Artist Once Again Known As Prince.

A *ki ahp,* or spirit shout, rises from my diaphragm as I attack the bag, and I am amazed to hear a shriek in return. I have startled a worker bee who has been quietly waiting to talk to me, causing him to scream with surprise.

"How long have you been here?" I ask.

"Sorry. I didn't want to disturb you. Daphne wants you upstairs for a screening," he says, after he recovers.

"When?"

"Now."

"Right. What *was* I thinking? Please tell her I'll be right up."

I stop my practice, grab a towel, and dab at my damp face. As I put on my shoes, I have another look at my target. With one shoe on and one off, I gimp over to the practice bag and paint on another white stripe, about two inches above the last. Not yet good, but most assuredly better. Then I grab the last slingback and totter out into the corridor, hurriedly stretching the uncooperative strap up and over my sweaty heel as I go.

Note to self: Keep a reserve pair of shoes a half size bigger in the dressing room. All those chagis *make your feet swell.*

"Where are you headed, Kate?" asks Christine as she crosses my path.

"Third floor. I've been invited—or should I say summoned?—to another episode of *Wednesday Afternoon at the Movies* with Daphne."

"I don't follow, sorry."

"Whenever Daphne needs to put over an important concept about a scene, she makes us watch a film that has elements of what she wants. Last time it was *Butch Cassidy and the Sundance Kid*."

* * *

"And today," Daphne says, nodding to me slightly as I slip into a chair, "I want you to take a look at *The Hunger*. Catherine Deneuve and Susan Sarandon as lesbian vampires. Never mind what you think about the film as a whole. Focus on the relationship between the two women."

I'm sitting in the dark with Charlotte. Charlotte plays Lacey Boudreaux, who I've been flirting with since Kirk married Amber before Christmas. As Daphne sees it, Charlotte will be Deneuve to my Sarandon. In the film, Deneuve portrays a very chic vampire who, with her paramour (David Bowie) prowls Manhattan's late-night clubs and discos in quest of fresh supplies of A, B, AB, and O to feast on. When Bowie starts to age rapidly, he goes to see Sarandon, a gerontologist. She watches him turn into an old man in just a day's time, but is unable to help. With Bowie no longer very appealing as a bedmate, Deneuve stashes him in the vault (with her other exes), and pursues Sarandon as her new lover. The lesbian seduction scene, considered kinky when the movie was first released, is still steamy more than twenty years later.

"We'll definitely be accused of Sweeps Lesbianism, but I don't care," says Daphne when the lights come back up.

"I don't know what that is," says Charlotte.

"Sweeps Lesbianism, my dear Charlotte, is the networks' habit—not just our network, all of them—of airing trumped-up lesbian romances during Sweeps and using them to titillate whatever tendencies toward porn-lite our Daytime viewers might have. Almost all of the affairs are short-lived, and the characters rediscover their heterosexuality once the Sweeps period ends."

"Oh," says Charlotte vacuously.

"But that's not what we're about here. Kate, even though this takes place during Sweeps, you're not going to snap back to heterosexuality once the regular season resumes, so they can eat my shorts. I need a good end to my story."

"Fine by me. Who could argue with that?" I respond.

"You don't have to be gay to find them erotic," says Daphne. Charlotte looks reassured. "Which is exactly what I'm looking for," Daphne continues, "a white-hot love affair between two women that the lady at the ironing board can relate to."

The lady at the ironing board . . .

Aka a woman between eighteen and forty-nine years of age—and preferably in her twenties or early thirties. She may be a cliché, but she is still

Daytime's #1 target demographic. Even after half a century of soap operas, advertisers still avidly court her, because she's the one who buys the detergent, the diapers, the peanut butter, the mascara, and the breakfast cereal that is hawked during the commercials. Holding her interest at midday isn't easy. There's the baby, the phone, and the radio—which all may be going at the same time—not to mention lunch. If she's a true queen of multitasking, she might also be checking her e-mail or bidding for something on eBay. And she is armed and dangerous. She has a clicker, and she knows how to use it. If we don't grab her from the top of the episode and keep her hooked, we'll lose her to another soap or to a talk show.

Daphne gives us each a script. "We're shooting the first love scene tomorrow," she says. "Do you want me to have them clear the set?"

"Nah. Let 'em watch," I say nonchalantly, perhaps with more bravado than I really feel.

The truth of the matter is that they'll watch anyway. I know Trent wouldn't miss this for anything. Even if Daphne clears the set, he'll be up Mzee's ladder and peering down from the rigging. Priscilla and Vladimir will figure out a way to watch because they'll undoubtedly have some form of filthy wager going—so they may as well have front-row seats.

"If it's okay with Charlotte, I'm sure the boys are all dying of curiosity," says Daphne with just the trace of a smile. Charlotte shrugs and looks blank—alas, this is all too common.

Wednesday night

My nose is assaulted as I walk in the front door.

"Eeew! What's that smell?"

"Nietzsche can't keep his food down. I'm thinking maybe he's bulimic."

"So what you're telling me is that I'm sharing my house with a farting Dane, a bedhog bulldog, a script-eating poodle, and a bulimic dachshund—this is all making me crazy."

"It's not that bad, really."

"Isn't it?"

Thursday

I'm trying to prepare for the hot and heavy scene with Charlotte when Nigel comes bursting into my dressing room. "Rrrrr-road trip!" he bellows, as if it were a rallying cry.

"Excuse me?"

"Pack your bags, Miss Kate, we're headed for the Big Easy."

"I have no idea what that is."

"New Orleans. There's a soap convention there this weekend. Since we're into vampires, what better place than Lestat's hometown?"

"Indeed. I could use a little fun. Is Ms. Lauren joining us?"

"Nope—she's too young to drink. I told Daphne I wanted to bring Trent along with us. She thought that was a fine idea."

"Bravo!"

"*Laissez les bons temps roulent*—let the good times roll."

"How will we rendezvous?"

"We're takin' the red-eye—see you at LAX, American Airlines first-class check-in, at eleven P.M. tomorrow evening. Oh, and don't forget. Sunday afternoon when we come back, the two of you are going to have just enough time to change your clothes and head straight to the *Soap Opera Digest* Awards."

* * *

"Quiet in the Peanut Gallery, please," says Marty. "We are now shooting the vampire lesbian love scene on the autopsy table. . . . Jeez, I can't believe I just said that. No wonder people don't believe me when I tell 'em what I do for a living."

INT. MASON SALISBURY'S EXAMINING ROOM AT THE MORGUE—NIGHT

          DEVON
   (trying to maintain her professional demeanor)
It was good of you to come down here this evening, Ms. Boudreaux. I'm sure these have been very difficult weeks for you.

          LACEY
      (actively flirting)
First Juliette, then Hamilton. Thank you for being so understanding.

For those of you keeping score at home, the body count in the current storyline is now two. It was the late Juliette Dupuy Boudreaux, Hamilton Boudreaux's wealthy second wife, who fell out of the closet the night we dressed Bill up in drag and I punched him in his Richard Nixon mask. Poor Hamilton didn't get to spend much time as the grieving widower and heir to her share of the Dupuy fortune—he himself was found dead in yesterday's segment. Hope Canyon's homicide rate is right up there with another deadly small burg—Cabot Cove, Jessica Fletcher's hometown.

                    DEVON
What kind of relationship did you have with your ex-
husband and his new wife?

                    LACEY
Even after Hamilton and I were divorced, I still retained great affection for him. And of course for the
children's sake I thought it important to remain at
least cordial with Juliette. . . .

                    DEVON
So shared custody was not an issue?

                    LACEY
Not at all.

                    DEVON
Tell me, Ms. Boudreaux . . .

                    LACEY
          (placing her hand on Devon's shoulder)
Call me Lacey, please.

                    DEVON
          (fighting her urges)
I'm sorry, Ms. Boudreaux, I can't do that.

                    LACEY
Because you think I'm a suspect?

                    DEVON
          (avoiding the question)
Even if it weren't against department policy, it's
just not prudent.

Lacey languidly runs her fingers through her hair.

                    DEVON
What can you tell me about the bite marks we found on
Mr. Boudreaux's neck?

Lacey casually but deliberately opens the top button on
her silk blouse.

                    LACEY
          (feigning ignorance, badly)
Bite marks? Hamilton died of bite marks?

Despite her full, rosy cheeks, it's fitting that Charlotte is a vampire. She is beautiful, but there is a slightly vapid air about her that is draining. Behind her large green eyes there's often nobody home. She uses her lack of personality to great effect—which is to say that she spends a lot of air time looking lovely and gazing off into space. She utters her lines in a baby voice, her lips barely moving, her plump mouth a pert rosebud through which her dialogue seeps. But she's a perfect foil for Devon, and the audience totally gets the attraction.

DEVON

They weren't what killed him—the knife in the chest was the fatal wound. But the M.E. found a series of bite marks on his sternocleidomastoid and levator scapulae—these are muscles of the neck. Some were fresh, some were semi-healed.

LACEY
(now stroking herself and
looking straight at Devon's cleavage)

The only one who might know about those was Juliette, and she can't tell us anything now.

DEVON

Juliette had some of the same marks, but all of them were very fresh.

LACEY

Why would I know anything about those?

DEVON
(increasingly turned on)

You probably wouldn't. . . . But some of Hamilton's wounds were older—much older.

LACEY
(running her tongue across her lips)

How much older, Devon?

DEVON

(crossing the line and responding to Lacey's advances)
We're guessing, Lacey, that they had been inflicted during the time the two of you were still married.

LACEY
(seeing an opportunity)

Can you show me where exactly they were on the body?

                              DEVON
(mesmerized despite herself, pulling her long hair aside and
        pointing to exposed spots on her own neck)
    Here . . . and here.

                              LACEY
   (exposing Devon's other shoulder and caressing her neck)
    Were there any here?

                              DEVON
                (falling fast and breathing heavy)
    Yes, yes.

The camera comes in close.

                              LACEY
        (lifts up Devon's hair and blows on her neck)
    What about here?

                              DEVON
                (surrendering to the moment)
    Yes. Yes. Yes.

Lacey presses up against her from behind. As Devon turns,
she kisses her on the lips, first softly, romantically, then
more ardently as Devon responds. There are kisses, many
kisses. Lacey then moves on to Devon's neck and shoulder.
Devon leans back onto the autopsy table, then pulls Lacey
down on top of her. When the camera pulls back, we see bite
marks on Devon's neck.

"And cut," calls Marty. "Whew! Allofasudden it's warm in here. Can,
um, someone help me unfog my eyeglasses, please?"

Gotcha, Marty! I just wish you really believed I was acting.

In playing a love scene with someone of the opposite sex, the fact that
you might be gay has absolutely nothing to do with whether the scene
works. You summon up the same sexual desire from within to sell what
your character is feeling. Rock Hudson did it. So did Montgomery Clift. So
did Marlene Dietrich. And it's no different if you're straight and playing a
love scene with someone of the same sex, as Deneuve and Sarandon made
perfectly clear.

"Loooooovely, ladies. That was hot." Daphne's voice comes out of the
ether, over the PA. "But I can't help but add, Kate, that it wouldn't have
been nearly as electric with you in short hair."

"Yes, but—"

"I haven't said no to the haircut, but I want to think about it a little more. As far as the scene goes, it was exactly what I wanted. My guess is that the guy from network Standards and Practices is about to put me on his speed dial—but as far as I'm concerned, that's his problem, not mine."

"What's the big deal?" Charlotte asks. "It's not like we were naked or anything."

"Everyone at network is jumpy," says Daphne. "Soap operas—all of us—are in the crosshairs of a potential investigation by the Federal Communications Commission. The FCC microcephalics in Washington, it seems, are determined to crack down on what they call 'broadcast indecency.' Lesbian sex in a morgue would probably strike those prudes as debauched, or at the very least a breach of etiquette."

"Shit!" Marty exclaims. "We'll be back to the days of *Ozzie and Harriet*—married couples in single beds—soon!"

"Okay, okay," I say. "New paragraph. I have a question about vampire rules of engagement."

"What is it, Kate?" Daphne asks.

"How many bites from a vampire does it take to turn the vic—the bitee—into a vampire? I'm trying to figure out why this wouldn't now make Devon a vampire, since she's been bitten by Lacey."

A babble rises up from my fellow cast members arrayed around the set. This is an issue about which everyone seems to have an opinion.

"In *Dracula* it's three bites," says LaTrisa.

"But even after a bite or two, don't you already have . . . issues?" asks Tiffany. "It's like a gradual thing, isn't it?"

"All it takes is one bite." The confident voice weighing in belongs to petite, slender Lauren Elizabeth Fielding. "One bite and your head morphs," she says authoritatively. "I watch *Buffy* religiously. One bite and you're in Fangland."

"Yeah, well, there are all kinds of ways to become a vampire," declares Vladimir. "Committing suicide, being a witch or warlock . . ."

"Having sex with a vampire . . ." adds Kirk.

"Or by being the seventh son of a seventh son," says Richard, "but isn't all of that beside the point?"

"What the fuck does it matter?" asks Priscilla disdainfully.

"The question Kate has asked is not a trivial one," Daphne says curtly as she emerges from the booth. "It affects the storyline greatly. Kate and Charlotte: Get touched up if you need to, but stick around, please."

Daphne huddles briefly with the new Maggie (the XXIV) and the head writer, then addresses the cast. "I suspect we will never come up with a definitive answer. For our viewers, however, we must eventually make it clear what the 'rules of engagement' are, to use Ms. McPhee's phrase. Unfortunately, there's no way to clarify the issue in today's episode without tossing out a lot of what we've shot, and that's unacceptable—what we have is just too good. I don't want to lose that footage, but we certainly cannot leave people with the notion that Devon is now a vampire."

"So then, what are we going to do?" asks Charlotte.

"Makeup—please remove the bite marks from Kate's shoulder," Daphne says.

"So is it one bite or three, or should we split the difference and make it two? Inquiring minds want to know!" says Trent, winking at me.

"We'll leave that question hanging for today, Mr. Winterfield. We are going to reshoot only the last bit of the scene, using a slightly different camera angle. Kate, Charlotte . . . the camera will pull back over Lacey's right shoulder rather than her left, so the sightline of Devon's neck is blocked. Our viewers will get to worry about this over the weekend."

Thursday night

"Looo-ucy, I'm home!" I call in my very best Desi Arnaz hak-sent.

I'm greeted by the four philosophers, all wagging their tails.

"How'd it go—with Charlotte and all?" Mark asks.

"It went," I say with a shrug. "Actually the scene was really hot, but nobody in the crew was impressed because they all think I'm gay."

"So they think there was no acting involved," he says.

"Right. Then we got into a big discussion about how many bites it takes to turn someone into a vampire."

"And the answer is . . . ?"

"And the answer is 'stay tuned.' We're vamping about vampires. Oh, and just so you know, I'm going out of town for the weekend. They're sending me to a fan meet-and-greet in New Orleans. I'm leaving on the red-eye tomorrow night."

"And you're returning . . ."

"Sunday. Sunday midafternoon—but it's just a touch and go. I'll be home to change clothes and then I'm off again. Sunday night is the *Soap Opera Digest* Awards. It's a be-there-or-be-square command performance."

"I'll get my tux cleaned."

"Sorry, I've already been issued a date. Nigel wants me to go with Trent. And besides, this is probably no place for a civilian."

"I see."

I head toward the kitchen in search of some tea—it's been a long day and I'm drained. I walk in just in time to see Nietzsche heaving—again.

"Mark . . . I thought you were gonna take Nietzsche to the vet."

"Didn't get a chance to, sorry."

"And don't you think it's time to take the Christmas tree down? It's almost Valentine's Day."

I bend down with a paper towel to deal with the latest episode and chance to look up. "Mark, come in here, please. Take a look at the cupboards—somebody's been gnawing on the cabinetry. The dogs are eating my house!"

Saturday morning

THE RED-EYE FLIGHT is as painless as air travel can be these days. I even get some sleep, but not nearly enough. There's a car waiting to whisk us to the Windsor Court Hotel, and just as Nigel promised, I'm ushered into a cushy suite with fresh flowers, a balcony with a grand view of the Mississippi, and hot and cold running everything. (Someday I want to ask why in good hotels the housekeeping staff folds the corners of the toilet paper into a V.) I have enough time to freshen up but not nap before it's time to leave.

In the car on the way, Nigel tries valiantly to prep me, even though by now he knows I'm hopeless. "Now, Kate, remember, this is like a game of cat and mouse. Fans who are here want to be one up on their friends at home, so they're going to ask you about what's going to happen to Devon over the next few weeks. Your job is to give them hints and tidbits, but not give away the show. We wouldn't want me putting my hand over your mouth to shut you up again like in Anaheim, now, would we?" he warns.

"No, Dad, I guess 'we' wouldn't."

"Good. So you can tell them that your romance with Lacey will keep going," Nigel says.

"But not that you eventually put a stake through her heart," says Trent.

"Exactly," says Nigel.

"Can I tell them how much I'm looking forward to that day?" I ask archly. "Charlotte's insipid *tabula rasa* is making me nuts. Can I tell them that every time we're on camera together, I am transfixed as I watch my very life force get sucked into her empty vortex?"

"Why, Miss Kate! That's not kind," says Nigel with mock horror.

"Yeah, but it ain't wrong," says Trent. "Charlotte's another Black Hole."

"Well, Conrad Barbera, the network's new head of Daytime, is a tabloid kind of guy," says Nigel, "and so her Black-Holeiness isn't really any concern of his. But—"

"Actually, Nigel, I think you've just come up with her nickname," says Trent. "Charlotte is hereby dubbed 'Her Black Holiness.' "

"Hah! Most excellent! I love it!" I say enthusiastically. "You were saying, Nige . . . ?"

"Barbera could care less if she's literally one of the walking dead on camera. The twits in Standards and Practices may be all worried about the FCC coming down on us, but as far as Barbera is concerned, it's all about ratings," Nigel continues. "His job security rises and falls with viewership, and the 'Cop Bangs Vampire Murderess' storyline is huge."

"Happy to oblige," I say with only a smidgen of sarcasm. "What if they ask whether I become a vampire?"

"Dance around it. Trent, you can tease the idea that you might be the father of Jennifer's baby, and tease Philip's mob connections with Laszlo, but don't give away his involvement in the embezzlement scheme."

"Righto."

The car pulls up to the deliveries entrance to the shopping mall, and we are escorted through crowds of people to a collection of tables under a big banner that reads NEW ORLEANS LOVES *LIVE FOR TOMORROW*! There are what seems like a zillion people milling about in such a small space. It's a bit daunting, and Nigel picks up on my hesitation—even in Anaheim I always thought the crowds were there to see Lauren, not me. "I won't be far, Kate," Nigel whispers soothingly in my ear. "If you get into trouble, just shoot me a look and I'll be right over." He wishes me luck, and then Trent and I begin pressing the flesh.

"Hello, I'm Kimberly," says a self-conscious young woman.

"Hi, Kimberly, I'm Kate."

"You look so much better in person . . . not at all like you look on television."

As soon as the words leave her mouth, Kimberly realizes that what was supposed to be a compliment came out badly and blushes deep scarlet. "It's okay, Kim," I say with a reassuring laugh. "I know what you meant, and I thank you for it. I'd better talk to my lighting guys, though! So . . . you look like you want to ask me a question—what is it?"

"Are you . . . are you . . . are you going to marry Lacey?"

Not under this administration, I think to myself.

Okay—this is the kind of stuff Nigel said to avoid.

"Actually, Kimberly, it's a little too soon to tell. Lacey and Devon are still in the early stages of their romance, and that will continue for a bit, but the murder of Lacey's ex-husband Hamilton and his new wife, Juliette, hangs over their relationship. I think Devon would have a real problem with that, don't you?"

"Oh, yes, of course she would."

"And who have you brought with you today?"

"This is my boyfriend, Broussard," Kim says.

"A pleasure to meet you, Broussard," I say, shaking his hand.

"He doesn't watch," says Kim disapprovingly.

"If you ask me, she takes your show too seriously," he complains. "I'll come home and find her in tears because some character died. Worst than that, she gets upset over the idea that some nonexistent guy is having a fictional affair."

"Now I bet you'd like a photograph. . . ."

Next!

"Hi there, Kate! I'm Heather, and these are my sorority sisters, Haley, Morgan, Madison, and Shelby. Even though we're in class when *Live for Tomorrow* airs, we never miss a show. We tape it and watch it in the evening. I confess that we fast-forward through the commercials, though."

"The Gerber baby food representative won't be too upset, but as far as the Clairol people are concerned, your secret's safe with me. Where do you go to school?"

"Tulane University. Kappa Kappa Gamma."

"Oh my goodness! I met some of your sorority sisters at Disneyland not too long ago. They were from USC."

"Oooh, this is so rad!" exclaims Morgan. "Did you meet someone named Chelsea?"

"I do believe I did." I take a good look at Morgan. "Matter of fact, she looked very much like you. Are you related?"

"That's my twin sister!" she squeals, whipping out her cell phone. "I'm calling her right this minute."

And so it goes for several hours, till we get to "Hi, I'm Gary, and all I want to know is whether you've thought about your immortal soul."

"I beg your pardon?"

"Homosexuality is a mortal sin, and a grievous offense to our Eternal Father. You must repent before your God."

I suppose we should have seen this one coming.

"This country has lost its moral compass. We have become slaves to the pleasures of the flesh, including all manner of abominations, above all homosexuality. It doesn't matter at all if the law of the land in some states lets you people get married—you will have to answer to a higher power for your perversion. Almighty God will never condone what you do."

Listening to this tirade in New Orleans, one of the most tolerant cities in the United States, is surely ironic, but I don't like the way this is headed. I throw Nigel a sharp look. He comes over with a security guard and Gary is quietly but firmly escorted off the premises.

A veritable gaggle comes up to the table en masse. "Good afternoon to all of you! I'm Kate McPhee."

"Pleased to meetchew! I'm Maureen, and this here is my mother, Doreen, and my daughters, Corrine and Noreen."

The family resemblance is unmistakable—they come from a gene puddle, not a pool. They have the same hair, the same eyes, the same chins, the same teeth—or lack thereof.

"We've come all the way from Ponchatoula to see y'all. Ponchatoula is the Strawberry Capital of Louisiana."

Judging by the family before me, even if the dentists in Ponchatoula are terrific, they're as lonely as the Maytag repairman.

"I'm flattered. And who else have you brought with you?"

"These are my cousins Willette, Josette, Claudette, and Mavis." I suppress a giggle, which would have been at Mavis's expense. "Mavis is adopted," adds Maureen, feeling the need to explain why she isn't one of the 'Ettes."

Willette looks like she's expecting a baby, but since they are all somewhat overweight, I dare not ask.

"My goodness! The whole family. You all fit into one car?"

"Took Earl's truck," says Claudette. "Course, he might not be too pleased when he wakes up and finds it gone."

"With the way that man sleeps, we might be back before he wakes up," quips Grandma Doreen. "He surely does spend a lot of time lyin' up there in that bed!"

"Now, Doreen, don't go raggin' on Uncle Earl that way," says Mavis.

"Just never you mind, Miss Mavis. I don't care if he gets so mad when he finds out the truck's gone that he jumps up and bites his lazy-ass self. We all love the show," Doreen continues, "and we love you in it."

"Why, thank you. Thank you very much," I respond. "Tell me what you like the best."

"I love Devon's independence," says Doreen firmly. "I love it that she's strong and that she can go up against the guys."

"I love it, too," says Corrine.

"Reminds me of those great romantic pictures of the forties," says Doreen. "I surely loved those movies."

"Me, too," I concur. "Still do."

"When I was young, my favorites were Claudette Colbert, Joan Crawford, Barbara Stanwyck. I even loved that scrawny no-ass Yankee, Kate Hepburn," she adds with a smile. "Damn if she wasn't uppity with Spencer Tracy—all the time! Those were strong women who didn't make drooling fools of themselves for every man who came by."

"But it seems to me the men were better then, too," says Josette. "The cowboys are all gone—the ones now seem watered down. Considerate and understanding, but bland."

"Like they've all turned into Alan Alda or something," adds Willette.

Note to self: Score one for the Steel Magnolias! The 'Eens and the 'Ettes—and Mavis, of course—are fabulous. These women, like so many who watch us, have a practicality, a resilience, and a sense of humor that get them through what in many instances is a hard-knock life.

Corollary note to self: Be not too quick to judge people by their dentistry.

Just as I finish signing autographs for the 'Eens, the 'Ettes, and their entire extended family of magnolias, Nigel steps forward. "Okay, everyone," he calls, clapping his hands. "On behalf of *Live for Tomorrow,* thank you all for coming today. I know we'll see many of you tomorrow morning for breakfast on the river. Now I have to get Kate and Trent on to their next event. Good night."

Once in the car, Trent and I erupt into a spontaneous duet of moaning. "Next event? What next event? You didn't say anything about a next event!"

"Dinner, of course," says Nigel. "And it's going to be faaabulous."

• • •

"So . . . you've never been to New Orleans, Kate," Nigel states flatly as we arrive at Commander's Palace.

"How'd you know?"

"Because you're pronouncing it 'Nyew Or-leens,'" says Trent, laughing and imitating my British accent. "It's N'awlins, chile!" he adds, honey dripping from his voice.

"Knoohrrlinntz," I try. Too harsh. "Shit. How do you get that syrupy glide in your voice?"

"Miz Kate, sugah, that's why God invented bourbon," explains Nigel.

In Creole cuisine, bourbon isn't just something you drink; it's a cooking staple that goes into everything, like potatoes in Russia. And it certainly does loosen whatever is clipped and Anglo-Saxon in the speech pattern. Trent actually talks me into having the crispy alligator with sugarcane-bourbon barbecue sauce as an appetizer. I follow with boneless duckling with bourbon smashed sweet potatoes. For dessert we share chocolate-bourbon pecan pie and bread pudding with bourbon sauce. And after a flaming bourbon-laced café Pierre, I'm gliii-din' with the best of them and that syrup is rollin' through mah conversation.

And like Ol' Man River, once we leave Commander's Palace it jus' keeps rollin' along . . . through three jazz joints and finally through the hotel's Polo Club Lounge. . . .

Sunday morning

8:15! 8:15!! 8:15!!!

. . . which explains why this morning my head won't fit through the door, and why I have eyes like tiny surgical incisions as we rendezvous in the lobby for the *Delta Queen* fan riverboat breakfast.

"Good fucking morning," I say to my traveling companions. "What is it about N'awlins—did I say it right?—that makes setting fire to a cup of coffee seem perfectly reasonable?"

"It's below sea level?" offers Nigel. Impeccably dressed and groomed, it's not fair that he doesn't look the slightest bit hungover, even though he kept up with us throughout the night—at least I think he did.

"And which of you bastards is going to claim responsibility for pouring that last *café brûlot* down my throat?" I demand, trying very hard not to move my head at all. "Not only was I still drunk at four thirty A.M., but thanks to the coffee I was a wide-awake drunk!"

"Seemed like a good idea at the time," says Trent, very quietly. His eyes, like mine, are slits.

"And at the time, Kate, you didn't seem to mind in the slightest," adds Nigel primly. "*Au contraire,* you thought it was such a swell idea that you bought a round for those rowdy Tulane boosters at the table next to us. If you care to recall, in their copious gratitude they helped you learn the Tulane fight song."

Oh, it all comes back to me, alas. "Green Wave, Green Wave, hats off to thee," I involuntarily begin to sing.

"Hold that line for the Olive and Blue," Trent continues softly. "We will cheer for you. . . . Crap—I can't tell if I'm hung over or still drunk," he admits. "Did we really do that?"

"Oh yes indeedy," Nigel confirms. "But wait. There's more. Then the two of you broke into a really off-key *a cappella* rendition of 'Ode to Billy Joe.' It was so painful to listen to that by the time you were done, forget Billy Joe McAllister—I was ready to jump off the Tallahatchie Bridge myself! But . . ."

"But what?" I'm afraid to hear what comes next.

"But I could have doubled my salary by taking photos of the two of you and selling them on the Internet," he says with a smile.

"Show a little compassion, will you, Nige?" I plead. "You're dealing with two really impaired individuals here. I've no idea how I'm going to survive this breakfast."

"But I do," he declares confidently. "Kate, you can do this," he says, grabbing my shoulders and launching into caretaker mode. "What you have here is a two-hour problem. I know you both feel rotten, but all you have to do is bolt down a bit of eggs sardou and fried potatoes, and be nice to the fans."

My stomach flip-flops. "Sorry, but the thought of food is absolutely revolting."

"Actually a good greasy breakfast will help," Nigel says, almost maternally. "Ballast. And as soon as we're on the river, I'll get the bartender to make you a Virgin Mary with a bit of Gatorade thrown in."

"Bleah! I couldn't, Nigel. I couldn't possibly."

"I don't wanna hear it, Kate. You need fluids."

"Draw two, innkeeper," says Trent weakly.

"After we dock, we'll stop at a drugstore for some Pedialyte, then head straight to the airport for the trip back to LA."

"Isn't that baby formula?" asks Trent.

"Not quite. It's what they give kids who are severely dehydrated," Nigel explains, "and I think you both qualify, my children."

"Thanks, Dad."

"Once we're airborne, I intend to keep pouring liquid down your gullets all across the country. I don't care if your kidneys are floating and your bladders are doin' the backstroke by the time we're over East Jesus, New Mexico. You're gonna keep drinking. I need you guys recovered—no, not just recovered, but *scin-till-a-ting*—by tonight for the *Soap Opera Digest* Awards."

"You're all heart, Nige," Trent says.

"I'm a publicist," Nigel shoots back. "I have no heart—I just put up a good front and pretend I have one 'cause it makes it easier to do my job. What are you wearing tonight, Kate?"

"Ralph Lauren, black silk, long, halter top, very linear, very understated."

"And very elegant, I'm sure," says Nigel. "Trent, the car will come for you first. Then you'll swing by and pick up Kate. Kate, you absolutely **must** be ready on time. You're due on the red carpet at six forty."

"But the show doesn't start till seven thirty."

"Yes, but my dear, you have to be seen and talked to before then."

"Ah yes, the media circus," says Trent.

Sunday night

Nothing quite prepares you for this business of being on display on the red carpet, which is to say being on display and being judged. It's a little like being part of the Miss America pageant, with all of us in the Evening Gown Competition, followed, of course, by the Answer-the-Same-

Question-We're-Asking-Everyone-Else Competition. Evening gown–wise, I should have known better than to go head-to-head with Meredith and the three blondes—Alison, Amber, and Tiffany—not to mention every other lead actress in Daytime. My "very simple, very linear" dress seems "very plain" next to all of the beaded and spangled gowns I see around me.

I grip Trent's hand tightly as we tread the red rug, brave the flashbulbs, and run the print and on-air media gauntlet. To me the red carpet looks like a runway—at the end of it you either lift off or crash and burn.

There's no way I'll be airborne at the end; I'm in the middle of girlie-girl nirvana. Trent and I walked off the plane from New Orleans a couple of hours ago, went home, got dressed, and came over here. (And much as I hate to admit it, Nigel's drown-a-hangover-in-Pedialyte cure had both of us feeling pretty much human by the time we landed.) It's clear to me now that the other women I see around me spent the entire day just getting ready for this evening. They've obviously kept a squadron of personal stylists, manicurists, hairdressers, and makeup artists busy for hours on end.

Consequently, the girlie-girls are a lineup of total perfection, each one more flawless than the last. But I don't think it would have mattered in the slightest if I'd done exactly what they had. All the stylists and hairdressers and face painters in the universe couldn't transform me into one of those paragons of femininity.

A local entertainment reporter shoves her microphone in front of my face. "And here come Trent Winterfield and red-hot Kate McPhee from *Live for Tomorrow*. How does it feel to be here this evening, Kate?"

"Speak in French when you can't think of the English for a thing," the Queen said sternly to Alice. "Turn out your toes as you walk—and remember who you are."

As I mouth inane replies to banal questions from journalists, I'm aware that I'm swelling up like a jumbo jet. No matter what I might have done earlier today, tonight I'd still be a big sweaty hulk, an ungainly Airbus trying to maneuver among the Learjets.

And of course, they sit everyone from the same show together, so when we finally enter the theatre I'm surrounded by the flower of *Live for Tomorrow* womanhood, and I feel more out of place than ever. It's all I can do not to abort the Airbus takeoff and run for the car, but just for good measure, I feel a monster blister coming up under the heel strap of the sandal on my right foot. Trying to walk out of here is gonna be painful, either now or at the end of the evening. I exchange air kisses with my flowery cast mates, then swell up some more. As they always are, the four of them are polite to my face, but as they continue to whisper to one another, I can just imagine what they're saying.

NARCISSUS (ALISON)

I think she comes from a different kind of garden.
She's certainly not like the rest of us. Maybe she's
a cactus.

TULIP (TIFFANY)

I think she's a wildflower! I don't think I've ever
seen a proper garden flower with that kind of blossom.

NARCISSUS (ALISON)

Certainly not here. And did you notice her petals?
What a peculiar color!

DAISY (AMBER)

No fragrance, either! I think she's a fungus.

NARCISSUS (ALISON)

Just look at her leaves!

TULIP (TIFFANY)

Not like ours at all.

DAISY (AMBER)

Just what are you, Alice?

ALICE

I guess you could say I'm a Katarina McPheeyana Devo-
nensis.

SNAPDRAGON (MEREDITH)

Looks like a common dykeweed to me.

Only Lauren Elizabeth leans over and says, "The rest of these broads are all
overdone. I think you look quite chic."

ROSEBUD (LAUREN)

I think she's pretty!

SNAPDRAGON (MEREDITH)

No one asked you, bud!

Lauren herself is looking very sophisticated in a simple Narciso Rodriguez
that is the color of champagne. The outfit is more than just a lovely fashion statement: it's a declaration of independence—or a coming-out party,
of sorts. She is obviously on the brink of womanhood, and it should be
clear to one and all that her days of playing Mallory as a flat-chested, rather
plain vanilla junior high student are pretty much over. Either Daphne will
have to let Mallory age up, or Lauren will have to give way to a younger
actress.

Monday morning

The rehash of who won what, whether or not it was deserved, and how that affects handicapping the Daytime Emmy nominations takes up most of the conversation in Gossip Central the next morning.

"I don't know why they had to change the Emmy nominating system," snips Alison. "It seemed to be working fine."

"I think the problem was that the old way tipped the scales in favor of shows with a larger cast," explains Richard.

"Yeah, like us!" says Trent.

"I don't understand how it's supposed to work," says Amber.

"We have to do our own prenominating in each category—within our own show," says Richard. "The top two vote-getters in each category become *Live for Tomorrow*'s candidates for possible Emmy nomination. All shows get two candidates per category, tops."

"Then what?" Amber asks.

"Then they're reviewed by a screening panel—a jury of your peers," says Trent. "Not that you have any, Amber. You are truly *sui generis*."

"Isn't that a munificent swine?" asks LaTrisa with a mischievous twinkle.

"Swine? Me? Sooey what?" says Amber with something of an adolescent pout.

"I intended no offense, truly," LaTrisa says.

"Nor did I. What I meant, dear Amber, is that you're in a class by yourself," says Trent grandly.

"Then why didn't you say that?" Amber cries.

"He did!" exclaims LaTrisa.

"Successful double entendre presumes the preexistence of single entendre," decrees Richard slyly.

"Hey guys, have you seen this?" Nigel comes in waving a printout from one of the soap websites. "May I quote? 'The fashion report card from last night's *Soap Opera Digest* Awards is mixed. There were hits and misses abounding; there were sights for sore eyes—and eyesores. Kudos to *LFT*'s very popular Lauren Elizabeth Fielding—obviously all grown-up now—and Kate McPhee for understated elegance. And Trent Winterfield wears his Hugo Boss tux with a casual panache worthy of Pierce Brosnan's 007.' And there are your happy smiling mediagenic faces and impeccable attire on the red carpet."

Applause breaks out in Gossip Central as Trent stands, bows, and blows kisses to his imaginary adoring public. "Wait, I'm not done!" says Nigel. "There's a photo of Meredith, too, with a caption that reads, 'What *was* she thinking?' It continues, 'Meredith Contini made quite a fashion statement—or shall we say misstatement—in a garish and unflattering ruched and ruffled fuchsia gown that could have been mistaken for casket lining.' "

"Fits the vampire theme, at least," LaTrisa wisecracks.

"Eeew ouch!" Ruben, who has wandered in for some caffeine and conversation, winces. "We're all gonna pay for that one! I told her that dress was a bad idea, but of course the Queen is never gonna remember that I said so."

"Okay, back to this Emmy business," says Alison. "What happens with the screening panel?"

"Each soap places ten people on the panel, and the candidates from each show get a reel together," Richard explains. "The screening panel looks them over and culls the nominees from that group."

"But that's where it gets gory," says LaTrisa. "Most candidates never get past the panel. You figure there are ten shows, with a max of two candidates per category, or up to twenty in all. The panel whittles that down to just five nominees for each award, and then the Academy voters cast their ballots."

"I'd like to thank the members of the Academy," Trent intones in a falsetto, fluttering his fingers in an impersonation that is clearly intended to sound like Meredith.

"Pbbbbblttt!" I can't resist razzing him, but of course, he asked for it.

"So who's putting a reel together?" Alison asks.

"Lauren Elizabeth. Me," says Trent. "Vlad. Carlos was a maybe. Meredith, of course. She does every year."

"Kate, you really should, you know," LaTrisa urges.

"Yeah, you should," Trent agrees.

"I think it's a splendid idea," says Richard.

"I dunno," I say dubiously. "The idea of looking over old footage and confronting my past mistakes is just dreadful."

"We'll help," LaTrisa offers.

"Okay, McPhee Emmy Coconspirators: my quarters—now!" says Trent.

Trent, Tri, and I shoehorn ourselves into Trent's dressing room. "You know, guys," I say as we settle in, "I still don't know about doing this. I feel stupid, like I'm honking my own horn."

"Get over it, girlfriend," states LaTrisa. "Honk away! You've done terrific work this season, and that should be acknowledged—celebrated, even."

"But I don't . . ." Through the wall we hear the shrill voice of Meredith on the phone. From the sound of things, she's having another meltdown. Trent holds his index finger to his lips, trots into the bathroom, and returns with three water tumblers. We invert them against the wall and press our ears to the cool, smooth glass.

"*Casket lining! They said my dress looked like casket lining!* You **have** to get that taken off the Internet, you hear me? You **have** to! . . . Well, there must be something you can do. Oh God, Renato, you are so useless!

"And Renato, don't forget that we've got the hospital fund-raiser tonight. Yes, you have to go. It's an ark event—married couples two by two. It's important that we're seen there. Why? Because our products are in the goody bags for all the guests. Product placement is everything—*everything*. How many times do I have to say that?

"What? Polo match? I don't want to fuckin' hear it. . . . Well, they're just going to have to get along without you for the second half. Chukker? Whatever. What? Then find a sub—surely somebody else can play that stupid game.

"And tell Carmen to make sure your tux is cleaned and pressed—you looked like shit the last time. What? Whaddaya mean we won't have a chauffeur—wherethefuck is Jesus? Call him back and tell him to get his shiftless ass back to work. Day off? Because why? What's the Bentley doing in the shop? Make them give it back. No, you will *not* call a car service. Meredith Contini would *never* be seen in a Lincoln Town Car.

"Now, Renato, about this nomination reel for the Emmys. You have to help me pick the shows. I've already watched all my tapes and marked the ones I can't use. What do you mean why? Don't you understand anything? Because my hair's no good . . . I've been working on Alison and Tiffany not to submit this year, and Amber's too stupid to tie her own shoes. It'll be just my luck that it'll come down to me and Kate. . . . What the fuck do you mean, Kate who? Dammit Renato, we've been married for twenty-seven years and you know nothing about my work. Kate McPhee is the English backstabbing bitch who's been playing Devon Merrick. Yeah, the one I had the run-in with about the bangs. That fag Nigel has been trotting her dyke carcass all over the country to promote her. Really pisses me off."

I pull my glass away from the wall. I've heard quite enough, thank you. "Okay then," I say softly, "now that that's settled, I think one show that should be on the reel for sure is the one in the bar with Kirk."

"Right," says Trent.

"But don't forget the autopsy table with Charlotte," adds LaTrisa.

Tuesday/Early March

A memo is posted on the board in Gossip Central:

Congratulations to our
Live for Tomorrow Pre-Nominees

Live for Tomorrow has forwarded the following pre-nominees to the NATAS Emmy screening panel for their consideration:

Outstanding Lead Actor:
  Trent Winterfield/Philip Salisbury
  Vladimir Kovacs/Laszlo Szekely

Outstanding Lead Actress:
  Meredith Contini/Regina Abell
  Kate McPhee/Devon Merrick

Outstanding Younger Actress:
  Lauren Elizabeth Fielding/Mallory Abell

Outstanding Supporting Actor:
  Carlos de la Fuente/Enrique Morales

The final list of Daytime Emmy Nominees will be announced live on the *Today* show on March 11.

Daytime Emmys will be telecast from Radio City on May 15.

24

A week later

DON'T SHOOT. It's me, the Emmy Pre-Nominee," I say as I turn the key in the door. Silence. Well, silence except for four galloping dogs. "Mark?"

Nothing. Nothing until I see the note on the pillow:

Dearest Kate,

 I know it's short notice, but I've gone to Toronto.

 Emergency rewrite/theatrical release. Stupid teen comedy, but at least it's not television. Screen credit—gotta start somewhere.

 I'm sorry to leave you with the 4-leggeds. I know they're a handful, but I can't take them with me. I'll be back for them, I promise. Extra 40 lb. bag of Science Diet in your closet.

Mark

I wander back into the living room and slump into a floor pillow in front of the Christmas tree. Drusilla crawls into my lap. "Well," I say to her, leaning back against the couch, "so much for that. I guess it's just you and me and the guys." As if on cue, the guys, quiet for once, come and cluster themselves around me. Kierkegaard sits, or rather half sits, on the couch—fanny and hind legs on the cushions, front feet on the floor. Hobbes begins insistently nudging my elbow. "Yeah, I know," I say to him. "I should take it down one of these days.

"So maybe he was never going to be the great love of my life," I explain, addressing myself to Sartre, who is at eye level, "but even so . . ." He gives me a consoling poodle-kiss in my ear, which Kierkegaard attempts to match from the other side, except that when he's done, the whole side of my face is wet.

"What are you doing, Neetch? Are you sure this is wise?" The doxie is attempting to claim half my lap and share it with Drusilla. To my surprise, she lets him but insists that I scratch behind her ear as a quid pro quo.

"This all started as a way to get over Rafe. It was supposed to be fun. It was never supposed to be anything heavy or serious. You all heard it. So I put this question before the Committee," I say to the group, "I ask you . . . now that he's gone, how come I don't feel any better?"

A bit of melancholy comes over me. I turn on the tree lights, pour myself a glass of wine, and throw a little Norah Jones on the CD player. Before I get too downhearted, however, I pick up the phone and call Christine.

"He's gone," I say.

"Well surprise-surprise," she says. "You okay?"

"Sort of." It's an honest answer. "Took off for Toronto on a rewrite gig. Don't know how I'm going to manage with the dogs."

"Wait a minute—he left the dogs with you?"

"Yes."

"Kate . . . Listen up. I'm not a dogophobe, I like dogs, I love dogs, but this group was running amok when there were two of you—what the hell are you going to do all by yourself?"

"That's what I'm trying to figure out."

"I have one word to say to you."

"Which is—"

"Outplacement. Find another home for them, together if you can, separately if need be."

Kierkegaard puts his very large head on my shoulder, rendering me nearly horizontal.

An enormous puppy was looking down at her with large round eyes, and feebly stretching out one paw, trying to touch her. "Poor little thing!" said Alice, in a coaxing tone.

"Oh I couldn't," I say, grabbing one of the doggie toys in the living room and tossing it lightly. My quartet of philosophers goes scrambling after it at full cry.

Hardly knowing what she did, she picked up a little bit of stick and held it out to the puppy: whereupon the puppy jumped into the air off all its feet at once, with a yelp of delight, and rushed at the stick, and made believe to worry it. Then Alice dodged behind a great thistle, to keep herself from being run over.

"Oh you could," Christine says firmly, mocking my voice. "You must."

"I'll think about it," I say, "but he said in his note that he's coming back for them. See you in the morning."

"Okay, you guys, stay here," I say to the menagerie after I hang up. "I've gotta go think about this, and to do that I need coffee."

I head down to the Starbucks. "Hey Sondra—gimme a Venti hazelnut latte with an add-shot, please."

"Thure thing. How ya been thoin', Thevon?—I mean Kate."

"I've been better, Sondra. I seem to have inherited four dogs, at least temporarily."

"Oooh! Puppies!"

"They're very sweet, but they're entirely untrained, and I'm gone all day long and they're wrecking my house. *And* I've got mountains of mail piling up at the studio that I have no way of dealing with because I have no time and nobody else knows enough about the show to . . ."

"Tooo what?"

"Answer them." An inspiration begins to form in my head. "Sondra, let me ask you a question."

"Okay."

"How'd you like to become my personal assistant?"

"Yeth."

"Just part-time."

"Yeth."

"You can keep working here if you want to. There's just one catch—the tongue bolt's got to go."

"Thtay here. Be right back." Sondra retires to the loo and returns unbolted.

"When do I start?" she asks.

Next morning

Sondra shows up at my house at 8:30 A.M.—still boltless—bringing me a fresh latte and a chocolate croissant. Already it's a good day. If I'm not mistaken, there is even a little less hardware in her ears and eyebrows as well. "Today is a day to get your bearings," I tell her. "Take the dogs for a walk—you can take the little three together if you like, but whatever you do, walk Kierkegaard by himself, or you'll be airborne before you get to the corner. Then make a list of stuff you think needs doing around here. Let's see about getting a handle on my domestic chaos. Later in the week we'll get to work on the fan mail."

I skip off to the studio thinking I've made a baby step toward being a grown-up. I leave dressed in my grubbiest sweats with no makeup at all, knowing that Charlie and Christine will put me right before I have to present myself to the camera. I'm just through the studio gate when my cell goes off. "Kate, this is Sondra. You need to come home right away—the fire department is here."

"I can't possibly, Sondra. I have a long day on set. Why is the fire department at the house?"

"Because it's on fire."

. . .

When I arrive, Sondra is herding dogs out front and the firefighters are just mopping up. Even out in the open air, everything smells dank, acrid, and sour. "Ms. McPhee, I'm Captain Frank Bernardo, LAFD."

"Thank you for coming so promptly, Captain."

"Happy to be of service, ma'am, but you should really thank Ms. . . ." He looks at Sondra. It dawns on me that I have no idea what her last name is.

"Huffnagel," she says. "Sondra Huffnagel."

"You really should thank Ms. Huffnagel here. Quick thinking on her part—she called us, then got your dogs out of the house."

"How bad is it?"

"Could have been much worse. Oh, and I just want to add that my wife loves the show."

"Thanks, always good to hear. Sondra, have you seen Drusilla?"

"No, Kate, and I feel terrible about that. I tried to find her when I rounded up the dogs, but then the smoke got too thick."

"Who's Drusilla?" one of the firemen asks.

"My cat."

"Let me check with my men. If there are no hot spots, we'll go back in and look for her."

As Captain Bernardo and I proceed toward the front door, I fear the worst. My head is downcast as I walk, because I'm afraid that I'm going to find a crispy lump instead of a live cat.

Obviously my body language must have given me away. "Don't give up hope," the captain says as we cross the threshold. "Cats are pretty resourceful. . . . Holy shit! It's March, Ms. McPhee. Please tell me that's not a Christmas tree."

"It is, or rather, it was," I say guiltily. What's left is a blackened broomstick. The skeletal remains are glistening, and droplets of water are trickling off the charred stub ends of the branches, like tears.

"I'm afraid you're gonna be camping out tonight, Ms. McPhee."

"I beg your pardon?"

"And lots of nights to come—as in camping out in someone else's house. This is a red-tag situation—the damage here is too extensive to let you stay. You'll want to get your personal effects out of the house and get it boarded up."

"But—"

"The tree was obviously Ground Zero of the fire. Leaving it up so long constitutes negligence; you're lucky I don't write you a citation." The captain strides across the sodden carpet toward the tree carcass, then picks up something from the floor. "Do you have any idea what this is?" he asks as he hands it to me.

Newly homeless person that I am, I start to laugh. I laugh until tears flow down my cheeks, because that's all there is to do.

The captain has handed me a singed plastic pancake that used to be the Meredith Contini doll at the top of the tree. Her red dress may have vaporized, but the perfect red sandals are now embedded in the congealed puddle of shriveled peachy tan polystyrene. The recognizable, intact head—with tiara—sits square in the middle. Since it's Meredith, it's no surprise that every hair is in place.

"Meredith had a *really* good meltdown this time!" I say, dabbing at the corners of my eyes.

"Wow!" Sondra is wide-eyed, looking at the pancake. "Looks like the Wicked Witch of the West after Dorothy threw water on her."

"Bingo."

Just then I hear a soft scritching noise from the bathroom. "Droos?" I call. More scritching, and a soft meow of complaint. "Drusilla!"

I run to the bathroom, open the door, and pick up a very cold, very wet but otherwise uninjured cat.

"Here's a towel," Sondra offers.

"Thank you."

"You're welcome."

"No, not for the towel, for everything! None of the animals would be alive without you—I'm so glad you're here. But now it's going to be a very long day, and I'm going to have to ask you to take on a great deal. Can you handle it?"

"What's next?"

"I've got to get back on the set. When I left, Marty said they'd try to work around me, but by now I'm sure that my absence is holding up the taping. Sondra, do you have a driver's license?"

"Yes."

"Good. It's going to be cozy, but you and I and all of the quadrupeds are going to get into the car and drive to the studio. You're going to drop me off, find a place to board the dogs and Drusilla for the night, come back to the house, pack up my toiletries, grab all the clothes and take them to the cleaners to get the smoke smell out, call a board-up company, and then check back with me. Okay?"

It looks like a clown car from the circus as we cram ourselves into the still-lopsided Honda. As we start out, Sartre, Kierkegaard, and Hobbes are in the back; Sondra is driving. Drusilla and I are in the shotgun seat, and

Nietzsche is between my feet. Kierk, however, is unhappy with the seating arrangements; he keeps trying to climb in front, causing Sondra to commit impromptu right-hand turns. Finally it's just easier (and safer) to trade places with him, so Drusilla, Nietzsche, and I climb in back. Even with a seat all to himself, the Dane is hunched forward. His nose is up against the windshield, and he's panting so much that he's fogging up everything. To solve the problem Sondra opens the sunroof, and he gratefully extends first his nose and ears, and finally the entirety of his huge blocky head, out the top. The imperturbable parking guard maintains his poker face when we roll into the studio lot. As we do, however, I'm aware that a news van is streaking across the pavement on a trajectory to meet us in front of the building.

By the time we come to a full and complete stop at the curb, a camera-man, a sound guy, and a reporter with microphone are poised and ready. I peek at myself in the rearview and cringe. I'm a fright—no makeup and straggly unwashed hair. My baggy grey sweats are covered with hair—feline and canine—not to mention coffee stains, drool, and slobber. But there's nothing for it; there's no way I can avoid facing them without looking like I'm running away.

The reporter extends her microphone in my direction, and the camera-man zooms in on my naked face. "Yes, we're here with Devon Merrick, or should I say Kate McPhee. Congratulations, Kate."

"Ah, thank you."

I have no clue what's going on here.

"The Daytime Emmy nominations have just been announced, and it's a very good day for *Live for Tomorrow*."

What?

"Indeed."

"How does it feel to be nominated with your fellow cast members Meredith Contini, Trent Winterfield, and Lauren Elizabeth Fielding?"

Nominated? Me? Steady there, Katiegirl. Team player time.

"Uh, fine. It's a great honor."

"Do you think of your nomination as a victory for gay women every-where?"

Think—what would Nigel want you to do here? Dance. He'd want me to dance.

"Well . . . ," I begin, "the fact that Devon Merrick has been so well re-ceived shows that our viewers want to watch good drama with interesting characters."

Sidestep. Sidestep. Swoop and parry. Sidestep and sashay.

"And I think that's a victory for everybody."

And blah blah blah. What can I do to get this woman out of my face?

Suddenly Kierkegaard starts on a basso profundo woofing jag. The cameraman pans away from me and points the handheld at the car. "And as you folks at home can see," the reporter continues, "for Kate McPhee, this is a family affair. She's brought her dogs and a young woman I can only assume is her companion to the set of *LFT* to celebrate her nomination. And now, back to you in the studio."

Aaaaaaaaaaaiiiiiiiieee! Companion?

Much as I dread it, it's only fair that I have a conversation with Sondra about this, since I can only imagine how it's gonna play on the evening news.

⋯ ⋯ ⋯

"Good morning, finally!" I say as I head into Gossip Central.

"Good afternoon," says Christine, correcting me.

"Yeah, I guess that would have to be right."

"Oh mymy, I seem to have my work cut out for me today," she says, surveying the damage that is my face. "Funny, you don't look like a nominee."

"Tell you what—let's burn your house down and see what you look like afterward!"

"Never mind, Kate. Let's get this urban renewal project under way."

"I'm going to have to find a new place to rent, you know."

"It's not going to be possible, Kate. You're gonna have to buy a house."

"What do you mean?"

"What do you mean, What do I mean? Mark ran off and left you with the original unrentable household—that's what I mean! You are a landlord's worst nightmare. No property owner in his right mind would take you on as a tenant. I can see the ad now," Christine says:

Wanted to Rent:
   1-bedroom house for single woman with 4 unruly dogs and 1 spoiled cat.
   Require huge closet space.
   Modern wiring essential. Overhead sprinkler system desirable.
   Need 6-foot fence (8-foot preferable) and vast yard with room for 4 dog runs, one extra large.
   Oh, and almost never home. Deaf but vigilant neighbors a plus.

"Point well taken. This is probably going to be a little more difficult than I thought."

Once I'm renovated and camera ready, I leave Gossip Central and I detour on my way back to my dressing room and decide to pay Rhonda a visit.

"Hey Rhonda!" I say as I lean into the doorjamb of her office. Rhonda's office is neat and clean, except for nine-foot-tall stacks of scripts and soap mags which leave the place cozy but slightly claustrophobic.

"Hey yourself, Ms. Nominee. Congrats, by the way."

"Thanks. Got a question for ya. Actually, it's a favor to ask."

"Anything."

"Don't say that."

"Too late."

"Can I crash at your house tonight?"

"Of course."

"Aren't you going to ask why?"

"Nope. If you want to tell me, tell me."

"Meredith short-circuited on the top of my Christmas tree."

"It's still up?"

"Was."

"You put Meredith on top of your tree?"

"Didn't have an angel. The lights around her legs fritzed out and the tree caught fire."

"And your house is . . ."

"Charbroiled. Medium well. Being boarded up, even as we speak. I'm looking for a place to stash me and the four-leggeds, at least on a temporary basis. It's going to be a fortune to board them."

"You're more than welcome to my pullout couch for as long as you like. In terms of your four-leggeds, I can only solve the smallest part of your problem, which is to say cat yes, dogs no. You shouldn't chew on your hair, you know."

"It keeps my hands away from my throat. I'm still trying to get Daphne to let me cut it. Maybe I'll chew it off. She won't be able to reprimand me for that."

"No, but Charlie will. You stand a good chance this year, ya know," she says.

"Yeah yeah yeah. It's a nice thought, but the truth is that you don't know, and neither do I."

"I'll be there, you know," she says. "Dinner's on me if you win."

I sit on her desk, eat her M&M's, and ponder how many of my problems winning the Emmy would solve—if any.

"I have to figure out what to wear," I mumble through purple and green chocolate candies and gaze at the TV screen, where *Live for Tomorrow* plays endlessly as rehearsals turn into takes, and takes turn into scene changes, and thence into magic.

"You've got a couple of months—plenty of time to figure it out—but if I were you, I'd stay away from anything that even vaguely resembles fuchsia casket lining," she says with a smile.

Sondra returns to pick me up, bearing an overnight bag for me and Drusilla in a new cat carrier. "Dogs are at the Ritz Pet Hotel," she says.

I open my mouth to question her about it, but she beats me to it. "Cage free. Animal socializers play with them every day. Filtered water."

Ka-ching! The owner of the Ritz Pet Hotel must already be on his way to Hawaii—on my nickel.

"Platform beds. Aromatherapy to help them sleep," Sondra continues. "Music is piped in, but TV is optional."

By the time she's done, I have just one question. "Do they have a room for me?" I ask.

"They're gonna bathe them there, too—they all smelled like smoke. Had to get them to the vet first, though, because the kennel wouldn't take them without proof of their shots."

"You got all of them shots?"

Ka-ching ka-ching!! The cash register in my head tallies up the damage. Both the vet and the owners of the Ritz Hotel are probably on their way to Bora Bora by now, first class.

"Had to, Kate, yes. Oh, and Nietzsche has a UTI," Sondra adds.

"A what?"

"Urinary tract infection. That's why he was peeing so much. They ran some tests. Then the vet gave him a couple of shots and some antibiotics to continue the treatment. The drugs should also help with the hole in his stomach lining."

"My bulimic dachshund has an ulcer?"

"No. They did an X-ray. Doc thinks he probably swallowed something— maybe a chicken bone. . . ."

"We never gave him bones—they're bad for dogs."

"Could have been a piece of wood."

"My God—the cupboards! One of them was gnawing on the cupboards."

"Coulda been him. Coulda have been one of the others and he just ate the splinters that fell to the floor. In any event, something poked a hole in his stomach. He should be fine—eventually."

Ka-ching Ka-ching Ka-ching-ing-ing-ing! Forget Hawaii. Forget Bora Bora. The vet and the owners of the Ritz have now each bought a private yacht that sleeps twelve and are cruising the Greek Islands with a live-aboard French chef.

The Honda begins making a series of unhappy grinding noises as we drive up Santa Monica Boulevard. I suppose that's not surprising, since I have no clear recollection of putting any form of liquid—gas, oil, water— into any of its various orifices in living memory, but all of the idiot lights on the dash are reading normal.

"The problem seems to be in the transmission," says Sondra. "How long have you been driving on the donut?"

"The what?"

"The mini-spare."

The specter of Erwin Saunders flits through my memory bank. "Since sometime in the fall, I think."

"Oh Kate! Don't you know that driving around for too long on one of those things wrecks the tranny?"

We limp and lurch along toward the Starbucks where Sondra works, and on the way I mention the possibility that she might be IDed as my "companion" when my nomination is reported. "You've done a remarkable job today," I say as we pull up. "Whatever I'm paying you, it's not enough." As she gets out I give her a hug.

Flash! A paparazzo captures the moment—ambush journalism at its finest.

"Oh Sondra, I'm so sorry!"

"It's okay, Kate, really," she says. "Let 'em think what they want."

"But your boyfriend . . ."

"Don't have one."

"Your parents . . ."

"Orange County. Button-down conservative. They can't think any worse of me than they do already."

At that point I decide to walk in with her. In case there's a reporter trailing the photographer, it's not fair for her to have to deal with that by herself.

But there isn't. The photog was just a lone wolf. Sondra greets her coworkers and dons her green apron. "There's a small bulletin board in the corner," she says. "You might want to put up a message about needing a place to live."

As I'm putting up the note, I become aware of a woman looking over my shoulder.

"You need a house?" she asks. "My name is Gudrun." Gudrun is petite, attractive, and wearing earrings that look like tiny double-bladed hatchets.

I explain the situation. "Hey—we love dogs," she says with a smile. "Janice here and I own a house in Benedict Canyon. Our last tenant just moved out. It's got a sturdy fence and a large yard. You're welcome to come look at it and see if it will work for you."

Okay, they're obviously a gay couple. Was that just a lucky shot, or do they think I look butch? And if they do, is that a good thing or a bad thing?

"Anything to help a sister," says Janice, scribbling down the address.

"I'll drop by and see it tomorrow. Interesting earrings by the way, Gudrun."

Ethics check, Katiegirl. Sisterhood is powerful, but I feel like a bit of an impostor.

It's now apparent that they think I'm gay. Is it tacky—or worse—to let them continue to think that in order to maybe get a house where I can put the dogs?

I'm still thinking about that as I jump back into the car and head for Rhonda's. The car now sounds like a bucket of bolts. Guiltily, I nurse it into the parking lot of a minimall on Santa Monica Boulevard, where it finally gnashes to a halt.

Okay—no need to panic. Just call the rental company. How could they know this is my fault? Tell 'em to pick it up and leave me another one.

I open the glove box to fish out the papers. Papers? What papers?? Nothing, well, nothing except parking citations. Was this Hertz? Avis? Alamo? National? Instant amnesia—no clue. I'd call a cab, but that would just put off the problem to the morning, when I'd have much less time to deal with it. But hark. Out of the corner of my eye I see the sign: RAINBOW RENT-A-CAR—BY THE DAY, WEEK, OR MONTH.

Twenty minutes later, I'm out the door and jangling the keys as I head for the new Jeep Cherokee Limited in the postage-stamp lot. I inhale the new car smell of the pearl grey leather as I climb in, or rather up and in. The helpful staff has already deposited Drusilla on the passenger seat, where she complains, but only halfheartedly. Wait! What's that in the back of the Jeep? The helpful staff has also transferred the remains of Meredith's gift basket.

Note to self: Ask Sondra to help me buy a car.

25

Aꜰᴛᴇʀ ꜱᴘᴇɴᴅɪɴɢ ᴛʜᴇ ɴɪɢʜᴛ at Rhonda's, I head into the studio early in the morning. My first scenes aren't till much later in the day, but Daphne has asked me to work with a couple of actors who are auditioning for a new character: Dr. Marcello Bertone. Dr. Bertone will be our Mafioso M.D., a doctor who has a regular practice with regular patients, but also leads another life on the QT. He treats gunshot wounds, helps mobsters and their women find solutions for inopportune pregnancies, uses treatment of legitimate clients to cover illicit drug activities, and works closely with Laszlo and Trent.

The audition scene has Devon investigating the doctor for his illicit activities, and him responding by threatening to kill me.

INT. NEW HOPE MEDICAL CLINIC—EVENING

                    DEVON
    So, Dr. Bertone, a patient of yours is dead under mys-
    terious circumstances.

                MARCELLO #1
            (age twenty-eight, blond, green eyes)

    I'm not sure how mysterious the circumstances are, De-
    tective Merrick. Ms. Demetrios died of a ruptured
    appendix.

                    DEVON
    When a seventeen-year-old girl dies of a ruptured ap-
    pendix without first complaining of abdominal pain, I'd
    call those circumstances mysterious.

                MARCELLO #1
            (his voice rising)

    Nonsense.

                        DEVON

We'll see what the medical examiner has to say about
that.

                    MARCELLO #1
                      (yelling)

You're going to order an autopsy on Athena Demetrios?
You can't be serious.

                        DEVON

Oh, but I can be—deadly serious.

                    MARCELLO #1
                (at the top of his lungs)

You'll live to regret this, Detective—but not for
long.

Well, that didn't work. He's cute, but someone should tell him that loud is not an emotion. The only weapon in this guy's dramatic arsenal is to increase the decibels. Thank you. Next!

INT. NEW HOPE MEDICAL CLINIC—EVENING

                    MARCELLO #2
        (age thirty-three +/–, brown hair, blue eyes)

You're going to order an autopsy on Athena Demetrios?
You can't be serious.

                        DEVON

Oh, but I can be—deadly serious.

                    MARCELLO #2
      (yelling even louder, grabbing me by the shoulders
                  and shaking me)

I'd think very carefully about that if I were you. The
members of the Demetrios family have been my patients
for years.

Ah, a bit of improv—let's see what happens here.

                        DEVON

As have several other prominent families, Doctor,
families with inconvenient maladies they'd like to
hide from the police.

                    MARCELLO #2

Ah, er. Um.

Blank stare. It would appear that you can deal with your own improv, Marcello #2, but not with mine.

> MARCELLO #2 (CONT'D)
> (flailing wildly, and screaming at the top of his lungs)
> You'll live to regret this, Detective—but not for long.

Yeah right. If he flapped any more, he'd take off. Don't call us, we'll call you. Next!

INT. NEW HOPE MEDICAL CLINIC—EVENING

> MARCELLO #3
> (black hair, mid-thirties—dark, mesmerizing eyes)
>
> There's nothing mysterious at all, Detective Merrick. Athena Demetrios died of a ruptured appendix.

Right from the top he's not doing it by rote. He's making it his own.

> DEVON
> A seventeen-year-old girl has died of a ruptured appendix, Doctor, without first complaining of abdominal pain. I'd call that mysterious—if not outright suspicious.

> MARCELLO #3
> (dismissively)
> That, Lieutenant, is nonsense.

> DEVON
> (pulling rank)
> That's not your decision to make, Doctor. We'll see what the medical examiner has to say about that.

The eyes of Marcello #3 lock on mine and I think I perceive the slightest nod of acknowledgment. I feel an electric shock go down my backbone. Immediate intimacy, vital for auditioning, is born of necessity. We have to be able to dive right in and interact on a level that is very personal and close to the bone—even with people we don't know very well, if at all—but this is something much deeper than that. It's as if my spinal cord were a long wire—like the thickest string on a double bass—that he has strummed into some harmonious vibration with his own being.

> MARCELLO #3
> (casually)
> Do you have children, Detective?

                    DEVON
              (caught off guard)
Why no, Doctor, I don't.

But I'd love to have yours, Marcello—whatever your real name is. Oooh—where did that come from and how did he do that? He pulled me out of character there with just a simple question. Get back into Devon, Kate, quickly.

                  MARCELLO #3
      (cool, almost clinical, authoritatively)
If you did, you'd know that teenage girls don't tell
their parents everything. And some of them don't
tell them *anything*. It's hardly unusual for a young
girl to hide symptoms from her parents.

                    DEVON
          (now enjoying the verbal fencing)
And from her friends as well? We checked with the
girls in her class. Athena never said a word to anyone.

                  MARCELLO #3
            (calmly, as if teaching)
You must understand that Athena was a very quiet,
withdrawn child. You can't be serious about ordering
an autopsy on her.

                    DEVON
                  (levelly)
Oh, but I can be—deadly serious. Athena Demetrios may
have been quiet and withdrawn, but last I looked,
that's hardly ever fatal—and I don't think she died of
a ruptured appendix, either.

                  MARCELLO #3
                  (firmly)
In other words, you, a police officer, are choosing to
reject the diagnosis of an experienced physician—the
diagnosis of Athena's own doctor.

                    DEVON
              (not backing down)
When you put it that way, Doctor, I guess you could
say that I am.

> MARCELLO #3
> (softly, speaking very slowly and deliberately, raising one eyebrow and taking one step toward me)

Now Ms. Merrick—Detective—I'd think very, very carefully about doing that if I were you. . . .

Oooh! That quiet, underplayed menace is dead on. This guy really knows what to do with the material.

> DEVON
> (directly, looking into those fabulous eyes and taking a step toward him)

You're not threatening me, are you, Doctor?

> MARCELLO #3
> (casually, backing way off)

Certainly not, Detective—may I call you Devon? It's just that the Demetrios family have been patients of mine for years.

Damn, he's good! And gorgeous, too!!

> DEVON
> (toughly, circling around him)

As have several other prominent families in Hope Canyon, Doctor—and by the way, it's still Detective Merrick, and pardon me if I don't call you Marcello— families with inconvenient maladies they'd like to hide from the police.

Marcello #3's eyes flare, then go neutral, even benign. Cool!

> MARCELLO #3
> (demurring, taking offense at being misunderstood)

You mistake my meaning, Devon—I mean, Detective. I've known Nestor and Hera Demetrios since before Athena was born. They are devout, deeply religious people. They've suffered a tremendous loss, and they'd be absolutely devastated at the idea of their little girl being cut open.

> DEVON
> (unswayed by his argument)

There's no other way to prove that a crime has been committed. And if their daughter was murdered, I'm sure they'd want to bring the murderer to justice.

Marcello #3's eyes flash with menace. He takes a step toward me, fixes me with a chilling look, and cocks his head to one side with a half smile.

MARCELLO #3
(coolly, offhandedly)

I think, Detective, that you're about to go poking your nose where it doesn't belong.

DEVON
(not cowed)

And I suppose you're willing to take it upon yourself, Dr. Bertone, to tell me where my nose does and does not belong?

Marcello #3 takes another step toward me until we are all but touching. The air between us is so electric that I'm surprised a spark doesn't jump the gap. Suddenly, I realize that this harmonious vibration thing has another name. Most people call it love at first sight.

MARCELLO #3
(very softly)

I believe you'll find that you'll live to regret this, Detective Merrick—but not for long.

As he speaks, he cups my right cheek very tenderly in his left hand, then runs the back of his right hand slowly and ever so lightly under my chin, extending his index finger as if it were a knife and he was slitting my throat.

Dingdingdingding! Ooh, Daphne, we have a winner! We have a winner!! Tell the rest of the Marcellos to go home. Give this man the job!

Never mind!! Give this man my phone number!!

"Thank you, Devon; thank you, Marcello." Daphne's voice brings me back to earth. "Please stay here, Marcello. Kate, they need you upstairs right away. Go get touched up and get on the set ASAP."

• • •

"Christine Christine Christine!" I yell exuberantly, skipping into Gossip Central. "Did you see the auditions? Did you watch them?"

"Didn't get a chance to, Kate. I was facedown over Vladi's nose hairs. Were there any good ones?"

"No, there were no good ones. But there were two dreadful ones and one absolutely fantastic one—Marcello Number Three—and he's so . . ."

. . . he's so just right for me. He's tall and dark and handsome, well, not exactly, certainly not in the pretty-boy/Bradley sense of the term, but he's got cheekbones to

die for. We locked eyes and it was electric and I know he felt it, too, and I bet he's absolutely fabulous in bed. . . .

Before any of these words leave my lips, I stop in mid-sentence because I realize I no longer have Christine's attention. She is gazing off toward the doorway.

"Hey there! You found me!" she says.

"Hey yourself, and yes I did, Madam Sinclair, but it wasn't easy," comes the response, accompanied by a hug and a kiss on the cheek.

Oh.

"Kate, I'd like you to meet my husband, Wyatt Sinclair."

Oh. Life is cruel indeed.

"Actually," he says, with his eyes cast downward, "we've already met—downstairs."

Well now, Katie, let's see how good an actor you really are.

"Yes. Yes, we have. Until we were formally introduced, I only knew you as Marcello Number Three. I'm Kate McPhee. You really nailed the audition, Wyatt."

"With your terrific help. That was fun down there, and yeah, I think I've got this gig, assuming the contract stuff gets worked out. Seems I'm about to be killed off as Dr. Ian Glenullen on *Denver General,* only to be reborn as Dr. Marcello Bertone on *Live for Tomorrow.*"

"Wyatt's a Lead Actor nominee as Ian Glenullen," says Christine, "and you have him to thank, at least in part, for your nomination, Kate. He was one of *DenGen*'s reps on the Emmy screening panel. I told him to vote for you."

"I would have anyway," he says with a warm laugh, then lowers his voice to a stage whisper, "and if I'd had my way, Kate, you would have been the only Lead Actress nominee from *Live for Tomorrow.*"

"Why, dear," says Christine with mock seriousness, "didn't you find Ms. Contini's reel compelling?"

"Reels."

"She sent more than one?" Christine asks. "I didn't think you could do that."

"Ah, but she did," Wyatt says. "Actually, a reel and a DVD."

"Okay, the reel was the montage of scenes where her hair looked good," I say, half in jest. "What was the DVD?"

"Ms. Contini seemed to think it would help the panel greatly if we each got a copy of her episode of Lifetime's *Intimate Portrait.*"

"You're joking," I say.

"I only wish I was," he replies.

Daphne comes in just as Christine is finishing me up, but she's looking for Wyatt Sinclair, not for me. "I thought you'd like to know, Wyatt, that I just rang off with your agent. We've come to a verbal agreement, and we'll make the official announcement tomorrow. I'm delighted that you're going to be our Marcello."

"I figured it would work out. It's a great part, Daphne, and I'm looking forward to it."

"I'm not asking you to give away any state secrets," she continues, "but can you tell me when *DenGen* is going to kill off Dr. Glenullen? I want you to start as soon as Ian's heart stops beating."

"I've already taped it, so . . ."

". . . So it should air early next week," Daphne says, not being one to let an actor complete a sentence if she thinks she can do it faster. "That will fit well with what I have in mind."

"Which demise did they go with, honey—mineshaft or unopened parachute?" Christine asks. The back of my neck suddenly begins to prickle. If I had hackles like Hobbes or Nietzsche, they'd be raised now, and I realize that I am bristling at my dear friend's use of the term *honey,* even though she's talking about her own husband.

Now, stop it. Stop it right now, Katie, I say to myself sternly. She's perfectly entitled to call him honey *or* sweetie *or* snookums *or any other term of endearment she cares to use.*

I continue to be unsuccessful at getting the small hairs on my neck to behave. My long curls hide that fact that underneath I look like a porcupine from the shoulders up.

What is it about this situation that's unclear to you? I ask myself harshly as I continue my autolecture. You're being possessive about something that's not yours.

"Neither. Flesh-eating bacteria," says Wyatt with a warm laugh and a gorgeous grin that I choose to believe is pointed straight at me.

"I advise you to leave off this minute!" said Alice to herself, rather sharply. She generally gave herself very good advice (though she very seldom followed it).

"I don't think that's been done before!" Christine giggles.

As she touches him lightly on the forearm, I am aware that there's a dark side of me that could be perfectly capable of coming over the table at her if I let it loose. I feel color rise in my cheeks—first rose, then cerise, and finally deep scarlet.

That's right, blush—shame on you, Katiegirl! This man is Christine's husband— the dear woman who gave you hot tea and a warm shoulder when you needed it most, the woman who put you back together not once, but twice, and would do it again in a heartbeat. If there's one guy in this entire universe who's off-limits to you, he's it.

"Well, I don't really die, they just leave me without a face. . . ."

"Which means that they're going to recast the part," says Daphne.

Meredith, perhaps aware of the presence of fresh meat, glides in and re-gally asks Daphne to introduce her to the newcomer.

"Wyattttt," she says effusively with her brilliant Crest Whitestrips smile. "I'm Mehrreddithhh. I'm so pleased—dee-lightt-edd—that you are joining our little family. Forgive me for not staying longer, but Regina Abell is needed on set, and I have to save her voice, so I'll just say, 'Wellllllll-commmme to my worrrlllddd.' "

It is in fact a carbon copy of the gushy and entirely counterfeit welcome I received so many months ago. Even though Christine has surely been giv-ing Wyatt regular bulletins about life down the *LFT* rabbit hole, I feel duty bound to give him the same warning Trent gave me. Selfishly, I also want to keep this conversation going a little longer. "Don't take it personally," I say to him, batting my eyelashes despite myself as Meredith moves off down the corridor. "That's what she says to everyone."

"You'll be fine, Wyatt," Trent chimes in, "as long as you recognize that it is indeed her world, her Gahrden Pahrty. At the pahrty, there are just two rules. . . ."

**"Know your place,
and stay in it!"**

Much to Daphne's dismay, this last is chanted as a chorus by the en-tirety of Gossip Central. It's confirmation, if anyone needed it, that Mere-dith has alienated almost everyone in the cast.

* * *

At the end of the day I aim the Jeep toward Benedict Canyon to meet up with Janice and have a look at the house that she and Gudrun have offered me. It is funky, not fancy, but tidy and well maintained, in a Birkenstocky/ whole-wheaty kind of way. And it has an enormous back yard—with a solid fence. It will definitely work.

"Well, whaddja think?" Janice asks good-naturedly.

"It's great—the dogs will have a place to run and there's a lot of room in-side, too."

There is now just the small matter of how much my conscience will yip at me about landing a place to live because these two well-intentioned women think I'm gay, even though I'm not.

"So you'll take it?" she asks.

"Yes, yes I will. But . . . but there's something I think I should be up-front with you about. It's a bit awkward, so forgive me if I . . ."

"If you're going to tell me you're not gay," she says, "we already know."

There you go, it's out there.

"I . . . I . . . I . . . If you and Gudrun want to offer the house to someone else, I understand," I say.

"Not at all, but thank you for being willing to come forward," she says warmly. "Gudrun and I talked about it. What we want is for gay women actors to be offered all kinds of roles regardless of their personal sexual preference, and it seemed hypocritical to penalize a straight woman for doing the same thing, especially one who can play gay so convincingly."

"Thank you."

"We decided that what really mattered was that you had made Devon an intelligent gay woman, not a stereotype. It's important for that image to be out there in the media."

"You must understand, though, that that choice is pretty much out of my hands," I respond. "On *Live for Tomorrow*—or any daytime drama, for that matter—characters change and evolve in response to the arc of the story. If they turn me into a lesbian mobster or a lesbian homicidal maniac, I'll be able to raise objections and maybe make some minor improvements, but I really have no say in the decision."

"Fair enough. But for the time being, thanks for making Devon so much fun to watch."

"Okay, I'm curious. How did you know I wasn't gay? Was there something, some signal I was sending out that tipped you off? I'm interested because it's something I may be doing in front of the camera as well."

"It was the earrings."

"I beg your pardon?"

"The earrings. You complimented Gudrun on her earrings the other night."

"And . . ."

"Do you remember what they looked like?"

"They were like little antique silver hatchets."

"That's the sacred double-bladed ax, the labrys, an ancient feminist symbol that dates back to Greek mythology. It was used by early matriarchal societies as both a weapon and a harvesting tool."

"Wow. Women were into multipurpose tools even then," I say.

"Like you might use a nail file as a screwdriver, when you have to," Janice continues. "The labrys was also the scepter of the goddesses Gaia, Rhea, Demeter, and Artemis. It was carried in battle by Amazon warriors—you can even see Lucy Lawless wielding one on some *Xena* episodes. Amazon, by the way, translates as 'a match for men.' Today it's a pretty common lesbian symbol of strength and self-sufficiency—and truth seeking."

"And when I didn't recognize it . . ."

"Right."

A week later

MY LIFE IS STILL IN BOXES, but with Sondra's help I've moved into Benedict Canyon. I wake early to the sound of chirping birds and smell of doggy breath, and it's all good. Today I have my first scene with Wyatt. Daphne apparently liked what we did so much that she wrote our improv into the script.

INT. NEW HOPE MEDICAL CLINIC—EVENING

We go through most of the scene like two prizefighters circling each other, trying to get position. Wyatt takes a step toward me, fixes me with a chilling look, and cocks his head to one side with a half smile.

                    MARCELLO
              (coolly, offhandedly)
      I think, Detective, that you're about to go poking
      your nose where it doesn't belong.

                    DEVON
                (not cowed)
      And I suppose you're willing to take it upon yourself,
      Dr. Bertone, to tell me where my nose does and does
      not belong?

                    MARCELLO
                (very softly)
      I believe you'll find that you'll live to regret this,
      my dear Detective Merrick—but perhaps not for long.

Wyatt once again cups my cheek in one hand and pretends to slit my throat with the other, and that same marvelous vibration runs the length of my spine—which is a relief, in a way, if only to indicate that what I felt before wasn't a fluke. What happens next is an improv inspiration that I think will serve the storyline well. I go with it, knowing Daphne will cut me off at the knees if she doesn't like it.

> DEVON
>
> Tell you what, my dear Dr. Bertone. The autopsy on Athena Demetrios is going to take place, and neither you nor her parents can stop it. But if you think it would make the family feel any better about it, you're welcome to be present—not to participate, but to observe. Think it over and let me know by this afternoon what you decide.

> MARCELLO
> (with his hand under my chin,
> tilting my face upward and closer to his own)
> I don't need to think it over. I believe, my dear Detective Devon, you've made me an offer I can't refuse.

Perhaps it's my imagination, but I sense that his hands linger at my face longer than is necessary for the scene. I look into his eyes. Is it possible that this isn't all me, that he feels some attraction for me as well, or am I reading more into this than is there?

"And cut!" says Marty. "Nicely done, you two. Set up for the next scene. We are moving to the Demetrios home set. Wagons ho! Get those cameras outta here. Head 'em up and move 'em out! Not you, Wyatt."

"I'm here, Marty."

"Stick around. This is your conversation with the bereaved parents, where you tell them that their kid is gonna be sliced and diced."

"You have such a way with words, Marty," I say with a laugh.

"So where is everyone else? Lord, spare me from day players! Where are the parents of the stiff? I need Nestor and Hera up here on the double!" he bellows into the intercom.

Daphne comes out of the booth and nods to me. "I looooove your addition to the dialogue, Kate. The autopsy scene will have an added layer of intrigue with Marcello there. You'll be able to watch him to see how he reacts as it unfolds. We shoot that tomorrow; I've just told the writers to tweak the script to incorporate Marcello into the scene. Oh, and Kate—make sure that the business office has your new address. The script will be messengered over to you this evening. And give them the license plate of your new car, too. The parking attendant seems to think that some infidel in a Jeep is parking in your spot."

"Ah, he misses the three-and-a-half-wheeled Honda. How sweet! And Daphne . . ."

"The hair, Kate, yes, I know. Soon. Soon."

* * *

INT. MASON SALISBURY'S AUTOPSY SUITE—DAY

All of us are outfitted in scrub suits, gowns, gloves, and clear plastic face shields.

                    MASON
          (speaking into a tiny microphone on an earpiece,
                like a hands-free cell phone)
          This is the autopshy of . . .

Richard walks around to the foot of the corpse, but needs to hold on to the table for stability. He reads the name on the toe tag, and continues.

                    MASON (CONT'D)
          . . . the autopshy of Athena Hestia Demetrios, age
          fourteen. Preshumed cause of death:

Richard stealthily consults a clipboard on the table where his instruments are placed.

                    MASON (CONT'D)
          . . . acute peritonitis due to a ruptured appendix.
          Let the record show that present for the prosheedings
          are Detective Devon Merrick, HCPD, Assistant District
          Attorney Jamila Benton, and . . .

Richard looks at Wyatt as if seeing him for the first time.

                    MASON (CONT'D)
          And who the hell are you?

They're letting that go? It's time to step in and give Richard a hand.

                    DEVON
          Dr. Salisbury, allow me to refresh your memory. This
          is Dr. Marcello Bertone.

Richard's face brightens as the light dawns and his brain finds his place in the script.

                    MASON
          Ah yes, and Dr. Marcello Bertone, personal physhician
          to the decedent. Pleased to meet you.

                    MARCELLO
          Likewise.

Wyatt gives me a wink, turns away from the camera, crosses his eyes, and gives a very sotto voce faux hiccup.

<pre>
                            MASON
Let's get shtarted. Weight of the body: ooooh, I dun-
noooo. . . . What's that look like to you, Ms. Benton?

                           JAMILA
Call it fifty-one kilos—one hundred twelve pounds.
</pre>

Richard picks up a large scalpel.

<pre>
                            MASON
I am now making the Y-shaped incision in the trunk. I
will, ah . . . ah . . .

                          MARCELLO
                   (Wyatt bails him out)
Then I believe, Dr. Salisbury, what you will do is
peel back the skin, the muscle, and the soft tissues
from the chest wall, and pull the flap up over Athena's
face.
</pre>

Richard is grateful, but astonished at the source.

<pre>
                            MASON
Quite sho. Hand me the . . . the . . . the Stryker saw
if you would please, Dr. Bertone, so I can open the
rib cage.
</pre>

After Wyatt hands him the saw, there is an odd moment of silence. Richard
seems unaware that he is supposed to continue speaking.

<pre>
                          MARCELLO
I presume, Dr. Salisbury, that when you open the rib
cage . . .
</pre>

Richard reads a sticky note that he has pasted to the blade of the saw.

<pre>
                            MASON
Aha! You presume that when I open the rib cage, I am
going to open the pericardial sac and check the pul-
monary artery.
</pre>

Richard turns on the saw as LaTrisa winces.

<pre>
                       MASON (CONT'D)
And you preshume correctly. That's exactly what I'm
going to do. I am now opening the pericardial shac and
the pulmonary artery where it leaves the heart.
</pre>

Unseen by the camera but observed by me and I assume, by LaTrisa and Wyatt as well, Richard drops a sticky note into the "corpse."

```
                    MASON (CONT'D)
     I am insherting my finger into the pulmonary artery.
     Wait—what's thish?
```

"And cut. Commercial break comes here, people," says Marty. "Anybody who needs a quick touch-up, now's the time . . . not that we can see much of you anyway."

LaTrisa comes over to me. "Kate," she says, "it's happening again. He's not slurring too badly, at least not yet, but he's definitely in the bag."

"Does this happen often?" Wyatt asks.

"Yes," I say.

"No," says LaTrisa, in unison with my yes.

"Which is it, ladies?" he asks.

"It's yes," she admits. "I didn't know for sure whose side you were on. If Daphne catches him again, we're gonna be looking for another M.E."

"On some level he must know he's in trouble," says Wyatt. "Did you notice that he's got crib notes stashed all over the set?"

"Yeah, and if he gets any worse, maybe I can stick one on my face shield," I offer, striking my forehead with the heel of my hand.

"Places, everyone," says Marty. "Back up in five . . . four . . . three . . . two . . ."

```
                    MASON
     I have found a . . . a . . .
```

Richard reaches into the chest cavity and consults the note he has concealed there.

```
                    MASON (CONT'D)
     A throm . . . thrombo . . . thromboembolism—that's a
     blood clot to you—in the pulmonary artery. This surely
     would have caused shudden death.

                    DEVON
     How did it get there?

                    JAMILA
     Well, one thing's for certain, it didn't come from the
     appendix.

                    MASON
     Indeed not. The appendix is . . .
```

Richard peeks into the corpse, apparently looking for another note that he's hidden in there.

> MARCELLO
> I can see that the appendix is intact and uninflamed.

I shoot a look and a slight nod at Wyatt.

> MASON
> Dr. Bertone—do you know whether Ms. . . . ah . . .

> MARCELLO
> Demetrios. My patient, Athena Demetrios.

He gives me back the same look, with a half smile.

> MASON
> . . . Demetrios, the deceased, had suffered any bro-
> ken bones within the last year or sho?

> MARCELLO
> No broken bones, but she did have arthroscopic surgery
> when she blew out her patella skiing last winter. You
> should see residual scars at the anterior cruciate
> ligament.

Richard comes to the head of the table, lifts the chest flap, and looks at Athena's face.

> MASON
> Ah yes, here it is. I can see it clearly. Just so.

Wyatt shrugs his shoulders ever so slightly, and LaTrisa rolls her eyeballs.

> JAMILA
> But she was only fourteen years old. That may be where
> the clot was formed, but why would it break loose like
> that?

> MASON
> For a female her age, the most likely increased risk
> factor is oral contrasheptives. We'll run some teshts
> to determine the hormone levels in the body.

> MARCELLO
> (reluctantly)
> That won't be necessary.

> DEVON

Why is that, Doctor?

> MARCELLO

Because I gave Ms. Demetrios birth control pills about
six weeks ago.

> DEVON

Did her parents know?

> MARCELLO

Of course not. She came to me privately and asked for
them.

> JAMILA

How did she get the prescription filled?

> MARCELLO

There was no prescription. I gave her samples. So
you see, my dear Detective Devon, there was no
murder.

> JAMILA

But there is culpability, Dr. Bertone.

> MARCELLO

What there is, Ms. Benton, is gullibility, and I must
take responsibility for that. Not only had Ms.
Demetrios undergone arthroscopic surgery of the
patella . . .

Wyatt pats the corpse on the right knee and looks Richard in the eye. "Oh!
Patella! Right!" he blurts out.

> MARCELLO (CONT'D)

. . . she also suffered from diabetes and hyperten-
sion. From the smell on her clothing, I suspect that
she was a secret smoker as well.

> MASON

In other words . . .

Richard starts exploring the abdominal cavity of the corpse in earnest. In his
frustration he utters a faint "Damn!" just as LaTrisa clears her throat. Richard
looks up to see that she has affixed the sticky note over her name tag. Peering
through his face shield in an effort to read his own hieroglyphic handwriting,
Richard leans forward and falls onto the gurney and across the corpse.

"Cut!" Marty calls. "You okay, Doc?"

"Yes, yes, I am. Sorry about that." The brief halt gives him a chance to master the contents of the note on LaTrisa's name tag.

"It's an easy pickup," says Marty. "Start from, 'In other words,' Richard."

>   MASON (CONT'D)
>   So in other words, this child was a walking catalogue
>   of contraindications for oral contrasheptives.

"Whew," says Wyatt under his breath.

>   MARCELLO
>   Exactly. Her risk factors were so severe that I never
>   would have given them to her for herself. She asked me
>   for them on behalf of a friend, and I believed her.

Wyatt and Richard both appear to be rummaging in the abdominal cavity of the corpse.

>   DEVON
>   What friend?

>   MARCELLO
>   I'm afraid I can't tell you. Doctor-patient confiden-
>   tiality.

>   JAMILA
>   I'm not sure how much that shields you when your pa-
>   tient, a minor, is deceased, Doctor.

>   DEVON
>   Or maybe there was no friend, in which case we will
>   charge you, Dr. Bertone, with being an accessory in her
>   death, as much as if you had stabbed her in the back.

>   MARCELLO
>   She was a child, and I'll have to live with the fact
>   that my actions contributed to her death for the rest
>   of my life.

Wyatt finally locates and removes the last sticky note from the cadaver and affixes it to his name tag. All it has on it are the initials M.I.F.

>   JAMILA
>   How are you going to list the cause of death, Mason?

LaTrisa elbows Richard to make sure he sees that Wyatt has his next clue. Richard nods.

> MASON
>
> Heart attack. Ms. Demetrios died of a . . .

Richard leans in as he strains to read it.

> MASON (CONT'D)
>
> M.I.F. . . . (Richard looks puzzled over what the initials
> might stand for, then brightens) Massive Internal Fart.

> MARCELLO
>
> Myocardial infarction.

But Wyatt's correction comes too late; we have all lost it. Actors, camera crew, stagehands, we are all doubled over with laughter. "Cut!" yells Marty, who is laughing himself. "That's one for the outtake reel, but for chrissake, Dickie, if you're gonna do that, will you get better penmanship? Or bifocals. And Wyatt, much as I prefer Richard's pronouncement of the cause of death to yours, we do have to shoot that little segment over again."

> MASON
>
> Myocardial infarction. There will be no mention of
> oral contrasheptives. The truth of what happened to
> Athena shtays in this room. The Demetrios family has
> had enough heartbreak as it is.

"And for the last time, cut," says Marty. "That's a wrap for today. Time out: twelve thirty-nine a.m."

"Okay," says LaTrisa as we walk off the set. "The question is whether he can drive."

"The answer is, 'He can, barely, and he shouldn't,' " says Wyatt. "He's gonna be all over the road, and his reflexes are no match for the traffic on Sunset, even at this hour."

"Decoy him. I'll go pinch the keys," says LaTrisa. "I still remember where they are."

"Tri and I have done this a few times before," I say.

"You up for helping on this one, Wyatt?" LaTrisa asks.

"Sure. Absolutely," he responds.

I catch a fleeting glimpse of a retreating figure in green. "Shit! I just saw him going out the door—and he's still in his costume!"

"He'll be in his car before we can catch up to him. We've got no choice but to tail him and try to make sure he doesn't pick up a cop. If he does, it'll be all over the news tomorrow," says LaTrisa.

"Okay, two cars," I say. "Keep your cell phone handy, in case we lose him."

We run for the parking lot, still in our surgical greens, just in time to see Richard's Beemer heading out of the lot toward Sunset Boulevard. Wyatt jumps in with LaTrisa and she burns rubber in the Infiniti as she pulls out behind him, with the parking attendant waving cheerily as they depart.

I follow farther behind in the Jeep, the last member of our bizarre procession, and get the same jolly farewell wave. What can possibly be going through this guy's head? We have given him ample evidence that we are all lunatics, but it doesn't seem to faze him in the slightest. About ten minutes down the road, my cell phone goes off. "Kate, we lost him," says Wyatt.

"Where are you now?"

"Vee on zee Sunset Streep, Natasha. Right now ve passink Moose and Squirrel," says Wyatt, in a very good Boris Badinov Russian spy voice.

"Izz goot, Boris," I reply as Natasha, knowing they are at the statue of Rocky and Bullwinkle. "Most excellent 'otel, Chateau Marmont, on yurr right."

"Where Belushi OD'ed, and Jim Morrison dangled from a drainpipe, trying to Tarzan his way from the roof into his hotel room," says Wyatt in a normal speaking voice. "Where are you?"

"I'm several blocks back, but the truth is that we don't know if Richard's ahead of you or behind you. Just passing Ogden now. Oh, shit! I know where he is."

"Where?"

"I just saw someone in surgical greens going into Greenblatt's."

"You sure it was him?"

"Yeah, he still had the plastic shield down in front of his face."

"You mean he's been driving that way?"

" 'Fraid so. And for sure he didn't stop for kosher pickles or matzoh ball soup. My guess is that he's picking up a bottle of good cabernet—not that he needs anything more to drink this evening."

"Go in after him, Kate. We're at Carney's—the train car burger joint. LaTrisa's hanging an illegal U and we're coming around. We'll be right there."

I walk into Greenblatt's and start to shadow Richard from the Napa zinfandel as he peruses the Australian chardonnay. The clerk looks at me funny because I keep checking the door, hoping to see Tri and Wyatt, but my cell phone goes off instead.

"Hi. [pant, pant] I'm on foot, running."

"It's been a long time since I've heard heavy breathing, Wyatt. What happened?"

"LaTrisa got pulled over for the U-turn. The cop said I could go. I ran track in high school; I'll be there as soon as I can. What's happening on your end?"

"I'm playing hide-and-seek with Richard from one aisle over. So far I think I'm winning."

As my quarry makes his selection and weaves his way toward the checkout, I lag behind trying to be inconspicuous, as if that were possible. Just as Richard, still with his face shield in place, is completing his purchase, Wyatt comes bursting through the door. He is all huffy puffy from trotting down the Strip. With the register open, the pimply kid behind the counter takes one look at the three of us and hits the burglar alarm.

LaTrisa arrives and is corralled as a potential perp, just like the rest of us. She is followed in short order by the CHP, including the same guy who just finished giving her the ticket for the U-turn.

"You! Again? What the hell is going on here??"

"Kate," Wyatt whispers in my ear, "do you have a spare key?"

"To what?"

"To anything. Not your car key, though."

"Yes, here," I say, as I slip him my house key surreptitiously.

Wyatt makes body contact with Richard, which is easy enough to do, since we're all being detained on the gewürztraminer aisle while the highway patrolman tries to figure out what kind of commendation he'll receive for apprehending four members of the notorious Surgical Green Gang in act of knocking over Greenblatt's.

Eventually he sorts it out and tells us we are free to go. "Tri, Kate, hang back," Wyatt says softly. "Let Richard go out first."

"But he'll . . ." LaTrisa begins.

"No, he won't. I switched Kate's house key for his ignition key on his keychain."

Soon enough, Richard meanders back in. "I shay . . ." he begins.

We bundle him into LaTrisa's car. Wyatt drives Richard's Beemer, and I follow in the Jeep. "Garage door opener is over the visor," I say.

Richard has already passed out by the time we pull into the condo's garage on Holloway. The three of us haul him up the stairs, but LaTrisa and I leave Wyatt the task of undressing him and getting him into bed. As the two of us set up the coffeepot, she begs to go on from there. "Maybe, just maybe, I've still got what's left of a hot date tonight," she says. "At the very least I owe him an apology. Would you mind—can you take Wyatt back to the studio?"

"My pleasure, Tri. Now go catch up with your guy."

Wyatt and I jump into the Honda and head back onto Sunset. "Ladies and gentlemen, on your left we are now passing the Comedy Store," I say to him in the preachy manner of a tour guide, "where many famous comedians, including Jay Leno, got their starts."

"The Comedy Store sits on the site where Ciro's used to be," he replies, tour-guiding me right back, "where Desi Arnaz and his band played, and where Frank Sinatra once punched a photographer. The other two big nightspots of the time, the Mocambo. . . ."

"Frankie probably punched photographers there, too," I suggest.

"And the Trocadero," he continues, "were both farther west, on the south side of the street."

"How do you know all this?" I ask.

"When she was growing up, my mother loved movies and show business," he explains. "She's something of a Hollywood pop-culture historian, and I guess I absorbed a lot just listening to her."

"And on your right, the Argyle," I continue.

"Boutique hotel to the stars, as it has been for generations," he picks up. "Built in the 1930s, the Argyle was originally the Sunset Towers. Howard Hughes stashed some of his women there, just to keep them handy till he needed them. John Wayne kept a female there, too," he says.

"Did not."

"Did too. The Duke kept a cow on the balcony of the penthouse, so he could have fresh milk, at least according to legend."

"Must have been a helluva ride up in the elevator with Elsie," I say, "or did he make her take the stairs?"

As we drive along, I continue my narration. "And here on the right, we have the giant Virgin Megastore, which is important only because it sits on the location where Schwab's Drugstore used to be. Lana Turner was discovered sipping a soda at the counter at Schwab's."

"Was not," he says.

"Was too," I counter.

"Was not. Lana Turner was discovered not at Schwab's, but at the Top Hat Malt Shop, which used to be located on Highland Avenue across the street from Hollywood High School. Lana, who was born Julia Jean Mildred Frances Turner, was sippin' a Coke and cutting typing class when Billy Wilkerson, publisher of the *Hollywood Reporter,* saw the way she filled out a sweater and fell in love with her mind."

"Remind me never to play Trivial Pursuit with you!" I exclaim with a laugh.

"If it makes you feel any better, another famous blonde was supposedly discovered across the street."

"Do tell."

"That corner over there—the one with the Pollo Loco fast-food chicken emporium—is where the legendary Garden of Allah apartment complex used to be," he says. "Many of Hollywood's wildest party animals hung out there—Errol Flynn, F. Scott Fitzgerald, Hemingway, Sheilah Graham, Ava Gardner, Clark Gable, Orson Welles. Tallulah Bankhead used to swim naked in the pool, and Marilyn Monroe was supposedly discovered there."

"Nude?"

"Could be."

"It's very sad that they tore it down to put up that dreck. In London, and in most of Europe actually, it's harder to do that."

"Joni Mitchell sang about it in 'Big Yellow Taxi.' " He begins to sing, "Don't it always seem to go . . ."

"They paved paradise, and put up a parking lot!" we croon in duet.

Singing assertively off-key, we drive up to the studio gate and into the empty parking lot at about 2:30 in the morning, waved through by the ever-smiling attendant. I pull up next to his Lexus. "I guess I don't have to ask which car is yours. Nice work tonight, Dr. Bertone, by the way, and if Richard doesn't say thanks for all of your quick thinking, he should."

"I'm not sure he'll say much more than, 'Oh shit! My head!' in the morning."

"Remind me to buy him a supply of Pedialyte. And Doctor . . ."

"Yes, my dear Detective Devon . . . ?"

"May I have my key? Otherwise I can't get into my house."

"Oh, sure." Wyatt fishes in his pocket and finally produces the key. "Good night, Kate. Despite all the melodrama with Richard, I actually had a lot of fun tonight. I laughed more than I have in years."

And with that, he leans over as if to give me a kiss on the lips, which I'm more than ready to give back, but then just touches his forehead to mine.

Three days later/late April

I

T'S CROWDED IN GOSSIP CENTRAL, not just with regulars but with day players as well, since the Athena Demetrios funeral scene will be very well populated. As Christine sits me down in the chair, I look around for Wyatt. "Don't you do his makeup?" I ask.

"Are you kidding?" she replies with a smile. "I make him go to Debra. It's just too absurd to put eyeliner on your own husband."

Suddenly there is a ruckus at the Queen's station. Meredith is upset about something. "My Gawd, Kevin, what have you done to me? This looks all wrong!"

"But Meredith, I'm using your products, and I'm using your color palette you gave me. These are your colors."

"But . . . but . . . I'm orange! Even people on *Entertainment Tonight* don't come out this color. And the lipstick—this can't possibly be MAC Bombshell."

"But it is, really!" he says defensively.

"Kevin—why don't you just show her the tube?" says Trent with a wink.

"Meredith—Ms. Contini—here, see for yourself," Kevin says, waving the tube under her nose and winking back at Trent.

"Time to funeralize Athena," Marty booms over the PA. "Everybody upstairs—now—and I do mean *everybody*!"

"Funeralize?" I say incredulously. "Funeralize? I don't think that's a word."

"Oh, but it is!" says LaTrisa, switching off her perfect Marlborough School for Girls diction and putting on a deliberately exaggerated black southern accent. "In the South people get funeralized all the time."

"Ah, well, yes, of course," says Meredith dismissively.

I try not to gape at her in astonishment, while LaTrisa just shakes her head.

INT. ST. NEKTARIOS GREEK ORTHODOX CHURCH—DAY

Amazing. We have one and only one church set, and it gets a lot of use. It is hardly recognizable as the mission-style church where Burke and Jennifer got married several months ago. This time the set designers have turned it into a dusky, exotic Greek Orthodox cathedral, full of smoke and mystery. Long-bearded day players in priestly vestments are swinging silver censers on long chains. For the show, however, they are dispensing not incense, which would be customary, but dry ice instead, because it gives off more "smoke" and doesn't make us all gag.

"Everybody into the pews," says Marty from the front of the church. "There are gonna be a few changes to how this is gonna go, so listen up, people. The show is running long, so we're gonna cut down My Big Fat Greek Funeral. Instead of using the entire service, the guys are gonna get some cutaway audience reaction shots. . . ."

"Ah, Marty, I don't think it's an audience in a church," says LaTrisa, who is seated next to me.

"Yeah, whatever. The cameras will be on all of you spectators in the bleachers, while the priests are up front here, saying the holy mumbo jumbo over the body. Then we're gonna get the conga line filing past the casket."

"Oh, what a surprise!" Trent whispers in his Nathan Lane falsetto as I endeavor to contain myself. "The lining is white, not fuchsia!"

"Questions?" Marty asks.

"I don't think the casket should be open," says Meredith, who is just arriving on the set.

"That's not a question; it's an opinion," says Daphne firmly, toggling her chin. Her tone of voice clearly indicates that the subject, unlike the casket, is closed; there will be no further discussion. "Let's get this scene moving. Marty, a little reorganization, please. Make sure all the young people who would have been Athena's classmates are seated together on the right side of the church, all except for Mallory, who will be on the left with Regina."

"You got it, boss lady."

"Oh, and Kate, come see me after the scene—let's talk about that haircut of yours."

We rearrange ourselves in the pews and then finally, when the crew has finished the reaction shots, we all queue up to pass the casket and pay last respects. Wyatt goes by and as his lips move, we see him mouth the words *I'm sorry* to the dead girl. It's a small detail, but it's perfect. Meredith is next up. Unlike the rest of us, who are wearing simple, even severe black or navy blue, she is clad in frilly burgundy, with chandelier earrings and a Jackie O–style pillbox hat. She had been insisting on a veil, until Ruben pointed out that it would make it very difficult to dab the tears from her eyes. Now she pauses until Wyatt has moved on, then goes forward, bowing her head before the deceased and daintily patting at her eyes with a delicate lace-edged hankie. In a companion gesture, she shakes her shoulders in a movement that is supposed to indicate that she is sobbing. In point of fact, however, she looks more like someone sitting on one of those vibrating beds in a cheap motel.

Lauren Elizabeth is right behind her in a spare and smashing Michael Kors black dress. The dress is all line and cut—and it again makes it clear she's not a little kid anymore. When she stands before Athena's body, she goes off script. Slowly and reverently she bows deeply to the casket, then softly places her hand on the shoulder of her friend. She kisses the large cross that lies on Athena's chest, kisses Athena herself on the forehead, and then lets a solitary tear roll down her cheek. It's a singularly heartrending and powerful moment—so powerful that Meredith serves up a withering glower as the scene concludes, then quickly leaves the set.

"Extraordinary work, Lauren," I say to her as we head back downstairs.

"Thanks, Kate," she says. "I did some research on how a mourner should behave at a Greek Orthodox funeral. What I did is absolutely authentic, but I think Meredith is a bit frosted. She seems to have stomped off in a huff, not that I care."

"Never mind. Grief at a young age is tough to deal with, and you conveyed your sense of loss beautifully, and without any dialogue. I found it very moving."

"What's this about a haircut for Devon? You finally gonna lose your ringlets?"

"I've been nagging Daphne about it for months," I say, "and the response was always no-no-no, or at least wait-wait-wait. Now it seems there may be a yes in my near future. I'm headed up there to talk about it now."

I'm about to knock on Daphne's door, but it is ajar and I hear the sound of loud voices from within. Make that loud voice, singular. And the voice I hear is Meredith's.

"Daphne, it's so unfair of you to let that girl get away with that."

"Get away with what?" Daphne's feeble attempt at naïveté falls quite flat, so flat that I suspect that's exactly what it was meant to do.

"You know exactly what I'm talking about," Meredith declares firmly. "That scene at the casket."

"I don't understand," Daphne replies halfheartedly.

Of course you do, you Machiavelli, I say to myself. Now you're just playing dumb.

"Lauren wasn't following the script, and she did it on purpose. I kept waiting for someone to stop the scene," Meredith continues, "but no one lifted a finger. How could you?"

"How could I what?"

You're not giving her an inch, are you, Daphne? You're pushing her over the edge, and you're doing it deliberately—but why?

"How could you let her use cheap histrionics to upstage me like that? How could you stay in the booth and do *nothing*? Nothing!"

"Actually, Meredith, I thought that scene was spectacular, and that Lauren showed why she deserved her Emmy nomination. Not only that, she showed why she deserves to win."

"And the dress!" Meredith continues as if Daphne had not spoken. "That dress was much too old for anyone playing my daughter. She should have been in a school uniform—a plaid jumper, little white socks, and saddle shoes."

"Catholic plaid and saddle shoes?" Daphne says incredulously. "Meredith, this was the Greek Orthodox funeral of her best friend. And besides, unless you want to set the clock back to 1957, no one wears that shit anymore."

"Well, I still think she looked much too old to play my daughter."

"Actually, Meredith, that's something I've been meaning to talk to you about. The time has come for Regina to get a little older."

Ah, now we come to it. This is Daphne's hidden agenda.

"Ooooooooohh," Meredith moans. It is a deep and guttural sound, like a wounded, cornered animal.

"Lauren Elizabeth Fielding will be eighteen in just a couple of weeks," Daphne states. "That's just a fact. She may be petite, but she's already a 36C, and the idea of her playing a thirteen- or fourteen-year-old is getting more ridiculous by the minute. We're taking a beating in the media because of it."

"Ooooooohh," Meredith moans again, this time even more deeply.

"During May Sweeps I'm going to age her up to match her real age," Daphne explains. "At that time, it will be appropriate for Regina to age up a little as well."

"Ooooooohh," Meredith moans yet again, but this time the sound has undertones of a growl, and comes right from the diaphragm.

"Five years," Daphne states flatly. "Regina has been thirty-five for the last fifteen years. It's time for her to be forty."

"Nooooooooooohh!" There is one final low-pitched sound—this time even more vicious and primal—that emanates from Meredith's solar plexus. "This conversation is over!" she snarls in an otherworldly voice several octaves deeper than I would have believed she had. There is a small thud, like a bird striking a windowpane. Then she throws open the door and storms past me, a deranged Medea mad with jealousy and betrayal, spittle flying from the corners of her mouth, her Jackie O pillbox hat wildly askew atop her burnished copper tresses which, for once, are in disarray.

I sweep into Daphne's office in her wake. "That went well," I say with an ironic half smile. "I was waiting outside and couldn't help but overhear. She looked like the Incredible Hulkette when she left."

"Kate, you're going to cut your hair," Daphne says calmly, choosing not to acknowledge that anything had happened between her and Meredith.

Daphne's effort to pretend that nothing is amiss is betrayed by the array of bright green edamame beans on her shoulder pads, and on the top of her frappéd, shredded-wheat hair. More are scattered across her desk; several float in her teacup; one has affixed itself to her computer monitor. Only two remain in a small bowl, which formerly resided on the credenza but now rests at the base of the windows.

"And you are going to cut it on the air."

A week later/early May

I'M SITTING ON THE DECK in Benedict Canyon, lingering over a cup of tea in the soft morning air, when my cell phone goes off. "Kate? It's Lauren. Quick—turn on your TV—*Regis and Kelly*, Channel 7. Meredith is on, or rather, Regina is on."

"What do you mean?"

"It's weird. Friends of mine from New York called as they were watching it live and told me to check it out. They said that when it aired there, it looked as if she was on the air as Regina Abell."

"In what way?"

"She kept referring to Meredith Contini in the third person."

I grab the clicker and turn on the tube.

"Hi, we're back," says Regis, "and Kelly, as part of our countdown to the Daytime Emmy Awards, we're here with Meredith Contini. Welcome, Meredith. Let me ask you now—as a veteran of *Live for Tomorrow*, you're no stranger to the Daytime Emmy Awards program. How many times have you been nominated?"

"Well, Regis, Meredith has been nominated so many times she's lost count."

"And out of all those nominations, how many times have you won?"

"She won just once."

A confused look crosses Regis's countenance, but he presses on. "And this year," he says, "you're going to be the master of ceremonies, or should I say mistress of ceremonies?"

"Actually, Regis, Meredith prefers the term 'host.'"

His confusion deepens, but when you're live, you're live. You keep going. "She does?" he says.

"Yes," Meredith says.

"Who does?" Regis asks.

"Meredith does."

"And it would be host, not hostess," he reiterates.

"Yes, she thinks that's better."

"Who does?" Regis says, trying it one more time.

I don't know—Third Base!! The two of them are on the brink of launching into an inadvertent sequel to Abbott & Costello's "Who's on First?"

"Meredith."

Poor Regis looks like he's hearing things—or wishes he was.

"So tell me, Meh—" he begins, then deliberately avoids any reference to a name, "how do you feel about being nominated with Lauren Elizabeth Fielding and Kate McPhee, your two costars?"

"Well, you know, Regis," she begins, "the evolution of both of those characters has certainly been, ah, interesting this season . . ." She tosses her hair. ". . . but I'm not sure I approve of some of the choices they've made."

"In what way?" Kelly asks.

"To be honest, I find Devon's English accent incongruous in Hope Canyon, and Mallory, well, like any little girl, she has a rebellious streak in her that surfaces at the worst possible moment."

"I'm not sure I understand," Regis says, in what may be the understatement of the morning.

"We just finished a scene last week," Meredith continues, "which should air today, I believe, in which my daughter insisted on wearing clothing and makeup that was much too old for her. It was a scene in a church, and I thought she was completely inappropriate. She behaved badly at the funeral service. Kissing the corpse. How dreadful."

"And we'll be back, after these messages. . . ."

Another week later

"Hey there, Grasshopper," says Jay as I kick at my practice bag in the rehearsal room. "You're really coming along!" Jay looks terrific, as usual. His tight Joe's jeans and black tank top enhance his slender, muscular build.

"Indeed I am, Sa Bum," I admit. "See my stripes?" Slowly but surely, Jay has taught me the lazy girl's way of martial arts, and the horizontal stripes on the kickbag chart the rising elevation of my right foot in delivering a roundhouse kick. "I started at Danny DeVito; this was Prince; and now I think I'm up to Mickey Rooney!"

"Next stop: Shaquille O'Neal, and after that, Yao Ming!" says Jay with a laugh. "Seriously, we have to start working on getting you ready for the big vampire fight scene. Daphne wants you to take on the whole lot of them in the grand finale of the vampire storyline."

"That should be fun," I say grimly.

"A little enthusiasm would be nice. Come now, where's my best fighter?" he asks, putting a fraternal arm around my shoulder. "Besides, it's not often you get to demonstrate one of the great martial arts truths of Hollywood!"

"Which is . . . ?"

"In a martial arts fight in front of the camera, no matter how out-numbered you are, your enemies never come at you in a pack. They attack one by one; the rest of them patiently wait their turn, dancing around in a threatening manner so they get knocked off one at a time."

I laugh because he's so right.

"Even the Nazis in the Indiana Jones movies don't gang up on Harrison Ford," he adds. "As Hollywood truths go, that's right up there with the fact that at night, you always go looking for burglars, murderers, and other felons alone."

"With only creepy music to accompany you," I add, "and unless you're me, women investigate only when wearing their most revealing lingerie."

"And all foreigners speak English," Nigel says, coming into the room, "even when they're alone, except that they have very bad accents." He waves a sheaf of magazines. "Thought you'd like to see the new *Vanity Fair*," he adds, handing me a copy. "They did a piece on the lead-up to the Daytime Emmys. Meredith's little appearance on *Live with Regis and Kelly* has had some fallout in print."

My mouth drops open as I read. It seems that Lauren Elizabeth has got-ten a little of her own back after Meredith's cheap shot at her on air. "Nigel, that's toxic!"

"I know—my phone's ringin' off the hook," Nigel says. "Everyone wants an official reaction from the show, but so far Daphne hasn't said any-thing."

"Lauren's become the poison ivy at the Garden Party. She's not behav-ing like a proper guest," I say. "I particularly like the part where she says, 'Meredith should look in the mirror and face reality.' "

"Pffft!" Jay snorts derisively. "If there's one thing that woman absolutely cannot do, it's that!"

"That's nothing. It gets worse, much worse," Nigel says. "She really lets Meredith have it—right in the birth certificate. Listen to this: 'I've been playing Mallory for the past five years. I'm just about eighteen and she still wants me to play her daughter as a little kid. In her mind, I shouldn't even be wearing a bra yet.' "

"Well, that part's true," I say. "I heard her tell Daphne that Mallory should have been wearing a plaid school uniform and little white socks at the funeral."

" 'Meredith refuses to let me grow up,' " Nigel says as he continues read-ing, " 'because she's still pretending to be the same age she would have been when Mallory was born. She tells everyone that if her daughter ages, it's not good storytelling, because it destroys the myth. There's a myth all right: Meredith is well into her fifties, and she's still trying to playing thirty or so—*that's* the big myth! And what keeps it afloat is equal parts La Mer face cream, Botox, and formaldehyde.' "

"Smokin'!" says Jay.

"Indeed. I'm gonna go with that as my personal favorite, too," Nigel says.

"Any words of wisdom, Nige, if they call me for a reaction?" I ask.

"Yeah, Kate, don't answer the phone. It's real good time to keep your head down and not be available for comment. Networks execs, even bright ones, tend to get real stoopeedo in crises not of their own making, and when shit like this hits the fan, it's never evenly distributed. Under the circumstances, 'no comment' is just okay. 'Could not be reached for comment' is bulletproof."

"Are they coming at you for not having prevented this?"

"Not yet," he says, "but it's a distinct possibility. You know how it works in this biz—finger-pointing is a blood sport."

"Hang in there, my friend," says Jay. "I'll give you some free lessons in self-defense if you need 'em."

"Thanks for the offer, but frankly, Jay, my mouth is my best weapon of self-defense. Always has been. Always will be." Nigel looks Jay up and down with a great deal of manly admiration that stops just short of outright sexual interest. "Jay, you are so *faaabulous*," he sings with over-the-top theatricality as he heads for the door, "are you *sure* you're not gay?"

Jay, in good-natured jest, attacks the bag with a holler and a leaping high kick that would leave Shaq rubbing his jaw, if not absolutely out cold. Nigel winks and closes the door.

"Yeah, right—like I could have forgotten that you're good at this," I say. "Let's get to work."

"Now, Kate, as I understand it, the setup is going to be this: the vampires are going to lure you into an ambush under the guise of perpetrating a break-in at Meredith's house. Whatshername—the one who plays Magda the tutor . . ."

"Selena."

"Yeah, sorry. Selena is going to pretend to see intruders, so that Regina will make you come to the mansion."

"How many of the undead will I be dealing with?"

"Nine."

"Whew! Who are they?"

"Lemme see—Daphne wants some real stunt guys, four of them including Bill. They'll do most of the intricate stuff. Then there are the vampire converts—Bradley, Vlad, and Priscilla. . . ."

"Basically anybody who was fucking Tiffany," I add, unable to resist.

"Right—but then I'd have to be in the scene, too." He grins.

"Let me guess—Priscilla and Vladimir are already pissed off."

"Well . . . yeah. A mere woman is not supposed to be Bruce Lee at their expense, especially if she's supposed to win. They're taking this personally as an affront to their masculinity, Priscilla especially."

"But wait! That's only seven." I laugh. "Listen to me—*only*!"

"Plus Selena and Charlotte."

"Shit! I have to kill them all? What a carnage!"

"Nope. The only one you have to kill is Charlotte. You knock the rest of them out, and deal with her last. When she dies, the spell on them is released and they revert to their nonvamp selves."

Soap opera logic. Nothing like it.

"Anybody else on my side, Carlos maybe?"

"No. It's you against the world, babe. But for the first time, you get to use weapons."

"Of mass destruction?"

"No, of the fourteenth century. You get to play with a medieval jousting lance."

"Swell."

"The lance will be what you'll use to kill off Charlotte—you'll put that through her heart."

"How are we going to prepare?"

"Because you really take them on in series, rather than all at once, I'll have you rehearse with individuals. After that we'll put the whole thing together."

First up is Bradley Davidson, who joins us in the rehearsal room. Bradley is the latest in the long parade of pretty boys who have played Nicholas Duncan. Like all the others who have preceded him, he is gorgeous and severely undertalented. And like all the others, he stands around mumbling dialogue, leaning against the scenery, and being picturesque, thinking he's invoking Clint or early Marlon. Egotistical and frustratingly popular, he gets ten bags of mail a day. Go figure.

"Magda is going to capture you briefly and tie your hands behind your back, Kate," explains Jay. "When Bradley comes at you, kick him in the throat, then head butt him. Bradley, when you feel Kate lightly tap your forehead, snap your neck backward and grunt."

We practice the move. "Unh," he says softly as Bill tiptoes into the room.

"Do it like you mean it," Jay orders. "Louder. Hello, Bill."

"*Unh!*" says Bradley.

"Better, but louder still. Again."

"*UNH!*" says Bradley reluctantly. To make that sound you have to contort your face, and he really hates doing that.

"Okay. I'll buy that one. But Bradley, you seem to have forgotten something."

"What?"

"After you take the head butt and grunt, you're supposed to fall backward. You're knocked out cold, remember?"

"Oh, sorry."

"Again. Kate . . . once Bradley's fallen, crouch down and jump-hop through your hands. This will bring your wrists in front of you. Then cut the rope with the sword on the wall, and go straight to dealing with Bill."

God, I love Bill.

"Okay, Kate," says Jay. "A middle-side-piercing kick to the right, a checking block to your left, knife-hand. Then pivot with your left foot, this way. It's like a dance. Then move your left foot outward; upward block with a twin palm. . . ."

"Can't I just shoot the sonofabitch, like Indiana Jones with the guy with the knives?"

"Ah, I think that solution is a little too permanent, Kate," says Bill with a laugh.

We work through the routine till Jay is satisfied, then he brings in a trio of his Korean pals. "Kate, meet Eugene, Henry, and Gregory. They're my buddies, and they've done this with me a lot. Trust them the way you would trust me. Okay," he says to them, "I'm gonna go with snippets from three different forms. We're using pieces of *Choi Jong, Yoo Sin,* and *Choong Moo.* I'll give Kate her moves. Your job is to look as scary as possible and go down when I tell you to.

"Gregory will be up to bat first," Jay explains. "Greg, you'll recognize this from *Choi Jong.* Kate, when Gregory comes at you, block him with a circular block, using your right inner forearm. Stay in left walking stance for a middle punch with your left fist, then go to right walking stance for a rising block with the right. Circular block with the left, then middle punch with the right fist. Greg, go down when she taps you with the right the third time."

"My pleasure," he says.

"Don't mention it," I respond.

"Eugene, you're the next 'victim.' This is *Yoo Sin.* Kate, give him a middle crescent kick with the left foot, followed immediately by a middle-side-piercing kick, also with the left. Come back into a sitting stance, then give him a middle crescent kick with the right foot, followed immediately by a middle-side-piercing kick with the right to finish him off."

"Hotcha! The old one-two, one-two," I say.

"Henry, I saved *Choong Moo* for you," Jay continues.

"You're too kind." Henry is large—formidable, even. I surely would not want to be on the wrong side of a fight with him in earnest.

"Kate, when Henry comes at you, extend both your hands upward as if to grab his head. Then kick to the left with your right knee, and pull both hands downward. Lower the right foot right away, then move your left quickly. He'll go flyin' right over you."

"Promise?" I ask.

"Promise," Henry says with a smile.

"Kate, the order of attack will be as we just went through it—Greg, then Eugene, then Henry. But I'm gonna put Vladimir—he'll have a knife—between Greg and Eugene, and Selena between Eugene and Henry. After Henry comes Priscilla. Charlotte's last."

"What happens with Selena? We haven't talked about that," I ask.

"Selena will be easy," Jay states. "She has to be. She's got no experience in stunt stuff. You'll fool around a little, then take the bust of Meredith off the desk and clobber her on the head with it."

"Crude, but effective."

"Priscilla is the wall-turn thing, and after that there is just Charlotte—Lacey—remaining. This is where you use the lance as a stake, Kate," Jay says.

"I have another idea," I tell him. "Could Props come up with an ax—a double-bladed one that looks antique?"

"Sure. The guys there will do anything for me."

"I'll draw you a picture of what I have in mind."

I have one small scene before I continue with Jay, so I head down to Gossip Central and slip into Christine's chair.

"Hey there, Miss Kate. Have you seen *Vanity Fair*?"

"Yeah, Nigel came and found me in the rehearsal room."

"Needless to say, it's all anyone is talking about around here."

"Have you seen Meredith since it came out?"

"No, thank God. Can you imagine?"

"I try not to. . . ."

"You settling in to your new house, finally?"

"Yeah. Doesn't quite feel like home yet, but it's getting there. Sondra's a big help."

There have started to be these awkward silences between Christine and me that never used to be there. I was always so open with her about my personal life, but the idea that I'm desperately attracted to her husband is a tough topic to introduce into the conversation. And an even tougher one to dance around.

I'm feeling guilty, but on the other hand, nothing has really happened. So I thought he almost kissed me when we got back to the parking lot after we took care of Richard. So what?? He didn't. We touched foreheads. Big deal. The rest of it is probably nothing more than my hyperactive imagination joining forces with my underexercised libido.

"Isn't this about the time that Rafe and Leslie's baby was due?"

"Zing—yes! Where did that come from?"

"I dunno. It's just that you haven't talked about it for a while, and I figured you must be holding back, but I know you must still be thinking about it."

"Not all that much, really."

Actually I've been thinking so much about Wyatt that I've pushed Rafe and Leslie into the back recesses of my brain.

"Well, it does look like you're sleeping better, at least. I haven't had to haul out the tea bags in a while, and the circles under your eyes aren't needing nearly as much concealer. You know," she says, as she dabs a little MAC Malt shadow on my eyelids and some Swiss Chocolate into the crease, "you never did tell me how you found out about the two of them."

"I didn't find out as much as figure it out," I say. "I'd been at her apartment one night—Rafe wasn't there or anything like that—but there had been a phone call at two in the morning. She didn't move to pick it up."

"That was it?"

"That was it. 'Aren't you going to answer that?' I'd asked her, and she said, 'No, don't worry about it. It's okay.' When I was driving home I started to mull it over, because she had seemed flustered. I tried to puzzle it out. I thought, 'Usually when your phone rings at two A.M., it's not good news. You might not like answering it, but you wouldn't ignore it, either.' "

"You were Devon Merrick even then; you just didn't know it."

"Why wouldn't Leslie answer a phone at two in the morning? What reason could there possibly be—unless she knew who it was, and knew that I shouldn't hear who it was?"

"And the only person that could have been was Rafe."

"And then it hit me that all the time I'd been confiding in her about how he didn't want to sleep with me, she'd been fucking him. When I realized that, it was like getting punched in the gut—all the air went out of me. I had to stop driving, pull to the side of the road. Just to make sure I wasn't imagining everything, I called my brother, Daniel, and told him about my suspicions. He said I was living in a nest of vipers. Not long after that, I accepted this gig on *LFT*—which at first I was going to turn down—and fled to Los Angeles, which at the time was as far from London as I could get."

"Greetings, one and all!" says Alison as she comes in. "I bring a news bulletin from the front!"

"Let's hear it—spill!" says Charlie.

"Lauren's been fired."

Oh dear, Alison . . . I fear that there was a little too much glee in your voice.

"She most assuredly has not," says Daphne, walking in on Alison's announcement as Maggie trails behind and struggles to keep up. "Alison, whoever told you that is spreading malicious rumors—I won't have it!" she spits.

"Sorry, Daphne, but I stand by my story, as they say on the news. I got my information from a very reliable source," says Alison quietly. "Lauren was fired by Conrad Barbera—personally."

Daphne's face clouds as she turns on her Ferragamo heel and heads back to her office at something akin to a gallop.

"Hoo-ee!" says Trent. "We're having fun now. I'd give anything to be a fly on the wall when she gets old Conrad the Barbarian on the phone."

"What I heard was that after the stuff in *Vanity Fair* came out, Meredith paid Conrad a little visit," says Alison, "and demanded Lauren's head on a platter. And she screeched and yowled and rolled on the floor until he gave it to her."

"Who is Conrad Barbera?" Amber asks.

"Oh sweetie, it's a name you should remember, if only for your own protection," says Alison. "Connie is the network head of Daytime."

"And if you see him, you'll recognize him instantly," says LaTrisa. "Flat head, eyes low on the side of the skull. Short, stubby body, gaudily patterned, with brightly colored beadlike scales, talonlike claws."

"Prehensile tail used for social climbing," Richard contributes. "Changes color whenever protective coloration is required."

"Venom is produced in the glands of the lower jaw," Nigel offers, "the jaw that houses large, jagged teeth. . . ."

"And a forked tongue," Trent adds.

"Highly territorial in behavior. Aggressive and combative in breeding season but can disappear into cover with considerable speed," Nigel continues. "Characteristic threat posture is to tilt the head upward, expand the throat, and open the mouth."

"Yes, and while copulating, the male holds the female's head in his jaws," says Kirk.

"Has to," says Tiffany, "otherwise he wouldn't get any at all."

"Gee . . . is he single?" asks Amber.

Seconds later, Lauren Elizabeth Fielding comes into Gossip Central, accompanied by Rhonda and a burly, grim-faced security guard. Lauren is carrying a Bottega Veneta leather overnighter; Rhonda has a pile of clothes over her arm, and the guard is toting a cardboard file box.

"I guess you all heard what happened," she says, "but I couldn't leave without saying good-bye."

"We'll miss you—I'll miss you," I say sincerely. "But I hope to see you in New York—on the Radio City stage, taking home the Emmy."

"That would only be poetic justice, kiddo," says Trent, "the best revenge of all. I'm calling my bookie and putting money on it."

"Thanks for the vote of confidence. I guess I'm sorry it turned out this way—for you guys, because I know that this makes your job harder, at least till the dust settles," she says, "but I don't feel bad about saying what I said. The old witch had it coming."

"What's with the escort?" Amber asks.

"Well, Rhonda came with me out of the goodness of her heart, to help me haul my junk. And Mr. Barbera sent this kind gentleman and his service revolver along with me, to protect me from all the muggers and rapists lurking in the corridor—*and* to make sure I didn't take anything that wasn't mine, *and* to make sure I left the premises in a timely manner."

"I bet that by the time you go through the gate, they're already painting over the name on your parking space," says LaTrisa.

"Do you know what you're going to do now?" I ask.

"I've got several interesting possibilities. . . ."

"Yes . . . ?" I say encouragingly.

"That I can't talk about just yet," Lauren responds, censoring herself. "Both my agent and my publicist will have my ass for breakfast if I open my mouth today." And with a wave and a hug, she's gone.

"I don't know about her agent," says Nigel, "but her publicist is lovin' every minute of this."

"I don't understand."

"She really put herself on the map by going off on Meredith in *Vanity Fair*," Nigel explains. "How many people knew her name yesterday, and how many people know her name today? If I'm a booker at Leno or Letterman, I'm desperate to get her on the show, and I'm on the phone several times an hour, hounding her people till I get yes for an answer. Her Q factor just took a quantum leap, and if they play it right, it's gonna go a lot higher. Come to think of it, I bet her agent is lovin' it, too. She's hot now—she really gave him something to sell. This might be the A-plus career move of all time."

"So you think she did it on purpose?" Trent asks.

"It's a distinct possibility. Lauren may be only eighteen, but she's been in showbiz longer than most of the rest of you. She always said she was destined for bigger things, and she's got really savvy management. The kid's no dummy. Could be that she saw her shot and she took it."

"Kate," says Ruben, "we need to talk about what you're going to wear in the fight scene. The raincoat and pantsuit just ain't gonna cut it. I have new orders from Daphne—I'm supposed to glam you up."

"What do you have in mind?"

"*The Avengers.*"

"I can't be Uma Thurman—she's about two feet taller than I am."

"Not the movie, the TV series. Uma's fine, but I've always loved the original."

"Diana Rigg. My kinswoman!"

"So . . . how do you feel about a catsuit?"

"Love it!"

Next day

Ruben has found me a black catsuit with an off-center zipper, high neck, and brown trim, which he pairs with Christian Louboutin ankle boots with needle-pointy toes and a stiletto heel. I'm about as far from cabbage roses as I can get, but still a little unsure about how I look until Wyatt passes by, doffs a hypothetical bowler hat, whistles softly, and whispers, "Mrs. Peel, we're needed."

Damn. Every time I think it's just me and I'm making all this stuff up, something like that happens. I could swear that he's flirting with me. On the other hand, it could be that I'm projecting, reading more into each little interaction than is really there— I'm very good at that. As someone said, if all you have is a hammer, everything looks like a nail.

"You sure you're not going to miss these curls, cherub?" Charlie asks as he starts working on my long brown tresses for the last time.

"Careful now, Kate. One lousy haircut can really put your career into the tank," Amber opines. "Think about poor Keri Russell. She had the longest bad hair day in history after she cut it for the second season of *Felicity*. I think she's still trying to live that down. And look what happened to Faith Hill. . . ."

The last thing I want to do is get into a hair discussion with Amber.

"Nope. I'm good. Short really suits Devon's character."

Jay comes by and gives me final instructions. "Remember: See. Think. Do," he says. "They'll come at you one-by-one. Deal with them the same way—as if it was nine small scenes strung together."

"What about Priscilla and Vladimir?"

"Brains can sometimes do what brawn cannot achieve, Grasshopper," he says with a smile.

"C'mon . . . make my day," says Marty. "Get this thing done in one take, can we?"

```
INT. ABELL MANSION—NIGHT

               REGINA
Thank you for coming so quickly, Detective Merrick.
Magda was positive she saw someone opening a window to
break in. Look—the window is still open! I'm sure
there are burglars in my home. I'm terrified, Detec-
tive, terrified, not just for me but for Mallory as
well.


               DEVON
Do you have a safe room in this house?
```

Finola Hughes and Digby Diehl 287

REGINA
Yes, of course.

Meredith tosses her hair at me.

DEVON
Then what I want you to do is take Mallory and go get
in it. Now. Take your cell phones with you. Both of
you.

Yes, Mallory was supposed to be in this scene, but as of now we don't have
a Mallory, so we had to figure out a way around it—and this was it. Of
course, this also cut Meredith's involvement in the scene down considerable, but since she's the one who got Lauren canned, she's gonna have to
live with that.

REGINA
But Magda . . .

Meredith presses the backs of her hands together in an "inverted prayer"
position. Why? I dunno.

DEVON
I'll send her along after I've spoken with her. Now,
don't argue. Go!

As I begin looking for burglars—alone—the creepy music shows up, just as
it should. I find Magda/Selena in the study, where the walls are conve-
niently decorated with medieval weaponry.

MAGDA
Ah, good evening, Detective.

She speaks with her back to me, so I cannot see her fangs until it's too
late. Experienced police officer and self-defense expert that I am, knowing
there may be burglars in the house I manage to stand with my back to the
open windows and to both of the room's half-open doors. While I am talking to Magda's back—doesn't everyone?—the room fills with eight more
vampires, who stand patiently behind me until Magda turns around,
shows me her incisors, and ties my hands behind my back. And then, it's
Showtime!

First up is Bradley. As we practiced, I dispatch him while still tied up. No
problem there, even though his grunt is positively anemic. Then comes
Bill, and after him, Greg. So far, so good.

Vladimir comes at me next, brandishing a knife in his right hand. I raise
my forearms in front of my body and step toward him as he slashes at me.

```
                          DEVON
        Put the knife down, Laszlo. I don't want to hurt you.
```

With my left hand, I chop him lightly in the neck, which is supposed to make him look stunned. Then I grab his neck and his right wrist, pushing the knife away from my body. At this point he's supposed to take a fall. He doesn't.

"See. Unh. Think. *Unh*. Do," I murmur as we tussle. "This is where you're supposed to go down."

"Make me," he responds through clenched teeth. "Otherwise it doesn't look real."

Swell. I'm now in a wrestling match with someone who outweighs me by about seventy pounds.

"You—*unh*—made a bet with Priscilla again, didn't you?"

"What do you mean 'again'?"

"I was watching secretly while you were—*unh*—screwing Tiffany on camera," I whisper. "I know you won that bet with Priscilla fair *unh*d square." Vladimir is temporarily stunned by my revelation, and I use that moment to knock his legs out from under him. Next!

After Choong Mooing Henry into unconsciousness, I bonk Selena and face off against Priscilla, who grabs me from behind. He's supposed to let me wrestle free from him as he tries to bite my neck, but he keeps holding me tightly instead—not just to piss me off, but also to win the bet. "Let me loose, you slow-talking, camera-hogging sonofabitch," I say softly between grunts.

"Got a problem, dyke?" he responds sotto voce.

"Eeeeooow . . . true colors, eh?" And with that, I jab the stiletto heel of my boot into his instep, and break free. "Who's the girl, now, hands up! *You!*" Picking up the scripted action, I dash toward the corner of the set, run halfway up the wall using the handy little camouflaged steps placed there for my convenience, kick through a turn, and come back at him from above. I make contact—perhaps a little harder than I'd intended, and he falls over.

On to the big climax, the catfight with Charlotte.

```
                          DEVON
        Give it up, Lacey. It's over.

                          LACEY
        Think again, my love. The time has come for you to
        join us.

                          DEVON
        Never. As much as I love you, never.
```

And with that, Charlotte throws me to the carpet on my back and comes at me from between my legs. As she bends over, I put my left foot into her right hip and pull her down toward me, locking my legs around her neck. Her face hovers just above my pubic bone. There is only my leather catsuit between her fangs and me—if Standards and Practices didn't like the autopsy table, they won't like this, either.

Pulling back to break free, she grabs the ax off the wall and comes at me with it. Props has done a wonderful job of replicating a life-size version of Gudrun's labrys earrings. Charlotte swings the labrys at me a couple of times, finally striking the shaft on the edge of the desk, sending the blade head flying. We wrestle for the stake until I take it from her and drive it through her heart, ending the vampire threat to Hope Canyon and terminating our relationship with extreme prejudice.

I look at her with a profound sense of loss and regret. I had no choice but to kill my lover, but the loss pains me greatly. A keening moan comes from my throat as I pick up the scissors from the desk set and begin chopping off my hair.

A N HOUR AND A GLASS OF MERLOT LATER, I'm sitting in Sally Hershberger's very comfy chair at the John Frieda salon. I have put myself in the hands of LA's best stylist, and Sally is wielding her magic scissors to complete the cut I started on the air as I grieved over Lacey's demise and my role in bringing it about. When she's finished, she twirls me around in the chair—and I love it! I am sporting a very piecy Klute-meets-Meg-Ryan do. I feel good! The new, improved, au courant me will roll out at the Daytime Emmy Awards telecast on Sunday—Daphne has worked the schedule so that the on-air haircut was my last appearance before the awards show.

Next morning

Trent and I board an American Airlines flight to New York. He carries a Prada weekender and short garment bag over a Jil Sander evening suit. I have a small Louis Vuitton roll-on suitcase and two garment body bags. The new luggage is courtesy of Sondra, who slowly has been cleaning up my personal life. She's going to be house-sitting for me while I'm in New York. The bags contain my two possible awards show gowns. In one is a dramatic Vera Wang chiffon one-shoulder Grecian-style gown in a riveting ocean blue, which has the most wonderful fluid swingy movement when I walk. In the other is a Reem Acra ball gown, a confection with beautiful embroidery and beadwork in the bodice, and a slightly off-the-shoulder neckline. It's a luminous pastel, a mysterious pale shade where ivory, peach, and mauve all come together. The full skirt is accented with more beadwork, and when I'm in it, I feel very pretty.

Which to choose? Indecisive for weeks, I was even thinking about a third alternative—a white Yves St. Laurent tuxedo—and wearing it naughty, which is to say with nothing underneath. After continually torturing Rhonda with the problem I'd finally consulted Ruben, whose first wisdom was to leave the tuxedo at home. "Kate," he said, "the tuxedo looks great on you, but it's the safe choice, too predictable—exactly what they'd expect from a lipstick lesbian. You want to wow 'em, really shake 'em up out there. As far as the two dresses go, you really can't lose. You're gonna look terrific either way. Since your hair will be short and styled maybe a bit messy, you can lean toward the quasi-girlie with the ball gown, but I believe the Wang should be your first option. That blue is hot, almost cyan—the intensity will really pop on the red carpet. And the cut is classic—it's Ava Gardner in *One Touch of Venus*. No, it's better than that. It's Action Goddess Dressing—it's the Angelina Jolie/Jennifer Garner way to go," he said. His final piece of wisdom: take both dresses.

I've been looking forward to a little free time in the city at least as much as the awards themselves. Ever since I hit the Big Apple with a Shakespearean touring company one summer while I was still in drama school, I've had a love affair with New York. It ignites my very essence, and for the first day Trent and I are in town, it's playtime. We settle into our enormous suites at the Carlyle, then run riot in Manhattan, dancing through the streets in our I ♥ NY T-shirts and sampling everything. While we're still uptown we hit the three Bs—Bergdorf, Bendel, and Barney's. I get my face painted in each establishment, trying out looks for the show to see what goes with the two dresses and the new hair, which I'm loving more each minute. At the cosmetics counter I buy some of everything—a little Anna Sui, some T. LeClerc, Delux, Kevyn Aucoin. It's all in the name of research; for the Emmys I've decided to get a stylist in to do my makeup, and even though I know she will bring a huge case of her own stuff, I want to have an idea of what I want before she begins.

Already laden with shopping bags, Trent picks me up by the scruff of the neck and physically removes me from Boyd Chemists before I get painted yet again. We cab it downtown to SoHo and the Village, making raids on Language, Costume National, Fragments, and Jeffrey. We take a break at Tea & Sympathy, then soldier on to Stella McCartney, Patricia Field, Alexander McQueen, Scoop, Max Mara, Balenciaga, Alberta Ferretti. For the day we are bloated label whores, high on consumerism and the infectious energy of the most satisfying city in the world. In short, we are happy. We max out our credit cards, then run to Canal Street to buy a cheap bag to put all our stuff in. We eat dinner at Florent in the Meatpacking District wearing our new goodies, Trent in head-to-toe Gucci, and me in a funky mix of McCartney, McQueen, and Balenciaga.

We stay out in the Village till four A.M., crash until noon, then order heavy breakfasts with a side of Pedialyte from room service. Because it's the Carlyle, they'll send someone out to get that stuff for you. Trent will be a presenter, so he leaves me behind to rehydrate while he goes to rehearsal. I play in my new acquisitions until he returns. He comes back groaning about the lame dialogue they have given him in the script but triumphantly produces true swag—one presenter's goody bag to which he was legitimately entitled, and a second pinched just for me. "Not to worry," he says, accurately reading the concern on my face, "no one will go without. There were extras, and besides, there's always someone who doesn't pick theirs up." The snagged swag in the bag is choice—Maui Jim sunglasses, TechnoMarine watches, Bulgari fragrance, a Tiffany sterling silver key chain, Sonya Dakar skin-care products, and three Pilates sessions at Equinox (New York or West Holly)—worth more than a grand all told, easy.

We take it slower that night, hooking up with Rhonda and two of her high school chums from Queens for dinner. Amazingly enough, they are not blow-dried, but rather naturally curly. Rhonda grew up in Floral Park (a name which, she says, is a lie twice over), but her years in Hollywood have worn away most of her New York accent. Her pals, however, still sound like the old 'hood, and I wallow in the juiciness of their language as we laugh and laugh over cocktails at the Mercer. As happy as I am to be laughing with good friends, another thought crosses my mind: Wyatt must be just getting into his hotel room. Christine has stayed behind in LA.

On Sunday morning I debate myself yet again about the dresses, and decide for the last time that Ruben is right. I'm finally at peace with my choice, ready to tell Roxanne the makeup artist that I'm going with the blue one-shoulder as soon as she shows up. Except that I wait and wait and wait, and she never does materialize.

Left to take matters into my own hands, I begin the makeup process myself and continue fussing long enough that Trent starts to get restless and twitchy. "Kate," he says, looking dashing in the Jil Sander suit even though he is pacing up and down, "there's no sense in me giving the producers a coronary. They have enough stress stroking all the other egos in the building without me adding to it. I've gotta go—I'll see you over there." It's probably a good call, since he's due to present early in the program.

As I'm putting on the gown, Roxanne finally arrives to do my makeup; she'd gone to the wrong hotel. "Too late," I say to her.

"Looks like you really didn't need me anyway," she replies. "You did fine. Let me just highlight your eyes a little more—no charge—and rev up the color on your mouth a bit. We don't want it to look like that dress is wearing *you*." She kicks it up a notch—I particularly like the NARS Red Lizard on my lips—and I can really see the difference. Roxanne gives me a final once-over and a thumbs-up and pushes me out the door.

Only after the concierge folds me into a cab do I realize that in rushing out I've forgotten my credentials, but there's no going back. I'll barely make the opening of the show as it is. I roll up to Radio City dreadfully late. The hot blue dress does indeed pop against the red carpet, but no one is there to see it. Everyone is already inside. It takes me a moment to talk my way in and convince people I really belong there—with my new hair I don't look like the dyke with the major curls they had been expecting. Because we are at the top of the program, the usher holds me at the back of the theatre briefly, then leads me down to my seat while the applause swells for Meredith, who is grandly making her entrance to begin her duties as host. As we walk toward one another, she onstage and me in the audience, her mouth is slightly agape and I emit a small shriek of laughter—more of a hoot, really. The usher looks at me in surprise. "You okay, Ms. McPhee?" she asks as she taps the seat filler on the shoulder.

"Oh yes, fine, really," I respond as I take my seat with a giggle. For a moment, at least, Meredith and I are the only people in Radio City Music Hall who realize that the two of us are wearing the same dress, except that mine is ocean blue and hers is her favorite shade—relentless raspberry.

"Okay," I say to myself with a certain degree of satisfaction. In the acting business, you never outgrow the comparing game that you played when you were a girl. "There are no zaftig action goddesses. I really do look better in it than she does." This is the first time in a long time that I've let myself come out on the positive side of the judgment scale.

At the commercial break the usher comes and finds me; the seat filler is right behind her. "Ms. McPhee, would you come with me, please? Mr. Barbera would like a word with you."

"Do you know what this is about?"

"Sorry, ma'am. No, I don't. He's waiting out in the lobby for you."

* * *

"Time is of the essence, so please forgive me if I skip the niceties," he says brusquely.

A pleasure it is meeting you, too, sir. Conrad, you may be the network's reigning czar of Daytime, but LaTrisa and the others were right: you resemble a giant Gila monster. What they neglected to mention, however, is that you have a voice like Kermit the Frog.

"I have an enormous favor to ask," he continues. "I'm hoping you brought another dress with you."

"I did."

"Thank God. I need to ask you to go back to your hotel and change your clothes."

"Because Meredith and I are wearing the same dress? They're the same style, but they're completely different colors. It's not that bad, Mr. Barbera."

"Meredith Contini seems to have a different opinion. She's insisting that if you don't change, she'll stop the show to change into something else. Since we're airing live, that's something I'd really prefer to avoid."

Oooh, Meredith, this is way over the top, even for you. Making me put on a jacket for a scene in a church is one thing, but forcing a nominee out of the theatre for a wardrobe change by threatening to hold a primetime live telecast hostage—during Sweeps, no less—is quite another.

The Gila monster looks uncomfortable; he obviously does not like the corner Meredith has backed him into. The only way he can really solve his problem is by passing it on to me. I mull my options briefly. It doesn't take me long to realize that they are severely limited. I don't have much of a bargaining position—still, I feel I should make my feelings known. I don't want to give him the idea that I'm rolling over for the diva. "Let me be clear, Mr. Barbera—"

"Conrad, please . . ."

"Let me be clear—I'm doing this because *you* asked *me*, not because *she* asked *you*."

"Understood."

"Not to put too fine a point on it, but if she'd had the nerve to ask me directly, I would have told her to go fuck herself."

Speak truth to power, as the saying goes. I wonder what he would have done if I hadn't brought a spare dress.

"I appreciate your candor. Take my car and driver. Malik will wait at the hotel and bring you back as soon as you're ready. Oh, and Kate . . ."

"Yes?"

"I owe you one." He smiles warmly.

Yeah, and if you live up (or down) to your reputation, Conrad, I won't assume that you'll find it convenient to remember that if I ever try to call in the favor . . . but for now, you seem to understand and even on some level appreciate where I'm coming from.

As Malik wheels the Lincoln back uptown, I watch the awards on the mini-TV in the back. Trent announces the Emmy for Outstanding Achievement in Multiple Camera Editing (and yes, he was right; his scripted dialogue is dreadful) and hands the statuette to someone from *The Bold and the Beautiful* just as the Carlyle's white-gloved concierge opens the door for me.

I dash upstairs, pull the Reem Acra out of the closet, and hold it up in front of me with one question in mind: How bad does makeup that was meant to go with bright, clear, almost-but-not-quite-turquoise blue look with delicate pastel?

The answers are

a. it's less than ideal; and

b. but so what. There's no time to completely redo it.

I slither out of the dress and leave it in a heap on the floor. "Oh, Vera, I'm so sorry, but I don't have time to hang you up," I say in apology to Ms.

Wang and her lovely gown. I dive into the ball gown and contort myself to do up the zipper and all the hooks. I stand in front of the mirror, look over at the clock, critically regard the match-up between the face and the dress, and look at the clock once again. I decide to settle for toning down the lipstick, something I can easily do in the car. I blot off Roxanne's NARS Red Lizard and then realize that only one color will do. I confidently reach for the MAC Bombshell and run back out the door.

Malik ushers me into the Lincoln and very carefully makes sure that the dress is tucked in there with me—all of it. I fill up the back seat all by myself. "You look lovely—again, Ms. McPhee," he says encouragingly. "I left the television on for you," he adds.

"And the Emmy for Outstanding Performance by a Younger Actress goes to . . . Lauren Elizabeth Fielding of *Live for Tomorrow.*"

"Yesssssssssssssss!" In the rearview I can see Malik grinning broadly as I whoop, holler, and clap wildly in my seat. From the Radio City audience there is more restrained applause, except from the *Live for Tomorrow* contingent, whose madly high-fiving reaction mirrors my own. The in-house applause is followed by a slightly awkward silence, and then the stentorian voice of the announcer: "Accepting the award on behalf of Ms. Fielding is her costar, Meredith Contini."

"Noooooooooooo!" I screech from the back seat. "Anybody but you!"

"My daughter Mallory—Lauren Elizabeth—could not be here this evening," Meredith begins, "but I'm sure she'd want me to thank the producer of our show, Daphne del Valle. In particular I think she'd want to thank Daphne for giving her this magnificent opportunity to work with such a splendid cast. And I have to assume that she'd want to especially express her gratitude to her on-air mother for . . ."

It's not about you, Meredith. It really isn't this time.

Malik picks up his cell to reassure his boss that we are headed back to Radio City. "Malik . . ."

"Yes, Ms. McPhee?"

"Please call me Kate. Malik, would you try to find out from Mr. Barbera if he knows why Lauren isn't here?"

"Yes, Ms. Kate." A pause. "Mr. Barbera tells me that Lauren Elizabeth Fielding got a great offer from Joel Silver and is filming in Spain."

Well done, Lauren! Take that, Meredith!! What goes around, comes around—and karma has a marvelous penchant for whapping you upside the head when you're still looking the other way.

Malik begins to chuckle. "What's so funny?" I ask.

"Mr. Barbera he says, quote, 'Tell Ms. Kate she's gonna laugh her ass off—it's a *Tales from the Crypt* vampire comedy.' "

I laugh so hard that tears form and I begin to worry about my mascara.

"Malik, please let Mr. Barbera know that he's absolutely correct . . . and that my laughing ass was last seen going out the window at Fifth Avenue and Seventy-first Street. I presume it was headed for the Frick Collection . . . either that or the Central Park Zoo."

I stop laughing when I realize that all this time the traffic hasn't moved an inch. To the contrary, we appear thoroughly mired in a classic midtown Manhattan gridlock. Despite a cacophony of taxi horns, nothing budges— in our case because we can't. We are hemmed in on all sides. Fifth Avenue is southbound only, and there are cars and buses up against our bumper both front and rear. To our left is Seventy-first, a one-way street jammed solid with cars headed toward us. They are trying to nudge their way forward so they can make the turn onto Fifth, and although they're having no success right now, they're all going to make it eventually. They have to, because there's no place else for them to go—on the other side of Fifth is Central Park.

And there we sit, for a good twenty minutes, then more.

"Damn!" I say to myself. "If I had known how long we were going to be stuck in traffic, I could have brought all the stuff I needed to tone down my makeup."

I settle instead for MAC Bombshelling my lips as perfectly as possible. Malik picks up his cell, speaks softly in Arabic, then rings off. "I'm sorry, Ms. Kate," he says, shaking his head slowly from side to side, "we'll be here awhile. Police have everything blocked off at Fifty-ninth."

"What's the trouble?"

"Bomb threat in the Trump Tower, big-time," he responds.

"Oh dear."

"When The Donald said, 'You're fired,' apparently somebody took it personal," he explains.

On the tiny screen the cameras pan the Radio City audience as the announcer's voice comes up over the orchestra. "We'll be back," he says in prelude to a commercial break, "with the presentation of the Lifetime Achievement Award."

This year's Lifetime Achievement Award honors a group of soap opera veterans, men and women who began in the earliest days of their shows. Many of them have been in the business for thirty or forty years, and they wear those years proudly, regally even. They are grey-haired and aristocratic, the matriarchs and patriarchs of their programs. They still appear from time to time, but where once they connived and caroused and canoodled—much as we still do—they are now the soap opera equivalent of fine china, dusted off and brought out for ceremonial occasions.

They have become the resident keepers of tradition and voices of reason, and even though they are in their sixties and seventies—at least—the camera loves them still. Best of all, they have retained a delightful twinkle that is compelling to watch, perhaps because they remember their lines better and put more zest into their performances than the blank Bradleys and insipid Ambers of today. They are a living lesson in the art of aging gracefully. It's a lovely moment to see the entire audience on its feet in tribute, but I can't help wondering what Meredith—who is closer to their age than she is to Bradley and Amber—must be thinking.

The cameras once more pan the crowd as the announcer intones, "When we return, the award for Outstanding Performance by a Lead Actress in a Daytime Drama." I'm bummed. Without really counting on winning, I had wanted to experience the giddy anticipation of shifting in my chair, listening to see whose name would be called. Instead I'm a prisoner on Fifth Avenue, and absolutely powerless to do anything but watch on television. The show must go on, and in this case it's going to go on without me.

The announcer introduces Tony Geary, who struggles to rise above his wooden dialogue with a certain amount of good humor before reading, "and the nominees for Outstanding Lead Actress are: Nancy Lee Grahn/Alexis Davis, *General Hospital;* Kim Zimmer/Reva Shayne, *Guiding Light;* Deidre Hall/Marlena Evans, *Days of Our Lives;* Kate McPhee/Devon Merrick, *Live for Tomorrow;* and Meredith Contini/Regina Abell, *Live for Tomorrow.*"

There is the sound of tearing paper; Tony reads the result for himself, looks up, and smiles. "And the Emmy goes to: Kate McPhee!"

That's me. That's my name he just read! "Aiyeeeeeeeeeee!!"

Malik begins honking the horn in celebration, and is immediately joined by the drivers of the surrounding vehicles. Even though I know the others are honking not for me but because we've gone all of about three feet in the last forty-five minutes, it still sounds like they're playing my song. Amazingly enough, the traffic starts to move.

Tony looks around expectantly to see where I am, but of course, I'm not there. *I'm here, I'm here! I want to say. We just went by Tiffany's and traffic is really moving. I can see the spire of St. Pat's. Vamp for just a moment, Tony—I'll be right there!!*

"Accepting on behalf of Ms. McPhee," booms the announcer, "is her costar and fellow nominee, our host, Meredith Contini."

Meredith glides up in "our" dress. She flicks her hair, embraces Tony, and takes the statuette from him. "I understand Kate is stuck in traffic," she coos, cradling the Emmy gently in her arms, "so it is with great pleasure that I accept this award on her behalf. I know that she would want me to thank our wonderful producer, Daphne del Valle; our writers, who keep giving us such terrific material to work with; and all the other members of our cast and crew who work so hard every day, making Hope Canyon such a fascinating place to be. And I'm sure she would want to express her appreciation to the fans. Let me tell you, I can't say enough about our fans. We love you. We wouldn't be here without you."

There is applause from the audience for the fans. Like Evita on the balcony, Meredith raises her arms in acknowledgment. In the background, the piano starts tinkling softly.

Oh my God—despite the piano, she's taking the applause as encouragement to continue!! They're not clapping for you, Meredith, any more than the cabs and buses were honking for me when Malik started tooting the horn!

"You know," she says colloquially, "our fans are what keep us going. Whenever I've been nominated and l—lo—los—t . . . ah, not won, our terrific fans have always been there for me . . ."

The piano becomes more insistent.

". . . sending me letters, visiting my web site, www.meredithcontini.com, giving me encouragement, suggesting new product lines, and bringing me oatmeal cookies and stuffed animals. . . ."

The rest of the orchestra joins in.

"There has always been this terrific outpouring of support . . ."

The orchestra grows louder.

". . . And it wasn't just my fans. My husband Renato has seen it all—I love you, honey. . . ."

What???!!! How did Renato the polo player get into this?

"And all of these years, my agent has stood by me. . . ."

Now she's thanking her agent? And am I imagining things or is she now fondling rather than cradling that statuette?

The music reaches a crescendo as Tony hooks her by the arm and gently but firmly leads her off the stage. I angrily switch off the TV as Malik nears Radio City. He flashes every piece of official credential he has and we are waved through the police cordon, straight to the entrance, where Rhonda and Nigel are waiting. "Congratulations, Kate!" Nigel says as Malik pulls me and my dress out of the car. "Did you see that Meredith—"

"Yeah, I saw it," I say. "Made me want to puke."

"With that fitted bodice? You couldn't. It's not physically possible," Rhonda says with a laugh. "Let me take a look at you. . . . Fabulous dress, but I would have given anything to see you and Meredith side by side—the pink and blue twins!"

"Listen up, Kate," Nigel says with determination as Rhonda and I are laughing. "Get serious for a moment. We're going to take you backstage to play Meet the Press, and that's something you absolutely do not get to talk about."

"What—that Meredith made me go back and change my clothes?" I ask.

"Precisely."

"Well, then, how am I supposed to explain why I wasn't there?"

"The Janet Jackson Memorial Wardrobe Malfunction?" Rhonda suggests.

"Dance around it," Nigel barks sternly. "Swoop and parry. Sidestep and sashay. And that's not coming from me. That's from Conrad the Barbarian himself."

A round of flashbulbs goes off in my face as I enter the press briefing area. Someone hands me my Emmy, triggering another round of flashes.

Gee . . . you think they'd be upset if I asked what happened to the cold dead hand they had to pry it loose from?

"Where were you, Kate, when you heard that you won?"

Whew! Something I can answer.

"I was in a car, stuck in gridlock at about Fifth and Sixty-ninth; nothing was moving. As I understand it, there was a bomb threat at Trump Tower. If we'd been just a little closer, I would have jumped out and run for it—even in this."

"Someone thought they saw you in your seat at the top of the show in a different dress. Why did . . ."

Oh shit.

Suddenly, there is a cheer and a shout and a new round of flashbulbs goes off. *Saved.* In comes the winner of the Outstanding Lead Actor Emmy—it is Wyatt, who has been honored for his portrayal of Dr. Ian Glenullen on *Denver General.*

"Wyatt! With the Emmy, any regrets about leaving *DenGen* for *Live for Tomorrow?*"

"None whatsoever," he says. "Marcello Bertone is such a rich part," he says, sidling over to me and putting his arm around my waist, "and I'm looking forward to getting him into trouble, just so Devon Merrick here can investigate me."

Blam! The flashbulbs explode. Under the circumstances it's perfectly legitimate to give him a big hug. He hugs me back. *Okay—that's not a for-the-cameras hug; that's a for real embrace.* We pose for a whole bunch of pictures as the photogs have a field day with two actors from the same show.

"Ms. McPhee . . . Kate . . . tell us about your dress."

"It's by Reem Acra, and it's pastel silk with pearl-and-rhinestone beading. . . . I feel like a baked Alaska in it."

"She looks like one, too," Wyatt quips, "most edible!"

While he is speaking, Daphne triumphantly comes in clutching a statuette of her own. I can tell she's chuffed. This one is the biggie—*Live for Tomorrow* is the Outstanding Drama Series for the year. She's wearing a navy blue smoking jacket paved in bugle beads over satin pants with a tuxedo stripe. She looks armor-plated (which is appropriate), but for once there is no food on her clothing. She must have paid someone else to chew it for her. As she looks at the two of us side by side, it seems I hear something click inside her head. The gears are surely turning. She nods ever so slightly, then takes her place to pose between us as the flashes continue to go off.

"Daphne . . . Ms. del Valle . . . with so many Emmys already to your credit, does the thrill of hearing them call you the First Lady of Soap Opera ever diminish?"

"Are you kidding?" she exclaims. "Who could get tired of this? Wyatt, when I first talked to you about coming over to *Live for Tomorrow,* what great confession did you make to me?"

"I told you that I hated soap opera," he volunteers somewhat sheepishly.

"And how did I respond?" she asks.

"You said, 'So do I,'" he laughs.

"You must understand," she says to the press, "I don't see what we are doing as soap opera. I never have. To me it's always about realistic portrayal of character. The show may not be exactly like real life as we live it, but it's a lot like the real-life jungle inside the human heart. My job is to put that jungle on the air.

"Whether you watch the soaps or work in them, you quickly come to understand how real the characters are to our fans. To our viewers, our characters have become friends and family. They know how the characters ought to behave, and they love the show because they tune in to see something that looks like genuine emotion up there on the screen every day. When we allow one of them to do something out of character, believe me, we hear about it. Soap opera viewers become intimately familiar with the characters in a way that primetime viewers never do—because they can't. Even long-running nighttime shows air just once a week, and even then there are reruns."

"Where do the ideas for your storylines come from?"

"From out of my head, but the raw material is all around me. All I have to do is pay attention. *Live for Tomorrow* is on with a new episode every day. In other words, there are more hours of *LFT* in any given year than there are in a hit primetime series over the length of its entire run. That means the characters have to work, and work consistently—in the long term as well as for a given episode. I may manipulate story for character, but I would never do the reverse."

"Can you give us a hint as to what's going to happen next?"

"Well, we are the number-one daytime drama, and I am most fortunate to have the Outstanding Actor and Outstanding Actress in my cast. And if you think that all happened by accident, think again. I can't give you

details as yet, but look for us to build on the popularity of these two characters."

"Have you found a new Mallory yet?"

"No, but ask me again a week from now. And now, Wyatt, you can go
celebrate with *DenGen* if you feel you must, but *LFT* is going to party like
there's no tomorrow upstairs at the Rainbow Room."

Same night

WE MUST BE SELLING one fuck of a lot of soap—our reigning Gila monster has bludgeoned the network into springing for a really big-ticket bash. Perched on the sixty-fifth floor of Rockefeller Center, the Rainbow Room is a living time capsule, an Art Deco masterpiece where it's still 1938. It looks as though Fred and Ginger might appear at any minute, and with a big band playing standards from Ellington and Glenn Miller, it sounds like it, too. The dance floor slowly revolves, so that the panorama of Manhattan's necklace of lights twirls around couples as they dance.

Daphne, Wyatt, and I, each of us clutching our winged statuettes, are the last ones to join the party. Cast and crew from the network's all-girl talk show and from our sister soap are here as well, but *LFT* is center stage—most assuredly first among equals. Cristal is flowing and there is an unbelievable cold buffet, but I wince as I see Daphne grab a plate, heap it with shrimp, then ladle a huge dollop of cocktail sauce over them, a sure harbinger of red doom for her bugle beads. "Congratulations, Kate," Trent says, giving me a hug. "Why weren't you up there—what the hell happened to you?"

"It's weird and it will take a while to explain it," I reply, looking around for Meredith and/or Conrad Barbera. "Can I tell you about it later?"

"Congrats to you too, Wyatt," Trent says. "I told myself before the show that if I didn't win, I wanted it to go to you."

"Thanks," Wyatt responds, "but this one might just as well have had your name on it as mine. I bet the next one is going to be yours."

"Excuse me, gentlemen," I say, "you two can carry on the Alphonse and Gaston routine without me. There's someone I want very much to meet."

I walk over to a window, where a solitary silver-haired woman is seated in a wheelchair. Edith Oakley is drinking in the Manhattan skyline. "Ms. Oakley," I say, coming up behind her, "I'm Kate McPhee." The figure does not move, and for a moment I fear that she has fallen asleep in her chair.

No, that's a lie. For a moment I fear that she's croaked.

"Ms. Oakley?"

"Mmmph . . . ah! Speak a little louder, dear. I'm not wearing my hearing aids."

"Ms. Oakley," I repeat, raising my voice, "I'm Kate McPhee, and I just want to say—"

"Wait just a minute, dear. This isn't going to work. I'll put the damn things in. . . . There, that's better. I don't like wearing them when it's noisy like this, because they pick up not just you but everything else in the room as well—voices, clinking glasses, shuffling feet on the dance floor. I get the Tower of Babel in my ear—it sounds like the entire universe is trying to shout at the same time."

"Ms. Oakley, I'm Kate McPhee, and I'd like to tell you personally how much I respect your body of work, not just on the show but throughout your career."

She is something of a legend. Prior to coming to daytime television, she'd already had a lengthy and acclaimed career on Broadway and in film. When *Live for Tomorrow* debuted, Edith Oakley spoke the first words of dialogue that went on the air, and her presence in the cast gave the fledgling show some much-needed credibility and gravitas. She portrayed Norma Corrigan Abell, a woman whose machinations were at least as devious as those of her rebellious daughter Regina. Edith still plays the same role today, as does Meredith, so get those pencils ready: it's time to do the math. In thirty-five years she's seen her daughter go from age twenty to age thirty-five.

"I wanted to apologize to you for not being in the audience when you were honored this evening," I explain, "but even if I'd been there I'd have figured out some reason to come over and introduce myself."

"Meredith said you were stuck in traffic. . . . Have you noticed that she's not here?" she asks with a sly grin. I pull up a chair next to her and arrange my dress. We proceed to have a real conversation that touches on acting technique, the Westminster dog show, the latest theatre in London, cast gossip, fashion, politics, AIDS, and *The DaVinci Code*. Not only does she still have all her acting chops, she still has all her marbles, too.

When the band takes a break and the noise level dies down, Edith removes her hearing aids once again. "It's not enough that they bring me more sound than I can process. The damn things itch like crazy, too!" she exclaims, rubbing her ears vigorously. "They make anti-itch cream just for hearing aids, but they want twelve bucks for the stuff and it doesn't work all that well anyway. I've found something better to use, but with these weensy evening purses, I didn't bring any with me."

"Well, there's nothing in mine but some MAC Bombshell and double-stick tape to keep my boobs from falling out of this dress, but I bet some-one around here has some. What is it?"

"Astroglide."

Actually, it's a good guess that someone up here is probably packing, in case they get lucky after the party, but I'm not about to run around the Rainbow Room making inquiries. And the question of how a woman her age discovered that a sexual lubricant would keep her hearing aids from itching will go unasked, at least by me. Nevertheless, I can't help smiling at the idea.

"What? Why is that funny?" she asks. "I'm old, not dead. And besides, we are always the same age inside, as somebody said."

"The somebody was Gertrude Stein," I say kindly. "And my mother had another saying. . . ."

"Use it or lose it!" we recite in unison, then start laughing.

The two of us continue our merry conversation until Trent comes up and asks me to dance.

"Go trip the light fantastic with him, dear," she says, patting my hand. "I had a splendid time talking to you, but this is your night. Congratulations. Enjoy!"

"I enjoyed our time together immensely, Edith," I say sincerely. "I hope to see you very soon back at the factory."

"When you do, I'm sure it will be when they trot me out either at Christmas or at another one of Regina's damned weddings," she says. "They both seem to come once a year."

"You looked pinned down over there," Trent explains as we dance. "I came over to bail you out."

"Thanks, but actually, we were having a terrific chat. I know that old age comes in a lot of different flavors, and I know we don't entirely get to choose, but that one's not so bad."

As the last strains of "Satin Doll" fade away, Trent excuses himself to head for the bar, leaving me momentarily standing by myself on the dance floor. "May I have this dance, Detective Merrick?" Wyatt asks.

He firmly takes my hand.

"Certainly, Dr. Bertone," I reply as the Big Band launches into "Moonlight Serenade."

This could be dangerous, Kate, I tell myself. It's late. There's champagne. A breathtaking view. Romantic music. He's gorgeous. He can dance. He's holding you very close in his arms.

"I was wrong earlier," he says.

"About what?" As we dance, I can feel his chest rise and fall against my own. He breathes deeply, absorbing my scent, as if he's trying to inhale me.

"You not only look like a baked Alaska, you smell like one, too!"

"That's a good thing, right?"

"A very good thing indeed," he says, pulling me closer.

As the dance floor revolves, we rotate past Daphne, who is locked in earnest conversation with Conrad Barbera. The Barbarian gives us two thumbs up and resumes talking, but I keep my eye on Daphne, whose raptor head swivels to track us as we go by. If her cranial gears were turning in the press room, they're whirring in hyperdrive now.

With another quarter turn around the circle, I catch a glimpse of Trent, who is slipping out the door with Tiffany. "Looks like Trent found himself a consolation prize," says Wyatt.

"Wonder if she's got any Astroglide."

"What?" he asks in astonishment and stops dancing for just a moment, until I explain about Edith Oakley's hearing aids.

"And you, Doctor, what did you find?"

"I'm not sure yet," he replies, "but it's all good so far. Let's get out of here."

"Is this when I'm supposed to say, 'Your place or mine?' " he asks when we get to the street.

"Mine's the Carlyle," I say.

"Okay, yours then," he says. "I'm at Morgan's, which certainly isn't bad. . . ."

"But it ain't the Carlyle, either."

My hands tremble as I open the door to the suite. I have no idea what's going to happen when we get through the door.

At first I kept telling myself that these tingly feelings were just me projecting all my frustrations and longings onto him. I even wondered if there was something so deeply perverse in my psyche that I had deliberately gone out and chosen Mr. Completely Unavailable as Mr. Right. This is a married man whose wife is my dear friend. She'd never given me any clue that there was something wrong between them. Nevertheless, there are these sparks, as there have been from the first day I saw him, and now it seems very clear than I'm not imagining the attraction, which at this point is so electric that it's palpable. And Christine is 2,400 miles away.

What happens is the world's most amazing kiss . . . and another . . . and another. As I undo his hand-tied bow tie and open his collar, his lips brush against my ears, the nape of my neck, my shoulders. . . . "Hold still!" I whisper as I fumble with the button.

He does, finally, and then grasps my shoulders firmly as my hands rest at his waist. We stand facing one another. "I hate you, you know," he says very tenderly as he kisses my hand and presses it to his cheek.

"Yeah, I hate you too," I say softly. "Head over heels, I hate you."

"I was afraid of that," he says.

"What are we going to do about it?" I ask.

"Every time I start to think about that, it comes out wreckage," he acknowledges sadly. "You should know that I'm not a player, Kate. I don't make a habit of this. In fact, this has never happened to me before. For the longest time I used to revel in the security of my marriage and how lucky I was that Christine and I were forever. With all the uncertainty of the acting business, it was the one sure thing in my life—the only thing I knew would never change. Even with all the beautiful women on *Denver General*, I was bulletproof. God forgive me, but there were times when I flaunted that in front of people whose marriages I knew were rocky."

"Ah, the sin of hubris," I say. "This is a bizarre comeuppance for me, too. I'm sure Christine told you about how my boyfriend Rafe ran off with my best friend Leslie, but only after they'd been sleeping together for a long time before I caught on."

"Actually, no."

How marvelous that she kept my confidences—which makes all this that much more painful.

"Well," I continue, "I suppose I can't really leave it at that now, can I?" I give him the midlength version of the Rafe-and-Leslie saga, ending with me swelling up at the dreadful Christmas party, the pregnancy, and the acres of tea bags Christine dispensed in the process of putting me back together. "And here I am. . . ."

"Thinkin' hard about how it might feel if that shoe is on the other foot," he says, picking up on my train of thought.

"She doesn't deserve this," I say.

"Neither did you," he says.

"What went wrong between the two of you?"

"What goes wrong with any married couple? In the old days they used to say, 'We grew apart.' It's not like we started having hideous fights or anything. There was just a day when I realized that Christine and I had become more like roommates than lovers. Unfortunately, that was right when I auditioned with you."

"Unfortunate? Unfortunate!" I exclaim with feigned dismay. "So I'm unfortunate, am I?"

"Well," he says softly, turning me around and nuzzling my neck from behind, "you must admit that it's a damned inconvenient feeling, this hatred."

"It is indeed."

"Do you think if we ignore it, it will go away?" he asks.

"No, but . . ."

"But what?"

"But much as I would love to think that all thoughts of Christine—yours and mine—would evaporate in the mad rush of unzipping and unhooking and unbuttoning, I know it doesn't happen that way. She'll always be the unseen presence, the woman who isn't there. After what happened to me with Rafe and Leslie, I can't do that to her. It's monstrous."

"So I'm a monster, am I?" he asks, mimicking my mock horror and commencing to tickle me.

Whatever martial arts technique Jay has ingrained in me kicks in. I cross my arms and seize Wyatt's hands, which are still at my rib cage. I lift my arms, thinking to pirouette out of the hold, but instead am rewarded by a loud *rrrrrrrrrrrrippp* at the seams of the dress.

I head for the bathroom to check the damage. It will take some doing, but it's fixable. If I leave it on, though, the tear will just get worse, so I shuck the dress in favor of one of those marvelous terry robes. When I come back out, I find Wyatt examining a sizeable scratch on his right wrist. "Did I do that to you?" I ask, taking his paw in mine.

"I think I'm going to need some lessons from Jay," he says.

"I think you're going to need a Band-Aid," I say, returning to the bathroom.

I place his hand in my lap to examine the scratch and notice a distinctive ring on his right hand. It consists of interwoven filaments of white, yellow, and rose gold in a Celtic knot pattern. "It was my great-grandfather's wedding ring," he explains, "and then it belonged to my father."

"It's lovely."

"My great-grandfather gave it to my father in 1940."

"Wait a minute! Your father must have been a baby in 1940."

"Precisely. Sinclair is a Scottish name, but my great-grandfather was living in London at the time. My father was his first grandchild, and as it turned out, his only grandchild."

"How come?" I ask as I dab a little Polysporin on the gouge I made in his wrist.

"It was the Blitz, and my great-grandmother had just been killed in a German air raid. My grandma gave birth to my father just a couple of days later. My great-grandfather was going through great joy at the birth of this baby—even as he was mourning the loss of his wife."

"What a dreadful combination of emotions to deal with."

"He was also trying to wrestle with the fact that his son, my grandfather, didn't know about either event because he was at sea with the Royal Navy. All this time the Luftwaffe was still coming over every night—it was bad. When they finally ordered all the children out of London, my great-grandfather took his wedding ring off his finger and gave it to his daughter-in-law. The Celtic knot is an unbroken thread. It means both eternal life and great love between people who will remain eternally connected even if they are separated—either by distance or by the grave."

"Wow," I say as I peel the Band-Aid off the paper.

"I always had the sense that Great-Grandfather knew or sensed something when he did that, because neither he nor his son survived war."

"So your dad never really knew most of the men in his family. They all died when he was little."

"Yeah, when he and Grandma came to the States after the war, they were very short on relatives, which may explain why he married my mother. She's Italian and comes from a huge family. I modeled Marcello on my Uncle Gino."

"Scottish-Italian—haggis with tomato sauce—interesting cuisine," I say, sticking the Band-Aid on his hand.

He winces. "Interesting family dynamic, too. Made for great fights at the dinner table. Mom would cook tons of food and talk at him a mile a minute, and Dad would just sit there and stew. He turned redder and redder until he finally turned purple and exploded. Anyway, my grandma held on to the ring until my dad was old enough to wear it. It came to me when he died last year."

I look out through the curtains and am amazed to discover that it is no longer dark. We have talked the night away. He gathers me in his arms.

"Wyatt," I say, "I can't. . . ."

"Do this to her. I know. Neither can I. I still hate you, though."

"And I you."

And with that, he releases me and leaves. I'm too tired to think about how amazing the night has been, but I fall asleep smiling.

Two days later

Trent and I are running lines in his dressing room when we hear Meredith on the phone. By now I know the drill and run into the bathroom for two drinking glasses.

"Yeah, Renato, be sure and have Jesus pick up a stack of *People* magazines. Their photographers were all over the place at the Emmys, and there's bound to be a big spread with some good pix of me. Yeah, it's due out today. . . .

"Oh, and Renato, check with Carmen. What? Well, Graciela then—whathefuck happened to Carmen? Actually if she's new, that may explain it. Ask Graciela what she's doing to my fuckin' underwear, 'cause she's ruining it. I gotta believe she's boilin' it or sumpthin'. All of a sudden the bras are all baggy and the panties are too tight. . . . No, it's not all in my imagination. I'm tellin' ya—my *chichis* are swimming but I have a perpetual wedgie in the *culo*. Yeah, goodbye."

Meredith slams down the phone as Trent and I look at each other, but then look away before we start to laugh. This is much too delicious for words.

"Asshole. I'm married to an asshole." Obviously she's still talking to somebody. But who? "Renato is an idiot and an asshole, not like you, my lover."

"Meredith, maybe you've . . . Is it possible that . . ."

Whose voice is that?

"What are you trying to say, my love? Stop beating around the goddamn bush!"

Ah, it's the voice of Kirk, the raspberry tart's paramour.

"I just thought maybe you've . . ." he begins.

"What? . . . Shit no, I haven't gained any weight! You know I never eat anything. Use that little brain of yours, lover. If I was getting fat, the bras would be too small now, wouldn't they? It's like I'm a victim of gravity. Everything that used to be in my boobs is now in my ass. You know, you're really starting to piss me off. You can go now."

       • • •

"Extra! Extra! Read all about it!" Rhonda sings as she comes into Gossip Central. "Get your red-hot copies of *People* magazine here. Step on up now. . . . Get 'em before they're gone." She flings a copy at me while I'm seated at Charlie's station.

"Let me see too, cherub," says Charlie. "I never got to see how your hair looked on the big night."

"She looked terrific—page seven, Charlie," Rhonda says. "I think you'll be pleased, Kate; I think Daphne will be pleased; I think even Conrad the Barbarian will be pleased . . . but the Queen—she's gonna be pissed."

When I get to page seven, I can see why. There is a great deal of attention given to my mysterious absence and that of Lauren Elizabeth Fielding. Meredith is barely mentioned in the text, but the pictures are even worse, at least from her point of view. The lead image is a photo of Wyatt and me standing side by side backstage after the show. The caption reads, LOOKING LIKE THE TOP OF THE WEDDING CAKE, THE NEWLY CROWNED KING AND QUEEN OF DAYTIME. There are a couple of red-carpet photos of other nominees, including a dapper-looking Trent, and a great shot of all the Lifetime Achievement winners, but there is nary an image of Meredith to be found.

Nigel comes in right after Rhonda. "You saw it?" he asks.

"Yeah," I reply. "How come they blanked Meredith? I mean, she was the host, after all."

"If you're covering celebs, you live or die by the escalator," Nigel explains. "If you're a celeb or a celeb wannabe, the Golden Rule is that you're only news if you're in motion. Things have to be changing in your life, personally or professionally. You're news on the way up, like you and Lauren Elizabeth, and, okay, Paris Hilton. And you're news on the way down, like Michael Jackson or Whitney Houston or Martha Stewart who is on her way up again any day now."

"Any story editor will tell you: if you stay the same, it's not news," says Rhonda. "If you're stuck at the bottom, nobody cares; if you're fixed at the top, it's a snore. You're a statue and pigeons crap on your head, but you're still there. As the leading diva of Daytime, Meredith has been standing at the top of the escalator for so long that there's not much left to say."

"I guess 'She's Still on Top' isn't much of a headline," I admit.

"Now, some people spend their entire life on the escalator—they're up/down, up/down, up/down, and whichever way they're moving, they sell copy," Nigel says. "Marilyn Monroe was one of those."

"Shit, Nigel, I think she's still on the escalator even though she's dead," I say.

"Yeah, her and Princess Di," says Charlie.

"Don't forget Elvis," says Rhonda.

"Pushing people *up* the escalator is what PR is all about. And of course," Nigel adds, "there is always that sleazy component of journalism that generates motion and sells copy by pushing stars *down* the escalator—whether it's really moving or not."

"I don't understand," Charlie says.

"Sometimes it's just a little shove and gravity takes over, as in, 'Guess who checked in to Betty Ford?' " says Rhonda. "And sometimes they just make up stuff outright. Hell, they've had guys in the *New York Times* doing that. Mostly, though, they publish half truths and innuendo, or photos of celebs looking crappy in no makeup while they're walking the dog in the rain. Then they feel free to speculate on why they were out there, or with whom."

"Excuse me a minute," Nigel says as his cell phone goes off. ". . . I'm on it, Conrad. I'll be right there." He leaves for a couple of minutes and then comes back with a dreadful look on his face.

"Who died, Nige?" Rhonda asks. "Connie can't be too upset; the stuff in *People* looks great."

"Nobody yet, but when they find me floating tushy side up in Hansen Dam, you'll know why." He tosses me a copy of the *National Enquirer.* "Check out page three. The only good news is that you're not on page one."

"I'm in the *National Enquirer*?"

"You and Meredith both." Some photographer, an enterprising fan in all likelihood, sold a picture to the *Enquirer* of me in the blue dress, rushing along the empty red carpet to get to Radio City. The scandal sheet juxtaposed it with an unflattering image of Meredith onstage in the pink dress, mouth agape. Because both photos are black-and-white, it's even more obvious that the two gowns are the same. There is a third photo of me in the ball gown, and accompanying text about how it's now obvious why Kate McPhee changed her clothes.

"What happens now?" I ask.

"Cloudy with chance of screaming," Nigel replies. "My phone is already ringing. Yours will be ringing shortly. I advise you not to answer it."

"Ni-gel!" Meredith screeches as she barrels into the room. "How could you let this happen?"

"If I'd known it was going to happen, I might have been able to get some damage control going, Meredith, but clairvoyance has never been my strong suit."

Ruben comes wandering in and immediately wishes he hadn't. "You!" she yowls before he can escape. "*You!*"

"Me?"

"Yes *you,* Ruben. You could have prevented this entire thing."

"What entire thing, Meredith?"

"Show him, Nigel," she commands. "Show him!"

Ruben looks at the *Enquirer* and appropriately furrows his brow.

"First there was the *Soap Opera Digest* Awards, and the dress that they called 'casket lining,' " she spits, waggling her finger at him.

"I *told* you not to wear that dress," he says, cutting her short.

"And now this!" she continues, as if he had not spoken. "It's all too much."

"Meredith," Ruben says calmly, "get a grip. I asked you what you were going to wear in New York and you refused to tell me, remember?"

"Well, it's *still* all your fault, Ruben. You should have told me that Kate was in Wang. And now," she continues, "and now you can't even get my clothes on camera to fit right."

"What on earth are you talking about, Meredith?" Ruben asks, his face the picture of choir boy innocence as Uta the seamstress scurries through Gossip Central with a load of clothes over her arm.

"You know that new Max Mara you picked out for me?"

"The vermilion one, right? You loved it."

"I did, but the top's too big and the skirt's too small."

"No way," he replies, shaking his head. "Can't be. You tried it on yesterday and it fit great."

"I know it looked fine yesterday," Meredith acknowledges, "but I put it on again just now. The top was huge and the bottom fit me like it was the casing and I was the bratwurst."

"Go put it on again and come right back," Ruben orders. "I want to see."

"I swear you're trying to drive me crazy!" Meredith stomps her foot and shakes her hair as she heads back to her dressing room.

"Well, she's got that right," Charlie whispers to me.

"Yeah, she really fell for it," Ruben says.

Meredith returns shortly thereafter in a smashing red Max Mara suit.

"Lemme see," Ruben says. "Turn around. . . . You look terrific. I've got some Sigerson Morrison heels in mind. . . ."

"I'm telling you, Ruben," she says. "I tried it on before and it was all wrong."

"I think you're imagining things, Meredith. It couldn't fit better."

"Hey, you look like one hot tomato, Mer!" Wyatt exclaims approvingly as he comes into Gossip Central. "Fits you perfect, too."

"It . . . well it does, doesn't it?" she says, her face softening in midsentence. As always, Meredith's ire dissipates instantly at the drop of a compliment. "You're going to kidnap me in this outfit, you know," she says coquettishly.

"I am?" Wyatt asks.

"That's going to be our new A storyline," she says smugly, glaring at me.

I don't think I'm imagining the edge in her voice that is equal parts "Neener neener neener," and "Take that, bitch!"

"Daphne told me herself," she adds. "I'm going to be the centerpiece of a mob kidnapping plot."

"What am I going to do with you once I kidnap you?" he asks.

"You're going to hold me prisoner in your hospital," she says sexily as she automatically flicks her hair and bats her eyelashes at Wyatt. "Doesn't that sound fabulous?"

Okay, I tell myself, this is a real good time to rehearse not being jealous. First of all, with Meredith, flirting is nothing personal. It's nothing more than a habit, like cracking your knuckles. And second, since we came back from New York, both Wyatt and I have been practicing being just pals—in the same way that Trent and I are pals. It's too soon to tell if we're any good at it or not.

Amber comes in walking bowlegged, looking like she just got off a horse. "Hey," she says, "anybody know how a pregnant lady walks?"

Okay, return with me now to a plot point of yesteryear. Jennifer Abell, Amber's character, married Burke Chaney, Kirk's character, when she was already pregnant with Philip Salisbury's baby. Trent, Mafioso scoundrel that he is, refused to marry her.

"They don't walk; they waddle," LaTrisa says, "but not like that. Meredith, you've been pregnant—how do pregnant ladies walk?"

"Oh, it's been so long. . . . Er, ah, I *never* waddled," she says as she flees for the sanctuary of her dressing room.

"All pregnant ladies waddle, eventually," says Carlos as he comes into the room. "When the kid gets big enough and that bowling ball head starts pushing on the bladder, every mama waddles." He breaks into an exaggerated duck walk. "It looks like this!"

"Still the *payaso*, eh Carlos?" I say. "I haven't been on a good Krispy Kreme bender since that night we put Bill in a Richard Nixon mask and a dress."

"Hey, *mi buchera predilecta!*" he says. "Welcome back from the Big Apple. I hear you brought some hardware home with you."

"I did indeed, and I trust that you, as the ranking officer of the Hope Canyon PD, have been keeping an eye on things in my absence."

"Except that while you were gone, without the coffee and the donuts I've been missing out on two of the four basic food groups."

"That is ridiculous," says Amber, trying to imitate Carlos's waddle. "That can't be right."

"Actually, that's pretty good, Ambarina. *¡Muy bien!* Take it from me! My wife is pregnant; my sister is pregnant; my sister-in-law is pregnant. . . ."

"Is that what they mean by a ménage à twat?" Amber asks brightly—or dimly—take your pick. Both her French and her mathematics are sorely deficient, as is her attempt at humor.

"You've been a busy boy, Carlos," I say. "Sounds like your *chilito* has been workin' overtime!"

"I don't like being pregnant," Amber declares somewhat petulantly. "I'm too young to have a baby."

"Well fiddle-dee-fuckin'-dee," Daphne snaps as she comes into the room. "Do they ever shut up on your planet, Amber?"

"I'm too young to be a mother, and anyway you must admit, Daphne," she says with a pout, "that motherhood is just not very glamorous."

"Look at Kate Hudson—it works for her. If she can handle it, Amber, so can you."

"You're not actually going to make me have it, are you?" she calls as she practice-waddles down the hallway.

"The writers are still working on it," Daphne replies, cutting her off. "Now, can we please break up the party and get some real work done around here?" Her face is like molten lava, and it looks like a good time to make oneself scarce.

One week later

```
INT. HOPE CANYON POLICE DEPARTMENT—NIGHT

                    BURKE
I'm looking for Detective Merrick.

                    DEVON
               (not looking up)
You found her. (softening as she sees him) Oh, hello,
Burke. I haven't seen you since the wedding. Is there
something I can help you with?

                    BURKE
I want to report a missing person.

                    ENRIQUE
               (getting out the form)
Name. Date of birth. Physical description.

                    BURKE
My wife, Jennifer.

                    ENRIQUE
She's expecting, isn't she?
```

BURKE

Yes. I woke up in the middle of the night and her side of the bed was empty. I thought maybe she went downstairs to read or something, I went back to sleep, and when I woke up this morning, she was nowhere to be found.

DEVON

Can you tell me why you waited till nightfall to report her missing?

BURKE

I figured she'd come home sooner or later. Maybe she'd gone to her sister's or something.

ENRIQUE

And you didn't find it odd that she didn't call?

BURKE

I did, but . . .

DEVON

Let's be honest here, shall we, Burke? Did you two have a fight last night? Is that why her side of the bed hadn't been slept in?

BURKE
(reluctantly)

Yes, but . . .

DEVON

Her car was gone as well?

BURKE

Yes.

ENRIQUE

And you tried calling her cell?

BURKE

Of course. No answer. Nothing.

DEVON

And you called Regina?

BURKE

No answer there, either.

                           DEVON

    I don't like it. Enrique—call the phone company and get
    the records for Jennifer's cell phone. If she hasn't
    been receiving calls, maybe someone's been using it to
    call out.

                        ENRIQUE

    I'm all over it, boss.

                         DEVON

    Burke, you and I are going to pay a visit to Regina's
    house and see what we can find out.

"And cut," Marty says. "Lunch break. Go grab yourselves a sumptuous repast, after which we shall break into the Casa Abell."

    EXT. ABELL ESTATE FRONT DOOR—NIGHT

                         BURKE

    There's no answer.

                         DEVON

    That's odd, isn't it? It's a school night, right be-
    fore final exams. Certainly Mallory and Magda should be
    home.

                         BURKE

    I believe they're off skiing in Gstaad. . . .

"Oh please . . . it's June," Kirk says, breaking character. "What the hell are they doing skiing in Gstaad?"

Daphne's voice comes over the speaker, like the voice of doom. "Don't be a wiseass, Kirk," she hisses. "Mallory will be skiing in perpa-fucking-tuity, until we get a replacement for Lauren Elizabeth. And I had to send Magda with her, because we're still fighting about, pardon me, we are still *discussing* whether the Queen will let her daughter be old enough to go skiing or even go take a shit by herself."

"Sorry, Mom," he says, blowing a kiss toward the booth, where Daphne's figure can be dimly seen. "I'll try to behave myself."

"Kate," says Marty, "we'll cut Kirk's line at 'Gstaad.' Just say your tag line and then we'll set up the interior."

                         DEVON

    Let's go have a look around the back.

"Sounds like Meredith and Daphne are *mano a mano* about the new Mal-lory," I say.

"Yeah, this is the Clash of the Titans; we'll see who blinks first," Marty says.

INT. ABELL ESTATE—KITCHEN—NIGHT

                          DEVON

No sign of forced entry.

                          BURKE

Looks like they left in a hurry, though. Everything is still out on the—

                          DEVON

Don't touch anything! I want to get the guys from the lab out here right away.

Devon's phone goes off.

                          DEVON
                    (on the phone)

Yeah, Enrique, whaddaya got? . . . Okay, and you traced the numbers. . . . That's very interesting. Put a tail on him—now! And keep me posted.

                          BURKE

Have you found her?

                          DEVON

No, but her cell phone has gotten some use since she's been missing.

                          BURKE

Well, she didn't call me. Who did she call?

                          DEVON

I'm afraid you're not going to like the answer. There were a whole lot of calls made to a number registered to Philip Salisbury.

Devon's phone goes off again.

                          DEVON
                    (on the phone)

I'm all ears, Enrique. He went where? . . . No. Stay on him but do not apprehend him. I repeat: Do not apprehend him. Burke Chaney and I are on our way.

                          BURKE

Oh God, Devon, please tell me she's okay.

DEVON
I wish I could, but I think we may have located her.
Sergeant Morales and his men have tailed Philip Salisbury to the Cañon Perdido Hospital. Let's go see if
we can find her.

"And cut," Marty says. "Alrighty then," he says to the techies, "let's set up the hospital. Stat!"

"You were saying . . . ?"

"Hold it a sec, Kate. Yoo hoo, oh yooooo hooooo," he halloos into the PA. "Down there in Maaaake-Upppp . . ." he continues in a singsong, "you know who you are, people. I need Philip, Laszlo, Marcello, Jennifer, and Regina, aka Trent, Vlad, Wyatt, Amber, and Meredith. Get your keisters up here—now!"

"As I was saying before I interrupted myself, when Lauren Elizabeth took over the part of Mallory a few years ago," Marty explains, "Meredith made them change Mallory's 'official' birth date—it was pushed up six years. Lauren was tiny, and when she was thirteen it wasn't too tough to buy the idea that she was still in grade school."

"But aren't they now looking for a sixteen-year-old who looks thirteen?" I ask.

"Nope," Kirk says. "Meredith is being a hardass about it. She's holding out for another Lauren—Lauren like she was when she started."

"Last fall Mallory was pregnant and lost the baby in a car crash, and now Meredith wants her daughter to be a little kid again?" I say incredulously.

"Precisely," says Marty. "And Daphne wants to go the other way entirely. She's looking for an actress even older than Lauren, so she can SORAS Mallory up to be in her early twenties."

"SORAS?"

"Soap Opera Rapid Aging Syndrome," the two men say in unison.

". . . Which explains how soap offspring who were 'born' in 1992 turn out to be twenty-two rather than thirteen today," explains Vladimir, who has just arrived for the scene.

Vladimir looks like he has a hangover—but then he always looks like that. It's part of his charm and attraction, both on the show and off. His dark, almost Egyptian eyes slope down, and his voice sounds like he smokes a pack of Marlboros daily. He's perpetually unshaven, with that sexy three-day stubble. There is an exotic and musky aroma about him—he smells how I imagine a souk would. The women love him. I don't love him, but he's been growing on me, mostly because he really inhabits the role of Laszlo—intensely. And so, despite his friendship with Priscilla, we've reached an accommodation of sorts, because of the acting.

"The truth of the matter is that as characters, children are a pain in the ass," Marty says. "When they're little, they can't instigate action on their own. They can be cute, and they can be pawns or victims. That's pretty much it."

"Well, the little urchins do have their place," says Trent as he walks on set. "Estranged parents or vindictive grandparents get to fight over them for custody; they can die of some horrible disease or accident; or they can be the objects of paternity suits. And they're decorative at weddings."

"But the little brats are a pain in the ass as actors, too," Marty says. "They usually come with a gorgon of a stage mama attached at the hip, and we can't work 'em to death till two in the morning like we can with you big people."

"Score one for accuracy, Marty," Wyatt says as he arrives, touching me lightly on the shoulder. "You didn't call us grown-ups."

"Until they're in their late teens," Kirk continues, "from a story standpoint no one knows what to do with kids. They're too young to be involved with anyone romantically, so there's this difficult middle period when they stop being adorable and progress to being annoying. SORAS just fast-forwards them through the awkward phase."

"Meredith doesn't want any part of SORASing Mallory, because it will make her seem that much older by comparison," Trent says.

"And there it sits," Marty says. "Neither she nor Daphne will give an inch. You can't imagine the screaming matches."

Actually, Marty, I can.

Kirk and I stand to the side and spectate as they set up the next shot. Trent, Vlad, and Wyatt are all ready. Amber shows up shortly thereafter, looking visibly upset.

"Oooh, Amber," Trent says, "I think your big baby shower scene will be coming up soon!"

"Zip it, Trent," she says, devoid for once of her characteristic pep squad effervescence.

"Mymymy, aren't we crabby today!" Trent responds. "Wrong time of the month—oh, sorry. When you're PG, you don't have a time of the month."

"Strapping on this watermelon is the pits, but if Daphne says I have to have this kid, I swear I'm gonna talk to my agent. Can't they just put me in the Witless Protection Program instead? Then when I come back, I'll have left it with some woman in Arkansas or something," she says.

"C'mon, Amber," says Wyatt, trying to jolly her along, "you can't stay an ingenue forever."

"Sez who?" she shoots back. "Meredith seems to be pulling it off."

"Speak of the devil," Vlad says.

"Why Meredith," Daphne says in passing as she heads for the booth. "How good of you to join us. This is the earliest you've been late this year."

INT. CAÑON PERDIDO INSANE ASYLUM—DAY

Laszlo and Philip are bringing Regina and Jennifer into
the building by force. **Meredith is wearing the red Max Mara
suit.** Marcello Bertone is waiting for them. Various extras
are wandering in the background, exhibiting strange facial
tics and babbling like the semifinalists in a glossolalia
contest.

LASZLO
I've got some new patients for you, Dr. Bertone.

MARCELLO
Welcome, ladies. We'll do our best to make you comfortable. You'll find hospital wear—but no sharp objects—
in your rooms. Get them out of here.

REGINA
You can't do this to me!

"No, I mean really," Meredith says. "Daphne, you said that Marcello was
going to kidnap me and put me in his hospital. . . .This isn't a hospital."

"Ah, but it is," Daphne insists from behind the glass. "It's a mental hospital, Meredith. 'Look around you, all you see are sympathetic eyes,' " she
sings—badly. " 'Stroll around the grounds until you feel at home. . . .' "

" 'Here's lookin' at you, Mrs. Robinson. . . .' " Vlad says with a grin.

"I've never, ever heard Mom sing before," Kirk whispers, then gives a
stage sneeze.

"Coo-coo-ca-choo," I say.

"Hey hey hey," says Marty. "Shall we continue?"

MARCELLO
Can't I?

Regina struggles.

LASZLO
Give her a shot of Thorazine, Doctor; that will calm
her down.

Jennifer begins to struggle as well.

LASZLO
Her too.

PHILIP
No! It would endanger the child—*my* child.

```
                    MARCELLO
He's right, Laszlo. I certainly can find a nice padded
lockup for her, though.

                    LASZLO
Keep them here until we find where Regina has hidden
the financial records. I know they're somewhere on the
estate.
```

"Cut!" says Marty.

"Oh you Snidely Whiplash, you!" Kirk says puckishly to Vladimir as he walks off the set. "Keeping those two women against their will like that!"

"It's a rotten job but somebody's got to do it," he replies with a grin.

"So Kate," Kirk says, slipping an arm around my waist and copping a feel in the process, "want to go to my dressing room and, ah, run some lines?" He says this last with an unmistakable leer, even as he's looking straight at Meredith.

"No, she doesn't," Wyatt says firmly, taking my arm.

32

Five weeks later

THE MEXICAN STANDOFF between Meredith and Daphne continues. As part of her power play, Daphne has kept Meredith stashed in the Cañon Perdido loony bin, and Amber in there with her. Thus the A story-line is in a holding pattern. Consequently the scriptwriters have been working overtime to give us all something to do, but they're running out of material. We've been through nine fruitless visits from the three mobsters—Vlad, Trent, and Wyatt—trying to get information out of the two sisters about the location of the "secret financial records"; Carlos, Kirk, and I have made four unsuccessful raids on the hospital looking for Regina and Jennifer. We're all treading water until Meredith and Daphne reach some kind of agreement over how old Mallory is going to be.

INT. CAÑON PERDIDO INSANE ASYLUM—NIGHT

                        MARCELLO
Welcome again, Detective Merrick. This is, what, your fifth visit?

                        DEVON
And I'm going to keep coming back, Dr. Bertone, until I find Regina and Jennifer. We know they're here.

                        MARCELLO
         (walking with her as she begins searching)
All you really know, Detective, is that you and your men have searched this place from top to bottom and come up empty each time. Here—let's take the stairs, that elevator is out of order.

The camera holds on the elevator.

One week later

Mallory is still skiing in Gstaad. She must be schussing on the glaciers by now. It's the middle of the summer, and the natives are getting restless. Trent and I are in his dressing room when we hear a ruckus through the wall. I race to the potty and return with the two tumblers. Drinking glasses up!!

"Ya know, I've just about had it with you, loverboy," we hear Meredith shout. She is almost loud enough that we don't need the glassware. "It's unbelievable that you're taking Daphne's side in this, Kirk."

"Oh, I don't know, Meredith, my sweet. I think it's unbelievable that you're not able to look in the mirror and realize how old you are. You have to face reality, Mer. Your daughter can't be eight years old!"

"Ooooooooooh," she growls. "She put you up to this! That freak, that mobile-chinned walking napkin with . . . with . . . with **bad hair**. . . . She put you up to this, didn't she?" There follows the sound of breaking glass.

"You missed me, you old bitch," he says, "and no—Daphne didn't put me up to anything. Common sense did it, all by itself."

"You can go now. Dismissed," she responds.

"No problem. I was just leaving," he says.

"And don't bother coming back. Even a good fuck isn't worth this."

"Why Meredith, I'm shocked. *Shocked,* I tell you."

"Why?"

"Whatever gave you the idea that you were a good fuck?" he says, slamming the door on the way out. There follows the sound of more breaking glass.

Meanwhile, back in the loony bin . . . "I need Devon, Regina, Marcello, and Laszlo—Kate, Meredith, Wyatt, and Vladimir. Upstairs now, please," says Marty over the intercom. The writers, more desperate now than ever, have decided to throw me into the asylum with the rest of the lunatics.

* * *

INT. CAÑON PERDIDO INSANE ASYLUM—NIGHT

                    MARCELLO
Welcome yet again, Detective Merrick.

                    DEVON
Dr. Bertone, nobody's fooling anyone here. Save us all
a lot of trouble. Just tell me where I can find Regina
and Jennifer Abell.

                    MARCELLO
      (walking with her as she begins searching)
How many more times will it take to convince you that
they're not here? This way, please. That elevator is
still out of order.

The camera holds on the elevator.

                    DEVON
              (watching Marcello's eyes)
     As it has been every time I've been here . . . and that
     may be the only place in this building that I haven't
     seen.

Devon thumps on the elevator door, and hears a faint thumping in return.

                    DEVON (CONT'D)
     Doctor, let's have a look inside that elevator.

                    MARCELLO
     (producing a large hypodermic and jabbing it in her arm)
     I'm so sorry you said that, Detective.

Devon collapses in his arms.

                    MARCELLO (CONT'D)
     Sleep well, my dear detective. Sleep well.

Marcello urgently flips open his cell phone.

                    MARCELLO (CONT'D)
     Szekely, it's Bertone here! Devon Merrick got suspi-
     cious of the elevator. I had to give her a shot.

Split screen with Laszlo.

                    LASZLO
     Keep her juiced up. I'll talk to Philip about what to
     do next and get back to you.

Pan to ELEVATOR INTERIOR—NIGHT

They have rigged the set so that the staircase where Wyatt and I remain is next to the cutaway of the elevator. Meredith, now clad in raspberry scrubs, stands with her back to the camera. She bends down and places a folded piece of paper in the corner of the elevator, then turns around and stands up.

"You ready for the sob scene, Meredith?" Marty asks.

"I will be shortly," she replies.

"Just a minute," Marty says, "the light's not quite right." A lighting techie comes on set, quickly makes some adjustments and disappears. I don't recognize him right away. He must be a new guy; he's wearing baggy overalls and has a baseball cap pulled down over his face. Got a great ass, though.

"That's better. Okay, Meredith," Marty continues, "They want you already in tears when the cameras start to roll."

Meredith turns her back to the camera once more and goes to unfold the piece of paper in the corner. "Aaaaaaaaaaaaaaaaaaaaaaaaaaaaaaaaaaaah!" she screams.

"What's wrong, Meredith?" Marty asks.

"Aaaaaaaaaaaaaaaaaaaaaaaaaaaaaaaaaaaah!" she repeats. *"Someone has stolen Fluffy!"* she says, gesturing to the unfolded paper.

Wyatt and I turn to look. Sure enough. Instead of her beloved photo of dear departed Fluffy, there is a picture of Scooby-Doo.

"You know, we can actually use that scream," says Daphne acerbically from the booth. "Very good, Meredith. That's the most authentic emotion I've gotten from you in quite some time."

"Break!" Marty calls. "Bring on the tea and sympathy—please!"

Meredith stomps off and grabs her cell phone, just as Kirk trots through the set, carrying a baseball cap and a jumpsuit. "Renato, drop everything and get over here," Meredith demands on the phone. "You're taking me to lunch."

As I return to Gossip Central, Rhonda comes in shepherding two visitors. "Kate, I'd like you to meet some very special guests. This is Emilia Contini, and Cosima . . . I'm sorry, Cosima, I'm going to mangle your last name, I'm sure of it."

"Cosima Ortega y Ochoa y Orvieto de Contini," she says, laughing. "It's a mouthful, I know."

"Her professional name is Cosima Santiago," says Emilia. "She's an actress, like her mother."

"Is that Contini as in—" I begin to ask.

"This is Meredith's sister and daughter," Rhonda explains.

There is no mistaking the family resemblance in either woman. But for her black hair, Cosima is a replica of her mother, right down to the spool of bangs across her forehead. Alas, the years have not been kind to Emilia. Her grey hair presides over a face well corrugated by time and care. I'm guessing she's about twelve years older than her sister—it's as if she could be the Dorian Gray self-portrait that Meredith keeps in her attic.

"How . . . unexpected. What are you two doing here?" Meredith asks on her way through. She does not look at all glad to see them.

"Hi, Mom," says Cosima, exchanging air kisses with her mother.

"Hello, Emilia," says Meredith rather frostily. "What brings you here?"

"We came to take you to lunch, Mom," Cosima answers. "Surprise."

"I'm sorry, that's not going to be possible. I have a lunch date with my husband."

"Surely Dad wouldn't mind if we tagged along," Cosima suggests affably.

"Rhonda," Meredith says curtly, "please order some lunch for Emilia

326 S o a p s u d s

and for Cosima. I'll settle up with you later." And with that, she turns on her heel and swans off.

"I think she had a bad morning," Rhonda offers.

Emilia waves off the attempted apology. "It's okay, I'm used to it," she says with resignation.

"We're just about to order from Jerry's Deli," I say to the Continis. "You're more than welcome to join us."

Daphne comes in behind them with Maggie on her coattails. "Thank you. I will," she says, assuming I was speaking to her. "Get me a grilled pastrami and cheese," she barks to Rhonda, who looks quite astonished, since Daphne almost always dines alone. "On rye, of course. Make sure it's Swiss, not jack. Who are you?" she asks in the middle of ordering lunch, suddenly realizing there are strangers in our midst.

"Daphne, this is Meredith's sister, Emilia Contini, and Meredith's daughter, Cosima Ortega y Ochoa y . . ."

". . . Y Orvieto de Contini, but my stage name is Cosima Santiago," she says, laughing easily. "It's just a lot more straightforward."

"It's a good stage name," I say. "It's memorable, and it's fun to say."

"Thanks," Cosima replies with a smile. "My mother picked it out for me." She turns to Daphne and gracefully offers her hand for Daphne to shake. "Needless to say, you're a legend in our household, Ms. del Valle. It's a great pleasure meeting you."

How can that be? I ask myself. This young woman must be about twenty-two years old—I have to assume that throughout her childhood she's been raised by a string of much put-upon nannies, and yet she seems to be a self-assured and perfectly pleasant human being.

"Extra Thousand Island dressing. Maggie, if you want anything, for chrissake speak up now," Daphne states flatly as she perfunctorily shakes Cosima's hand. She says nothing to the two visitors, but I can see her cranial gears starting to turn once again.

"Extra sauerkraut . . . You look just like Meredith," Daphne adds. "Side of bagel chips and ranch. Iced tea . . . You both do." Fiddling her chin ever more vigorously, Daphne looks back and forth between the two Continis as if she were watching a tennis match, or rather, as if she were a peregrine falcon deciding which budgerigar to seize for an entrée. "Make that a Diet Coke instead."

Finally she taps her pen on her clipboard, and then hands it to Maggie without looking at her. "Ms. Contini, please forgive me," Daphne says, addressing Emilia, "Ms. Santiago and I will be dining in my office. If you'd follow me, please." Cosima looks at her aunt, shrugs, and leaves with Daphne and Maggie.

Once she disappears, Emilia finally allows herself to look crestfallen. "I'm so sorry," I say. "We're not always this rude. Our manners are usually at least a little better than that, all of us. I'm sure you must be disappointed. This started out as a nice family outing, and look what's happened to it."

"We were just trying to celebrate our birthday," she says somewhat sadly.

"And here Daphne's gone and hauled her off. How nice that you and your niece share the same birthday—maybe you can still do dinner together instead."

"No—*our* birthday. Meredith's and mine."

"Sounds like your dad got busy at about the same time each year," Rhonda says with a half smile.

"No—**our** birthday. Didn't she ever tell you? We're twins."

A week later

THE STALEMATE BETWEEN Daphne and Meredith continues. There has been no move to compromise on either side; hence, Mallory is still skiing in Gstaad. Meanwhile, Daphne has devised a love story for Wyatt and me. The romance does a lot more than just put her two Emmy winners on camera together. It also further deprives Meredith of time before the camera and punishes her for continuing to hold out for a young girl to play her daughter. And it has the added bonus of easing the desperation of the writers who are trying to keep the A storyline alive. Until Daphne and Meredith work out a solution, other than continued fruitless visits to the hospital, there isn't too much more to put on the air without abandoning the storyline entirely. Since I'm still a lesbian, it took a little contrivance to set up, but nevertheless, I'm about to get my first on-air kiss since my scene with Charlotte in the morgue.

```
INT. CAÑON PERDIDO INSANE ASYLUM—NIGHT

                         MARCELLO
                      (on the phone)
       I tell you, Laszlo, this situation is making me ner-
       vous. I'm holding a police officer against her will.
       What? Yeah, there are drugs I can give her so she
       won't remember a thing, but I can only do that for so
       long before causing permanent brain damage. . . . What
       do you mean, you don't care?

                          DEVON
                     (moaning, groggy)
   Ugh. Ahhh . . .
```

                              MARCELLO
                     (continuing in a whisper)
I am a doctor, Laszlo; I still have some ethics left.
And you know what? When there are cops swarming all
over this place looking for her, it will be me, not
you, who will have to deal with them. And if they find
Detective Merrick doped up with my meds in her veins,
why do I think that you won't be sending one of your
high-priced suede-shoe lawyers to bail me out? So
hurry up and find the records at the mansion. The clock
is ticking here. . . .

                              DEVON
Ugh. Ahhhh . . .

                              MARCELLO
She's coming around. I've gotta go.

                              DEVON
                     (in a drugged fog)
Where am I?

                              MARCELLO
                     (sitting by her side)
You're here. You're with me.

                              DEVON
          (opening her eyes, but still lethargic)
Who are you?

                              MARCELLO
It doesn't matter who I am.

I look into Wyatt's penetrating eyes and just dissolve. He gives me the same
little nod he gave me during his audition.

                         MARCELLO (CONT'D)
Do you know your name?

                              DEVON
No, I . . .

                              MARCELLO
You are . . . Woman.

He caresses my cheek.

                              DEVON
                    (dreamily, compliant)
        I am Woman.

                              MARCELLO
        And I . . . I am Man. And there is nothing else that
        matters in the entire universe except you and me.

He nods again, gathers me into an embrace, and kisses me, first gently, then ever more deeply. *Oh shit. All that "just friends" stuff just went right out the window.* The kisses feel just like the ones in the Carlyle on Emmy night—so much so that it's unclear whether Marcello is kissing Devon or Wyatt is kissing Kate. A minute and a half later, an eternity on television, we're still at it, but since no one's hollered "cut," we keep it up.

Finally Marty ends the scene and says, "Jeez, cut already. Will someone throw a bucket of water on these two so we can separate 'em?"

"Not just good, very good," Daphne says. "Finally I have something real to put on the air. I loooooove it!"

"Wyatt!" I whisper as we head off down the corridor. "We have to talk," I say urgently.

"Can't right now. Daphne wants me to run an audition scene with somebody."

"Then when?"

"Tonight—in the parking lot—after we shut down," he says, moving along at a gallop.

I'm left to face Christine by myself.

"Wow!" she says, fanning herself as I walk back into Gossip Central. "I was watching you two on the monitor. I thought I'd gotten used to watching Wyatt in love scenes with actresses on *Denver General,* but that almost looked real!"

Oh . . . what can I possibly say to that?

"But then I said, 'Nah, that's why they won the Emmys. They're just two very good actors, doing what they do best.' You sure had me wondering for a while, though."

I feel like a traitor, a betrayer of trust. I feel like I always thought Leslie should have felt when she got involved with Rafe.

Mercifully, a diversion appears as Amber slips into Debra's station next to me. "Hey Amber," I say, "looks like you've finally got the pregnant lady waddle knocked."

"Or knocked up," chirps LaTrisa from the other side.

"It sucks," Amber says. "I feel fat. I feel ugly. I hate being pregnant. I really do."

"Why?" LaTrisa asks. "Women bloom when they're pregnant. They get this luminous glow. . . ."

Suddenly, Christine drops the mascara and bolts from the room.

"What?" LaTrisa asks. "What did I say?"

"I don't know," I respond, jumping up to go after her, "but you touched some kind of nerve."

I find Christine in "our" stairwell, head tucked into her folded arms, sobbing. "Looks like it's my turn to get the tea bags," I say. "What happened back there?"

"I'm fine," she says.

"No you're not. What's goin' on?"

"I'm fine, really," she says, trying to shake it off. "It just that . . . Never mind, it's silly."

"What?"

"Well, there was Amber crabbing about having to play pregnant and how much she hated it, and LaTrisa going on about how pregnant women get all glowy and . . ." And the sobs return and take over her body once more.

"Hey now," I say, putting my arm around her shoulder. "Hey now."

Christine produces a tissue and blows her nose. "I'm sorry," she says.

"Your feelings are your feelings," I say. "Never apologize for them. You know how it knocked me for a loop when I found out that Leslie was pregnant. I felt like something had been stolen from me—something that was supposed to be mine."

She takes a deep breath and looks me in the eyes. "Yes, but even if it's not with Rafe, at least you can have a child, Kate. I can't. Wyatt and I were trying for a while. Nothing. We've been to a slew of doctors and they've all said the same thing. It's not possible. And now to have one woman complain about having to playact at being pregnant and another going on and on about how radiant you get . . . Well, it just got to me."

"Of course it did," I say, hugging her as tightly as I can manage. "Of course it did."

Now I really feel like shit, I say to myself. I'm lusting after my friend's husband while comforting her over not being able to have a child. I'm a child-ready husband stealer!

. . .

The parking lot is empty. I'm sitting in the Jeep as Wyatt pulls his Lexus into Bradley's empty spot next to mine. I'm just about to jump out and get into his passenger seat when he opens his door and climbs into mine. "You're gonna be covered with dog hair," I say. "Kierkegaard has been riding shotgun. It's everywhere—"

"Shut up, Kate," he says as he leans over and kisses me strongly. I automatically start to respond, but then push him away.

"Why didn't you tell me that Christine can't have children?" I demand.

"I'm glad she finally told somebody. I wanted to, believe me, but it wasn't my place to say anything," he says. "She's always been a very private person about stuff like that. She made me promise that I'd leave it to her to mention it."

I tell him about the incident with Amber and LaTrisa that sent her into tears. "It's killing her that she can't have a child," I say.

"And what exactly am I supposed to do about that?" he asks somewhat angrily.

"I'm sorry," I say.

"I'm sorry, too," he says. "About everything."

We sit in silence for several minutes.

"I had to face her after our scene today. I felt awful—I *feel* awful."

"Yeah, so do I," he admits. "What are we going to do about all this, Kate?"

"We're way beyond 'Dear Abby' here," I reply.

"It's not going to happen, but I long for something clean and simple, like in the movies," he says wistfully.

"You mean like, two years from today meet me in a café in, oh, I dunno, pick one . . . Budapest? Cairo? Singapore? Sounds like Bogart and Bacall in the opening scene of a bad sequel to *Casablanca*."

"Bogart and Bergman," he says. "Bogey and Bacall was *To Have and Have Not*."

" 'You know how to whistle, don't you, Steve? You just put your lips together and . . . blow.' "

He smiles and whistles softly, but I can see the tension in his face.

We sit side by side, staring straight ahead.

"I still hate you, you know," he says softly.

"And I you—head over heels, I still hate you, too."

A week later

```
INT. CAÑON PERDIDO INSANE ASYLUM—DAY

                    MARCELLO
Look, Szekely, in good conscience I can't keep giving
her the drugs much longer.

                    LASZLO
You've got to, Bertone—you don't have a choice. Be-
sides, I should think you'd want to. From what I hear,
she seems to have forgotten she's gay and fallen in
love with you.

Marcello socks Laszlo in the jaw and turns to the nurse.
```

NURSE
Here are Devon's meds, Doctor.

MARCELLO
(writing on her chart)
Put those back, Nurse. I'm changing her treatment pro-
tocol. Instead of those, give her two of these this
evening, and two more tomorrow morning. Now, where is
she?

NURSE
Out in the garden, Doctor.

EXT. CAÑON PERDIDO INSANE ASYLUM—DAY

Marcello and Devon are sitting on a bench, hand in hand.

MARCELLO
You seem to be doing very well today, Woman.

DEVON
Oh yes, Man, yes I am.

Marcello produces a plain gold ring on a string and dan-
gles it in front of Devon's face.

MARCELLO
(softly)
Woman, I want you to listen very carefully to my
voice. Your body is relaxing. Focus on your breathing.
Inhale . . . exhale. That's good, very good.

Wyatt places his hands on my head, rests his thumbs on my forehead, and
then makes small circles right between my eyes.

MARCELLO (CONT'D)
Now, close your eyes, Woman. Feel your chest rising
and falling with each breath. You are at perfect rest,
Woman, perfectly calm, perfectly still. You are going
into a deep, deep sleep. That's it. Now, what is your
name?

DEVON
I am Woman.

MARCELLO
And I am Man, and you trust me in every way, don't
you?

> DEVON

Yes, Man, I do.

> MARCELLO

And you know that I would never hurt you, don't you?
Now, I'm going to give you the ring you just saw,
Woman. Touch it, slip it on your finger.

> DEVON

Yes, Man.

> MARCELLO

Now take off the ring and give it to me.

Devon hands him the ring. He kisses it.

> MARCELLO

Woman, in a little while I'm going to put it in your
pocket. Keep it with you always. Whenever you change
your clothes, you will remember to take it with you.

> DEVON

Yes, Man.

> MARCELLO

Now Woman, listen carefully. You will be leaving here
soon. You will not remember how you got here, and when
you get out into the world, you will not remember me
until I call you and say some special words. Do you
understand me?

> DEVON

Yes, Man.

> MARCELLO

I'm going to call you on the phone and say, "I hate
you, Woman." Then you will put the ring on your finger.

**Wait a minute! He was supposed to say "I love you, Woman." He changed
that! Marty's keeping the scene going, and I can't really stop it myself without giving away the show.**

> DEVON

Yes, Man, I will.

> MARCELLO

I would tell you I love you, but I would be afraid
someone else would say that to you. Do you understand?

                              DEVON
Yes, Man, I do.

                            MARCELLO
You will not remember this conversation, and you will
not remember that you were in a trance. You've just
been sitting here, listening to me read to you. Do you
understand, Woman?

                              DEVON
Yes, Man, I understand.

                            MARCELLO
I'm putting the ring in your pocket, Woman.

Marcello kisses Devon on her closed eyes.

                            MARCELLO
Now Woman, count backward from ten—very slowly—and
then open your eyes.

                              DEVON
  10, 9, 8, 7, 6, 5, 4, 3, 2, 1 . . .

Devon opens her eyes, and she is alone.

"And cut!"

Next day

M EREDITH COMES ON THE SET waving a sheaf of papers and screaming at Daphne in the booth. "Absolutely not! I absolutely will not
have it!" she yells. "Under no circumstances will I allow you to hire Cosima
to play Mallory!" she insists, with a toss of the hair and a stamp of the foot.

Daphne, looking vexed, exits the booth, Maggie on her heels. "My contract," Meredith shouts, brandishing the papers, "my contract gives me
right of approval on any actress who is going to play my daughter. . . ."

"I don't believe that's correct," Daphne says with exasperation. "I believe
that you have to be *consulted,* but that you don't have final say."

"Wrong!" Meredith sings. "Wrong-wrong-wrong!" she trumpets. "It's
very clear—black and white—see?" She shoves the top page under Daphne's
nose. "I absolutely will not allow my daughter to play my daughter. My
daughter is too old to play my daughter."

"Curiouser and curiouser," said Alice.

Daphne peers through her half-frames. "Maggie," she says, twisting her
chin like a screw top, "take these papers and make me a copy of them.
Now!" As Maggie scurries away to do as bidden, I swear I see the slightest
glimmer of a smile on Daphne's face.

Next day

Whump! Whump! Whump-whump-whump! A gnome fills my dressing room
with sacks of mail. "There's lots more where this came from," says Nigel,
"and there's a stack just like this for Wyatt, too. We're getting monster positive feedback on the Devon/Marcello–Man/Woman storyline."

Alison comes into Gossip Central with news. "We have a new Mallory—finally!" she says. "My friend over at network told me that Daphne has hired someone named Kendall Gilman for the part. Meredith okayed her."

"What else do you know about her?"

"She's fourteen, and she's four feet six inches tall."

"Talk about small for your age!" Trent exclaims. "Even the gymnasts her age are taller than that! When she's a little older, we can set up a storyline romance for her with a jockey at Santa Anita."

"Great idea, and then we can get Thor the Lovesick Wonder Horse back," I say. "That way, she and her mother can double date."

"When do we get to meet her?" LaTrisa asks.

"At the wedding—Regina's wedding," says Alison.

"Crap!" says LaTrisa. "I cannot believe she's marrying again; we should be bricking her up in an assisted living apartment in Florida."

"Regina's getting married again!?" Trent exclaims. "Be still my heart. Who's the lucky victim?"

"Bradley—I mean Nicholas," Alison says.

"But they aren't even dating!" I say.

"It will be a whirlwind love affair," Jay says as he pours himself a cup of coffee. "A shipboard romance, followed by a huge All-Skate rehearsal dinner at the Abell mansion, and grand whoop-de-doo wedding at the church. Daphne's using it to bring in all the old-timers."

"As she is required to do to meet their contracts," Daphne says crisply as she comes into the room.

"I have something special in mind for this wedding," she continues. "As Jay said, all the veterans of the show will be onboard for the rehearsal dinner. And for the wedding we are going to do something that hasn't been done on Daytime in quite a while. We're going live, at least for the East Coast. We'll tape the New York feed for the rest of the country."

"That would mean we're on camera at ten A.M.!" Alison moans.

"It would indeed," Daphne says. "If that's a problem for you, my dear, have your agent call me in the morning—I'll be awake." And with that threat hanging in the air, she departs.

Two days later

Now that we have a Mallory on the horizon, Daphne is letting Regina out of the loony bin. After all, if she's going to get married, she can't still be locked up. Today is a rehearsal day. We need to set up her "rescue" from the elevator, where she's been stashed since the stalemate began. Jennifer will escape in a laundry truck shortly thereafter, with Philip's clandestine assistance. The elevator shot will be a bit complicated. I'm to clamber up to the top of the set, rappel onto the top of the elevator, cut a hole in the roof, drop a rope into the elevator car, and pull Meredith out.

```
INT. CAÑON PERDIDO INSANE ASYLUM—DAY

                     DEVON
              (talking to herself)
  Okay, Regina's in here somewhere. What do I remember?
  I remember a sealed box. . . . What kind of a sealed
  box . . . ? A big sealed box.

Devon sees the elevator with the OUT OF ORDER sign.

                 DEVON (CONT'D)

             Big sealed box . . .

After trying to pull open the doors, Devon dashes to the
top of the building, looks into the elevator shaft, grabs
a blowtorch (an insane asylum always has one handy, right?),
then rappels down to the top of the elevator car, lights
the torch, and gets to work on the top of the elevator.
```

"And cut," says Marty. "Okay, Meredith. Get in the car now, please."

Twenty minutes later, I'm still cooling my heels on top of the elevator, waiting for her to show up so we can do our scene together. Finally she graces us with her presence.

```
INT. CAÑON PERDIDO INSANE ASYLUM—DAY

I am standing on top of the elevator car, where the techies
have just removed the "hole" I have "blowtorched" into the
roof. Behind me is a cameraman with a handheld, who will
shoot over my shoulder and down through the hole at Mere-
dith.

                     DEVON
        (peering into the darkened elevator)
  Anybody in there?

                     REGINA
  Don't hurt me—who is it?
```

"I can't see her," says the camera guy.

"Meredith," I shout down into the car, "the cameraman can't see you. You're going to have to move to your right so you're on camera."

"And again," Marty says.

```
                    DEVON
          (peering into the darkened elevator)
    Anybody in there?

                    REGINA
    Don't hurt me—who is it?
```

"I still can't see her," says the camera guy.

"Meredith," I say, "you need to move to your right even more—as it is now, you're not in the shot."

"One mo' time," Marty says.

```
                    DEVON
          (peering into the darkened elevator)
    Anybody in there?

                    REGINA
    Don't hurt me—who is it?

                    DEVON
          (blanking momentarily)
    I am . . . I am . . .

                    REGINA
    Who is it, please tell me.

                    DEVON
    I am . . . I am Detective Devon Merrick of the Hope
    Canyon Police Department.
```

And we wait, and we wait, and we wait . . . and finally. . . .

```
                    REGINA
    Is that really you, Detective Merrick? Oh thank God!
    I've been terrified, I tell you, terrified.
```

I look down through the hole and see her face tilted up toward me. She's doing this thing that drives me crazy, where she's trying to look beautiful on camera—mouth sexily agape, wide-open eyes. And it irritates the life out of me, as it always does, because it has nothing to do with the material or the emotion behind it. "Oh shit!" I say in frustration. "Meredith, would you please have the decency to look *terrified*? And you're going to have to be *terrified* a little faster. Come in with your line sooner—do you think you can manage that? Otherwise I'm just standing up here on top of the elevator contemplating my navel."

"Don't tell me how to act, Kate," she says, flicking her hair and attempting to maintain her unruffled demeanor.

"Well, somebody better," I shoot back. "It's about time. It's a rotten job but somebody's gotta do it."

"Kate, it's not your place to comment," she says archly.

Ah, the old know-your-place-and-stay-in-it gambit. I'm not behaving the way a proper guest at the Garden Party should. Well, fuck it—I've had it. What I really want to do is take the blowtorch and make her melt, just like she melted on top of my Christmas tree.

But instead I slide down through the hole on the rappelling rope and land in the elevator car, right front of her. "It's like this, Meredith," I explain sarcastically. "The whole idea of acting is to take what you've experienced in real life and use it to create a realistic portrayal on camera. The trouble with you is that you've got it all backward. You can't take the way you behave here and apply it to how you live your life. The world is not your oyster, and it ain't your Garden Party, either."

"Ooooooooooh," she says, her voice lowering an octave.

"Well well well, who rattled your cage, Meredith? Was it me?"

"Ooooooooooh . . ." It's the same otherworldly growl she made in Daphne's office when Daphne told her she wanted Regina to be forty rather than thirty-five. I half-expect her head make a complete revolution on her neck, à la Linda Blair, and her mouth to gush forth pea soup.

"You know, Kate, ever since you won the fuckin' Emmy, you've been so goddamn full of yourself. . . ."

"Despite your making me go change my dress—excuse me, *our* dress—that didn't exactly come out the way you'd planned, did it, Mer?"

Meredith rises slowly and comes at me with her claws bared.

"See. Think. Do," I say, repeating Jay's mantra as I extend my foot in a roundhouse kick. In a well-aimed near miss, it whizzes just past her right ear. I'm sure she felt the breeze as my toes went by.

Meredith dissolves instantly in tears. "Dafff-neee!" she wails. "Dafff-neee! She attacked me. I was savagely attacked by Butchy the Vampire Slayer!"

"Alrighty then," says Marty. "We're rrrrrready to rrrrrumble!"

"That's enough. Both of you," Daphne says. "Marty, we need to reblock this scene, and we need a bigger hole in the top of the elevator. Let's move on to the next."

"And we'll now turn our attention from female mud-wrestling to *Name That Dad*!" Marty says. "Jennifer and Philip on set, please—I need Da-Da and the Little Mama. Let's go, please."

I stand to the side to watch the paternity scene between Amber and Trent. Dressed in her blue loony bin wear, Amber waddles onto the set—by now, it's become second nature to her and she's doing it all the time, even when she's not on camera. "Oh Kate, nice kick," she says. "Real nice kick, Butchy!" she adds with a giggle.

Jay comes over and gives me a thumbs-up. "Perfectly placed *chagi*, my butchy grasshopper," he says with a grin. "You got good extension, too. I think you may be up to Tom Cruise by now!"

Trent arrives on the set and pats me on the back. "Yo Butchy!" he says. "Way to kick ass and take names!"

"Dafff-neee!" Meredith whines again. "I hope you intend to do something about this."

"Back off, Meredith," Daphne replies menacingly. "Not now. Right now I've had it with the whole fucking lot of you." She has that look in her eye that strikes fear in the hearts of all of us.

Well, all of us except Amber. "Daphne," Amber says, "I have to tell you that I'm really tired of being pregnant."

Hideously poor timing, Amber. Even Meredith is backpedaling because Daphne looks like she's about to blow.

Daphne turns scarlet, then purple.

"Daphne, I . . . This pregnancy thing . . ."

Oh shit. Only someone as clueless as Amber would ignore all the warning signs of an impending volcanic eruption on Mount del Valle.

"Daphne, I want to know how much longer I'm going to be preg—"

"Amber," Daphne says softly, but with steely determination. "The answer is that you're not going to be pregnant any longer at all."

"Oh thank you, Daphne. Thank you so much!"

"Just have your agent call me in the morning."

Two weeks later

WYATT HAS NOT BEEN IN THE STUDIO since he hypnotized me in the garden. He's been in North Carolina—one of Conrad Barbera's pals had asked to borrow him to shoot a TV movie. To account for his absence, our storyline has had him on the run in the wake of the rescue of the Abell sisters from his sanitarium. To keep the idea of our romance alive, Daphne has had me investigating his disappearance, unsure whether to consider him a missing person or a fugitive from justice.

I miss seeing him, but in any event we have been busy with the lead-up to Meredith's wedding. Meredith, of course, has been in her element, especially since Bradley—Nicholas Duncan—proposed by moonlight on bended knee two episodes ago. From her perspective, the hiring of diminutive Kendall Gilman to play her daughter and her betrothal to a man about half her age are proof that she's still just a slip of a girl herself. Today we're shooting the rehearsal dinner with the entire *Live for Tomorrow* cast, both past and present, in attendance. This segment will be taped and will air tomorrow at about the same time that we'll have our final run-through for the live broadcast. The day after that, we'll be up live for Meredith's wedding.

This morning Meredith calmly inhabits her celestial throne in Gossip Central, being made beautiful for her rehearsal dinner. Even on an ordinary day, getting Meredith ready for the Garden Party can take up to four hours, but because today is such a special occasion, we're lookin' at five-plus, easy.

It takes about two hours to style her hair. First, it is washed with color enhancing Capelli di Regina Shampoo in Flaming Cinnamon, and conditioned with Capelli di Regina texturizing, volume-enhancing rinse. The hair, including the hot dog bun on the forehead, is then set on Velcro rollers the size of the Alaska pipeline and dried under a heat lamp.

Then come the extensions. And since today is so very special, more are being added. Shiny titian extensions are being braided into the underlayers of her hair, producing the voluminous coif that is her trademark. If one were to run a hand over Meredith's head—not that one would ever be so impertinent—one would feel the bumps and ridges where the extensions lurk. The crown of the helmet is finished off with her own Contini Velvet Glove hairspray to ensure that it won't move an inch until the following morning, when the entire follicle fox-trot will begin anew. The only portion of her tresses given leave to move are those locks that must slinkily glide around her shoulders whenever she makes a gesture or statement of weight. Without Meredith's famous hair acting, alas, there probably would be no acting at all.

For the moment, Meredith has her eyes closed and appears to be serenely in repose. Her chubby worker bee is carefully taping excess skin from her baggy throat around under the nape of her neck. The worker bee is sweating; it's a tricky job and she doesn't want to upset the hair extensions. Meredith, however, is completely unperturbed. Her full chest is gracefully rising and falling, and one can see the skin from her neck unfurling into youthful smoothness.

Next is the kabuki mask. The makeup bee drywalls, sands, putties, trowels, and plasters a perfect surface, then sandblasts MAC foundation from throat to hairline. Once this foundation has been applied, powdered, and set, it's the perfect canvas to apply the face of Regina, and the bee begins the arduous task of painting on the mask of Venus. Brows, eye sockets, lash lines, cupid's bow, brow bones, cheekbones, nostrils, and lips are all daubed on to accentuate or diminish and create perfection.

The result is still magnificent. Meredith when she enters her cocoon is truly an embryo; when she emerges in full drag, she is every inch the beautiful butterfly, looking younger than the college interns who deliver our scripts. It's amazing that the conversion process continues to work after all these years, but it does. Hell, considering that in its natural unsurgeried state her face would look just like her sister Emilia's, it's a fucking miracle.

Having been a witness to the transformation, I pour myself a cup of coffee, snuggle down in the couch, and wait to be called. The coffee is so hot that it spitefully hits my empty stomach and reminds me I haven't eaten since midday yesterday. Food! I am completely inept at hunting and gathering. Even with Sondra stocking my fridge, I can't seem to remember to eat before leaving the house. Now famished, I resort to the tactic I have seen my fellow cast members use quite successfully in the past: I whine.

"I'm so hungry," I whimper. Before I can take another sip of coffee, the deli menu is making the rounds and Trent is taking notes on a pad. He picks up the phone and places the order, using a special voice he reserves for those who are hard of hearing, those who are deaf between the ears, and those who are still several hundred night classes away from mastering the English language. "Greek omelette sandwich, Chinese chicken salad, pasta primavera, salmon salad, tuna wrap . . . extra balsamic, extra lemons, sauce on the side, no oil, egg whites only in the omelette," he instructs.

We at *Live for Tomorrow* are a culinary nightmare, a collection of dietary prima donnas—nobody orders the food the way it appears on the menu. Hence the order, when it arrives, will be wrong—it always is—but we never return anything because we are paranoid they will spit into it. The flurry of activity has awakened Meredith, who asks if someone could be so kind as to request for her a no-fat soy latte and a no-fat sugar-free chocolate muffin. She keeps her voice at a delicate whisper and smiles at Trent as if he were her lover surprising her with a caged nightingale as a gift. Trent nods and adds the pretend food article to the long list.

He winks at me as he hangs up the phone and turns back to Meredith. "You are looking very slender these days, if I may say so, Meredith," he drawls impishly. "It's about time you got Bradley to settle down with you—again. How many times is it now you've been married to Nicholas?"

"Oh, Trent, you tease!" Meredith giggles girlishly and brightly turns to face him, pushing her worker bee in the chest to get her out of her way. "I've married Nicholas Duncan only once, but that was several Bradleys ago; this will only be number two. There was one time in between when it almost happened. We tried to profess our love for each other, but then his bastard twin sons turned up with assault rifles, remember?"

"How could I forget that most Chekhovian of scenes?" nods Trent, gravely.

Chekhovian? Chekhovian, as in Anton Chekhov? I ask myself, and look at Trent quizzically. Nyet—that plot is not Chekhovian in the slightest. No trains or suicides or manic-depressive sisters.

He brushes his index finger to the side of his nose to validate my suspicion that he is twitting her, but she has no clue. Meredith is writhing gently in her conversion pod, languidly gesturing with underwater hand signals, as if conversing with a deep-sea diver. "It was such a dramatic day," she continues. "Three contract players were shot dead—mistaken identity on the twins' part. That all came out in the trial afterward, because Daphne decided she wanted to keep the twins for a while, so they needed to be innocent. I used that show in my Emmy nomination reel that year." She bats her eyes and continues. "The Nicholas we had at the time was such an accomplished actor, marvelous at emotion. He could really cry."

"Pepper pot," LaTrisa hisses in my ear.

"Real tears," Meredith continues, oblivious. "I got concerned at first that he was truly upsetting himself."

I snigger, John Belushi to Meredith's Blanche DuBois. In the wake of the *chagi* incident in the elevator car, there seems to be no point in trying to hide my feelings about Meredith, in part because it's all I can do to keep hiding my feelings about Wyatt from Christine—indeed, from everybody. I have good friends, wonderful friends in the cast and crew—Trent of course, LaTrisa, Rhonda, Nigel, Mzee, and dear sweet Charlie—but there is no one I can tell about my feelings for Wyatt. These are dear folk with whom I would share almost anything about myself. Over the months I've told them about Rafe and Leslie, but I can't bring myself to talk about the fact that I've fallen hopelessly in love with my friend's husband and he with me, and there's absolutely nothing we can do about it.

It's not that I'm really fearful that they would tell anyone else (well, maybe Charlie would share it with Don), but the weight of the matter is too great to put on a friendship. It's about the same as suddenly handing a friend a giant boulder and expecting them to hold it indefinitely. The weight of that boulder of information changes everyone who carries it, and of course it's that much heavier when everyone knows all the people involved and sees them daily. By putting it on Trent or LaTrisa, I would change not only my relationship with them, but also their relationships with Christine and with Wyatt—and I don't think I have the right to do that.

"He used the inhaler," LaTrisa continues, jolting me out of my self-absorption, "and if that didn't work, he stuck pepper in his eyes."

Meredith's worker bee shoots us both a look as we titter quietly, then glances at the clock on the wall. Meredith's marathon storytelling is setting us all back big-time. I shrug, what can you do? Only an earthquake could stop her now. I pray for a small 6.0.

"There was the scene, at the end," Meredith goes on, "where I was holding the hands of the dying priest and the blonde kindergarten teacher and the blonde cheerleader as they were all bleeding to death. I held their hands and told them God forgave them for their sordid triangle of love and that they would enter into the kingdom of heaven. And then the priest gave his two loves the last rites. Even though he was gasping for breath, he managed to cleanse those two trollops of mortal sin.

"And you know the thing that was so touching? The camera held on me the entire time. Throughout his entire monologue, the camera slowly crept in on my face. And then . . . and then at the last possible moment, as they all breathed their last, I closed my eyes and I looked up to the heavens as a tear rolled out of my right eye . . . No, my left eye, my downstage eye. It was perfect."

At this point Meredith has grabbed both Trent's hand and her worker bee's hand and is earnestly clasping them to her fleshy bosom. Her eyes are cast up, as if reliving that electrifying moment. She gasps. She is Jennifer

Jones in the *Song of Bernadette;* she is reborn. We all burst into spontaneous applause. Yes, we do. But Meredith isn't finished. We stop clapping.

"Thank you. Yes, what a moment," she continues. "Then, after the paramedics had come into the church, as the bodies were being carried out, I laid a rosary on each one. And then I was left alone at the altar. I knelt before my God and asked forgiveness for their tortured souls. I humbled myself before the Lord and flung myself down, prostrating myself before eight million viewers. I was wracked with grief, inconsolable, my wedding day destroyed by the bloodshed."

But wait, there's more!

"Nicholas entered and knew not how to help his one true love. He stood there with an extraordinary blank expression on his face, one that said, 'I have lost everything, and it is all my fault, and my bastard sons have come back to haunt me.' Bradley did this all with one look—not an eyebrow raised, not a murmur—just the slow tensing and releasing of his jaw. He was masterful, masterful. The camera slowly pulled away from him, revealing me lying delicately along the aisle before the altar, my six-thousand-dollar Vera Wang spread out around me like angel wings. Then the camera panned up into an overhead shot of these two broken people, lost to each other for good."

Meredith pauses. Surely she is finished, but alas, she continues. "Lost to each other for good. But no—there is a second chance. There is always a second chance! Tomorrow and tomorrow and tomorrow . . ." Meredith takes a deep breath. She pauses dramatically and opens her mouth; she is not done yet.

"Jesus Christ, woman, are you on crack?"

Who said that?

"There are forty crew members, thirty-five contract actors, twenty extras, ten Makeup, ten Hair, seven Wardrobe, sixteen writers, two medical supervisors, and two child chaperones all waiting for you to get your goddamn slap on and get your girdled, expensive, and expansive ass on set. You have twenty minutes, and if I do not see the whites of your paid-for eyes up there within that time frame, I am canceling your trip to Florida to hawk your gold-plated holiday geegaws."

All of our heads whip around in unison. Standing in the doorjamb is a terrifying apparition—Daphne. And she is righteously pissed. There is smoke coming out of her nostrils, and her hair has been whipped into a frightening sponge cake arrangement that precariously sits on top of her head in terror of its life. Her bifocals are perched at an odd angle on her nose and she is spitting and growling and chewing on a pencil, even as she is puffing on a cigarette—simultaneously—which accounts for the smoke. Because Daphne seems to both dress and apply her makeup in the dark, her figure is not the easiest of surfaces on which to bring one's gaze to rest. However, at the moment I find myself unable to stop looking at her. There is no question that Daphne spends good money on her appearance. The mystery is how her clothes manage to resemble leftovers plucked from a rummage sale at a dear little Catholic church hall in Pocatello.

I wonder who actually purchases this stuff for her, because I'd bet my cat that she has never stepped into a dressing room at Neiman's. She'd eat the sales assistants alive, for starters. My guess is that she walks into our wardrobe department, plonks down one of her hefty salary checks, and instructs Ruben and his staff to knock themselves out. I also imagine they do exactly as ordered, but until one of them sets up a cot in her closet, they can't be responsible for how she puts herself together in the morning.

Today she is wearing one of her faves: a crumpled pink tweed Chanel pantsuit that has obviously seen better days. She has paired it with a thin turquoise cashmere sweater, a peach-and-cream silk scarf anchored by an oversize brooch, and camel suede Ferragamos, which are somewhat down at the heel. Her garish earrings are black-and-gold—well, there's only one; Daphne always removes the other to accommodate the cell phone. She is gripping an Egg McMuffin under her elbow, which is also holding her script. I think of Karl Lagerfeld stabbing himself in the throat with his fan if he ever were faced with the vision before me.

At the end of the day Ruben ought to confiscate the Chanel and send it off to the Brentwood Royal Cleaners for special treatment, and I fixate on this matter only because I am too scared to look at anything else but her clothing and the Egg McMuffin. Nevertheless, I know that something is happening. I know this because I hear a soft rustling movement behind me. With trepidation I tear my eyes away from the breakfast tragedy and slowly, slowly peer back at Meredith. Blank. She has the blankest of all expressions. Her forehead is completely smooth; she is devoid of emotion. Her mouth is set in a straight, MAC Bombshell frosty pink line. She stares directly at Daphne, then glacially, fraction by fraction, she rises from her makeup pod. The rest of us do our very best wallpaper impression; we have all stopped breathing.

She grasps the arm of the chair with one hand and smooths a fine henna strand that has escaped from her bangs with the other. The smoothing hand is shaking violently, and she quickly brings it down and starts walking toward Daphne. Her four-inch Jimmy Choos clip-clop very deliberately on the linoleum. Daphne stares hard at her as she approaches. Meredith pauses, then speaks calmly and purposefully. "Yes, Daphne, your dancing poodle will be ready directly." And with that she gracefully swans out, emitting a cloying exhaust contrail of Contini di Notte mixed berry cologne behind her.

Daphne smirks a little, it seems, looks at all of us, remembers her McMuffin, and takes a large bite. "Hand me a Kleenex, someone." About fifteen people run into one another grabbing various paper products— tissue boxes, towels, cartons of napkins, anything to appease the monster— and offer them up to her. Too late. She wipes her mouth with the sleeve of the Chanel and exits. Brentwood Royal Cleaners will need a miracle.

I head up to the set and find Daphne still spitting and gnashing away. Maggie the XXVI has become a human lectern. This sweet young woman, fresh from her communications course at UCLA, is turning script pages to the rhythm that Daphne snaps with her fingers. She has dark circles under her eyes and her hair appears unbrushed. I suspect she was called in the middle of her shower this morning and charged right over here in response to Daphne's peremptory summons.

Daphne doesn't budge as Maggie continues flicking through the script. Finally she stops reading and just stares ahead into the distance. She does this when some genius thought is approaching. She turns to stare at the exit door. Something is going on inside her cranium.

"Maggie?" Her little assistant tenses and nods and holds the script forward in the manner of an eager choirboy offering up a goblet of wine to the congregation. "Maggie, have we called the cast up yet? Tell Marty to get this goddamn show on the road, and fast." Daphne snatches the script from Maggie and marches off to the booth.

The company begins to file in. En masse, a soap opera cast is daunting. The hunks mill around, pretending to talk about sports but secretly running their lines in their heads. The insecure male leads are patting their hair, checking their plugs. The evil characters lurk, silent and brooding, dripping with talent. The current blondes are squealing about Brazilian bikini waxes.

"I waited for more than an hour to get waxed over at Pink Cheeks, but it was so worth it!" Tiffany gushes. "Cindy even put Sergio's initials in the front—in rhinestones!"

"It was the funniest thing," says Alison. "Last time I was there, I saw Priscilla on his way out. He looked terrible."

"Don't say anything," says Tiffany conspiratorially, "but Cindy told me they had to pry him off the ceiling three times during his treatment."

The elders file in, the ones who started this back in the days of black-and-white, bowed by age and yet still carrying themselves with great dignity. A warm and comforting feeling of familial camaraderie ripples through my body at the sight of them, a feeling that radiates outward to embrace the rest of the members of the cast. We are all of us—veterans and newcomers alike—part of the great continuum of actors, people together who love what they do—no matter how well they do it. I give Edith a hearty wave when I see her, just as Trent arrives bearing my egg-white-omelette sandwich. "She didn't pay again," he announces to me between bites of his Chinese chicken salad.

"Who? What?" I say through a mouthful of cholesterol-free egg.

"Meredith—for her muffin and coffee. She never pays," he says.

Meredith, however, is still not on the set. Today was always going to be long, but now it's verging on gruesome. Trent and I sit in the shadows, munching our deli food and whispering funny things to each other about everyone. "There's Cooper. . . . Cooper St. James," Trent says, pointing to a handsome silver-haired man in the background. "He played Carter Wharton, the mayor. Haven't seen him for a while. He didn't make it last year, and I thought maybe they'd laid him off—or worse, that he'd kicked the bucket."

Just then a flurry of activity. A rumor that Meredith might be joining us. Trent and I swivel our necks to face the exit door. We wait. Nope. Nothing. We turn back. Marty is waving people around, seating and standing them, generally being a traffic cop. The set is a large white room filled with pink and blush roses, Regina Abell's favorite. Facing out to the fourth wall is a long table covered with white linen, where the rehearsal dinner will be served. Placed on it are candles, plates, glasses, and elaborate floral arrangements. It looks like Martha Stewart has catered the Last Supper. Devon isn't officially invited to the dinner, but I'm there in my official police capacity.

As the minutes tick by, I am more and more envious of Carlos, who has been given the day off because his wife went into labor. Her timing was pretty good; two days later she'd have been giving birth alone. The live broadcast airs the day after tomorrow, and Daphne wasn't about to let anyone out of that.

I hear a noise behind me and look expectantly to see if it's Meredith, but no, it's Uta the seamstress, and she doesn't look happy. She bustles in, laden down with sewing equipment and a small stool. Still no Meredith. I turn back to find that Trent is up on his feet socializing and making everyone laugh with evil suggestions. I finish my sandwich and go in search of caffeine.

Another twenty minutes pass; I now suspect that Meredith is sticking it to Daphne for embarrassing her in the Makeup room. Daphne is not on set. She left about five minutes ago. Marty is trying to jolly everyone along, talking to the cast and crew. The cameramen (and one woman) are leaning back in their seats, eating almonds and cashews. They keep snacks on the skirt of the cameras, usually cashews, unsalted almonds, dried apricots, figs, prunes, mints, and gum. It's our craft services. Everyone is allowed to help themselves; actors chip in now and again and replenish with whatever they like. I go over and grab a handful of cashews from Terry's camera. I ask him about his daughter, who studies tae kwon do, and we bullshit for a bit.

Suddenly the fire alarm goes off. We look at one another, then at Marty, who surely must know. He looks concerned as he speaks into his headset. "Hold on, everyone, we weren't expecting a drill," he says.

He talks into his headset again, trying to find out whether we should evacuate. "No, it's okay. Everyone stay where you are; they're investigating. Stay calm," he announces.

The alarm continues.

"Shouldn't we get our purses?" Alison mewls.

"Yeah, our purses," Trent agrees. "We might need them to fight the fire." He grabs Uta's sewing bag and does beefy fireman acting by pretending to use it to fight back enormous imaginary flames.

And then it happens. We hear yelling at first, loud, high-pitched, angry screaming. Then banging. Then the large fire door bursts open. No, it's not our fabulous men in yellow. It's Meredith—and she is screeching. Behind her is Daphne, and behind her is Ruben, the costume designer, bearing a velvet cape the color of cotton candy. Meredith has her tight, tight tulip-shaped skirt hiked up around her hips. She is tottering on her Jimmy Choos because Daphne is goose-marching her onto set. I look to see if there's a gun, but it is not evident.

"This is unthinkable, not to mention irresponsible and downright dangerous. You are crazy. You're a crazy woman. I'm having the head of Daytime down here tomorrow," Meredith is yelling.

"No. You want him? Let's get him now, right now!" Daphne urges. "Let's just call Conrad Barbera right this minute and tell him that we are an hour behind. We've been back from lunch for forty minutes, and you were down there plucking your chin hairs."

Chin hairs?

"How dare you? How dare you?" Meredith is red in the face and she's huffing and puffing.

"Yes, let's get him over here immediately," Daphne continues. "However, my suggestion is we use all this passion and outrage and get some real emotions going in your scenes for a change. Whaddaya say?"

"Daphne, you know you're being unfair," Meredith says frostily. "It takes me longer on days like this. This gown is very fitted and it's impossible to go to the ladies' room." It is evident that she can barely walk in it, but that's not unusual. She usually takes the elevator. Today, obviously, was an exception. Meredith is trying to mince her way onto the set in her outrageously tight frock. "I can't even sit in this dress, let alone go to the bathroom. Uta has to help me." Uta nods knowingly.

"Well, then, we're just going to have to change the blocking. No sitting for you," Daphne sings merrily. She snap-snaps her fingers at Marty; he mouths "no sitting" in affirmation.

"I *have* to sit. It's hours and hours. I must." Meredith sounds like a twelve-year-old arguing with Mommy at the supermarket checkout for a packet of Skittles.

"You can lean," Daphne suggests. "Lean on your leading man. . . . You've been doing it for years."

A sharp intake of breath from the assembled Dearly Beloved at that one.

"Clearly there is no talking to you. I will have my lawyer contact the network and you will be fired by next week."

"Perhaps, but I'm taking you with me, darling. Just think: We can get rooms next to each other at the SAG retirement home." While Daphne is cheerfully pointing cameras into their starting positions, cast and crew are milling around in stunned silence, pretending to be professional. We are all trying to figure out how we're going to be heard above the din of the fire alarm.

Makeup and Wardrobe continue to dance attendance around the Queen, making final adjustments to get her camera-ready. It's not going well. Despite the makeup bee's best efforts to powder her matte, Meredith is still so flushed around the gills that I wonder whether Priscilla hasn't slipped her some niacin.

"You're a crazy, mad, nasty woman," Meredith says in a tremolo. Not fluttering gracefully like a butterfly, as would be her custom when feeling self-assured, Meredith is shaking—quavering, actually—like a humming-bird. She looks to be on the verge of a meltdown, but Daphne appears quite determined not to let her have one.

"Yes, I thought we'd already established that," she replies, completely unfazed. Daphne continues her preparations for the scene, placing her bi-focals on her nose and calmly checking the shot list.

While Ruben and Uta are attempting to get Meredith squared away in her costume—in front of the entire cast, no less—she is vibrating in her stilettos. The shaking may be the onset of a case of the vapors. She is compacted into a carnation pink Versace corset dress that was designed with Catherine Zeta-Jones in mind, but Meredith's booty is too bootylicious for the dress. Now all of her air-puffed roundness has been squozen out of her midsection and pushed either north or south. Uta is forcing the tight skirt back down around her ass, and the effort is such that I half expect to see her ankles puff up as a consequence.

Meanwhile, Ruben has cut off the northern fat escape by jamming the velvet cape up under her chin and tying it around her neck.

"So we are finally ready, are we?" Daphne asks. "Come on then, let's get going before Meredith ages another moment."

As if on cue, the fire alarm ends abruptly. Meredith, if she could walk faster than a Chihuahua with its legs bound, would strangle Daphne at this point. Suddenly, Bradley ambles up to Meredith, takes her hand in his, and kisses it.

"You look simply ravishing, Meredith," he grunts, staring into her eyes. In his oafish way, he has struck upon the one thing that will bring Meredith out of the absolute red-hot fury that she's in at this moment. She looks up at Bradley. He is a good two feet taller than she is. He restates it in case she didn't hear, and because he's basically thick. "Simply ravishing."

"You are such a gentleman, Bradley. Thank you," Meredith says, exuding pure Garden Party politesse. If she had a little Chinese paper lantern, she would hang it from his nipple.

"Right. So, is everyone ready? No last-minute phone calls to agents? Okay. Then let's rock and roll." With that Daphne claps her hands and bustles off to the control room, grabbing Maggie by the arm.

"Crikey," I whisper to Marty as I quickly review my speeches.

"Yeah," he replies. Despite all the hubbub in front of him, he looks distracted. He stares off into the distance, wearing an expression that suggests he's taking a leak in the ocean. You know the one. What he is doing, however, is avidly listening on his headset to what is occurring in the control room.

"Hmm," he continues. "Quite a showdown."

"What's going on up there in the booth?" I ask urgently. "Did Daphne really set off the alarm?"

"Sounds like it. Apparently Meredith came out of her dressing room in her fur coat ready to leave, and Daphne grabbed her and manhandled her to the set," Marty concludes.

He nods to the booth and puts his hand up to count us down. "In five . . . four . . . three . . . two . . ."

The premise of the scene is that Nicholas's ex-wife Sylvia has shown up at the rehearsal dinner ready to cause trouble, with her two delinquent sons in tow. By the time I burst in, the drama is already well under way. Meredith is propped up against one end of the long table, while Bradley is gesticulating toward the actress who plays Sylvia, a scrappy, trailer-trash broad with terrible grammar.

NICHOLAS
It was love, Sylvia. [Bradley's face is devoid of any expression, as usual.] I loved Regina then as I do now. So help me God, as I will to my dying day.

Bradley grabs Meredith clumsily around the shoulders and draws her to him. Meredith does her best to totter over, resembling a pudding on pointes. She leans her head lovingly into his waist and shares a camera shot with his Prada belt. It's a fashion win, at least.

                    NICHOLAS (CONT'D)
      So, you go on now, Sylvia. Take your sons out of here
      and don't cause any more upset than you already have.

                    SYLVIA
      They're *our* sons and I ain't goin' nowheres.

The actress playing Sylvia sits right down at the head of the table, something Meredith longs to do and cannot.

                    NICHOLAS
      Sylvia, you're making a scene.

                    REGINA
      Let me handle this, Nicholas, my love.

Ever the Queen, Meredith sweeps into the fray, or hops, I should more accurately say. She clings to the side of the table and in a series of tiny hopping motions begins approaching the ex-wife. She shakes her head, causing her hair to rearrange itself into a perfect frame around her face. She is glorious in her fury, yet oddly not really furious. It's more mildly sexual, as though she really were coming over to stick her tongue down Sylvia's throat.

                    REGINA
      Sylvia, may I call you that?

                    SYLVIA
      It's my name, ain't it?

                    REGINA
      Yes, indeed. Then Sylvia, let me ask you this: What do
      you hope to achieve by making a spectacle of yourself?

Meredith flutters her eyelids and leans over the table to display her décolletage to Camera 2.

                    SYLVIA
      Well, I hopes this good-fer-nothin' here will give me
      chile support 'n I kin git off welfare. That's what
      I'm hopin' fer.

Bradley remains unmoved, and quite possibly unconscious.

                    REGINA
      Yes, in a just world, Sylvia, that is what should hap-
      pen. But nothing is ever fair, is it, Sylvia? Life's
      just not fair.

Meredith heaves herself away from the table and attempts to stand up-right, but it's not working. White-knuckled, she grips the back of a Philippe Starck chair. She mince-lurches along the length of the table, steadying herself from chair to chair, her tight skirt making it impossible to put one foot in front of the other. It's a long table, and Sylvia's at the other end of it. Suddenly, Meredith picks up speed and at the same time attempts to deliver her speech.

REGINA (CONT'D)

Nicholas and I are going to be married in the morning, and there is not one thing that you can do to stop it.

Meredith is now teetering along at an alarming rate, her feet and knees being propelled by the constricting silk shantung. She seems out of con-trol. Her voice sounds as it would if she were driving on a particularly bumpy country road.

REGINA (CONT'D)

You should look to yourself as to why these innocent young boys have taken up a life of crime. Where did you go wrong? What kind of a mother do you call your-self? I ask you that question—and only you and God know the true answer.

Sylvia furrows her brow, but it has nothing to do with the script. Meredith's tiny feet are going hell for leather; her constricted limbs, plump upper body, and huge hairdo have put her desperately off balance.

REGINA

Nothing you or your sons can do will stop my marriage tomorrow to Nicholas.

You've got to hand it to her—Meredith is still trying to appear sexy whilst resembling a Weeble wobble. She is about two feet from Sylvia and closing fast. She's headed for a major face plant. I have to think quickly. I impro-vise. Just as I see her Jimmy Choos lose contact with the ground, I charge in and grab her warmly—by the throat.

"Regina, stop," I command as I catch her midair. "This is the eve of your wedding. The beginning of a new fu-ture. Don't do something you will regret forever."

I push her backward and somewhat into balance. I hold her firmly by her shoulders and shake her gently.

"Think about it, Regina," I continue. "We cannot be vi-olent at our own rehearsal dinner, now can we?" I hate sounding parental, but at least I think I've restored her equilibrium. Time to get back to the script.

> DEVON
> I'd like to know your whereabouts over the past two
> nights. And yours, Nicholas.

I look over Meredith's hair—a difficult feat—and locate Bradley. He's supposed to come in with a line here, but he appears to be making mental airplane reservations and wakes from his reverie with a grunt.

> DEVON
> Exactly. Please, no one leave. I have a few things I
> want to talk to you about. . . .

I sweep the room with an enigmatic squint, and try to do my best Dirty Harry impersonation. Unfortunately, I catch the eye of Trent, who is eggplant-colored trying to suppress laughter. Bastard.

> REGINA
> Why, what has happened, Detective Merrick?

Meredith is actually totally on board with me and has followed my cue with the correct line, skipping right over Bradley, whose brain is still laboring to catch up—and failing.

> DEVON
> There has been a murder.

I let the statement hang in the air before continuing.

> DEVON (CONT'D)
> Olivia Landsdowne, the socialite, is dead, and I'm
> classing it a homicide.

A dramatic gasp from the Dearly Beloved ensemble. Bless them.

> DEVON (CONT'D)
> I don't want to spoil your wedding, Regina, but I'd
> like to let you know that Sergeant Morales and I
> will be at the church tomorrow, both for your pro-
> tection and to check for any signs of suspicious ac-
> tivity.

"And cut!" says Marty. "This is where we let 'em sell some Altoids and Viagra. Everybody stick around."

After Sylvia departs in a huff with her sons, I hang to the side as Edith and Meredith have a mother-daughter chat about marriage.

NORMA

Regina, as many times as you've been married, it still
does my heart good to see you so happy.

REGINA

Thank you, Mother. By this time tomorrow I'll be Mrs.
Nicholas Duncan! He's the right man for me; I just
know it. I'm so glad that you will be my matron of
honor.

NORMA

It's a shame that the rest of the Abell women are not
here for your big day.

Suddenly there is a hubbub and an off-camera voice is heard.

MALLORY

Oh, but I am here, Mom! And Magda too! We're just back
from skiing in Gstaad.

Kendall Gilman makes her debut as Mallory Abell. She is indeed a miniature person—Meredith now has a pixie for a daughter. Selena Romanova,
who plays Magda (the tutor and ex-vampire), enters right behind her.

MAGDA

It's so good to be home after all this time!

Suddenly, there is another hubbub and an unscripted off-camera voice
joins the scene. "And I'm here, too!" the female voice calls. "I may be
pregnant but I, Jennifer Abell, wouldn't think of missing my
sister's wedding!"

Are the planets in retrograde orbit? Has Daphne unfired Amber? I
look around for Amber and her all-too-familiar pregnant lady waddle, but
what I see instead is even more amazing. Cosima Santiago (or Cosima Ortega y Ochoa y Orvieto de Contini—your choice), now a honey blonde, has
strapped on Amber's old pregnancy padding and is waddling for all she's
worth toward the set. She's pretty good at it, too! Nevertheless, she doesn't
make it very far before the screaming sets in.

"Dafffffffffffffffff-neeeeeeeeeeeee!" Meredith screeches. "You can't!"

"I can, and I have," comes Daphne's very calm, even voice from the
booth. "You should be congratulated, Meredith. Your daughter's a fine
little actress. I had her audition with Wyatt and she held her own just
fine."

"My contract gives me—"

"Meredith, I'll loan you my bifocals so you can read the fine print, because I certainly did. Your contract gives you review and approval over one character: your daughter Mallory."

Meredith bunny-hops offstage with a toss of her freshly implanted hair extensions. "I'm calling my attorney."

"Do that, honey. And while you're at it, call Connie Barbera too. Both of them will tell you that there is absolutely nothing in your contract that gives you any say whatsoever in who plays Jennifer Abell. I checked with the network lawyers myself."

"Hoo boy. Break time. Ten minutes," Marty calls.

"And you! *You!*" Meredith fumes at Cosima. "My own flesh and blood—how could you do this to me?"

"Sorry, Mom, but I'm not doing it *to* you; I'm doing it *for* me," she says earnestly. "This is a great opportunity. There are only so many acting workshops you can take, so many bad equity waiver productions you can be in. I've been auditioning all over Hollywood for a couple of years now with nothing to show for it. Unless you're actually a working actor—being paid for what you do—nobody takes you seriously. You know as well as I do that starting out in the business, when the big break comes, you jump on it. That's what you did!"

Brava, Cosima, brava, I think to myself.

Edith Oakley wheels up next to me. "Did you get all that?" I ask her.

"Oh yes indeed. Got my hearing aids in; I caught it all. Kate, my ears may be shot, but my eyes are still pretty sharp."

"As is your brain, dear lady, as is your brain."

"Take a look at Cosima. Until today I hadn't seen her since she was a little girl. Meredith used to bring her to the set."

From what little interaction I've had with her, Cosima strikes me as pretty balanced," I reply. "Meredith seems to have done a good job as a mom, but I have to say that I'm surprised she ever brought her to the studio."

"Well, she didn't do it often, and when she did it was pretty much Show-and-Tell for the press. 'Take your daughter to work,' and all that. After the flashbulbs stopped popping, she'd hand her off to her sister Emilia. That woman pretty much raised her niece, from what I understand."

"Which goes a long way toward explaining why she's such a great kid. Did you know that Emilia and Meredith were twins?" I ask. Edith arches one eyebrow in astonishment.

"I just found out a few weeks ago," I continue. "Emilia and Cosima came by unexpectedly to take Meredith out for a birthday lunch. She blew them off to have a solo lunch with Renato. That was when Daphne got it in her head to hire Cosima. She wanted her to play Mallory, but Meredith put a stop to that. Cosima is a lovely young woman."

"Yes, and that's just it. Have you met Renato?"

"Haven't had the pleasure."

"Meredith's husband looks like the ineffectual, self-indulgent member of the deposed Cuban oligarchy that he is."

"Jeez, don't hold back, Edith. Tell me how you really feel about him."

"He has a face like a ferret, no, a weasel—weak chin, sloping forehead, ears that seem to jut out from his skull at an odd angle. Look at that child's profile—it's perfect."

Edith is right, of course. "But so what?" I say. "Cosima just drew the lucky numbers in gene pool lotto—all of her mother's, and none of her father's."

"Maybe, maybe not," Edith says. "Look at her profile again, then look around the room and see if you see another like it."

I scan the studio like a Savile Row tailor, looking over the men in the cast, sizing up their DNA and measuring them all to see how well they might look in a bespoke paternity suit.

"There—just there," Edith says.

"Bingo!" My gaze rests on the silhouetted profile of Cooper St. James, the erstwhile mayor of Hope Canyon. It's identical to Cosima's.

"You see the resemblance," Edith says. "Back in the early eighties, there was a storyline about an illicit romance between Regina and Carter Wharton, Cooper's character. I always thought there was some heat offstage as well as on."

"He still has a great profile and a full head of hair, but . . ."

"You should have seen him then! He was the *éminence grise* of the show. Cooper was a big deal at the time. There was always some young yum-yum in his dressing room, thinking she could get ahead by sleeping with him. Meredith was one of the few who wasn't underage. Pity. He could have been so much more than he turned out to be. Rumor had it he was hung like a horse, too."

"Are your ears burning yet, Richard?" I mutter, my eyes involuntarily tracking our current Imminent Grease.

"What?"

"Sorry."

"Since I was also having an affair with him—well, not *me*, Norma Abell— when I caught him in bed with Regina, I put a stop to it. It was quite a scene and I always wondered. . . ."

"About what, Edith?"

"There was some scuttlebutt around the cast that they'd actually done it on camera."

"Back then?"

"Come now, Kate. Both sex and television have been around for a very long time. Surely you can't believe that the younger generation invented the idea of pretending to do it on camera, and then *really* doing it on camera."

"Tiffany and Vladimir will be so disappointed."

"Excuse me?"

"Never mind. They really did it? Meredith and Cooper St. James?"

"Did it, yes, they did," Mzee says softly as he joins the conversation. "But since they did not see me, I was not there."

"Were you up in the rigging?"

Mzee nods almost imperceptibly.

36

Two days later/the day of the live broadcast

4:34! 4:34!! 4:34!!!
The time flashes on the ceiling as the alarm goes off. Drusilla, who is curled around my head like a living nightcap, complains as I lean over and bash the alarm button to restore silence. Eventually I crawl over the other warm hairy bodies to put my feet on the floor. Although I've apologized repeatedly to the four-leggeds about the fact that I simply cannot buy anything bigger than a king-size bed, I've been unable to convince any of them to adapt their sleeping patterns to fit. The dogs seem to find it necessary to maximize the space they occupy, a habit I suspect is nothing but doggie sarcasm.

It's dark, very dark, outside. It's dark inside my head as well. As I stagger into the shower, my brain is barely functioning. All I know is that after rehearsing for this live broadcast for the last two weeks, I'm more convinced than ever that Daphne is nuts. There have been days when we never got beyond "Dearly beloved . . ." Not a rehearsal has gone by when chaos hasn't erupted, including the final one yesterday. Alison tripped over cables. Bradley kept looking at the wrong camera. Priscilla was caught on-camera picking his nose in the background. Worst of all, we were a couple of minutes short.

Even so, Daphne's lunacy has already redounded to our ratings benefit. The notion that we are intrepid or crazy enough to go back to live daytime drama has attracted considerable media interest. All eyes will be on us today—and mostly they'll be on us to see how badly we fuck up. I have every expectation that we won't disappoint them in the slightest.

It's about 5:15 with just a hint of sunrise when I stop at the Starbucks and check in with Sondra. "Good morning, Sondra," I say as she hands me an extra-hot no-foam latte. "Great job on the fan mail, but there seems to be more coming in. You might want to think of selling me more of your time." On the way out I wave at my two landladies, Gudrun and Janice, who are earnestly perusing the *New York Times.*

Twenty minutes later I drive past the cheerily waving guard to pull the Jeep into the studio parking lot, resolving once more to do something about the remnants of the gift basket in the back. Meredith's car is already here.

As I head for Gossip Central, at least that aspect of the brilliance of Daphne's lunacy has become apparent. On this day of days, Meredith, who would quite truly be late to her own funeral, can't be tardy. We're going up live at ten A.M., and she has to be at the back of the church at the opening of the show. With an entire cast to prepare, it's going to be a very busy morning in Hair and Makeup. I have an early call because as a relatively minor player in the day's proceedings, it was decided to get me dressed and painted to get me out of the way. Meredith has an early call because it takes forever to get her ready for her close-up, Mr. DeMille.

Meredith is already luxuriating in her conversion pod, resting quietly in the crinoline underpinning to her Monique Lhuillier gown. Ruben wanted to make absolutely sure she could walk in it—nobody wanted to see the bunny-hopping performance at the rehearsal dinner repeated on live TV. From a preparation standpoint she's at the spatula, Spackle, and base coat stage. Her hair has already been washed and conditioned and extensioned.

I slip into Christine's chair. "Morning, Kate," she says brightly as she starts prepping my face. "Wyatt sends you greetings from North Carolina. He says the shooting is going well."

Ah, I say to myself, now I can talk about him.

Since he's been gone, I've bent over backward devising ground rules for myself about how to behave with Christine. The first rule was that I wasn't going to be the first to say Wyatt's name. Stupid, I know, but it's quite possibly a throwback to what I learned in my teenage years, when my mother guessed that I had a crush on Timothy, the boy who lived on the corner. When I asked her how she knew, she told me that I'd developed a case of "mentionitis." I'd managed to work Timothy's name into the conversation about eight times in ten minutes.

"And hello back to him, too. I bet he's not sorry he's missing this."

"He'll be home soon."

Gossip Central gradually fills as people arrive for the show . . . Vladimir, intense as always; Trent, my favorite clown prince; Jay; and even Priscilla. Carlos enters, bearing a huge box of Krispy Kreme donuts, all with pink icing. "It's a girl," he says proudly, "and she's beautiful, just like me." He then starts handing out cigars with pink ribbons, but only to the men. "Since we named her Catarina, after you, I guess I ought to give you one, too," he finally says with a huge grin, handing me a cigar. "For a *tortillera,* you've got at least as many *cojones* as the rest of these guys."

"She doesn't deserve one," Trent says, snatching it out of my hand and returning it to Carlos. "She's not, you know," he says.

"Not what?" Priscilla asks.

"Not gay," LaTrisa replies.

"Kate . . . ?" Jay asks.

"When she first got here she used to tell me all about how she was dating Matt, this magician," Charlie adds.

"We all had Christmas at her house," Richard offers. "She was living with this writer—nice guy, too."

"She's not a dyke," Kirk says. "I could have told you that the first day on the set."

All eyes are on me. All I can do is blush and shrug. The look on Jay's face is absolutely priceless.

Suddenly, Marty's voice comes over the PA. "Okay, do we know what time it is? The big hand is on the twelve and the little hand is on the nine. That's right! It's nine o'clock, boys and girls! One hour to Showtime, so everybody pee up—now! There will be no, and I mean absolutely *no,* potty breaks once we're live. So go now or cross your legs till we're off the air at eleven."

There is a brief pause, but I can hear that the mike is still open. "And this means you, Meredith," comes Daphne's voice as an addendum.

Meredith, who has already opened her eyes during the cigar discussion, now rouses herself from her pod and heads for the loo. Maggie comes through looking for Edith, Kirk, and Richard, and grabs a small trash bag on her way out. There is shrieking shortly thereafter.

"Aaaaaaaaaaaaaaaaaaaaaaaaaaaaaaaah! My hair! *My hair!*" Meredith comes tearing out of the bathroom at breakneck speed—those Jimmy Choos have never motored so fast. "It's chocolate. It's *chocolate,* I tell you! It's **CHOCOLATE!**" she yells. "What did you do to me?" she screams at the worker bee.

"Nothing, Ms. Meredith," she says. "We used the Capelli di Regina Flaming Cinnamon shampoo and conditioner like always, see?" She proffers the bottles for Meredith's inspection.

Meredith sniffs them and finds nothing out of the ordinary, but she's right about the hair color. Instead of being its customary burnished copper, Meredith's hair is definitely Ghirardelli bittersweet . . . well, most of it. The extensions, because they are acrylic and not real hair, are still henna sunset. She catches sight of herself in a mirror. "I'm two-toned!" she moans. "Do something, Charlie! *Fix it!*"

Charlie just throws up his hands. "No time, Meredith, sorry. If we started over now, we'd never have you ready by ten."

"Those of you who are in costume and in your war paint, get your hineys upstairs and on the set," barks Marty over the loudspeaker. "Let's fill these pews. We've got thirty minutes to airtime. Meredith, Uta, you can finish arranging the dress up here. Move it. *Now!*"

I come up to the set and have a look at the church. The set decorators have outdone themselves. There are flowers dripping from every corner; you'd never suspect that it's the same set we used for gloomy St. Nektarios, where Athena Demetrios was "funeralized."

Uta and Meredith materialize at the back of the church, and Uta busies herself straightening the crinoline and arranging the soft folds of the gorgeous cherry blossom pink gown.

"Oh, there you are, Kate," Maggie says as she hands me a cell phone from an armload that she is clutching. "Daphne wants you to have one of these. Have you seen Trent? I have one for him, too. Keep them out of sight, though!"

Cosima approaches us in her cerise wedding finery. "You too, Cosima." Maggie hands her a cell phone before going off. After checking with her agent and her attorney, Meredith has grudgingly accepted the idea that her daughter will play her sister, Jennifer. And now Daphne has put her in the wedding procession as a very pregnant bridesmaid.

"Places everyone. This is the big banana," calls Marty. "And we're live in five . . . four . . . three . . . two . . ."

Suddenly a sound like that of a large tabby being castrated with a butter knife fills the rafters of the enormous studio. Daphne decided that Nicholas Duncan, as a man with a proper Scottish last name, would have bagpipers at his wedding. Mercifully, she vetoed the idea of a kilt for Bradley. *Thwee . . . Thwee . . . Thwee-thwee . . . Thwee . . . Thwee . . . Thwee-thwee . . .* The sound of air rushing through a pig bladder to the strains of "Here Comes the Bride" may never have been what Richard Wagner had in mind, but nevertheless, it's how the live broadcast is beginning.

Bradley waits for his beloved at the altar as three generations of Abell women—Meredith, Edith, Kendall, and Cosima—are piped down the aisle.

```
                    MINISTER
Dearly beloved, we are gathered here in the sight of
God, and in the presence of this company, to join to-
gether Nicholas and Regina in holy matrimony. Nicholas
and Regina have written their own vows. They will give
them now.


                    NICHOLAS
Regina, so many people swore we weren't right for each
other. In just two weeks we've proved them wrong. It's
```

taken each of us a couple of tries to get it right, but
here we are. I pledge my love, my life, and my devo-
tion to you in front of our friends, family, and God.

He takes Regina's hand.

                    NICHOLAS (CONT'D)
I promise to love you, honor you, and cherish you, to
have and to hold, from this day forward, for better or
worse, in sickness and in health, for richer, for
poorer, until we are separated by death.

Damn, it's really working! Bradley's mouth was the only part of him that
moved while he was saying his vows, but he got them out. We might actually pull this off!!

                    REGINA
Nicholas, we've been together again for only two weeks,
but I know that my love for you is forever. I'm saying
this for God and Hope Canyon and the entire world to
hear: I love you, Nicholas Duncan. I will shout it from
the rooftops: I love you. I pledge to love and trust
you, to have and to hold, from this day forward, for
better or worse, for richer, for poorer, in sickness
and in health, until we are separated by death.

                    MINISTER
The ring is a symbol that illustrates a spiritual
truth. It is a never-ending circle. Let the ring remind you of your never-ending commitment to each
other. The ring is made of precious metal. Let your
rings speak of your loving relationship which grows
and becomes more precious with the passing of time.

The seven-year-old ring bearer steps forward, and Nicholas
removes one of the bands from its satin pillow.

                    MINISTER (CONT'D)
Nicholas, place your ring on Regina's finger.

Bradley drops the ring, but picks it back up and jams it on Meredith's finger.

                    NICHOLAS
Regina, from the day we met, I knew that you were the
one for me. As long as the sun rises and sets in the

```
sky, as long as I breathe, you will be the love of my
life and the source of my unending joy. I give you
this ring as a symbol of my devotion to you and as a
token of our abiding love.
```

```
                        MINISTER
Regina, place your ring on Nicholas's finger.
```

```
                         REGINA
Nicholas, our love has no end and no beginning. Our
lives are intertwined and inseparable. Take this ring
as a symbol of our connectedness, and as a token of
our abiding love.
```

"And we're down for the first commercial break," says Marty. "Way to go, everyone. Looking great so far. Two and a half minutes—if you're gonna cough, sneeze, or scratch your nuts, now's the time."

"And back up in five . . . four . . . three . . . two . . ."

```
                        MINISTER
If there be anyone present who knows of an obstacle or
has just cause why this couple should not be joined in
holy matrimony, let them speak now or forever hold
their peace.
```

In all the years of daytime drama, there may have been a handful of soap opera weddings where no one's lodged an objection, but in general someone always speaks up. I was amazed when the script had this one going off without anyone raising an objection, but then . . .

```
                        JENNIFER
          (patting her very large belly and
        surreptitiously closing her cell phone)
I do. I have an obstacle.
```

There is a collective gasp from the Dearly Beloved. Meredith looks wild-eyed at Cosima.

```
                        MINISTER
             (recovering as best he might)
```

```
State your objection, please, Mrs. Chaney.
```

```
                        JENNIFER
My husband, Burke Chaney, is not the father of my un-
born child.
```

Another gasp from the DB. It is followed, however, by stunned silence as the minister—and the rest of us as well—try to fathom what Cosima's ad lib has to do with the wedding of Regina and Nicholas.

The silence continues until I hear a faint buzzing that seems to be coming from Trent's pocket. He takes out his cell phone, flips it open, smiles, and looks up.

> "I am," he cries loudly. "I, Philip Salisbury, am the father of Jennifer's baby. Let the wedding go forward."

So that's it, I say to myself. Daphne has planned a few surprises for us all. No wonder the final dress rehearsal ran short.

"And we're down," says Marty. "This is a very short break, people—stay sharp."

"Just what the fuck is going on here?" Meredith shouts. "Cosima? What do you think you're doing, young lady?"

"Proving I'm your daughter, Mother."

"Daphne, I demand—"

I hear another cell phone buzz. Kirk quickly glances at his cell, then flips it shut.

"When you're live, you're live," Daphne says from the booth.

"Places, everyone!" Marty hollers. "Back up in five . . . four . . . three . . . two . . ."

> "Actually, you're not, Philip," Cosima says flatly. "**You**, Nicholas Duncan, **YOU** are the father of my unborn child!"

Bradley's jaw drops open. Un-fucking-believable. Bradley's face actually moved!!!!!!

> "Jennifer! It's okay!" Kirk says, coming to his feet. "I love you no matter whose baby it is. I love you despite everything, and it's obvious that Nicholas is in love with your mother. Look at the two of them. We'll raise the baby as our own."

*Mother? Ah, the raspberry tart has hit the fan now. **Mother?!** It didn't exactly sound like a slip of the tongue—Kirk's too much of a pro for that.*

> "Why, Burke," Meredith says delicately, fluttering her fingers, tossing her hair, but looking at Kirk with homicide in her eyes. "You know perfectly well that I'm not Jennifer's mother. I'm her sister."

> "Actually," says Edith from her wheelchair, flipping a cell phone shut, "that's not true, my dear."

Another DB gasp, this one bigger and better than the last. We're quite good at it, actually.

> "We were pregnant at the same time, don't you remember, Regina?" Edith continues. "And we went into labor at the same time. They told you that your child died in the incubator, but it was my child, *mine,* that died. I raised the two of you as sisters, but Jennifer is indeed your daughter."

One mo' time—let's hear that marvelous DB gasp!

> "And I know who the father is," says Richard, closing a cell. "It's him! I was just an intern when the two of you were in the hospital, but Carter Wharton is your father, Jennifer!" he exclaims, pointing to Cooper St. James.

"And we're into commercial!" Marty calls.

Daphne comes out of the booth, applauding. "Excellent, all of you!"

"AAAAAAAAAAaaaaaaaiiiiiiiiiiiiiiiiiiiieeeeeeeeeeEEEEEEE!" Meredith sounds exactly like one of the bagpipes.

"Mom—" Cosima begins.

"You!" Meredith shrieks. "Get out of my sight. I'll deal with you later."

"Come with me, child," Edith says gently to Cosima. "Let's let your mother have her meltdown. I suspect we've both seen enough of them. God knows I have."

"Daphne, you absolutely cannot do this to me!" Meredith hisses.

"Oh yes I can, Meredith. Your contract says you have dominion over who plays your daughter—your daughter **Mallory**. It's specific to her and her only. It says nothing about you having control over a daughter by any other name."

"I'll sue! I'll . . ."

"I think you'll do nothing of the sort," Daphne says at almost a whisper, "unless you want me to tell both Renato and Cosima that Cooper St. James really is her father."

"Ooooooooooooooooh." Meredith's voice becomes a growl and drops two octaves to *Exorcist* depth. "That's a lie, Daphne, a vicious lie."

"Is it?" Daphne asks coolly. "Cosima told me that you chose her stage name, did you not?"

"I suggested it, yes, of course."

"Kate, where's Carlos?"

"Aquí, mi jefe, aquí," he says.

"Carlos," Daphne says, working her chin overtime, "would you be kind enough to translate for us? How do you say 'St. James' in Spanish?"

"It's *Santiago,* Daphne," he replies. *"Santiago* is St. James."

"Coincidence, Meredith? I think not. Let us continue, shall we?"

"Back up in five . . . four . . . three . . . two . . ."

MINISTER

Have we satisfied all the objections to going forward
with this wedding? I ask again: If there be anyone
present who knows of an obstacle or has just cause why
this couple should not be joined in holy matrimony,
let them speak now or forever hold their peace.

Mercifully there is silence.

MINISTER (CONT'D)

Forasmuch as you, Regina, and you, Nicholas, have made
this covenant together, and have formed the bond of
holy wedlock, and have declared your love for one another before God and in the presence of this company,
by the authority vested in me as a minister of the
church and the power vested in me by the state of California, I now pronounce you man and wife.

"I'm going to be a grandmother!" Meredith wails as she tosses her bouquet over her shoulder.

If I don't catch it, two dozen cabbage roses, Casablanca lilies, alstroemeria,
lisianthus, and trailing stephanotis will hit me right in the face. I grab it
just as my cell phone goes off.

"I hate you, Woman," I hear Wyatt's voice in my ear.

"I hate you too, Man," I reply out loud. "Head over heels,
I hate you."

37

I GET TO MY DRESSING ROOM to find I already have visitors.

Whump! Whump! Whump-whump-whump! Whump! Whump! Whump-whump-whump! Whump! Whump! Whump-whump-whump! A fan mail avalanche is being delivered via mail gnome, with Nigel not far behind. "Nigel, help! What am I supposed to do with all this?"

"I hope Sondra's been eatin' her Wheaties," he says, "because this is absolutely huge. Congratulations, Kate: You and Wyatt are the new Supercouple of Daytime. I'm getting calls like crazy. It's not just *Soap Opera Digest*; it's *TV Guide, People*, and *Entertainment Weekly*. They all want to do a story on the two of you."

"Uh, that's great, Nigel. Fantastic news."

I guess. Famous, me? Famous, us?

Daphne arrives shortly thereafter. "Kate," she says, "I've only seen this a few times before in my career, and it's funny. Everybody wants nothing more than for these supercouples to get married. All the fans, all the web sites and magazines will push like crazy toward that end, or at least to get them into bed to consummate their loooooove and then get married in a huge storybook wedding."

Gawd. An on-camera love scene with Wyatt. An on-camera wedding with Wyatt. The kissing was bad enough. How am I ever going to pull that off?

"And so?"

"And so the truth of the matter," she says as she twists her chin like a doorknob, "is that fans are fickle. Once you finally have the big wedding or the big love scene, people start to lose interest. The romance of Luke and Laura was immensely popular. Their wedding brought in huge numbers for *General Hospital*, but after that . . . after that they were a lot less interesting—as characters. The same is true in primetime. Remember *Moonlighting*?"

"Ah, detective agency . . . Bruce Willis and Cybill Shepherd, right?"

"Yes. Everybody loved the banter and the cleverness between the two of them, and the romantic interest that burbled beneath the surface. But after it was out in the open, people stopped watching."

"And so . . ."

"And so the trick is to find something that the viewers want, and then not give it to them."

"What does that mean?"

"We're gonna tease this romance till it bleeds. Eventually Devon and Marcello will have a huge wedding—during Sweeps, of course. I've already started working on getting permission to use Greystone, the mansion where Luke and Laura got married, but I might do something different. This went so well today that I may even want to do it live. In any event, Devon and Marcello will be my star-crossed lovers at least till November, and probably till February."

"So, Daphne," I say with a wry smile, "you're a cynic after all. You don't believe in happily ever after."

"Oh but I do, Kate. I do! But you'll find that it makes very poor television."

Daphne and Nigel withdraw, leaving me with a room full of mailbags. I doff my beloved trench coat and climb into jeans and a T-shirt, then I grab my cell phone and hit #5 on my speed dial. "Hey, Wyatt, it's me," I say to his voice mail. "Thanks for the phone call at the end of Meredith's wedding—I assume that was you. A funny thing happened on your way to North Carolina—just thought you'd like to know that there are about a million fan letters waiting here for you when you get back. It seems we're the new Luke and Laura. . . ."

There is a soft knock on my door. "Kate, it's me, Christine." I flip the cell phone shut and go to open the door.

"Holy Moley!" she exclaims as she walks in. "What is all this?"

Bzzz. Bzzz. My cell phone starts to vibrate insistently on the table, but I don't dare pick it up. I'm sure it's Wyatt, who by now has seen my number as a missed call on his cell. *The revenge of Rafe and Leslie!*

"Aren't you going to answer that?" she asks.

"No . . . no. It's okay," I say uneasily. "Let's go get some lunch, shall we?" I gently lead her out the door, leaving my cell phone behind.

What a dreadful parallel! I can only hope Christine didn't notice.

· · ·

I return from lunch to see that I'd flung the trench coat onto the floor. My hand finds its way into the pocket as I pick it up, and I realize there is something in there.

Oh! I know what this is! I tell myself. This is the ring from the hypnotism scene in the garden of the sanitarium. I forgot to return it to Props.

Except it isn't. When I remove my hand from the pocket, I'm looking at interwoven filaments of white, yellow, and rose gold in a Celtic knot pattern. Wyatt has given me his great-grandfather's wedding ring. *"How did he . . ."* I start to wonder, then replay the scene in my mind. I finally remember that when he put the ring in my pocket, my eyes were closed.

I reach for my cell to call him again but realize that if Christine were to walk in again, there would be nothing I could say that wouldn't leave her absolutely destroyed.

Dearest Wyatt,

I wasn't ready for this, and writing is not my strong suit, so bear with me while I say what I have to say. I feel like I've been hit by a bus. You know how people always tell you that no matter how careful you are, no matter how many precautions you take, you can always step off the curb and get hit by a bus? Well, that's me. Blindsided. Just a tiny nod during your audition and—bam—that bus of yours sent me flying, and I landed with a splat on the deck. I've been there ever since.

Under almost any other circumstances, you'd never hear me complain about getting run over like that, especially since it's such a fabulous bus. I've never seen another quite like it—distinctive Scottish-Italian design . . . got a couple of miles on it, but it's been fanatically well maintained . . . piercing headlights . . . aerodynamically sound . . . and, I suspect, one helluva kick in the ass to drive.

I don't think it ran me over on purpose, any more than I sat myself down in the middle of the highway and dared you to hit me. Hell, at this point it doesn't really matter. I'm here, flat on the deck, and I have no idea how I'm going to survive pretending to be your lover and then pretending to turn it off when we leave the set. Actually, I think that for me at least, the true acting will begin when Marty hollers "Cut!"

There are no easy options for us. There may not even be any good options, only better and worse. For me, the choices of what behavior would be honorable, what would be ethical, and what would be kind chase one another around in my brain until my head literally spins. And usually the only thing that makes it stop is some really swell fantasy, like lying on a white sand beach somewhere, you nestled up against me, filling in one another's negative spaces, half dozing in the sun.

And that fantasy is what will have to sustain me somehow. I'm going to cling to it, because as moved as I am that you want me to have this ring, I can't possibly keep it. It's beautiful and it means so much to you and your family—I'd love to be able to wear it proudly and show it off, but the first person I'd want to show it to is the very person who could never see it on my finger. To Christine, there's no way that ring could be anything but what it would appear to be: the accusation that neither of us could deny. I think we both want to spare her the heartache of the double betrayal it would symbolize. She deserves so much better than that. The ring itself deserves better than to stand for that.

This walking away is painful, and what I'm asking you to do is painful as well. Go home to Christine and make a real effort to stay together. As much as I would love to spend the rest of my life with you, I couldn't build that life on the foundation of her unhappiness. So please, take back your ring. Cherish what it stands for, and know that not a day will go by without me wishing there was a way I could keep it, and you, forever.

Kate

PHOTO: © DENIZ UZUNOGLU

FINOLA HUGHES was born and educated in London. She originated the role of Victoria in the West End production of Andrew Lloyd Webber's *Cats,* and made her American film debut in *Staying Alive.* Perhaps best known for her role as Anna Devane on *General Hospital*—a role she played for seven years, winning an Emmy in 1991—Hughes resurrected the character on *All My Children.* Now the host of *How Do I Look?* for the Style Network, she lives in Los Angeles with her husband, artist Russell Young, and their sons, Dylan and Cash.

DIGBY DIEHL is the bestselling co-author of *The Million Dollar Mermaid* and *Angel on My Shoulder.* A noted book critic, he is currently working with Coretta Scott King on her memoirs. He lives with his wife, Kay, in Los Angeles.